Never Love a Scoundrel

DARCY BURKE

For Erica,
flat out the most hilarious and awesome person I know.

Without you my vocabulary would be free of such bon
mots
as shenanigans, nitcrittery, and that other word
I won't write here that ends with balls.

Chapter One

THE NUDE WOMAN draped across the table winked. A slow smile lifted Lord Jason Lockwood's mouth as he winked back. The Cyprian at the center of his drawing room was lovely and inviting, precisely what she ought to be in order to entice a paying customer. And though Jason wasn't one of them, there were plenty about.

As he turned away, she pouted her dissatisfaction. How far he had come from the days of his first parties, when the demimondaines had regarded him with a measure of fear and a smattering of revulsion—at least when they looked at his scarred face. The rest of him, they'd proclaimed to a one, was superb.

He turned from the drawing room, still smiling. There was nowhere he'd rather be than at a vice party in full swing, and nothing he'd rather do than host it. His own personal pleasure would come later.

Everyone wore masks, save the courtesans he invited to please his guests. A few inclined their heads in his direction, and he returned the gesture. Come and be entertained, but preserve your identity. Such was the unwritten contract of Lockwood House parties. There were some who disdained anonymity, but they kept entirely to the gaming room.

Mask or no, Jason knew precisely who attended his parties. One didn't gain entrance without revealing the little card emblazoned with a black L. A few young bucks attempted to sneak in now and again, but Jason's retainers were nothing if not vigilant.

He moved through a small sitting room where couples—or even trios—gathered together in shadow, sampling each other's wares before they decided to adjourn upstairs. Some gentlemen came to find pleasure with a demimondaine, but others brought their own female entertainment—and sometimes from their own class. It was one of the reasons secrecy was paramount.

But above all, his parties allowed people to be who they wanted to be whilst safely under the veil of concealment. It had once been the only way Jason could obtain companionship, before he'd established a reputation that had ensured women—at least of the Cyprian class—sought his favor.

The gaming room was the brightest lit in Lockwood House during a vice party. Men, and a few masked women, played at cards, dice, and billiards. The mood was lively, though it could become serious as the hour grew late and the wagers deepened.

Jason sauntered amongst the tables and began to notice something odd. Several people looked up from their cards or dice and cast a lingering glance at him as he passed. A few of them leaned close to their neighbors and exchanged words he couldn't hear. By the time he'd made his circuit and leaned against the wall to watch the next round of vingt-et-un, he felt distinctly uneasy. The sensation rankled him—there ought to be nowhere else he felt more comfortable than his own house during a party whose attendees wholly appreciated his generosity.

What the devil was going on?

Jason left the gaming room in search of his valet. He would know what was afoot, or if he didn't, he'd find out. He signaled a footman in the foyer. "Send Scot to my office."

The footman nodded. Jason's butler and Scot's twin, North, arrived just as Jason was pouring himself a glass of whisky.

North closed the door after he entered. "My lord, I heard you were looking for Scot. May I be of assistance?" He was as stoic and unflappable as Scot—or "The Scot," which was his original nickname—was animated and outspoken.

Jason turned toward North. "I should've sent for you as well, but I asked for Scot since he typically knows everything. What's going on tonight? People are looking at me . . . strangely." It had been years since anyone had regarded him with a sense of guarded interest or worse—fear. Or, worst of all, pity. And that was because Jason was careful to avoid Society, where he was bound to receive all of those sentiments and more.

North's mouth twitched slightly, but not with amusement. If Jason had to guess as to his butler's suppressed emotion—and he often did—he would say he looked uncomfortable. "I've heard a few rumblings. I was trying to glean more information before alerting you."

What dastardly deed would Jason be charged with now? The more staid members of Society liked to imagine that he was an utter scoundrel with the basest of desires, and that he fulfilled the base desires of others at his sin-laden parties (that part, at least, was true), and of course, that he was as mad as King

George. "Out with it."

"It seems Mr. Ethan Jagger, calling himself Mr. Ethan Locke now, was seen at St. James this past Sunday in the company of Lady Aldridge."

Jason stared at North as if the man had sprouted another arm. His bastard half brother had emerged from obscurity to escort a wealthy widow to church? "Why?"

"No one knows, my lord. Therein lies the mystery and why people are undoubtedly looking at you more . . . curiously this evening. As you can imagine, they are wondering where he came from, how he knows Lady Aldridge, and whether you and he are actually brothers."

Jason scowled before taking a drink of whisky. "Why do they think we're brothers? Because he gave himself some bastardized version of my name?" *Locke?* Though Jason supposed that sounded better than FitzBenjamin, which would clearly indicate he was Benjamin Lockwood's bastard. Jason would've credited Ethan with a sense of subtle class if he didn't know better.

"They are saying you share similar physical characteristics." North's mouth took on a grim set. "But I'd say it's the insistence of Lady Margaret Rutherford that you are indeed half brothers that has convinced people."

Jason's fingers clenched around the glass tumbler. "I should have guessed that old viper would have her hand in this." Margaret was a harridan of the worst sort—a cannibalistic harpy who fed on the miseries of others by spreading rumors and gossip for no apparent reason other than to bask in her own moral, social, or financial superiority. Seven years ago she'd provoked his mother into a mental collapse from which she still hadn't recovered. And though this gossip was ancient—a lifetime ago, people had speculated that Jason's father had sired a bastard—it was new and exciting again with Ethan showing his face in polite society.

Not only did Jason have to deal with the reemergence of his half brother, he apparently had to square off with that vicious bitch, too. He took another sip from his glass and his eyes found the portrait of his father—their father—hanging over the mantel. Jason kept it there as a reminder not to be a self-serving prick.

Ethan didn't have a copy of the painting. Perhaps that was why he'd turned out—if their verbal and physical brawl seven years ago was any indication—as selfish as their sire. And now that he was squiring a wealthy young widow about, Jason wondered if he'd also inherited their father's penchant for skirt-chasing. Apparently Ethan was quite good at it too, since Lady Aldridge hadn't been seen about town since her husband had died last spring. What had Ethan done to coax her out of her house? Dangled his "name" in front of her? Or simply employed his handsome face by smiling disarmingly? Something Jason could no longer do.

Jason glowered at North, who was well aware of the brothers' history. "I suppose he's trying to claim a place in Society? Maybe find a wealthy bride?" It made sense. Last time they'd met, Ethan had been a thief-taker. He seemed to do all right for himself, if his clothing was any indication. Jason had seen him now and again at pugilistic bouts over the years. Though they'd never spoken, Ethan's fashionable attire had communicated plenty.

"Perhaps, my lord." North's forehead puckered only slightly. "Do you find his association with Lady Aldridge suspicious because of the circumstances of her husband's death?"

The Earl of Aldridge had been found murdered on the banks of the Thames last spring. He'd been exposed as the leader of a theft ring that preyed on houses in Mayfair and fenced the stolen items. "It's interesting, given Ethan's occupation as a thief-taker. I think I'll pay a call on Lady Aldridge."

Both of North's eyebrows arched. "You'll go out?"

The man rarely looked surprised, and Jason took a fleeting moment to enjoy it before answering. "It's not as if I never leave Lockwood House."

The eyebrows fell to their normal location, and the reserved butler's façade was in place once more. "Of course not, my lord, but you haven't paid a respectable call in a very long time. Do you think it wise that you visit Lady Aldridge?" North was trying to be deferential and delicate, but they both knew what he was talking about.

Jason wasn't welcome in much of polite society because of the way he chose to live, whereas his half brother, who couldn't know the first thing about how to comport himself, apparently was. The corrosive anger he often felt with regard to Ethan pulsed through Jason. "You're worried I'll scandalize her ladyship with my presence?"

North's features were smooth, unruffled. "I'm not worried, no, my lord. Indeed, I think you should go."

A knock sounded on the office door. "Come," Jason

called.

Scot stepped inside. He and North were identical, apart from Scot's slightly longer brown hair, and the extra lines around his blue eyes, which weren't due to age—the brothers were only a few years younger than Jason's thirty years—but to the frequency with which he laughed. Other than that, they were mirror images of a six-foot-tall, athletically built Scotsman.

Scot registered his brother's presence and gauged—correctly that something was afoot. "You sent for me?"

"We're discussing Jagger's appearance in Town," North said crisply and without inflection as if he were delivering the weather.

Scot shot Jason a look of outrage that was extremely satisfying to behold. "Bloody awful." He crossed his arms. "What're you going to do about it?"

Jason knew he could count on Scot to help. Blessed with an ease in forming friendships, he was particularly adept at learning things, which was why he'd summoned him in the first place. "Gather information first."

He grinned and rubbed his hands together. "I'll look forward to it."

North, on the other hand, merely inclined his head slightly. It was his favorite and most often used gesture.

Scot elbowed his brother in the arm. "This'll be fun, won't it?"

North turned a beleaguered eye toward the man who was ten minutes his senior, but Jason knew the exasperation was an act. Mostly. "Do try to retain a modicum of propriety, will you?"

"When a situation calls for propriety, I employ it," Scot said, straightening his livery. He tossed his brother a taunting glare before turning his attention back to Jason. "One more thing, my lord. Miss Stroud is awaiting you upstairs."

Cora. Jason had forgotten about her in the wake of learning about Ethan. Like the other gentlemen who attended his parties, Jason sought entertainment and she was his. Though she wasn't his mistress. His father had kept more than one, and Jason made damned sure he didn't keep any.

"In the south blue room," Scot added.

Since Lockwood House offered a variety of chambers for party attendees, each bedroom—save Jason's, which was off-limits to everyone, even Jason didn't use it on these nights—upstairs was designated with a direction and a color for identification purposes.

Jason nodded before downing the rest of his whisky and setting the empty tumbler on the sideboard. "Thank you." He went to the door and then turned. "I nearly forgot. Keep an eye on Dilly tonight. I'd prefer he stayed downstairs. Last time he used the prop room, he broke a few things."

Scot laughed loudly. "I remember. The man has no finesse."

North shook his head almost imperceptibly. It was, Jason knew, an expression of humor, however small.

Jason departed the office and made his way to the massive staircase at the back of his foyer. He passed a masked couple as they made their descent. Engrossed in each other, they didn't acknowledge him, so he walked right on past.

His mind turned to his half brother. He'd always known they would have another confrontation, and it seemed the reckoning was near. Ethan would be back with his taunts and asinine declarations. Only this time, Jason would be ready.

What did Ethan want? Gentility? Respectability? Since Jason couldn't gain either, the thought of Ethan doing so thoroughly galled him. He was the reason Jason had been cast out, and it seemed the time might be ripe for Jason to return the favor.

ONCE AGAIN, LADY Lydia Prewitt was on a fool's errand. Aunt Margaret was rabid to learn all she could about Mr. Locke's sudden appearance in Society, starting with the nature of his relationship to the young and recently widowed Lady Aldridge. And since Aunt Margaret had threatened to return Lydia to her father in remote Northumberland if she failed to discover the truth, Lydia had no choice but to obey her directives.

Mr. Locke was of interest because he was the bastard brother of the notorious—and very likely mad—Lord Lockwood, who was neither seen nor desired in Society. Gleaning information about him was important to Aunt Margaret, as she firmly believed that knowledge was power. Which meant Aunt Margaret had to be the most powerful woman in London.

However, powerful wasn't the same as liked or admired, and Lydia had decided that she preferred the latter over the former. It was a sentiment Aunt Margaret didn't share, which had caused them to be at extreme odds of late—hence Aunt Margaret's threats to return Lydia to the middle of nowhere, also known as "home." Not that it was difficult to be at odds with Aunt Margaret. She was a singularly domineering and demanding person.

Aldridge House loomed before Lydia. Larger than most town houses, its façade spanned at least three of her aunt's house. A wrought iron gate separated a path leading to the door from the sidewalk.

Lydia arrived at the gate at the same time as a tall, well-dressed gentleman. She lifted her eyes to his face and stifled a gasp. A long scar cut down his left cheek marring what would have been a handsome visage. He tipped his head to the side so that his right cheek was angled toward her.

"Are you going to Aldridge House?" he asked.

"Yes." Lydia searched her memory for his identity. She prided herself on knowing everyone, but she was certain they'd never met. Then it hit her: the scar. She did gasp then. "Are you . . . Lord Lockwood?"

His gaze narrowed slightly.

Aunt Margaret had said that Locke and Lockwood were half brothers. There was also a rumor that they shared certain physical characteristics, which only gave credence to her aunt's declaration. Lydia studied Lockwood's features, trying to discern a resemblance, but she'd only seen Mr. Locke across a crowded ballroom. She supposed they were nearly the same height. Maybe. And they both had very dark hair. But, brothers? She couldn't say for sure.

The brim of his hat shaded his face from the weak afternoon sun finding its way through the mottled clouds, but she saw his right brow arch. "I'm afraid you have me at a disadvantage."

"Lady Lydia Prewitt. It's a pleasure to meet you." And a boon. When Aunt Margaret heard of this, perhaps Lydia would earn a reprieve from having to hunt gossip. "Are you here to see Lady Aldridge?"

He opened the gate and held it for her. "I hope to, yes. Paying my respects."

Lydia walked into the front courtyard and looked back at Lord Lockwood as if she could visually detect whether he was actually insane. He tipped his head up slightly, giving her a clear view of his features and she didn't doubt for a moment that he was a scoundrel. It seemed to be written in the wide set of his mouth, the alluring coal-black lashes spiking from his eyes, and of course that terrible scar. What was a mad scoundrel who avoided Society doing visiting Lady Aldridge?

Although Lydia had lost her taste for gossip-mongering, she couldn't quell her genuine interest in people. Especially enigmatic people who never ventured into Society with whom she now found herself. So she made small talk. "Awful business with Lord Aldridge. Such a tragedy."

"Mmm."

Apparently Lord Lockwood was not inclined to chatter. He waited for Lydia's maid to enter the courtyard and then he shut the gate. Lydia sent her maid a look and a slight nod. The maid took a position along the low iron fencing.

Lydia tried again. "Are you a friend of Lady Aldridge's?"

"I knew her husband." He didn't elaborate, and since his only interaction with Society gentlemen came from the scandalous parties he hosted, Lydia wondered if Lord Aldridge had been a guest. Several well-placed gentlemen were purported to attend Lockwood House's entertainments, which she found more than a bit hypocritical since Lord Lockwood himself was generally disdained as an utter blackguard for having them in the first place.

At the door, Lord Lockwood rapped on the wood. A scant moment later, the butler appeared. "I'm sorry, her ladyship isn't accepting visitors," he said.

Lydia was nothing if not persistent. Undeterred, she flashed her best smile at the butler. "If you let her know Lady Lydia Prewitt is calling, I believe she'd like to see me. I bring tidings from my aunt."

The butler looked at her as if she were an oddity. "Her ladyship isn't feeling well today. Perhaps another day."

Lord Lockwood pivoted so that he partially blocked Lydia. He handed the butler his card. "Would you inform her ladyship that I'm here? I'll wait." His tone was firm and brooked no disagreement. Lydia imagined he was used to issuing orders.

The butler gave a single nod and then closed the door.

Lord Lockwood might be a Society outsider, but he'd elicited more results than she. Apparently his name was still worth something, and because of that she was doubly glad she'd encountered him today. Aunt Margaret would be very annoyed if Lydia came home empty-handed, but now, thanks to Lockwood, she would not.

He turned to face her, still keeping the left side of his face slightly averted. "Do you visit Lady Aldridge often?"

"No." Like him, she found herself giving a brief response. However, she couldn't very well reveal that she was here rooting for information about why Lady Aldridge was attending church with his bastard brother.

Better to deflect the conversation back to him. "Have you seen Lady Aldridge often since her husband passed?"

He sent her a look that made her wonder if he thought *she* was mad. "No."

Attempting to smooth over any discomfort, she said, "Well, I suppose it's not odd that neither of us have seen her. She's kept to herself for the most part, hasn't she? Until recently." She watched him closely to see his reaction. Was he here because of his half brother? What was *their* relationship?

"Mmm." Again, the noncommittal utterance.

The door opened a small amount, and the butler's round face appeared in the gap. "Lady Aldridge thanks you both for stopping by and hopes to receive you soon, but she's simply too ill today."

Lydia stepped to the side so that she wasn't blocked by Lockwood. "Please convey my best to her ladyship."

"And mine," Lockwood put in.

The butler nodded before closing the door. Lydia glanced at Lockwood as she turned. "I do hope she's not terribly ill."

Lockwood pivoted, and they started back toward the gate. "Mmm."

"That's the third time you've done that," Lydia said. "But I suppose your conversation skills might be a bit out of practice."

She inwardly cringed and shot him a regretful look. She wasn't typically sarcastic—out loud, at least— except with the select few with whom she felt comfortable. Did that mean she felt comfortable with Lord Lockwood, of all people?

He slowed his pace and stared down at her. He didn't

appear angry, but with that scar and eyes the color of the Thames in winter—a dark, murky gray—he looked fierce. "Yes, they might just be," he said softly, with what she thought could be a touch of humor.

Lydia relaxed, but only briefly. She shouldn't leave yet. If she failed to gather even a sliver of gossip for Aunt Margaret, she might find herself on the next mail coach to Northumberland. Expulsion would make the six years she'd spent entrenching herself in London Society all for naught. She'd likely wind up married to a sheep farmer who lived thirty miles from the nearest village. Rural sheep farmers were fine and good for someone who loved the country and isolation. But Lydia loved the bustle and noise—even the smell—of London.

Fortified with the need to cling to the life she'd built in Town, Lydia gathered her courage and ignored her shame, two things she'd mastered under Aunt Margaret's tutelage, and made a nuisance of herself. "Forgive my boldness, but I'm afraid I can't let this opportunity go without asking. Why are you here? You're a recluse, and yet here you are calling on Lady Aldridge."

He gave a little shrug. "Perhaps I'm just thoughtful. Is there something wrong with that?"

"Of course not, but you must agree it's . . . odd."

"No, I mustn't agree." He paused, his gaze assessing her shrewdly. "You're going to tell everyone you've seen me here, aren't you?"

If Aunt Margaret had anything to say about it—and she unfortunately did—Lydia would tell anyone who would listen and even those who wouldn't. But maybe he didn't want her to. If he asked her not to tell, she'd agree, even though it would likely earn her Aunt Margaret's undying wrath if she ever found out. Hesitantly she asked, "Is your visit here a secret?"

"Not at all. Feel free to tell everyone you've met the mysterious and dastardly Lord Lockwood." His eyes bored into hers with exacting precision, as if he was daring her to do what he said.

She stared into his eyes, unable to look away. "Mysterious, yes, but *dastardly*? However can I draw such a conclusion after our brief encounter?" Because everything about him—from the notorious parties he hosted to the vicious scar delineating his face—said he *was* dastardly. And scandalous and dangerous and who knew what else.

They arrived at the gate. He opened it for her. "I'm sure you'll find the right word—or words—to describe me," he drawled, his voice carrying the barest hint of darkness.

Delicious.

Lydia stopped. Where had *that* word come from? Her gaze darted to his scar. She was oddly fascinated by it. His ruined face should be unsettling, and she imagined most people—especially young ladies—cringed from it. But she found herself wanting to touch it. The wound had to have hurt quite a lot. He tipped his face again, averting the left side from her inquisitive gaze. Questions burned her tongue, but for the first time in she couldn't remember how long she didn't release them.

She stepped from the courtyard, and from the corner of her eye saw her maid inch forward. Lord Lockwood held the gate open until she haltingly made her way through it. She kept her gaze carefully averted from his face as she went to stand several feet down the sidewalk.

Lord Lockwood latched the iron clasp of the gate and then turned to Lydia. Again, he kept his right side prominent, and she wondered if he even realized it or if it was simply habit. How long ago had he received the scar? Aunt Margaret would know. She knew everything. And she was going to be giddy when she heard Lydia had met the reclusive Lord Lockwood.

"It was a pleasure to meet you, Lady Lydia." His deep voice resonated in her belly and that word sounded in her head again like a warning: *delicious*.

Her pulse ticked up. "I do hope we'll meet again."

He smiled then, and Lydia's knees nearly melted. "You never know, but I shouldn't think so."

"Then I shall have to treasure this interlude always," she said, meaning every word. He carried an indescribable air. It was equal parts mystery and danger, but there was something else. Something that made her quivery and silly. "Though, I'll endeavor to ensure it isn't the last time."

He leaned slightly forward, his eyes gleaming. "I'll look forward to your efforts."

She inclined her head and slowly turned away from him. She was reluctant to leave, but what was she going to do, stand there and trade flirtatious banter with him all afternoon? That sounded heavenly, actually.

She passed her maid and after a few steps turned her head. Lockwood's back was retreating down the street toward his carriage, which was parked at the opposite end of Aldridge House. She willed him to turn and look at her, but he didn't. With an internal sigh, she turned back and continued on her solitary way.

Chapter Two

JASON STEPPED INTO Lockwood House and gave his gloves and hat to North, who gestured with his head to the left—toward the sitting room off the foyer.

"My lord, a Mr. Teague from Bow Street is waiting to see you."

Bow Street? Jason's gaze met North's in silent communication, then he turned and entered the sitting room.

A burly man with a balding pate and wearing a somber gray suit stood as Jason stepped over the threshold. He held his black hat in his meaty hands. "Good afternoon, my lord." His tone was deep and his words clean, though they didn't carry the clipped delivery of the aristocracy.

Jason moved into the room after closing the door behind him. Curiosity pricked his neck. "Good afternoon, Mr. Teague. How can I be of assistance today?"

Deep lines furrowed across Teague's forehead. "I'm afraid I'm here on a sensitive matter."

Jason's curiosity intensified. "Indeed? Let us be comfortable, then." He gestured for Teague to sit as he seated himself in a chair covered in rich burgundy damask.

Depositing himself back upon the settee from which he'd risen, Teague set his hat beside him. "I'd like to ask you some questions about Mr. Ethan Locke."

What had Ethan done to draw the attention of Bow

Street? Jason had wondered if he was corrupt, as some thief-takers were wont to be. How else did he sport the expensive, bejeweled rings Jason had spied on his fingers when he'd last seen him at the Bucket of Blood?

Jason relaxed into the chair and smiled. "How can I help?"

Teague set his hands on his knees. "Thank you, my lord. Can you confirm the rumor that he's your half brother?" His gaze was direct, probing even.

Jason saw no reason to lie, particularly when being honest might somehow cause trouble for a man who'd done more than his part in ruining Jason's life. He set his elbows on the arms of the chair and sat back. "As much as I'd rather not claim relation to him, yes, he is my father's bastard."

"I appreciate your openness, my lord. Have you been in contact with him?"

"Not recently. After my father's death, he and his mother found a new protector." Jason weighed whether to tell the Runner about their altercation seven years ago, but decided to wait and see if it was pertinent. "I only just learned he was moving about in Society."

"So this was a surprise to you?" At Jason's nod he continued. "Do you know where he's been the last several years?"

"Here in town, though not in Society. I see him at boxing matches now and again." Tension spiraled down Jason's neck. He enjoyed a good bout, but seeing Ethan at one never failed to ruin it. "He sponsored a fighter last spring."

"Yes, we've spoken to Mr. Ackley," Teague said.

Jason wondered if they'd also spoken to the other

man who'd fought for Ethan—Lord Ambrose Sevrin. But again, Jason kept that to himself. Perhaps Sevrin wouldn't appreciate being involved. Jason would talk to him, provided he was even in London at present.

Teague's lips pursed, and he glanced at the floor briefly. "Do you have any plans to contact Locke now that he's come out?"

"I might." *Especially now that I know Bow Street is investigating him. But what for?* "Do you suspect my half brother of some crime?"

Teague tipped his head to the side and was quiet a moment. "I shouldn't say, my lord. However, seeing as you are his relation and a peer, it seems I could trust you with a few details. Particularly since you are inclined to help." The last was said with the barest inflection of a question, but Jason understood. If Teague gave him information, Jason must do the same.

"I'm *eager* to help, Mr. Teague." Anything to put an end to Ethan's foray into Society.

"I'm sure you know that Lord Aldridge was found to be the leader of a theft ring. It was in the papers last spring."

Jason's pulse thrummed. "Yes, I'm aware."

Teague leaned forward. "The thefts stopped after his death, but they picked up again a month or so ago. Then Mr. Jagger—sorry, Mr. Locke—showed up."

Bow Street of course knew his real last name. "No need to apologize. His name is Jagger after all, not Locke and certainly not Lockwood. Do you suspect him of taking over Aldridge's theft ring?"

"His association with Lady Aldridge seems . . . odd. We don't believe she was involved with her husband's crimes at all, but she's kept almost entirely to herself since his death. Until she allowed Jagger to take her to church. We're simply trying to ascertain your brother's motives." He shook his head infinitesimally. "The timing of his appearance and the resurgence of thefts in Mayfair is simply too coincidental to ignore."

Jason didn't believe in coincidence. "I agree. Is he still a thief-taker?"

"Not for some time." Teague frowned. "I don't think he was a very honest one, either."

Jason snorted. "That's not surprising."

"May I speak plainly, my lord?" Teague asked tentatively.

"Please."

"You seem to hold your half brother in low regard. Why?"

Jason ran his hands along the curved gilt arms of his chair and offered a bitter smile. "Ethan was my father's favorite, as was his mother, and he took every opportunity to lord it over me and my mother. I wouldn't put anything past him. To say that we share a rivalry is an understatement. When my father died, he and his mother were finally out of our lives."

Teague seemed rapt. "You haven't spoken to him since then?"

"Just once." Again, Jason didn't want to divulge the specifics of that event. He only said, "He visited me to ask for some letters his mother had written to our father. I couldn't find them." He hadn't even bothered to look.

Teague frowned again. "Forgive the question, but if he's been absent from your life for several years, why are you certain he's capable of this level of wrongdoing?"

Jason gripped the arms of his chair as the old fury settled into his bones. "He made sure I was cast out from Society, that after my mother's public collapse, I too would lose my standing. All of London thinks me a madman, Mr. Teague, and I have Ethan to thank for that. He's ruthless when it comes to getting what he wants."

His eyes widening slightly, Teague leaned back against the settee. "I see."

Ready for the interview to conclude, Jason stood. "Then you also see how much I'd like to be of service to your investigation."

Teague plucked up his hat and levered himself to his feet. "I'm pleased to hear it, my lord. Do let me know if you learn anything."

"I will notify Bow Street at once." Jason led him to the door of the sitting room.

Teague inclined his head before putting his hat atop it. "Good day, my lord."

North showed him through the foyer and then outside. Then the butler turned to Jason with a questioning look.

"You heard that?" Jason asked, well aware that North sometimes eavesdropped, though his motivation was perfectly acceptable. He liked to anticipate needs before one even knew they had them and organize things with the best possible efficiency. He was a damned good butler.

North crossed the foyer to join him. "I did, my lord. How do you plan to proceed?"

Jason's mind worked. He would help Bow Street with their investigation. To do that, he needed to kindle some sort of relationship with Ethan. The thought turned his stomach. "Teague said Ethan's been invited to some events. Who the hell is extending him invitations?"

"I can find out, my lord."

"No, it doesn't matter. What matters is that I am invited to the same things." But how the hell was that going to be possible? Jason's invitations had dried up seven years ago. Anger ripped through him again. Ethan was effortlessly gliding into the Society that had exiled Jason.

"You could angle for a few invitations," North said. "You've become friendly with several gentlemen in prominent positions."

While that was true, they'd befriended him as the host of scandal-filled parties who provided them with all the gambling, liquor, and courtesans they could want. Such a relationship didn't precisely translate to sharing a drink at White's or exchanging pleasantries at Almack's, where he doubted he could even obtain a voucher. Anyway, he didn't really *want* to be included.

Still, if he wanted to help Bow Street, he had to do something. And if he thought about it, the idea of encountering the lovely Lady Lydia again held a certain appeal. She hadn't been cowed by his hideous face. In fact, if he hadn't been mistaken, she'd actually flirted with him.

He looked expectantly at North, suspecting he already had a plan. "What do you suggest? Even if people don't remember what happened here seven years ago, they certainly haven't forgotten the party I hosted the other night. And if they don't, I'll be having another soon. In short, I have no invitations, and no respectable person would extend one."

North's eyes gleamed with satisfaction. "In fact, you do. Just one, but that's all you need."

Jason stared at him blankly. "I do? What idiot is heedless enough to send me an invitation?"

"Mrs. Lloyd-Jones, my lord. She hosts a bi-weekly tea and always sends a card."

Good Christ, she wasn't an idiot; she was an old friend of his mother's. The only one who'd cared enough to visit after Mother's collapse. The only one who still wrote to her. Jason shook his head. *He* was the idiot for neglecting her. "When?"

"Day after tomorrow, if you'd care to attend."

Jason nearly laughed at the idea of attending a *tea*, but he had to start somewhere. "All right, I'll go. Send Mrs. Lloyd-Jones a note. I don't want to send her into a fit of apoplexy by showing up unannounced."

North's nod was brisk, an economic movement as efficient as he was. "Shall I assume you wish to cancel the next party?"

The vice party. What had started after Jason's removal from Society as a way for Jason to build his own circle of acceptance had become a well-attended and sought-after event by those in the highest echelons of the ton. He offered a haven for those seeking pleasure outside of Society's dictates, and he'd become accustomed to providing that support. Within that world, he was the arbiter of acceptability, the style-setter, the very king. And he had no plans to relinquish any of it. "Assume no such thing. Haven't the invitations already gone out?"

"Indeed. However, and do forgive my impertinence, but do you think it wise to have the party when you are trying to gain acceptance?"

He pinned his butler with a dark stare. "Acceptance is not my goal. Once I've concluded my business with Ethan, I'll be more than happy to return to my fiefdom here at Lockwood House."

Another quick nod, but this one dipped a bit lower, offering the faintest note of apology. "It's good that you're going to Mrs. Lloyd-Jones's tea. Perhaps you'll be able to change some perceptions about you and your family."

Jason was only mildly surprised by North's suggestion. Though usually stoic, he'd also been a supportive friend over the years. Indeed, Jason liked him and his brother better than just about anyone else. Which was why Jason teased him and asked, "What the devil's gotten into you? You aren't pining for some happy ending to this family tragedy? What has marriage done to you?"

North, who'd recently wed Lockwood House's housekeeper, Sarah, allowed a small smile. "You'd be amazed what the love of a good woman can do for you, my lord."

Jason barked a laugh. "For you, maybe." He turned and strode across the foyer toward his office.

North had probably only been teasing in return, but Jason couldn't ignore the underlying message: Love made things better. However, Jason didn't need any reminders that love had never found him and likely never would.

His mother had loved him in her overbearing and manic way, but her mind was fragile now and she often thought he was his father. At those times, she despised him.

Jason paused at the doorway to the drawing room. It

was large and airy, decorated in blues and browns with a touch of gold here and there. A pleasing environment his mother had once loved to entertain in. Now, it was the entry point to London's most notorious parties.

This room had been something else, too. Once, it had seen him break down in a way very similar to his mother's collapse, giving birth to his fear that he would end up just like her.

And maybe he would.

LYDIA'S AUNT MARGARET sat in her upstairs sitting room in a chair near the windows overlooking Davies Street below. Her eyes were narrowed as she read through her mail, which was piled atop her lap.

Eager to share her news and perhaps earn a smile from her aunt, Lydia hastened into the room. "Aunt, I have incredible news to share."

Aunt Margaret looked up, the dark irises of her eyes gleaming like tiny black marbles. Her lips were drawn tight, causing the flesh around her mouth to wrinkle more than normal. A lifetime of judging others had already carved deep grooves that did nothing to improve her fading looks and everything to indicate her character.

"Indeed?" Her mouth curved into an anticipatory smile. "Come, tell me." She inclined her head to the chair situated beside hers.

Lydia smiled with relief. Life was so much more tolerable when her aunt was happy. "I wasn't able to see Lady Aldridge—she's ill." Aunt Margaret's face fell, but Lydia rushed to add, "However, I encountered someone who made the trip more than worthwhile." Lydia paused for dramatic effect. "Lord Lockwood."

But Aunt Margaret didn't gape, nor did her eyes widen with excitement. No, her mouth tightened, and she looked . . . angry. "Where?" she snapped.

Lydia hid her disappointment. "At Lady Aldridge's. He also went to see her."

"He came out in the light of day to pay a call?" Aunt Margaret pierced Lydia with a look that would curdle most people's stomachs. However, Lydia was used to her moods and didn't flinch. "What did he say?"

"That he was there to pay his respects," Lydia said nervously. Why was Aunt Margaret perturbed by this? Seeing Lord Lockwood surely had to be a coup, especially since Lydia had actually spoken with him. And flirted with him—though she didn't want to disclose that. Some things were hers alone. Or at least she wished they could be.

"What else?" Aunt Margaret leaned forward, her chest, which only seemed to expand with age, rising and falling rapidly with expectant breaths. "There has to be more than that. You're not so silly as to believe him when he says he's there to pay his respects."

Why not? Did everyone need to have an ulterior motive like Aunt Margaret typically did? Lydia tried to ignore that she'd had the same reaction upon meeting him. It was going to take some time to banish the bad habits Aunt Margaret had instilled.

Lydia did, however, need to reveal some of what she'd learned. "Well, he hasn't been seeing her regularly. I'm fairly certain he hasn't seen her at all. He also said his visit wasn't a secret. In fact, he encouraged me to tell everyone I'd seen him." Which was why

Lydia didn't feel *too* bad about sharing this with Aunt Margaret.

Aunt Margaret leaned her head back against the chair, appearing at least slightly mollified. "So the reclusive Lockwood suddenly shows up to call on a widow who's been keeping company with his long-lost bastard brother. There's something more to this story," she mused.

Just as there was more to the story regarding Aunt Margaret's apparent dislike of Lord Lockwood. Lydia weighed whether to risk further irritating her by asking about Lockwood. Probably, Aunt Margaret would become even angrier, and then she'd start threatening Lydia with removal to Northumberland. Or, and Lydia really thought this was the likelier response, Aunt Margaret would relish the notion of regaling Lydia with exactly why she didn't like Lord Lockwood. Lydia knew precisely how to phrase her question.

"Aunt Margaret," she began, infusing her tone with just the right dose of anticipation, "I should be thrilled to hear the story of how Lord Lockwood became London's most reviled bachelor."

Her dark eyes sparking with gleeful intent, Aunt Margaret cocked her head to the side. "Have I never told you the specifics of that tale?"

Lydia shook her head.

"It's frightfully entertaining." Aunt Margaret smoothed her skirt and lifted her chin, like an orator about to launch an important lecture. "To adequately tell this story, I have to go back very far. Back to my own days as a debutante. I've never told you why I didn't marry."

Lydia had always assumed it was because she'd never

been asked, but didn't say so. "No, you haven't," she said with an excitement she didn't feel.

"I was on the verge of becoming betrothed to Lord Benjamin Lockwood—yes, the current Lord Lockwood's father and father to Mr. Ethan Locke."

Betrothed? Aunt Margaret had told her they'd courted, but Lydia didn't realize things had progressed that far. She pivoted toward her aunt in anticipation, no longer having to feign interest. "You never said." And neither had anyone else. Clearly, this wasn't common knowledge.

"No, it was rather . . . humiliating." The sparkly sheen in her eyes hardened to ice. "He was rigorously courting me when Harmony Millhouse showed up in Town. She was quite the toast. Nearly every young buck turned their attentions to her, but she had her sights set on Lockwood."

And she'd won him, too, but Lydia waited for Aunt Margaret to continue.

"She used every nasty trick she could think of to woo him away from me. Told lies about me. Offered him favors I would never have done without a trip to church—regardless of what she said."

Aunt Margaret had been the victim of gossip? Did that explain why she worked so hard to keep herself on the other end of it?

"Scarcely nine months after their wedding she whelped that brat. But I had the final laugh at her expense. Turned out Lockwood was as monogamous as she deserved. Which is to say, not at all. He took a mistress almost immediately, when she was fat with child, not that one can blame a man for doing that. But he never got rid of her, and a few years later, they had their own child—Ethan Locke."

Lydia immediately wondered how that had affected Lockwood—the current Lord Lockwood—but waited for her aunt to continue. Since this was the story of how he had become exiled from Society, she was bound to learn how he'd been influenced.

"Lockwood's care for his mistress literally drove his wife insane. Her jealousy was legendary, and she panted after her husband like a mare begging to be mounted." One could always tell how far into a story Aunt Margaret had fallen by the vulgarity of her descriptions. This was a tale she obviously loved to impart. "When Lockwood died, everyone expected her to return to the sanity of her youth, but she only worsened. She sought out other women he'd dallied with—Lockwood was incapable of remaining faithful, even to his beloved mistress—and berated them. She was obsessed. I felt pity for her son, but then he began to exhibit signs of her madness."

He hadn't seemed all that mad to Lydia. A trifle intimidating perhaps, but in a rather dark, seductive way. Lydia internally shook herself and focused on her aunt's tale.

"He was a quarrelsome child, often in trouble. He was even sent down from Eton for a time after he broke another boy's arm."

Lydia stifled her gasp. She had trouble reconciling the gentleman she'd met that afternoon with a violent young man, but reminded herself she didn't know him at all.

Aunt Margaret's eyes regained their feral gleam. "About seven years ago, Lady Lockwood snapped. No one knows precisely what finally set her off, but she utterly lost her senses in the middle of a supper party. Jumped up from the table and threw her food about like an ill-disciplined child. The footmen tried to escort her out, but she hit at them and shouted insults. It was an obscenely coarse display." And one her aunt had clearly enjoyed.

Another person would have demonstrated at least a modicum of pity—if only because it was expected—and Lydia assumed her aunt did so when relating this story to someone other than her. However, Lydia always got the unvarnished truth of Aunt Margaret's emotions.

Contrary to her aunt, Lydia felt sorry for Lady Lockwood. "What happened to her then?"

Aunt Margaret waved her hand as if she were batting away a pesky insect. "She was taken to some hospital. Lockwood disappeared for a time, to see after her, I imagine. The next we heard of him, he'd suffered a similar loss of his faculties at Lockwood House, ripping rooms apart in a mad rage. Then he showed up a month or so later sporting that hideous scar." She shivered in revulsion, her lip curling. "He went from Sought-After Husband to Social Pariah faster than you can say, 'Bedlam.'"

Lydia had to work hard to stay silent. Aunt Margaret's characterization was woefully unfair, but then she always drew her own conclusions and those conclusions became fact. Never had the cruelty of her "hobby" been more apparent. Lydia felt sick.

Aunt Margaret leaned forward, her gaze narrowed. "Don't you dare pity Jason Lockwood. He dug his own spot in the gutter. Scared his entire staff away with his mad behavior and then started cavorting with

Undesirables—demimondaines, dissolute rakes, the utter dregs of Society." She sneered in distaste. "Then came the scandalous parties. He turned Lockwood House into a destination worse than a gaming hell and more offensive than a brothel. He has no one to blame for his downfall but himself."

"How—" Lydia had been about to say, "can you say that when he was labeled a lunatic and lost all of his standing," but instead forced out, "pathetic."

Aunt Margaret sniffed. "Indeed." Her countenance suddenly turned fierce. "I mean it when I tell you not to pity him. He's not a victim, and neither is his mother. Yes, their madness is—I suppose—tragic, but that's precisely why they shouldn't inflict themselves on polite society. I can only imagine what Lockwood might do now that he's back. Throw his long-lost half brother into the mix and . . . " Her lips spread into an anticipatory grin. "There shall be no dearth of excitement this autumn."

Lydia couldn't find any of that exciting, but didn't say so. Instead, she glanced at the stack of correspondence in Aunt Margaret's lap. "What 'exciting' things are coming up?"

Aunt Margaret held up one of the invitations she'd been reading, "I need to attend a meeting with Mrs. Edgecombe on Thursday, so you'll go to Mrs. Lloyd-Jones's tea by yourself."

Happiness sang through Lydia's veins. She adored Mrs. Lloyd-Jones and enjoyed visiting without the pall of apprehension her aunt's presence caused. Lydia kept her tone even, though, when she said, "Yes, Aunt."

"Mrs. Lloyd-Jones is an old friend of Lady Lockwood's. You might see if she knows anything about Lord Lockwood." Aunt Margaret set the letters on her lap. "Although, I must warn you to tread carefully. While it's of course fine to talk about Lord Lockwood, I don't want you to seem too interested. His reputation is worse than black and I should hate for it to color yours. And above all, you must stay away from him."

Lydia kept her shoulders from sagging. She'd been looking forward to seeing Lord Lockwood and perhaps flirting with him again. Foolishly, she tried to use a bit of logic to help her cause. "Perhaps my encounter with Lord Lockwood will make me the talk of the town again. I was quite popular after my name was written down at White's."

Last spring, a mysterious, masked woman had been seen at a party at Lockwood House. Gentleman wagered on her identity in the betting book at the gentlemen's club, and some young buck had put her name down. Aunt Margaret had been horrified and had locked Lydia in her room for two days. But the young man had recanted, and Lydia had become inexplicably popular for a few weeks. It had been the best weeks of her life in London. People had spoken to her with genuine interest and had even offered sympathy for her plight. She'd do anything to recapture that—including befriend Lord Lockwood.

"Lydia!" Aunt Margaret barked. She leaned forward, her dark eyes spitting fire. "You were extremely fortunate things worked out as they did, but Society is fickle. Linking yourself to Lord Lockwood will ruin you, do you understand?"

Lydia didn't, but realized further argument was futile. She nodded.

"Good." Aunt Margaret inhaled, and her features relaxed. "Let us discuss Mr. Locke a moment. I was certain you were going to be introduced last night, but then you took a turn on the terrace with that worthless Goodwin. By the time you returned to the ballroom, Locke had already gone."

Hardly anyone ever asked Lydia for a stroll or a dance, and she simply couldn't summon an iota of regret. She could, however, come up with a tidy fib to rationalize it. "I'd hoped to learn what Goodwin's cousin thought of Locke's presence."

Aunt Margaret squinted at her. *"And?"* she drawled, dragging the word out thrice as long as it needed to be.

Lydia clasped her hands tightly in her lap. "I'm afraid Goodwin hadn't spoken to his cousin on the subject."

"Why should he?" Aunt Margaret laughed cruelly. "Goodwin's cousin is a bloody earl. He doesn't make time for his nothing second-cousin. You should have known that." She lifted her chin and glared at Lydia, delivering a visual set-down to go with the verbal. "You're a right nodcock sometimes. Have I not told you time and time again that knowledge is how we retain our place in this world?"

Lydia wasn't a nodcock ever, but again she bit her tongue. Things were always the way Aunt Margaret saw them. *Always.* "Yes, Aunt Margaret."

"Tonight," Aunt Margaret began in her clearest dictatorial tone, "you will make every effort to gain an introduction to Mr. Locke, and you'll angle for a dance. Lord knows you'll have plenty of space on your card. You will determine what he's doing with Lady Aldridge. And now that we know Lockwood is somehow involved, you'll query him about his half brother as well."

So many of these things were out of her control, not that Aunt Margaret cared. "I'll do my best."

Aunt Margaret nodded slightly, which had the effect of looking like preening. Or maybe it just felt that way because of the sycophantic manner in which Lydia felt beholden to address her.

Lydia turned her gaze toward the windows and the world beyond. Someday she'd have the opportunity to leave her aunt's web of gossip, but as each year passed without a marriage proposal, Lydia began to despair that she would become a jaded spinster. Just like Aunt Margaret.

Chapter Three

LYDIA SITUATED HERSELF on Mrs. Lloyd-Jones's settee. Her drawing room contained six ladies, including herself—a small affair, but then Mrs. Lloyd-Jones's teas rarely saw above a dozen visitors. It was early yet, perhaps others would drop by. For now the usual attendees were present: the hostess, her spinster sister, Miss Vining, who resided with Mrs. Lloyd-Jones, her close friend, Mrs. Yarrow, and three other matrons.

Of the six, Lydia realized just one had a living husband—Lady Trevett, who was also the youngest woman in attendance aside from Lydia and a somewhat formidable gossip in her own right. How sad that most of these women were alone. Lydia imagined herself thirty years in the future with no one to keep her company save a few friends. She wouldn't even have a young female relative to manage—not that she would ever do to anyone what Aunt Margaret had done to her.

But at least they *had* friends, something Lydia had very few of as a result of so many years dancing to Aunt Margaret's tune. She had one close friend and had begun to acquire a few others since trying to shed herself of her reputation for gossip. She'd only be able to continue on this path if she got away from Aunt Margaret, which meant she had to find a husband.

Next to Lydia, Mrs. Lloyd-Jones was deep in conversation with Lady Trevett, who was seated on a facing settee. They were discussing the previous night's ball, where Lydia had once again failed to draw Mr. Locke's notice and as a result had suffered Aunt Margaret's anger in the coach on the way home.

Lady Trevett leaned forward in her chair. "Lady Lydia, is it true you encountered Lord Lockwood the other day? I heard it from Mrs. Horwatt last night, but I didn't have a chance to find you and obtain the real story."

Lydia nodded. "Yes, I happened upon him outside Lady Aldridge's. We were both there to pay a visit. Unfortunately, she was ill."

Everyone exchanged pitying nods. "Such a shame about Lord Aldridge," Mrs. Lloyd-Jones said. "To lose one's husband is bad enough, but to lose him in such a fashion . . . " She shuddered delicately. Answering murmurs of agreement filled the room.

"How did you find Lockwood?" Mrs. Yarrow asked, her eyes wide. "Is he as fearsome as they say?"

Last night, Lydia had disclosed the details—well, not *all* of the details—of their encounter to a handful of people, but each time she'd grown more irritated by their questions. It was absurd, but her experience with Lord Lockwood felt personal. *Intimate.* She was inexplicably loath to share it.

To keep herself from glaring in response, Lydia turned her gaze toward Mrs. Lloyd-Jones. She seemed to be suppressing a smile. How curious.

Mrs. Lloyd-Jones addressed Mrs. Yarrow with a firm tone. "I can't imagine why he would appear fearsome."

Lydia inclined her head in agreement, glad for the support. "Indeed, he was a perfect gentleman. He held the gate open for my maid and me." Lydia strove to direct the conversation where she needed it to go: To Mr. Locke. "Did any of you speak with Mr. Locke last night?"

Mrs. Lloyd-Jones tipped her head to the side. "Mr. Locke? I thought you'd set your cap for Mr. Goodwin."

Lydia worked to keep the conversation on its necessary path. "It's difficult *not* to be interested in a charming gentleman who asks you to dance. But surely you must agree Mr. Locke is rather dashing. One only wonders where he's been hiding."

"Mr. Locke is quite handsome and terribly charming." Lady Trevett leaned forward, her eyes intent. "How is it Lady Margaret knows he is Lord Lockwood's son?" She quickly added, "I'm not questioning the veracity, of course. Everyone knows your aunt only speaks the truth." Lady Trevett was smart enough to know not to cast even a smidgeon of doubt against one of Society's most feared matrons.

Lydia cast a quick glance at Mrs. Lloyd-Jones. As a friend of Lady Lockwood's she could likely vouch for Aunt Margaret's declaration. However, when she said nothing, Lydia gave the answer she'd rehearsed. "My dear aunt could never reveal her source in this intimate matter, but she was familiar with the Lockwood family."

Settling back, Lady Trevett tapped her finger against her lip. "Ah, yes, I seem to recall . . . "

Mrs. Lloyd-Jones's butler appeared in the doorway. "Lord Lockwood, my lady."

Every head turned at once, and the resulting gasps were audible.

Lydia had reached for her cup, but was glad she

hadn't picked it up. She likely would have dropped it. The sound of breaking china echoed her thoughts and drew everyone's attention to Miss Vining, who stared open-mouthed at the door, her teacup in pieces at her feet. Suddenly Mrs. Lloyd-Jones's suppressed smile made sense—she'd known his arrival was imminent.

Lord Lockwood's intimidating figure filled the doorway. Lydia's heart hammered as she looked up at him. He was, without question, the most broad-shouldered man she'd ever seen. And quite tall, with dark hair, and of course that vicious scar running down the left side of his face.

"Good afternoon, ladies." His deep tone filled the drawing room as he stepped over the threshold. He offered a serene smile, which drew her to stare at his scar again. Did it pain him? How had it happened? Did he hate it very much?

Lydia shook herself from her fancy and caught sight of Lady Trevett's horrified expression. Goodness, couldn't the woman rein in her reaction? He wasn't ghastly to behold. Oh, but perhaps that wasn't the cause of her distress. It was simply his scandalous presence.

Mrs. Lloyd-Jones stood abruptly. She grinned and because Lydia knew her, she knew the welcoming expression was genuine—just as everyone else's shock was equally real. "My dear boy, do come in. I'm honored by your attendance. Indeed, I shall be the envy of every woman in Town." She gestured to the lot of them seated about the room. "All of us will be.

"Lord Lockwood," she said with a knowing smile, "I believe you've already met my dear friend Lady Lydia Prewitt."

He moved slowly closer, and the advance seemed somehow predatory. She attributed such nonsense to his size and ignored the way the drawing room suddenly felt quite small. And warm. "It's a pleasure to see you again, Lady Lydia." He bowed and Lydia wished she'd offered her hand. What would it feel like to have a man such as him touch her? He was vice and scandal incarnate. *Delicious.* Oh confound it, there was that word again!

She smoothed her skirt as if she could gentle the thudding of her heart. "The pleasure is mine, my lord."

"Would you care for tea?" Mrs. Lloyd-Jones asked as she sank back down onto the settee.

"Yes, thank you. No cream, and just a bit of sugar." He looked around at the shocked faces of the other women. "I hope it's all right I've invaded your drawing room." He turned his attention to Mrs. Lloyd-Jones.

Mrs. Lloyd-Jones poured his tea and stirred in a trifle of sugar. "You are more than welcome. Please, sit." She gestured to the rather feminine-looking, pale yellow-cushioned gilt chair situated very near Lydia.

He lowered himself to the edge of the seat, looking as if he feared he would break the piece. Perhaps he would. He was huge. Wild. Unlike any other gentleman Lydia had ever met. But then he wasn't a gentleman, even if he had given evidence to the contrary—holding gates open for her and her maid, bowing elegantly before her.

Mrs. Lloyd-Jones finished with the tea. "Lydia, be a dear and give Lord Lockwood his teacup."

Lydia picked up the cup and saucer and transferred them to Lord Lockwood. His fingers brushed against hers. Though they were both gloved, her imagination threatened to run away with itself from the slight contact—had he intended to touch her?

"Mrs. Lloyd-Jones's blend is excellent." Lydia mentally chastised herself for the inane comment. Lockwood likely didn't give a fig about tea!

Lord Lockwood's gaze was intent, and when it was combined with that ferocious scar, he looked utterly imposing, like some warrior of old. Thankfully, he shifted his heady regard to their hostess. "I must apologize that it's taken me so long to accept your kind invitation."

"Not at all, my dear. Though, forgive me for saying, your presence is most remarkable," Mrs. Lloyd-Jones said.

Miss Vining gasped again, and Lydia didn't suppose it was due to the footman who was cleaning up the mess of her broken teacup. Mrs. Lloyd-Jones threw her sister an exasperated glance. "Bridget, pull yourself together. We're being visited by Lord Lockwood, not Lucifer."

Lord Lockwood cradled his teacup in his massive hands, making him seem even more masculine, if that were possible. "I'm certain there are those—perhaps even in this room—who would argue there is no distinction." He lowered his voice and gave Mrs. Lloyd-Jones and Lydia a provocative stare. "And I wouldn't blame them."

Since Mrs. Lloyd-Jones had seen fit to address his attendance, Lydia saw no reason not to pursue the topic. "Why have you come today, Lord Lockwood? Is your presence here anything to do with the arrival of Mr. Locke in town?" Her heart fluttered as she waited for his response. Was it possible to offend a man who likened himself to Satan?

He returned her interest with a frank perusal. Lydia's flesh heated, but she blamed it on the boldness of her query.

"I've yet to make the acquaintance of Mr. Locke," he said. "Perhaps you can introduce me?" He sipped his tea while his eyes continued to bore into hers.

"This is hardly a suitable conversation," Mrs. Yarrow said, giving Lydia an insistent glare. Perhaps it wasn't polite to question a man about his rumored bastard half brother, but it wasn't as if they all weren't curious!

"It's quite all right," Lord Lockwood said, casting a knowing glance about the circle of ladies. "I'm aware of the rumors regarding Mr. Locke and myself."

Mrs. Yarrow's eyes widened and she blinked rapidly as her cheeks colored.

Lydia could feel the tension swirling about the room. Every single woman there wanted to ask him if Mr. Locke was indeed his bastard brother. Every woman but Lydia. She knew the truth, and not because Aunt Margaret had declared it. She knew it because Lord Lockwood's eyes told her so.

"How is your mother?" Mrs. Lloyd-Jones asked, effectively dissipating the current of anxiety. "Her last letter said you were visiting."

He busied himself with his teacup, keeping his eyes averted from everyone. "She's well, thank you." He looked up again and though he didn't reveal the slightest bit of discomfort, Lydia had the sense his mother wasn't as well as he claimed.

Mrs. Lloyd-Jones smiled with genuine warmth. Clearly she was an intimate friend of Lady Lockwood's, just as Aunt Margaret had said. "I look forward to when she returns to town. She mentioned that would be soon."

Lord Lockwood took another sip of tea. "Perhaps."

Lady Trevett set her teacup down with a clatter. "Well, I'm afraid I must go." She stood, smoothing the folds of her skirt with a flick of her wrist.

Lord Lockwood got to his feet. "I hope I haven't driven you away."

Lady Trevett pursed her lips and said nothing for a moment, as if she were trying to determine the best course of action. At length she turned to Mrs. Lloyd-Jones. "As always, thank you for tea." Then she looked—quite expectantly, as if she were trying to communicate with her eyes—to Lydia. "I'd be happy to drop you at home, dear."

There was no way Lydia was going to miss the opportunity to speak with Lord Lockwood. She tipped her head to the side and offered her a warm, grateful smile. "I appreciate your solicitude, Lady Trevett, but I do believe I'll stay a bit longer."

Lady Trevett's eyes widened briefly and then she moved closer to Lydia. "You mustn't stay," she hissed quietly. "To be in Lord Lockwood's presence could be detrimental to your reputation!"

Mrs. Lloyd-Jones was near enough to hear what she said. "Nonsense. We're having tea, and you can see that nothing untoward has occurred."

Lady Trevett pursed her lips and appeared at least somewhat chastened. "Indeed. Well, good afternoon." She inclined her head to all of the ladies. When her gaze met Lord Lockwood's, she blinked, gave a small nod, and scurried from the room.

When no one spoke, Miss Vining stood. "Please excuse me, I'm feeling a bit fatigued." She did look pale, but Lydia supposed it was due to Lord Lockwood's scandalous presence as opposed to being tired.

Mrs. Lloyd-Jones gave a tiny sigh, audible only to Lydia since she was seated next to her. "Shall I have dinner brought up later?"

"No, I'm sure I'll recover by then." She offered a wan smile and quit the drawing room.

With two of their number fleeing Lockwood's presence, an awkward silence seemed to settle over the room. Never one to allow such social discomforts, Lydia made her move.

She leaned slightly toward their scandalous guest. "Lord Lockwood, would you care to take a stroll in Mrs. Lloyd-Jones's garden?" It was a terribly forward invitation, particularly given his notoriety and Aunt Margaret's admonishment that she avoid him like the Black Plague, but she simply couldn't resist the temptation to flirt with him again.

He turned his head, giving her a better view of the scar that ruined the left side of his face. And it did ruin it—she could see he'd been a devastatingly handsome man before. In profile, when she could see just his right side, his features were very attractively arranged: a rugged chin, a full, yet masculine lower lip, strong cheekbones, and those storm-cloud eyes with those impossibly long lashes.

His lips twisted into an ironic smile. "Aren't you a bold little thing?"

"It's a character flaw, I'm afraid."

"On the contrary. I prefer it to mincing. Yes, let us take a turn." He stood. "Mrs. Lloyd-Jones, I'm going to escort Lady Lydia about the garden for a few minutes.

Do you still keep a collection of yellow roses?"

Mrs. Lloyd-Jones beamed. "You remember! I still have the one your parents gave to me when my youngest was born."

Lord Lockwood's answering nod was a trifle stiff. He held his hand out for Lydia. "Shall we?"

Lydia allowed him to help her up from the settee. His gloved hand was warm, solid. She imagined the rest of him was equally so and didn't chide herself for thinking it. But then she never scolded herself about such things. She got enough scolding from Aunt Margaret.

As he guided her through the drawing room, Lydia felt every pair of eyes follow their progress. Likely they would all discuss this interesting turn as soon as they exited the building. A footman held the door for them and they stepped out onto the bricked veranda.

Mrs. Lloyd-Jones's garden was compact, but well appointed. The rose garden was situated in the back right corner. Lord Lockwood took her arm—with his right one, was it to keep his "good side" toward her?—and led her down the stairs and along the path. The day was a bit cool, and Lydia briefly wondered if she ought to have taken her shawl. However, the heat of his touch seemed to infuse her, and she decided she didn't need it.

He looked down at her and their gazes connected. "I don't remember the last time I escorted a young lady for a stroll."

"I don't remember the last time 'Lucifer' was my escort."

He laughed. "Bold and cheeky, but then I already knew that from the other day."

She felt remarkably at ease with this social pariah.

Again, she wondered how he could be the mad, violent man Aunt Margaret painted him as. "One could also call you bold. Coming here, I mean. You indicated we likely wouldn't meet again, and yet here you are."

"Clearly the thought of seeing you has drawn me out."

Apparently there *would* be flirting. Lydia tried not to appear as thrilled as she felt. "I find that a bit hard to believe. You haven't shown your face in Society in at least six years, and now you've done it twice this week."

He glanced at her and she noticed he was still careful to keep his scarred side averted. "Longer than that, actually. Why did you settle on six?"

"Because that's how long I've been out and we've never met. Until yesterday."

They'd reached the rose garden. A few shrubs still sported a bloom or three, but most were heading toward dormancy for the winter months. She left his arm and went to sniff a butter-yellow bud with pale pink edges. When she looked up, she found him staring at her intently. Oh, he was scandalous all right.

Her pulse quickened. His interest meant she could perhaps get what she wanted. "You said you hadn't made Mr. Locke's acquaintance, but surely you've met your own brother."

His eyes narrowed. He walked toward her, stopping just two feet away. Not terribly close, but not that far either. Her heart continued to pound. Surely because she was being obnoxiously nosy. She refused to credit any other reason—she certainly wasn't afraid of him, no matter how intimidating his size or scarred features might be.

"Why are you so certain he's my brother? I've not

confirmed it. And I'm not lying when I say I haven't met Mr. 'Locke.'"

"You don't have to confirm it. You mask your emotion well, but I've made a habit of studying people." *Thanks to Aunt Margaret.* "Your eyes give a very slight twitch when he's mentioned."

The left corner of his mouth ticked up, pleating his scar. "How . . . observant. If I'm not careful, you're going to pry all of my secrets from me, aren't you?"

The way he asked the question, in that dark, provocative voice, sent frissons of excitement all the way to her toes. She suddenly wanted to know all of his secrets, and not because she wanted to share even one of them. "Will you at least tell me why you came today? You've spent so many years as a recluse."

"Would you believe I came here hoping to see you?"

Lydia could only stare at him as her entire body warmed. He'd left Lockwood House for *her?* She let out a shaky laugh. "You're bamming me."

His gaze was appreciative but held the slightest hint of challenge. "Given your superior powers of observation, surely you can determine whether I am or not." He gave a little shrug. "Perhaps I simply tired of my own company."

Now that she *knew* was untrue. "I don't believe for a moment you're tired of any company. You entertain plenty." Her pulse skipped—had she really just referred to his scandalous vice parties in the light of day in the middle of what should have been an extremely decorous and polite tea?

His lips curved up in a slight smile. "You caught me in a lie, how unsporting of you."

With every line they traded, she felt giddy, and had to

keep herself from grinning. "I could argue it's unsporting of you to lie in the first place."

His smile broadened, and her legs grew weak. When was the last time someone had flirted with her like this? *Never, ever.*

"Well, it's not as if it's appropriate for me to discuss the entertainments I host at Lockwood House with a young lady such as yourself. But tell me, what have you heard?" He stared at her in open inquisition, almost daring her to answer. Who could out-scandalize the other?

Lydia refused to cower beneath the mantle of propriety, not when she'd probably never get another chance to be alone with Lockwood. She moved infinitesimally closer. "Your parties are for a gentleman's enjoyment. You provide lavish food and drink, deep gaming tables, and women. Lots of women." She could only imagine what actually occurred, but this was the general understanding of his parties, with an emphasis on the women.

He also inched forward, closing the distance between them to a mere, disreputable foot. "You have the basic gist. I'd invite you to come see for yourself, but I'm afraid I don't extend invitations to ladies."

He slowly perused her form as if he were verifying that she was in fact a lady. Her skin heated, and the day suddenly turned balmy. Lockwood was not the typical gentleman she encountered—but there she'd done it again. He was no gentleman.

He abruptly turned and offered her his right arm. "We should return. It's shocking enough that you asked me for a stroll. We mustn't do anything further to damage your reputation."

Disappointment settled over her like a cold, spring rain. She took his arm, realizing their flirtation was over—at least for now. Instead, she tried to do what Aunt Margaret wanted her to and asked, "What will you do when you encounter Mr. Locke?"

"Why, I shall thank him," he turned his head to the side and brushed a long, masculine finger down the edge of his scar, "for giving me this."

His own *brother* had scarred him? There was a frigid edge to his tone, but it was natural that he harbor ill-will toward the person who'd disfigured him. He likely hated his half brother, and it seemed with good reason. Lydia found she hated him too in that moment—which was completely illogical given she'd never even made his acquaintance.

They were very near the house now. "I imagine you must want to exact some measure of revenge," she said.

He walked her up to the bricked veranda and then speared her with a heated look. "You'll just have to wait and see."

JASON LINGERED NEAR a vase of flowers on an ornately carved Chinese-motif table in Mrs. Lloyd-Jones's drawing room as she saw her last guest out. His first appearance in Society hadn't been a rousing success exactly, but it hadn't gone as poorly as he might've imagined. Yes, a few of the women had fled, but at least they hadn't fainted dead away, and there'd been only one broken teacup.

Mrs. Lloyd-Jones reentered the drawing room and

closed the door behind her. She was tall and possessed an elegant beauty that hadn't faded with age. Her dark brown hair was streaked with gray, and her coffee-brown eyes still sparkled with wit and intelligence. He had fond memories of her from his childhood—and there were precious few of those. He hadn't expected her to be offended by his attendance today, but he couldn't ignore the joy he felt that she'd actually embraced his presence. Consequently, he felt comfortable enough to be familiar with her.

"Are you certain you should close the door?" he drawled, reaching back to the way he'd worked to charm ladies before he'd been prevented from doing so by his scar. "I'd hate for your reputation to be threatened."

She chuckled. "My dear boy, I'm too old for such poppycock. Now tell me what the devil you're really doing here. When I received your note yesterday morning, I nearly fell into my breakfast." She went to the settee and sat, then patted the space beside her.

If he joined her, she'd be on his left side. She hadn't stared at his scar, not like the audacious Lady Lydia, so perhaps he could be at ease. But in the end, his feet carried him to a chair opposite the settee instead.

He settled himself into the velvety cushion and went about avoiding a direct answer to her question. "I admit I was surprised when your guests were so shocked upon my arrival. Why didn't you warn them?"

She chuckled and waved her hand. "We could all use a bit of excitement."

Perhaps perversely, Jason found he'd been happy to supply it, or maybe he was just charmed by Mrs. Lloyd-Jones's support. "I'm glad to have been of service, though I can't help but wonder if you'll be a pair of ladies short two weeks hence."

Her eyes narrowed shrewdly. "I shall not, if only because I'll force Bridget to attend. And you're procrastinating. Stop it at once and tell me what's brought you out of seclusion."

He flashed a brief smile. "It's not as if I've been lurking in a cave. I live in London, and I see plenty of people."

She gave him a rather maternal stare. "I'm well aware of your *parties,* which I never mention to your mother. I presume she knows nothing of them?"

He kept his face impassive, though he inwardly cringed. Mother would be horrified, but it wasn't as if she'd ever find out. None of the Bosbury Park staff— his estate where Mother had been installed with her doctor and companion the past five years—would ever upset her, and he now had verification that her sole correspondent wouldn't either. He exhaled softly with relief. "I appreciate your discretion."

She rested her hand against her heart and leaned slightly forward. "Your mother isn't as well as you say, is she? Otherwise, she'd be able to come back to Town."

"She's better, but no, she's not improved enough to return to London, and I doubt she ever will be. I trust you to also keep that private."

"Of course, you needn't even ask," she said, settling back and dropping her hand to her lap. "I would have visited her, you know, but her physician always deters me."

"It's probably for the best. Her health is still unpredictable." At Mrs. Lloyd-Jones's consoling look,

Jason shifted in his chair. He knew her pity was for his mother, but he couldn't help but feel a sliver was directed at him, given his own purported insanity.

She smiled at Jason, dissipating the dark moment. "You're a good son to see her so well cared for. I was so pleased you didn't let her languish in an institution. At Bosbury Park she can enjoy some semblance of normalcy." Mrs. Lloyd-Jones's expression froze a moment before her eyes widened. "Goodness, she's not aware of Mr. Locke's presence in Society, is she?"

Jason hid his surprise. Mrs. Lloyd-Jones clearly knew precisely who Mr. "Locke" was. He wondered how many people did. But he knew the answer to that—everyone, if they listened to Margaret Rutherford. "Mother knows nothing. I have the newspapers diverted and reviewed so she doesn't inadvertently see something that would upset her."

Her lips pulled up again in an approving smile. "Such a good son."

Jason let the tension ease from his frame. "I recognize that I owe you an explanation for attending your tea. I'm ready to reenter Society."

She cocked her head to the side. "Is this to do with Mr. Locke's equally unexpected grand entrance?"

Though he felt as though he owed Mrs. Lloyd-Jones at least a modicum of honesty, he didn't plan to reveal more than was necessary. He wasn't yet ready to publicly declare he and Ethan were half brothers, which was why he'd dodged Lady Lydia's questions. He certainly wasn't going to disclose the depths of his hatred for Ethan, or their enduring rivalry. "Does it matter why?"

She leaned forward and studied him intently. "You're

being frightfully secretive. It's very suspicious. That's not going to help matters now that you're out again."

"I'm not looking to impress anyone."

"Which is why you sit at the fringe of Society." There was a note of admonishment to her tone. "You must play the game if you want to achieve entrance, Lockwood."

She had a point, but he didn't need—or want—to discuss his strategies with her. For now, he only wanted to gain access to the same places Ethan accessed, and Mrs. Lloyd-Jones was his key. He inclined his head toward her deferentially. "You mentioned a ball at Lady Whitmore's tomorrow evening. Is there a chance you could secure me an invitation?"

Her eyes flashed surprise, but she recovered quickly. "I was going to say it would be difficult, but I wonder if it might actually be easy. People were salivating over your appearance at Lady Aldridge's the other day, and after coming here, they will be simply agog. Half of them will be scandalized by your reappearance, and the other half will be clamoring for your company."

He wished Lord Whitmore was one of the many members of the ton who visited Lockwood House, but alas, he was not. In any case, Jason wasn't sure if that would have helped or hurt. The men who attended his parties might insist on keeping him as far away from their homes as possible. "Which half does Lady Whitmore fall into?"

"I'm not certain, but I think it might be the latter," she said. "She's trying to increase her standing because she has a daughter coming out in the spring."

"Then she may not want me anywhere near her ball."

"Let me take care of it. I'll send a note as soon as I

get a response." She settled back against the settee. "What else can I do for you? Dare I hope that you might finally want to settle down with a wife? Your mother would be thrilled."

An image of Lady Lydia came to his mind—her porcelain-perfect complexion, pale blond hair, and gently curving figure. She was alluring, to be sure. There was something about her eyes. Dark, where the rest of her was light. Complex, where the rest of her seemed straightforward. Still, he had no desire to marry. That had been his father's disaster, and it wouldn't be Jason's. "I'm not in the market for a wife."

"You'll let me know if you change your mind?" she asked hopefully.

He smiled as he stood. "I would, though please don't be disappointed when I don't. Thank you, Mrs. Lloyd-Jones. Seeing you again has made me realize that perhaps I should not have kept myself so closed off. I do hope I'll be able to attend Lady Whitmore's tomorrow evening." He took her hand and pressed a kiss to her knuckles. "Will you allow me a dance?"

She smiled up at him, her eyes sparkling. "I insist."

Chapter Four

UPON ARRIVING AT Lady Whitmore's ball, Lydia immediately scanned the vast ballroom for her closest friend, Audrey Cheswick. Audrey was very tall—taller than some men—with brown, corkscrew curls that did their best to defy any hairstyle. Those traits alone would've made her somewhat easy to find, but it was her wallflower status that ensured she could be located at any given moment—provided one didn't mind skulking about the darkest corners of the venue.

There. Partially obscured by a column near the back corner. Lydia started a path to her friend. Free of Aunt Margaret's presence—though saddled with the expectation of learning all she could about both Mr. Locke and Lord Lockwood—Lydia sought out Audrey for a few moments' respite.

It took her several minutes to reach her friend because she was constantly stopped by people wanting to know about her encounters with Lockwood. By all appearances, he was the sole subject of conversation at the event; the ballroom was buzzing with little else.

At last, she arrived at Audrey's side. "Would it pain you to at least stand partially in the light?" she said without heat, a genuine smile curving her lips. Audrey was the only person with whom she could be completely unaffected—and that was only when they were alone.

"No, but what would be the point?" Audrey asked, referring to her dearth of success in Society. She lacked a certain grace expected of young ladies and was prone to nervousness when presented to "important" people. Her parents despaired of her ever finding a match and constantly tried to improve her polish. "And you drag me about plenty."

Lydia did, and she wasn't sorry for it. "It's good for you. However are you going to snare the duke of your dreams if you're lurking in the shadows?"

"I don't lurk. I reside. No one but you cares where I am." She shrugged then turned toward Lydia, her eyes gleaming with excitement. "Is it true you've seen Lockwood *twice*?"

Lydia nodded.

"How extraordinary," Audrey breathed. "I fear I might've fainted dead away if I'd met him."

"Oh, stop. You're made of stronger stuff than that. Even Miss Vining failed to collapse, though she did drop her teacup."

Audrey giggled softly. "Poor Miss Vining, his lordship's presence must have completely overset her." Her eyes were sincere when she added, "I hope she wasn't too adversely affected."

Lydia loved her friend's capacity for empathy. It was one of the reasons she was drawn to her. "I'm sure she was fine."

A commotion across the ballroom drew their attention.

"I think someone Important just arrived," Audrey said. "There's a murmur." She inclined her head toward the doorway where the majordomo was announcing arrivals.

His deep voice intoned, "Mr. Ethan Locke."

Every head turned, but Lydia couldn't see anything.

Perhaps Audrey, with her height advantage, could make something out. "What do you see?"

"Nothing. Everyone is mobbing the entrance. Poor fellow. Lockwood's bastard brother or not, no one deserves that kind of notoriety." It was that sort of statement that made Lydia wonder if Audrey really minded being a wallflower at all.

"I suppose I should go." Lydia didn't disguise the reluctance in her voice. The part of her that was trained to appreciate gossip wanted very much to partake in the spectacle going on across the ballroom. The part of her that wanted to simply be a young woman with her friend preferred to remain in the corner. However, doing that would only cause her heartache later. She turned to Audrey. "Come dear, it's time for us to join the throng." She linked her arm through Audrey's and pulled her forward before she could protest.

Audrey sighed and fell into step beside her. She knew better than to argue, and after all, like Lydia, she did want to find a husband. But then their reasons were very different. Audrey believed in love and fairy tales and a happy ever after, while Lydia wanted to be a valued and accepted member of Society. As soon as she finished her "Aunt Margaret work" for the night, she could turn her attention to attracting Goodwin for another dance.

It took her and Audrey several minutes to break through the crowd. When they finally emerged near the doorway, Mr. Locke was surrounded by a group of women—several debutantes and their prurient mamas. Lydia couldn't imagine they were driven to seek Mr. Locke's company by anything other than curiosity. While it was true that a bastard son of a peer could find success—Lydia could name a few with ease—Mr. Locke's manner and sensibility were as yet unknown.

His appearance suggested wealth. His black superfine jacket was cut in the latest fashion and a diamond pin flashed in the snowy folds of his impeccably wound cravat. Though his head was turned, she could tell his dark hair was artfully styled.

He pivoted toward them. His similarity to Lord Lockwood was astonishing. She was now certain they were half brothers, and everyone else would be too, once they saw Lockwood again. Was it the squarish chin? Similar, but not quite. The nose? No, Mr. Locke's was more angular. *It was the eyes.*

"There she is," said Lady Dunthorpe boldly from the circle gathered around Locke. All of them turned their attention to Lydia, including her quarry.

Locke moved forward through the circle. His gaze was purposeful, and his lips curved into a smile Lydia was sure could charm the hardest of hearts. "You're Lady Lydia?"

He was seeking her out? Was it because she'd met Lockwood yesterday? Whatever the reason, she could scarcely believe her luck—at last. "Yes."

"Shall we take a spin?" he asked with a dashing smile.

Lydia glanced at the dance floor. The set was nearly half over. "The next set?"

He presented his arm. "No, I meant a stroll about the ballroom."

No dance? Lydia suffered a jolt of disappointment. Hopefully she'd dance later. For now, she had to be satisfied that she'd drawn Locke's attention at all.

She shot Audrey an apologetic look. Audrey's mouth lifted in a small, knowing smile. She inclined her head as if to say, "Go on," and then retreated to the perimeter.

Lydia took Mr. Locke's arm, and he led her away from the goggling circle of women. "You do realize this is a bit improper since we haven't been formally introduced."

He exhaled softly. "Right, I should have realized. Do you want to stop?" His gait slowed.

"Not at all." She'd be forgiven such a transgression because people were too afraid of Lady Margaret's wrath to deride her niece. Not to mention, everyone was eager to solve the mystery of his sudden appearance and they'd pin their hopes on Lydia finding success.

"You were looking for me?" Lydia asked, curious as to why.

"I understand you had tea with Lockwood yesterday."

Her pulse quickened. Was she about to become the first person to hear him admit they were half brothers? "Yes."

Locke inclined his head toward people as they passed. Lydia didn't bother to register their identities; she was too intent on Locke.

"How was he?" he finally asked.

Overwhelming. And not in a bad way. "He was very pleasant—and honest." What did Locke want to know? He was proving every bit as reticent as Lockwood. Which wasn't surprising. The two men were circling each other like the cocks on the farm back in Northumberland.

He turned and led her along the back of the room where the doors were open to the cool night air. "And what did you discuss?"

"Mr. Locke, are you going to tell me why you're so interested in Lord Lockwood?"

He slid her an inscrutable look, and his mouth curved into an indulgent smile. "Don't pretend you don't know the gossip. Didn't it originate with your aunt?"

She didn't flinch from his gaze. "Are you confirming it?"

"If your aunt spread this information, and one can presume you are an intimate of your aunt's, shouldn't you already know the answer?"

What a pair of frustrating men! Neither wanted to come right out and *say* it. But Locke was right—she already knew the truth. She pursued a new avenue. "Why have you come to Town now?"

"If you tell me what you and Lockwood discussed yesterday, I shall tell you anything you want to know."

Anything? Aunt Margaret would be thrilled. Lydia, on the other hand, suffered a pang of anxiety. She'd so been hoping to permanently improve her reputation, and here she was, being asked to gossip about Lockwood. "He spoke briefly of his mother—that she is well and may return to London."

"Indeed?" His tone carried a hint of surprise. "I'm glad for him if that's true."

He was glad for Lockwood? While Lockwood likely wanted to exact revenge against him. The relationship between these two men was beyond curious. Lydia burned to know more—and not for the purpose of sharing what she learned. "He also said you scarred his face."

Locke didn't react. He merely slid her an amused

glance and said, "Did he?"

Lydia refrained from glaring at him in exasperation. "Did you? And before you attempt to evade answering me again, you did say you would tell me anything I wanted to know."

"I said *anything*, not *everything*. I can say I didn't realize I'd scarred his face." He gave her a mocking glance. "We haven't spoken of it. We're not exactly close."

Given the desire for vengeance that had burned in Lockwood's eyes, Lydia was certain he blamed his half brother. But perhaps there had been mitigating circumstances. Locke wasn't gloating about having done him harm, but neither was he apologetic. "How do *you* think he was injured?"

"He fell through a window."

She felt a pull of allegiance toward Lockwood, probably due to Locke's cavalier attitude. A thought occurred to her, one that might explain the divide between them. "Did you push him?"

His shoulder lifted in a slight shrug. "I might have."

Again, not even a sliver of remorse, but also no note of triumph. What had happened between these men? "Why?"

He was silent a moment as he turned her around and directed them back they way they'd come. "It's a very long story, I'm afraid. And somewhat tedious. Probably not very appropriate ballroom talk."

Probably not, but she didn't care. She was inexplicably fascinated by Lockwood. Perhaps she could goad Locke into telling her. She pretended to pout. "It's very unsporting of you to only give me half the story."

He laughed. And yes, his eyes crinkled attractively.

"Such a minx! We had a disagreement. Leave it at that."

She rolled her eyes in mock exasperation. "A disagreement? That's what fights are. Fine, if you won't explain, at least tell me why you've come to Town now and where you've been."

"I've been . . . around. And I've come to Town because my dear friend Lady Aldridge lost her husband."

If Lady Aldridge was his dear friend, why hadn't he been to visit her before? What did "around" mean? She bit the questions back in favor of showing the proper respect due to Lord Aldridge. "Such a shame what happened to his lordship. Frightening, too. To think that an earl could be involved in such criminal activity and then murdered." She shuddered.

"Indeed," he said. "Lady Aldridge is still quite bereaved. I believe I've finally convinced her to retreat to the country. She's been reluctant to leave the house where she and the earl spent so much of their time."

Lydia frowned. "I called on her the other day. Her butler said she was ill."

"She is, which is why I'm hoping she'll go to the country."

Lydia was about to ask how he knew Lady Aldridge in the first place when an older, broad-shouldered gentleman with dark gray hair stepped in their path.

"Locke. Lady Lydia." The Marquess of Wolverton gave her a slight bow.

Lydia's gut tightened. Wolverton never spoke to her. He was an Untouchable—one of the few members of Society whom Aunt Margaret had declared immune to gossip. She and Aunt Margaret stayed clear of him and went so far as to quash any rumors about him.

His appearance in their path gave Lydia more than a touch of anxiety. "My lord," she said with a curtsey.

Wolverton gave her a patronizing smile. "It's terribly rude of me, but do you mind if I steal Locke? I've a matter to discuss with him."

Wolverton and Locke had matters to discuss? This was a wonderful tidbit and one she could thankfully repeat to Aunt Margaret since Wolverton had addressed him in the middle of the ballroom.

Lydia gave her sunniest debutante smile and withdrew her arm from Locke's. She masked her disappointment, keeping her voice as pleasant as her face. "It's not rude at all, my lord. Mr. Locke and I had a delightful turn."

Locke inclined his head toward her and gave her a mischievous little grin. "We did. And I look forward to the next time."

"As do I." She transferred her smile to Locke. "*Soon.*"

They turned from her and strode away through the ballroom. Lydia pivoted, working hard to tamp down her anxiety. It had been a fruitful promenade in that she'd learned he'd argued with his brother and probably pushed him out of a window, which had scarred his face. This was undoubtedly new information since Lydia hadn't heard it yet, which would thrill Aunt Margaret, who'd demanded Lydia get to the heart of Lockwood's declaration that Locke had given him his scar. She scanned the ballroom for her aunt, but she was hard to find, being so petite. Failing in that search, she looked instead for Audrey. As expected, she was against the wall near where Lydia had left her.

Halfway to Audrey, Lydia was stopped by Lady Trevett. "Lady Lydia, I saw you strolling with Mr. Locke."

Lydia gave her a patient smile. "Yes, we discussed Lord Lockwood's visit to Mrs. Lloyd-Jones's yesterday."

Lady Trevett's eyes widened. "Did you? Did he admit they're brothers?"

"Why would he? Because we discussed Lockwood's shocking reappearance? *Everyone* is talking about that," Lydia said with a touch of impatience. It was dreadfully difficult to shed one's image as a gossipmonger when people continued to approach her for gossip. "Please excuse me, I see Miss Cheswick and wish to speak with her." Lydia gave her an apologetic, graceful smile and took herself off.

However, Audrey was no longer by the wall. Fortunately, a moment's scan revealed her in an alcove. She was turned away from Lydia talking to a gentleman. A very tall, massively-built gentleman . . . Lydia's steps slowed as she neared them. Tucked into the alcove they were practically invisible to anyone else, but Lydia had been looking for her friend.

Lydia came to a stop behind them. Her gaze settled on the scar disfiguring Lockwood's beauty—and goodness, was he beautiful in his evening attire. She'd never seen a man fill out a suit of clothing better.

He peered around Audrey. "Lady Lydia."

Audrey stepped back, allowing Lydia into their little circle. "Look who I've just met, Lydia, it's your Lord Lockwood."

"He's not mine," Lydia said quickly, an inexplicable shiver running through her frame. She focused on

Lockwood. "Did you sneak in unannounced? I didn't hear your name, and surely you'd be mobbed by now." She glanced back over her shoulder. Everyone seemed oblivious to his presence.

"I was allowed to enter through a side door. Miss Cheswick was the first person I encountered, and she seemed . . . approachable." He threw her a commiserative smile, and Lydia marveled at Audrey's aplomb.

"You see," Lydia said to Audrey with a wink, "I said you wouldn't faint if you met him."

Audrey's cheeks pinked, and she cast Lockwood an apologetic smile. "Please don't take offense. I'm intimidated by many people."

Thankfully he didn't look the least offended. "But not by me, I hope."

"Oddly, no," she said with a tiny head shake.

"I'm delighted, Miss Cheswick." He slid his gaze to Lydia. She stared at his eyes—they were the same shape as Locke's, but the gray was actually slightly different. Lockwood's were darker, stormier. Stormier? When had her thoughts turned so fanciful? When she'd met Lord Lockwood.

"Lady Lydia, would you care to dance?" He glanced at Audrey. "My apologies, Miss Cheswick, since we haven't been formally introduced, I can't ask you."

Score one social point for the elder Lockwood brother.

The set was finishing. If Lydia was right, a waltz was next. Did he know how? By all accounts, he hadn't been to a ball in ages. "It's a waltz," Lydia said.

"Is it?" He sounded careless. "Excellent." His gray eyes looked into hers with an intensity that made her toes curl. What was he about this evening?

She took his arm, and they left the alcove. With each step toward the dance floor, Lydia was aware of attention turning toward them, of heads turning, of conversation ceasing. By the time they took their places and the music started, the ballroom was almost deadly quiet, except for the strains of the waltz. As he swept her into the dance, the other couples remained still. For a few moments they moved about the center of the ballroom, his hand at her back, her hand on his shoulder, their fingers clasped. It seemed they were the only things moving in the entire world. Time had ceased to advance. Everyone around them was frozen in some eerie tableau.

But Lydia was most aware of him. His wide shoulders, his warmth, that jagged scar . . .

"Why do you stare at it so much?" he asked.

She shook her head and raised her gaze to his. "What?"

His eyes held the same intensity as they had in the alcove. "My scar. You always stare at it." His voice grew soft. "Does it make you uncomfortable?"

"No," she said the word before she even contemplated her reasoning. Why *did* she stare at it? She wasn't the least bit repulsed by how it looked. "It makes me sad. I wish you didn't have it. I wish I could make it go away, and not because it disfigured your face, but because it's a reminder of something I'm sure you'd rather forget."

She heard his breath catch. Her heartbeat doubled. She knew what it was like to want to forget, to erase memories from your mind and maybe create a history that could make you smile instead of weep. His eyes bored into hers and she thought he understood.

The moment shattered as other couples started dancing and conversation picked up again. She looked up at him, prepared to query him about his half brother, but the questions died on her lips. He was still looking at her in that intensely . . . *hot* way. Maybe whatever moment they'd shared hadn't broken apart. Maybe this was more than a moment.

Lydia's gaze locked with his as the waltz continued. For the first time ever she simply enjoyed the dance. She wanted to laugh at doubting his skill—he was exquisite. He moved gracefully and effortlessly for such a large man, but then his build was athletic. What did he do to achieve such results? Suddenly the questions burning her brain became far more personal. What did he do for leisure? How had he learned to dance so well? What made him happy?

But she said nothing. She was too afraid to ruin this blissful interlude where she was simply a young lady enjoying a waltz with a handsome man.

Unfortunately the music began to wind down. Lydia's pulse quickened with anxiety. She didn't want it to end, wished time would freeze again, and they could dance forever. Tears blurred her eyes. She never cried. Why now?

The music ended, and she blinked rapidly lest she break down. *Goodness, pull yourself together, Lydia!*

Reality forced its way back in as they made their way from the dance floor. People were openly staring again, and the sound in the ballroom came to a slow but definitive halt. Even the musicians remained silent.

And then Lydia knew why. Emerging from the throng of people to greet them as they exited the dance floor was the only other person who could cause such a furor.

She looked up at Lockwood, her arm clutching his as if she could give him strength. Later she would have to consider this sudden and surprising allegiance to him, but for now, she only hoped he was all right.

His eyes were dark and they fixed on the figure standing directly before them.

Locke's lips spread in a wicked smile. "Good evening, brother."

Chapter Five

SO THIS WAS how Ethan planned to go on? Jason knew they were going to have to admit the familial tie—they were too similar to hide it. But here, in the middle of the first ball Jason had attended in forever? The audacity didn't surprise him. Ethan would choose whatever suited him and damn anyone else.

No, what surprised him was Ethan's appearance in a bloody ballroom. He looked . . . respectable.

Lady Lydia's fingers dug into his forearm, drawing Jason back to the present. He forced his muscles to relax and his mouth into the semblance of a smile. "'Locke,' is it?"

Ethan cocked a smile in return and then bowed. Jason stifled the urge to kick him to the ground.

Lydia stood on tiptoe and whispered toward Jason's ear, "We should move off the dance floor."

All of Society was watching and wondering if he would suffer a mental break in front of their very eyes. Several were probably even hoping for it. He kept his features schooled into a pleasant mask. "Yes, we should."

"Lockwood, perhaps you'd care to take refreshment with me?" Ethan asked.

Jason would rather have dined with the devil, but since he'd come here to determine Ethan's motives, he went along. "I should be delighted." Had anyone noticed if that last word sounded strangled?

Lady Lydia steered him toward a doorway. "The

refreshments are through here."

The people surrounding them still stared, but the music began again.

He glanced down at Lady Lydia's blond head. What was she doing? She shouldn't be a part of this. "You should go," he said quietly.

Her answering look was full of concern. "I'm not leaving you with him."

She meant to protect him? Why? Given his experience, he was generally suspicious of people, particularly when they offered kindness. He couldn't begin to fathom why this young woman would want to come to his aid.

They moved into a room set with tables of food and drink. A handful of Society's finest were inside. Every single one of them turned to gape.

Ethan came around Jason's side—his left side. His gaze flicked to the scar he'd caused. "I assume you'd like something stronger than ratafia?"

"I'll drink whatever you're drinking," Jason said, hoping against hope a footman would come by with a large bottle of whisky.

Ethan inclined his head and a footman brought champagne. It would suffice.

After first presenting Lady Lydia with a glass, Ethan offered one to Jason. Their eyes met and Jason wrapped his fingers tightly around the stem of the glass as he accepted it. Ethan's eyes were like his, though the color was a bit lighter, more like their father's. In fact, looking at Ethan in this environment, in those clothes . . . he looked so much like their father as to be uncanny. No one would doubt their kinship. At least no one with decent eyesight.

Jason moved closer and kept his voice low. This was not the best place to conduct this conversation, but he simply couldn't contain himself. "What are you doing here?"

Ethan blinked, trying his best to look innocent, but Jason wasn't fooled. "Sharing a glass of champagne with my brother. Surely there's nothing odd to question about that."

Ethan was provoking him as he always did. Jason worked to keep his temper in check. This man had monopolized their father's time and affection, his very existence had contributed to Jason's mother's mental collapse, he'd demanded things that didn't rightfully belong to him, and he'd caused Jason to lose whatever tentative standing he'd had in Society following Mother's confinement. He'd ruined Jason's life.

He smiled blandly and sought to aggravate Ethan in return. "And that's the difference between you and me. I find everything odd about it. We may be blood related, but our relationship is not brotherly."

Ethan frowned slightly. "This isn't going the way I'd hoped. How disappointing."

He couldn't be serious. They'd practically killed each other seven years ago and now he wanted to be bosom brothers?

Contemplating what to say, Jason sipped his champagne and nearly choked as the false-sweet tones of Margaret Rutherford snaked through the room. "Lydia, dear, aren't you going to introduce me?"

Jason swung around so quickly that his elbow caught Lydia's shoulder and knocked her off balance. She grasped at his arm with her free hand. He reached for her waist and held her upright. Champagne sloshed from both of their glasses and a large amount splattered Jason's coat. Her gaze met his, and the pained surprise in their depths almost distracted him.

But then the grating voice came again. "Don't manhandle my niece!"

Her *what?*

He made sure Lydia was firmly on two feet and then let go of her as quickly as he'd grabbed her. Then he took a step back for good measure. He stared at Lydia's suddenly distressed expression. How could this witty and lovely young woman be related to that harpy? His gaze swept to the small, round woman he despised almost as much as the bastard viewing this entire proceeding with the undisguised interest of a bettor watching a fight.

A footman rushed to take Lady Lydia's glass as she brushed at the champagne saturating her glove. "Aunt Margaret, he wasn't manhandling me, he was saving me from disgrace."

Why was she defending him? Perhaps she hadn't accompanied him in here out of kindness after all. What if she was only aligning herself with him to support her aunt's destruction of his family? Her interest in him, her impertinent questions, her brash invitation to walk in the garden, even her support tonight . . . all of it led him to believe she was a copy of her aunt. Or maybe a puppet. Either way, he needed to be on his guard around her.

The same footman took Jason's glass and retreated from the room. The front of Jason's coat sported a wet mark that looked like an ever-spreading inkblot.

Margaret swept Jason with a razor-sharp perusal. After snickering at the stain on his coat, her gaze moved up and lingered on his scar. "It's been a long time, Lockwood." She flicked a look at Lydia. "I'm still waiting for my introduction to Mr. Locke, dear."

Lydia started as if she'd woken from a stupor and quickly moved between her aunt and Ethan. "Allow me to present Mr. Locke. Mr. Locke, this is my great-aunt, Lady Margaret Rutherford."

Margaret held out her stubby fingers and Ethan bowed over her hand. "It's a pleasure to finally make your acquaintance, Mr. Locke," Lady Margaret sang.

Ethan stood and released her hand. "I understand we have you to thank for celebrating our brotherhood with the masses."

Lady Margaret shot Jason a superior, taunting glance.

That was all he could stand. He could barely stomach the veiled taunts he was exchanging with his half brother, and he sure as hell couldn't endure Lady Margaret's gloating. His evening suit felt tight, hot, constricting. After so many years of mastering his reactions, he felt his control slipping, and he couldn't let that happen here. Not when all of London was watching—and waiting—for it. Thankfully, he could blame his hasty departure on the ruination of his coat. He gestured toward his soggy lapel. "Please excuse me."

Ethan looked as if he wanted to say something, but he merely inclined his head. "Good evening, Lockwood. I trust we'll meet again soon."

Jason looked forward to it—but it wouldn't be in the middle of a bloody ball. "Count on it." He gave Margaret no such consideration and stalked from the room without a glance in her direction.

His gaze, however, fell on Lady Lydia as he passed

her. She kept her eyes averted from his. *Good.* Whatever he'd imagined had passed between them on the dance floor went up in flames. That he'd enjoyed the company of Margaret's blood kin made his stomach roil.

When he shifted his attention to his path, he finally noticed the crowd of people that had gathered at the entrance to the buffet room. He flashed them all a counterfeit smile as he cut through their throng. They scurried to get out of his way. Sometimes it was helpful to be able to scare people away with only a tip of one's scarred head.

He made his way similarly through the ballroom. The music continued playing, but the sounds of laughter and chatter dimmed upon his entrance. He inclined his head as he passed the majordomo and exhaled heavily as he gained the cooler air outside the ballroom.

Tonight had not gone as planned, but he blamed himself. Next time, *he'd* orchestrate the meeting with Ethan, and it would go the way *he* intended. He'd underestimated the effect of putting himself on display, inviting Society's opinions and reactions. Furthermore, he hadn't imagined coming face-to-face with his mother's nemesis, which he should have done. But then nothing could have prepared him for learning that the young woman he'd flirted and waltzed with was her niece.

He descended the staircase to the foyer. As he neared the foot, a gentleman escorting a petite young woman drew his attention. His gaze fixed on Jason's scar. "Lord Lockwood?"

His ruined face was as identifying as if he'd strapped a calling card to his forehead. Jason gave him a patient, somewhat patronizing look. "I'm afraid you have me at a disadvantage . . ."

The man had the grace to don a slight flush and quickly avert his eyes. "My apologies." Then he brought his gaze back up and met Jason unflinchingly. "I'm Carlyle."

The name Carlyle sparked something in his memory. Then it came to him. "The former constable?"

He nodded. "The same."

Jason remembered the remarkable story of the constable who'd inherited a viscountcy, and now he recalled that Carlyle had taken a wife. Jason offered a bow to his companion. "Lady Carlyle."

She curtseyed in response. "My lord."

But there was more to Carlyle—he'd been a close friend of Lord Aldridge. Jason was suddenly pleased the man had recognized him. However, Jason couldn't interrogate him about a potential connection between Ethan and the deceased earl at the base of a staircase in the middle of a ball. "Carlyle, you should come to Lockwood House some time."

Carlyle glanced at his wife and drew her closer. It was the reassuring behavior of a besotted husband. He perhaps thought Jason meant he should come to a vice party, so Jason set Lady Carlyle's mind at ease. "Come for a game of billiards. I've an excellent table."

Still, he made a mental note to have North invite him to a party anyway, though he doubted the newly married Carlyle would attend.

Carlyle inclined his head and again met him eye to eye. "I would very much like to continue our acquaintance."

"I'll look forward to it." Jason moved past them and

nodded at a footman who rushed off to summon his coach.

Given his past life as a constable, could Carlyle be aware of Ethan's criminal activities? Jason looked forward to finding out. Perhaps tonight hadn't been such a disaster after all.

As Jason settled himself into his coach, he recalled the pained look in Lady Lydia's eyes when that harpy, Margaret, had surprised them. For a brief moment on the dance floor, he'd allowed himself to believe Lady Lydia might be different. Yes, she stared at his scar like everyone else, but not for the same reasons. She wasn't frightened of or revolted by him.

It was a genuine shame she was related to Margaret. But maybe there was more to Lady Lydia's story. He should know better than anyone not to judge someone based on familial relation. Perhaps he owed Lady Lydia the second chance he'd never been given.

FOLLOWING LOCKWOOD'S RATHER dramatic exit, Lydia had excused herself to dry her champagne-sodden glove. However, by the time she reached the retiring room, her glove had nearly dried. Even so, she appreciated the opportunity for a moment's reprieve.

She found a mirror to survey her appearance. Her hair was still in place and she looked the same as always. Too-dark eyes against her alabaster skin. But what did she expect? That an evening in the company of London's two most talked-about gentlemen would somehow make her look different?

The door opened and two ladies stepped inside.

Their eyes widened upon seeing Lydia, but before they could pounce on her with their rabid questions, Lydia excused herself and fled the room.

In the corridor, she turned away from the ballroom in search of a quiet place in which to take respite. She didn't want to gossip anymore. Not tonight. Not *ever*, but Aunt Margaret wouldn't allow that.

More importantly, she didn't want to gossip about Lord Lockwood.

She'd obeyed her aunt all these years in the hope that she would somehow find the life she wanted—a good marriage and standing in Society, but she couldn't willfully ruin someone else's life. Especially Jason Lockwood's. She thought of their waltz and shivered, though she wasn't the least bit cold.

What she needed right now wasn't the company of scandalmongers. What she needed was a moment alone with her thoughts. And the unexpected pleasure of her memories.

Her feet carried her to a door near the end of the corridor. Her heart picked up speed as she opened it slowly. One never knew what one might find behind a closed door at a ball. On occasion, Lydia had gone searching for scandal to report—at her aunt's behest— and had even found it a time or two. This time, however, she was just searching for solitude.

At first glance the room appeared empty. Exhaling, Lydia closed the door behind her and stepped inside.

"Lady Lydia."

She jumped as she discerned the tall figure of Mr. Locke standing in the shadows near the thick velvet curtains lining the window. If he hadn't spoken, she might never have seen him. "Mr. Locke, I'm sorry to disturb you. If you'll excuse me." She turned to leave.

"Wait. That is, if you don't mind, I would like to speak with you." He stepped away from the curtains. "We were interrupted earlier. I should appreciate the opportunity to finish our conversation."

What more did he mean to discuss? Was he going to disclose more information about Lady Aldridge?

Lydia's fingertips rested against the doorframe as she considered his invitation. To stay would mean more information for Aunt Margaret and she could perhaps count this night as her most successful ever. But it also meant risk to her reputation. If she was found in this room with Ethan Locke of all people, she'd be socially crucified.

Maybe not.

She'd survived being accused of attending Lockwood House with a blackguard last Season. In fact, she'd come out of that scandal more popular than ever. She turned back to face him with a smile. "Certainly, Mr. Locke, however we must be brief. I'm sure you're aware that my being alone with you like this is more than a bit scandalous."

His smile was vague. "I should have realized. It's a simple matter and shouldn't take too much of your time." He prowled toward the center of the room where the fire in the hearth and the lanterns on the mantel and on a table better illuminated his features. They might be half brothers, but their appearances were as much alike as if they were full blood. Locke, however, *looked* more approachable, likely because his face was smooth and handsome. "How well do you know Lockwood?"

Lydia watched his movements, her curiosity more

than piqued. This made twice Locke had sought her out tonight. "Not well at all. We've met less than a handful of times."

He picked up a carved wooden dog from the table with the lantern and studied it idly. "But you've formed an opinion, have you not? Just as you've formed an opinion about me."

She walked along the perimeter of the room, moving a bit closer to where he stood. "I don't have a clear opinion of either of you yet. I can say without hesitation that Lockwood is an excellent dancer. And you perhaps don't dance at all." She'd never seen him take to the dance floor, and he'd pointedly taken her for a stroll earlier.

He returned the dog to its resting place and inclined his head. "I knew you were intelligent. But you're not being completely honest." His voice dropped a bit, became soft, but there was an edge of steel that pricked her senses and put her on guard. His gaze was steady, holding hers in rapt attention. "You danced with him. You accompanied him into the buffet room. You stood by his side. I think you *have* formed an opinion about him."

Lydia glanced at the fire and pondered why he should even care. He and Lockwood were estranged, after all. She shifted uncomfortably beneath his frank stare, still unsure of his purpose. "Why should that matter to you?"

He paused and his gaze lost a bit of its intensity. He tipped his head back and forth as if weighing whether to continue. "Because I believe you're in a position to help me. Aside from the business about his scar, what else has he told you about me?"

Help him do what, spread rumors about Lockwood? Why else would Locke seek her out and ask what Lockwood had told her? Well, Locke was going to be disappointed because for some indefinable reason, she'd decided to protect Lord Lockwood. In fact, she already regretted telling Locke about his scar. "I must warn you, Mr. Locke, if your goal in entering Society is to somehow discredit or adversely affect your brother, I'll do my best to stop you."

Oddly, Locke gave a subtle nod of appreciation. "Excellent. I don't wish to discredit him. I wish for us to try to claim a brotherly relationship." His gaze darkened. "However, if you repeat that to anyone, there will be *unfortunate* consequences for you."

His words spread over her like a glacier moving across land, slow but very, very frigid.

His features immediately brightened. "My apologies. I don't wish to frighten you, only to stress the importance of my mission and the need for secrecy. I can see you wish to protect Lockwood, so my persuasion isn't really necessary, is it?"

Persuasion? Was that a new word for threat? Though he looked somewhat remorseful, his tone was still edged with steel, and it compelled her to agree with him. "No, it's not necessary. I would be happy to assist you with your brother." And she would, his threat notwithstanding. "But why me?"

"Because you've met Lockwood on more than one occasion—which is far more than anyone else in Society—and when I saw the two of you together tonight . . . " He shook his head, smiling. "And I can see you already care for him."

He was right. However, Lydia was at a loss for how

she could help, and she was still feeling particularly loyal to Lockwood. "What do you want me to do?"

"For now, I would appreciate it if you could determine his level of animosity." His tone turned a touch self-deprecating. "Although from his reaction earlier, I would guess it's still fairly high."

"You'd guess right." Though she felt no compulsion to aid Locke, she thought it best to warn him. "I think it's possible he may seek revenge for his scar."

Locke's eyes fixed somewhere to the left of Lydia and he frowned. Deeply. When his gaze found hers again, it was inscrutable. "Indeed?"

Lydia didn't think he needed or wanted an answer, so she waited. He looked away again, appearing absorbed in thought. When the silence stretched and she began to grow uncomfortable, particularly given the length of her absence from the ballroom, she said, "Have you changed your mind?"

He shook his head and focused on her once more. "No. I'll simply have to reassess how to proceed. I should like to speak with him. If you think you can arrange a meeting, I'd be grateful for your assistance. Otherwise, if you could, perhaps try to persuade him that I'm not the man—or boy—I used to be."

She wanted to ask why and how he'd changed, but she was out of time. "I can try, but you'd do better if you could perhaps demonstrate how you've changed." Anxiously, she glanced at the door. "I'm afraid I have to go."

"Remember," he said, and the steel was back in his voice. "You can't speak of this to anyone but him. I know you want to, but you can't."

Keeping a secret from Aunt Margaret would be a

risk. Lydia didn't doubt that she could do it, but if Aunt Margaret ever learned she'd withheld information like this . . .   Lydia didn't want to imagine it. Her punishments had lessened over the past few years, but this level of betrayal—which is precisely how Aunt Margaret would characterize it—would surely earn Lydia some sort of misery. Was keeping this confidence worth being exiled from London forever? A nervous jolt rippled through her as she turned her head to look at him. "I understand."

"Go ahead and leave the way you came," he said. "I didn't enter that way and I won't leave through there either."

Lydia exited the room and was nearly to the ballroom when she realized there had only been the one door. Just how in the world had he come and gone?

Chapter Six

JASON SAT AT his desk eating a late breakfast three days after the Whitmore Ball. He finished reading a letter from his mother's physician and set it aside. The familiar melancholy ache that always accompanied news of his mother settled over him. She'd finally stopped begging to come to Town—at least for now. The regular valerian tinctures had done their part, and she'd returned to her more complacent self. How Jason wished she could return to her *real* self, but he'd accepted that would likely never happen. He shoved his plate away, having lost his appetite for eggs and kippers.

North entered, Scot on his heels, and presented the *Times*.

Jason glanced up at his two most trusted retainers before taking the newspaper. The headline leapt from the front page:

Robbery on Curzon Street

Jason skimmed the article. Several items stolen. No one injured. In fact, no one could actually pinpoint *when* the items were taken. A silver piece was noted missing yesterday and a search of the house revealed other items were also absent. The residents—Lord and Lady Chauncey—insist their retainers are not to blame. Bow Street is making inquiries.

Robberies in Mayfair were not particularly

noteworthy. However, robberies that occurred when Ethan Jagger was about *and* being investigated by Bow Street gave Jason pause.

He looked up at North and Scot. "Is there anything else you know that's not written here?"

"Mr. Jagger was a guest of Lord Chauncey just over a week ago," North said.

Another "coincidence."

"I see. Excellent reconnaissance. Still no response from Ethan regarding the party tomorrow night?" Jason had issued an invitation after returning home from the Whitmore Ball. He wanted their next meeting to be on his terms in an environment where Jason felt completely at ease.

North shook his head. "Not as yet, my lord."

Perplexing. Jason leaned back in his chair. Ethan had sought Jason out at the ball the other night. He would presumably have jumped at the invitation to Lockwood House. "Who delivered it to the Bevelstoke?"

"Hennings," North said.

"I want to talk to him before I leave." Jason had an appointment with Lord Carlyle.

North inclined his head and departed.

Scot remained. "What do you have planned for Jagger tomorrow night?"

"I only mean to speak with him." Jason gave his valet a sardonic look. "You needn't worry we'll rip the house apart again." He stood and inclined his head for Scot to follow him. "Assuming he comes, I'll expose him to everything I have to offer."

"See what perks his interest?" Scot asked, falling into step beside Jason as they made their way to the foyer.

"Yes, and maybe find a vulnerability." Though Jason

suspected Ethan guarded those just as closely as he did.

"Hoping he loses his shirt at the tables? Or maybe drinks himself under one?" Scot chuckled.

Jason flashed Scot a smile. "Something like that."

North met them in the foyer with Jason's hat and gloves.

Hennings, a footman, came from behind the stairs and bowed. He was one of the youngest on staff and had only been in Jason's employ a few months. "My lord."

"I understand you delivered the invitation to Mr. Locke at the Bevelstoke?" Jason took his gloves from North and drew them on.

The boy's eyelid twitched. He looked nervous. "I did."

Jason smiled faintly, trying to put Hennings at ease. "Did you give it directly to Mr. Locke?"

Hennings shook his head. "No, I gave it to his man."

"His man?" Jason chastised himself for not conducting this interview immediately after the delivery, but that had been the day he'd gone to the Whitmore Ball and he'd been preoccupied. "Tell me about him."

Hennings eyes were bright, his face animated, and he spoke a bit too fast. "Odd looking bloke. He didn't say anything. Just nodded and took the note."

Interesting. "Odd looking in what way?"

"He was bald, my lord, and he wore an earring."

The baldness wasn't peculiar, but the earring was notable. Perhaps a criminal cohort? "Thank you, Hennings," Jason said and then added, "well done."

Hennings stifled a smile, bowed again, and took himself off.

"What're you thinking?" Scot asked as he took Jason's hat from his brother and brushed a speck of lint off the black wool. He presented the spotless item to Jason.

Jason took the hat and set it on his head. "I'm thinking I want you to spend some time hanging around the Bevelstoke and see what you can learn. Do either of you have any friends in service there?"

The brothers looked at each other. "Is Jemmy still with Mr. Ingle?" Scot asked.

North shook his head. "No, he left to care for Lord Anstruther's horses." He turned his gaze to Jason. "I'll think on it, my lord. I'm sure we'll come up with someone."

"Or I'll just make a friend," Scot said with a grin.

"Keep me informed." Jason turned and strode to the door, which North hastened to open.

A half hour later, he was admitted to Carlyle's town house on Brook Street, where he was shown into the viscount's office.

Carlyle stood from behind his desk. "Good afternoon. I hope it's all right that we're sitting in here. This seemed more a business meeting from the tone of your note."

Jason had purposely worded it that way in order to exclude Lady Carlyle. He didn't want to have this conversation in front of her. "This is fine, thank you." He removed his hat and set it on the edge of Carlyle's desk before sitting in a large, wingback chair.

Carlyle gestured for the butler to leave them. "I'll ring if we require refreshment," he said and then sat behind his desk. "To what do I owe the pleasure of your visit?"

Jason took in the surroundings. It was a very masculine room decorated with a trio of pastoral paintings from the middle of the last century, a large gilt-edged mirror, a pair of twenty-year-old chairs situated before a hearth with a low fire, and a sideboard with a collection of half-empty bottles on display. Something about it seemed off. He wasn't sure what he'd expected, but the décor didn't seem to fit the office of a former constable. It seemed the office of an aging viscount. But then perhaps Carlyle still hadn't quite learned to inhabit his new role.

The chair Jason sat in might be a bit old, but it was comfortable. He put his shoulders back against the seat. "I won't mince words. I'm here to discuss my half brother—Ethan Locke, as he calls himself."

Carlyle's nostrils flared. Jason inched forward. The man knew something and meant to share it, otherwise his face would've been impossible to read. He was a former constable after all. "You know him by another name?" Carlyle asked.

"Yes, and I'm willing to wager you do too. Jagger."

Carlyle leaned back in his chair. "I know Jagger. We've had dealings in the past."

Excellent. This was precisely what Jason had been hoping for. "Are you aware that Bow Street is investigating him?"

Carlyle's gaze turned inscrutable. "Yes, and I've told them what I know, which isn't much."

Jason's muscles tensed with frustration. He'd been hoping Carlyle would know something of interest. Still, he'd take what he could get. "Would you mind telling me what you told them?"

"For what purpose?" Carlyle's features broke into a

smile then. "Look at us, tiptoeing around the subject. Let us speak frankly. I am aware that you and he are estranged. Are you helping Bow Street, or is there a chance you want to reconcile with Jagger?"

Jason wasn't ready to speak quite so openly. Not until he knew the extent of Ethan's crimes—or if he'd actually committed any. Did that mean he'd consider reconciliation? Not on his bloody life. "You're correct that we are estranged. We're trying to determine how to proceed." That wasn't precisely a lie given their awkward encounter at the Whitmore Ball. "I'm not certain whether we'll reconcile or not."

"And you came here to see me because of my former occupation. You hoped I would shed some light onto Jagger's activities." The corner of his mouth ticked up. "Sorry, it's difficult for me to think of him as Locke."

Jason allowed an ironic smile. "I have the same difficulty. I'm curious as to how he went from thief-taker to alleged thief."

Carlyle lifted one shoulder. "Thief-takers are paid for recovering stolen goods and identifying the thieves. Some of them organize thefts so that they can easily return the goods and collect the reward—at the expense of their gang, of course. The practice isn't as common as it once was, but it still happens."

"Doesn't sound like that would make them too popular," Jason said.

"Perhaps not, but they prey on young, naïve boys who are eager for the promise of wealth—however small."

A wave of disgust washed over Jason. If Ethan was guilty of such treachery, he deserved whatever came to him. "Is that how Ethan became a thief?"

Another shrug, this time accompanied with a slight frown. "I don't know the details of your half brother's past. But I'd caution you to reserve judgment until you speak with him yourself."

Jason could just imagine that conversation. If Ethan were guilty of such a crime, he'd never admit it, especially to Jason. He narrowed his gaze on Carlyle. "You seem to think he might be innocent."

"I can't say for certain, but I don't believe he's taken over Aldridge's theft ring." Carlyle paused a moment. "At least, not willingly."

"What the hell does that mean?"

Carlyle pursed his lips together. At length he said, "Jagger works for one of London's worst crime lords—Gin Jimmy. I don't think his choices are his own."

Jason could scarcely believe what he was hearing. Ethan had utterly fooled this man. "Are you saying he was somehow forced into a criminal life?"

"As I said, I don't know the specifics of his past. I only know that the Jagger I've dealt with has been fair and perhaps even . . . regretful." He held up a hand when Jason opened his mouth. "Don't ask me more than that. A constable—even a former one—has to retain some secrets for the safety of those involved."

He meant to protect a probable criminal? Jason's plans for a partnership with Carlyle evaporated. "I hope you won't be the one filled with regret if it turns out you're defending a criminal."

"I'm not defending him, I'm merely giving him the benefit of the doubt. We don't know what he's doing yet." His features were grim, tinged with remorse. "I hope he's not what Bow Street thinks."

Jason curled his hands around the arms of his chair,

digging his fingertips into the soft velvet. He could hope all he liked, but that wouldn't change the facts, and Jason had more cause to believe that Ethan had turned to a criminal life than not. "I've known him since we were boys and it makes sense he would resort to thievery. He's always wanted more than he had. More than he deserved. I'm sure he'd do whatever he could to improve his lot." How many times had he taunted that *he* should have been born as their father's heir? That Father would've preferred it that way.

Carlyle's eyes flashed with irritation. "Who are you to say what he deserved? And shouldn't a man try to better himself, improve his station in life?" It was the sentiment of a man who hadn't been born to privilege.

"Legally." Jason stretched his fingers in an effort to release the building tension in his frame. "Ethan has always looked for the easy way to get ahead."

Carlyle briefly drummed his fingertips lightly against the edge of his desk. "I wonder what drove him to do that."

"Greed?" Jason was losing patience with Carlyle's attitude. "His mother was a whore who sold herself to the highest bidder. The minute our father died, she found a new protector—and it wasn't as if she was desperate. My father provided for her."

"I see," Carlyle said judiciously, revealing the patronizing forbearance of a lawman. Then he exhaled deeply. "I can see the old resentment between you runs deep, and I'm sorry for it. I only know your brother a little, but I would say that somewhere buried inside of him is a decent fellow trying to get out."

What if that were possible? What if Ethan was trying to change his fortune? What if he had made a series of bad choices and now found himself wanting to correct them? Jason couldn't fathom it. The Ethan Jagger he knew was selfish, spoiled, and cruel.

"I don't know what he said or did to convince you of that," Jason said, "but my experience with him is quite different. He taunted us—my mother and me—about how our father loved him more. He made sure we knew exactly what Father gave them, what he did with them, how he preferred them as a family to us, how Father said *he* should be the heir instead of me. Worst of all, he made sure my mother was aware of the love her husband felt toward his mistress. He was relentless, pushing her ever closer to insanity. There isn't a decent fiber in his being."

"He was a boy then, wasn't he? Surely he's changed."

"His years as a criminal have somehow rehabilitated his soul?" Jason laughed as darkness swirled within him. His patience with this interview had expired, and he hadn't even mentioned the robbery or discussed whether Ethan had been involved. He got to his feet. "Thank you for your time."

Carlyle also stood. He frowned again, but his features were creased with what Jason would characterize as genuine concern, as if the man cared about the brotherly drama playing out before him. "I'm not convinced Jagger's motives are evil, and I again urge you not to draw any hasty conclusions about his appearance. For now." His gaze turned dark and serious. "I assure you, if his activities are anything less than legal, I'll be the first to drag him to Bow Street."

Ten minutes later, Jason made his way from the town house. He felt certain there were things Carlyle wasn't telling him, but that only meant there was information to be gleaned. With North and Scot working their angles, and if he continued to work with Bow Street, he'd get to the meat of Ethan's activities.

Jason glanced down the street toward Lady Aldridge's residence and froze. Coming toward him, an ivory bonnet trimmed with green framing her angelic face, was the only person in Society who'd encouraged him, at least for a few moments—Lady Lydia Prewitt.

He considered hurrying into his coach, but to do so would have been blatantly rude. And despite Lady Lydia's relationship to Margaret Rutherford, he couldn't deny that he'd liked her.

"Good afternoon, Lord Lockwood," she called as she neared him. A footman trailed behind her at a discreet distance.

He bowed. "Lady Lydia. We keep running into each other." He noted that Aldridge House was just down the street. "Did you come from Lady Aldridge's?"

"Yes, but I'm afraid she's still ill." Her brow creased beneath the wide brim of her bonnet. She looked quite fetching today, with delicate blond curls framing her lovely face. "I'm on my way to visit Mrs. Lloyd-Jones next."

"Ah, just a few houses down the street, so I needn't offer you a ride." He felt a stab of disappointment, but reminded himself she was—for now—the enemy. Or at least aligned with one. And his enemy's friends were his enemies, weren't they? Still, he couldn't resist a bit of provocation. "Although inviting you into my coach would've been terribly improper of me." Particularly with her footman standing twenty or so paces distant.

She tipped her head to the side and gave him a coquettish grin. "Don't you like improper things?"

He almost laughed at her outrageousness—and she knew it. "I do. Which is why I shouldn't like you. Nor should I like talking to you in the middle of the street."

Her smile grew brighter, more genuine. "I suppose, but I'm glad you *are* talking to me. You could come with me to see Mrs. Lloyd-Jones," she said. "I daresay she would like that."

"I'm sure you're right, but I'm afraid I have other business."

She glanced away, but then nodded her understanding. "I imagine you're overwhelmed with invitations after your long absence."

Not particularly. He'd received a handful, but after his confrontation with Ethan at the Whitmore Ball, he hadn't accepted any of them yet. He supposed he must, though the thought of having to conform to Society's dictates gave him a headache. On the other hand, the thought of allowing Ethan to claim a place while he stayed on the periphery was too grating. He wasn't proud of his jealousy, but he also couldn't change it.

She touched his arm. "Lord Lockwood?"

The connection of her hand with his arm drew his attention more firmly than her words. It reminded him of their waltz, the single best moment of his recent memory. Dancing was one of the few things he actually missed about Society. "Ah, yes." He coughed. "I should go."

Her fingers closed around his coat sleeve. "Wait. I'm glad I met you here. I've been thinking about the other night quite a lot." Her cheeks flushed a delicate pink.

She'd been thinking the same thing he had? *Dangerous.* He hadn't tangled with a respectable young woman in far too long. Did he even remember the boundaries? He must, otherwise he would've swept her into his coach and kissed her senseless.

Kissed her? His gaze dipped to her lush lips. Oh yes, he wanted to kiss her, and the stiffening of his cock only underscored that fact.

Boundaries, he reminded himself. He reluctantly withdrew his arm from her grasp.

She didn't glance away this time, and he saw the disappointment reflected in her eyes. "I enjoyed our waltz."

Don't speak of it, he silently pleaded, *I need to keep you at arm's length.* "As did I, but I shouldn't expect a second. I wouldn't want to tarnish your reputation."

"Nonsense, dancing with you made me very popular."

"As did witnessing the scene in the buffet room." And then, because he needed to intimidate and discourage her, he tilted his face so that his scar was visible. "Tell me, Lady Lydia, how many times and to how many people did you recount that tale?"

She stared at him, her lush brown eyes wide. Her lips parted, and he wondered if she only just kept her jaw from dropping.

"You look surprised by my query." *And guilty.* His voice lowered, and he leaned close. "I know your aunt very well. I wondered if you were like her, and I can see from your reaction that you are. How . . . disappointing."

"I'm not," she said, her voice sounding a bit strangled. Her protest only made her look guiltier.

It was time to go before things became any more uncomfortable. "Good afternoon, Lady Lydia."

He climbed into his coach and didn't look back as he

drove away.

LYDIA'S LUNGS SEIZED and she was afraid for a terrible second that she was going to sob. She abruptly turned away from his departing coach and forced herself to walk to Mrs. Lloyd-Jones's house, though she really wanted to go home and bury her head beneath a pillow.

That had been such a lovely interlude until he'd accused her of being like her aunt. An accusation that was terribly and unfortunately true. Shame washed through her.

Slowly her lungs relaxed and she began to breathe normally. Had she really been on the verge of tears again? Perhaps she should cry. Maybe that would help. But the more she thought about it, the drier her eyes felt.

She trudged up the steps to Mrs. Lloyd-Jones's house. Her footman moved up beside her and rapped on the door.

She was shown directly to Mrs. Lloyd-Jones's private sitting room upstairs, where her hostess was sitting at her small secretary. She looked up as Lydia entered. "Good afternoon, dear." Her welcoming smile faded. "What's the matter? You look pale, as if you've seen a carriage accident. You haven't, have you?" She stood up and met Lydia, putting her arm around her shoulders and guiding her to the settee.

Lydia shook her head. "No, nothing like that."

"Tell me all about it while we're waiting for tea." She sat with Lydia on the settee and smoothed the skirt of her pale blue day gown.

Lydia removed her bonnet and gloves because she always did when it was just the two of them. There was nowhere she felt more comfortable. "I've just encountered Lord Lockwood."

Mrs. Lloyd-Jones's eyes lit with interest. "Oh? You looked rather dashing together waltzing at the Whitmore Ball."

"You're not playing matchmaker, are you?" Lydia asked.

"So what if I am?" Mrs. Lloyd-Jones lifted a shoulder. "You've made no secret to me about wanting to marry. And Lockwood is a good man, no matter what anyone says."

Lydia knew very well who "anyone" meant. Her aunt. "Regardless, it's not worth considering. I don't believe he's interested in me in the slightest." *Ha*, he'd made that quite clear.

Why did it bother her so much? Perhaps because he was only the latest gentleman to find her lacking. Goodwin had already moved on, or so it seemed. After dancing with her thrice in recent weeks, he hadn't paid her more than cursory attention since the prior week.

The tea tray arrived, and Mrs. Lloyd-Jones poured out. She gave Lydia a compassionate smile. "You *will* find someone."

How many times had Lydia heard that exact sentiment? Too many to count. And too many to believe it any longer. She'd had just as many offers here as back home: zero. Yet she had to keep trying. She thought of the cold, dark nights, the jostling carriage ride over thirty miles to the nearest town, and the dearth of anyone near her age, and she inwardly shuddered.

Mrs. Lloyd-Jones broke into her self-pitying reverie. "You should consider Lockwood."

Had the woman not heard her? "There's nothing to consider. As soon as he learned I was Margaret's great-niece, he couldn't avoid me quickly enough." And he'd been quite plain in the street a few minutes earlier on the subject of her aunt and gossip. No, there was nothing for her there.

Mrs. Lloyd-Jones sighed. "A vicious cycle, isn't it? You want a life of your own, but people make assumptions about you because of your aunt and you can't form the sort of relationship that could lead to more. We must find a way around this."

Lydia's stomach pitched again. They'd discussed this topic before, but for some reason it was just too . . . painful today. She forced herself to smile, and tried very hard to make it genuine to put her hostess—and friend—at ease. "I'll find a way. Eventually."

"In the meantime, I think I'll champion this Lockwood match. I'm sure he's not disinterested. You're the only young lady who's drawn his favor." She arched her brow at Lydia. "You don't mind, do you?"

Lydia didn't mind. She liked Lockwood. But his behavior wasn't encouraging. Furthermore, what sort of life would she have if she were married to him? He was reclusive and scandalous—not exactly the prime qualities Lydia wanted in a husband. "What of his reputation? His *activities*?"

"He'd give them up, of course. I don't think he'd continue to host his parties if he had something—or someone—else to fill his life."

Why had he even started hosting them in the first

place? She wished she knew more about his background. Aunt Margaret had told her some of it of course, but Lydia knew better than to take her tales verbatim. "That's relieving to hear. However, who's to say he won't submit to a fit of madness and tear his house apart again?"

Mrs. Lloyd-Jones frowned. "It was a sad time. His mother had suffered a total mental collapse. They were close."

"Were they?" Lydia asked softly, a new picture forming in her mind. One she understood all too well. He'd had a mother who loved him. And she'd been taken away. Just like Lydia's.

"Quite." Mrs. Lloyd-Jones sipped her tea. "Lady Lockwood took the death of her husband badly. She wore full mourning for over a year, and then never strayed from half mourning."

This didn't seem to fit with the woman Aunt Margaret had described. Would someone who was bitter over her husband's infidelity honor his memory in such a way? "Aunt Margaret said she was very jealous of Lord Lockwood's mistresses."

Mrs. Lloyd-Jones blinked in rapid succession. "What woman isn't? That doesn't mean she didn't love him. Indeed, if she was guilty of anything, it was of loving him too much."

Lydia couldn't imagine being that overwhelmed by emotion, likely because she tried very hard not to display any, which had become easier over the years. "But she went insane with it, didn't she?"

Mrs. Lloyd-Jones's expression turned sad. "Yes. I don't know how it happened or if there was anything that could have been done to prevent it. She manages all right now, in the peace of the country, but she's very fragile. She can't return to Town, to the life she led before. It's such a tragedy and not fodder for gossip." She was warning Lydia about spreading this information, and Lydia couldn't argue with her. The entire story seemed very tragic and not just because she'd met Lockwood and—as Mr. Locke had said— "formed an opinion about him."

What was that opinion exactly? That he was interesting. Refreshingly honest. Exciting. Was there a way at all she could attract him? He'd seemed at least moderately intrigued by her—before he'd learned of her relation to Margaret. Perhaps she could prove to him they were not that alike. "Rest assured, I don't wish to cause Lord Lockwood any pain. I will guard my tongue. Especially since you seem to think we'll suit." She gave Mrs. Lloyd-Jones a knowing smile and wink, hoping to interject a little levity into their tea. Things had turned far too maudlin, and Lydia endured enough of that living with her aunt.

"Oh, yes. You leave things to me, dear. I'll have you and Lockwood to the altar before the end of the year. And how happy that will make me." She beamed at Lydia.

Lydia wondered if it would make her happy, too. Then she pondered the notion of someone finding joy on her behalf and decided that alone would be enough.

Chapter Seven

THE FOLLOWING EVENING Jason took up one of his two favorite positions at Lockwood House during a vice party. He lounged in a dark corner of the drawing room that gave him an excellent vantage point from which to view people as they arrived and decided where to go or what to do first.

Some went directly through to the gaming room. Others surveyed the feminine wares on display. The drawing room was always well populated with demimondaines who—for a fee—would entertain his guests and, as the evening wore on, were usually in lessening states of dress. Still others arrived with their own entertainment—in pairs, or trios, or whatever combination they preferred—and simply made good use of Jason's facilities.

Jason's blood thrummed more than usual. His parties could always be relied upon to boost his mood. It was a combination of things, not the least of which was witnessing the ton's elite indulging their basest desires—and thinking about how he could ruin people with the things he knew. Though revenge against those who'd ostracized him would be sweet, it wasn't the reason he'd begun these parties, and, perhaps surprisingly, he'd actually befriended some of the gentlemen. It would be interesting to see how they reacted now that he was back in circulation. Perhaps he *ought* to drop by White's.

His eye was caught by a vivid scarlet gown sweeping

into the drawing room. Cora Stroud was immediately set upon by a young buck. Her rouged lips parted in a beguiling smile. She'd flirt, she'd tease, she might even give him a taste or two, but she'd save the best for Jason, as she'd done the past, what—five months?

He'd never had a consistent paramour before. In the early days, he'd invited women here—courtesans who serviced him for a price and treated him the way he'd been used to, before he'd been scarred and branded a probable lunatic. Some left as soon as they saw him, others endured their evening and then opted not to return, and after a time, some began to ask to be invited again, while still more clamored for an invitation. With an armful of beautiful women to aid him, he was able to increase his social circle—the only one available to him—and so he'd invited a handful of wastrels to make a party of it. Then it had simply become habit.

Cora's kohl-rimmed eyes found his, and she gave him a secret smile full of promise. Oddly, Jason's desire didn't stir, but he was distracted. Likely by the prospect of Ethan. He nodded toward her and then put her from his mind. He wanted to focus on the matter at hand. No distractions. Which is what he'd instructed his retainers as well, not that they were easily lured from their posts. Jason knew after one party whether a servant was going to succeed at Lockwood House. Watching the goings-on at one of his vice parties was not for the faint of heart, nor for the indiscreet.

Jason decided it was time to mingle. He moved through the drawing room, greeting guests who made eye contact with him through the slits of their masks. One couple came forward as he passed them. The woman clutched the man's arm, and dipped her head down and then up. Then she leaned up and whispered something into the man's ear. Despite her mask, Jason knew when he was being surveyed.

"We were hoping you might join us upstairs later this evening," the man said. Jason couldn't quite place him, but thought he might be a young man called Swindon.

"Though I'm flattered by your proposition, I'm afraid that's not where my interests lie." He offered a benign smile. "I do know some other gentlemen who come here looking for just that sort of thing, however, and I'd be happy to direct one of them your way. Or, I can have a member of my staff simply set something up for you."

Swindon bent his head and spoke softly near the woman's ear. Her mouth, just visible beneath her ebony mask formed a disappointed little moue, but she ultimately gave a slight nod.

"That would be appreciated, my lord. Thank you." Swindon inclined his head and then escorted his "lady friend" away.

A footman opened the door for Jason to enter the sitting room. It was a smaller, more intimate room, with scant lighting. When attendees wished for a quieter atmosphere or if they simply couldn't bother themselves to retreat to a chamber upstairs, they came in here for a modicum of privacy.

Jason passed a couple entwined on a chaise, the woman's hand clearly stroking the man's cock through his trousers. Privacy was not perhaps the reason they came in here. The drawing room was for looking. The sitting room was for *doing*.

He scanned the semidarkness for Scot, knowing that

he was more likely to be stationed in this room than anywhere else. Jason found his valet near the wall, flirting with a pale blond Cyprian. She gave Jason a provocative smile as he approached and then took herself off as she recognized that he wanted a word with his retainer.

"There's a couple in the drawing room. They're looking for a male counterpart to join them upstairs. Are Pinnock or Blickleigh here?" Jason asked.

"I think I saw Pinnock in the billiards room. I'll take care of it." He cast a lingering glance at the Cyprian, who'd gone to a man lounging in the corner and had just dropped to her knees before him. He exhaled, muttering, "Later."

Jason stifled a smile as he followed Scot to the gaming room where he spent the next half hour talking with various gentlemen and surveying the evening's participants. He watched Pinnock eagerly leave the hazard table in order to meet Swindon and his companion upstairs. And he witnessed Mrs. Ulmer, a widow who never bothered to wear a mask and was one of the few women Jason invited, accepting the invitation of a much younger gentleman to join him in the fantasy room. Such couplings made Jason smile because it reminded him of why he loved to host these parties: Anything could happen at Lockwood House.

But still no Ethan.

Just as Jason's frustration began to mount, a masked man stood from a table in the corner. As he made his way between the tables, Jason assessed his build and tried to determine his identity, but couldn't place him—only his mouth and chin were visible beneath the black mask covering the rest of his face up to his dark hairline. The man sidled up beside him without formally addressing him, as if they were close friends. Jason's neck prickled.

"Lockwood," Ethan drawled. "I'm honored to be included in one of your legendary parties. I feel as if I have . . . *arrived.*"

The pompous ass. "You fool yourself if you think entrée to one of my parties will somehow solidify your tenuous position in Society. But come, let's discuss it." Jason turned and led him into the corridor where they would skirt the rooms open to partygoers.

"Going to your office?" Ethan asked, trailing just behind him.

Jason threw a feral smile over his shoulder. "I can't think of a better place." It was where their fight had begun all those years ago. Where Jason had found the bastard looking for a secret drawer in which their father had purportedly kept letters from Ethan's mother.

A few minutes later they entered Jason's office, which was situated in the back corner of the house. Bookcases lined the interior two walls while a window graced one of the exterior walls, and a massive fireplace dominated the other. Above the fireplace hung the portrait of their father in his youth. Ethan looked disturbingly like him—sharp gray eyes, a firm mouth, and a perpetual sense of . . . something broiling just beneath the surface, as if he had a secret or was simmering with some strong emotion. The painting captured a young man in his prime, before he'd taken a wife and saddled himself with responsibility, not that he'd ever let that interfere with his preferences.

Jason moved to the sideboard. "Whisky?"

"Yes," Ethan answered from behind him. "New

desk?"

Jason nodded as he poured whisky into two glass tumblers. "Do you like it? I had it made special."

"What happened to the old one?" Ethan asked, his tone guarded.

Picking up a tumbler in each hand Jason turned. He offered a glass to Ethan. "I burned it." Jason had never found the letters Ethan had been looking for. He hadn't even searched. He'd simply had it broken down and fed to the fire.

Ethan accepted the whisky and whipped off his mask. Yes, the resemblance between him and the portrait behind him was unsettling. "Naturally." His tone carried a bite.

Jason took a pull of his favorite whisky. Rich with heavy oak undertones, it was distilled in the lowlands of Scotland by one of North's and Scot's cousins and it soothed his roiling temper. He went and leaned against the sideboard. "This isn't meant to be some sort of civilized meeting."

"It isn't?" Ethan asked with an innocence that didn't match the flint in his eyes. "Why the whisky then? In fact, why invite me at all?"

"Tell me what you're doing masquerading as a gentleman."

Ethan shrugged. He gazed about the room in practiced nonchalance—or what seemed practiced to Jason. There was still that undercurrent of energy, of barely-contained something.

"It's no masquerade," Ethan's voice had grown soft, but carried the edge of a sharpened razor. "I *am* a gentleman by birth."

"*Half,* but you haven't behaved as one."

Ethan turned his body toward him, as if they were squaring off. Memories of that night seven years ago swirled about the room and thickened the moment. "And you have?"

Jason let his own darkness creep in and sneered. "I've done what I must, given what you left me with." He turned his scar toward Ethan.

Ethan looked away. "I never meant for that to happen."

Jason gaped at him. Was he apologizing? What the bloody hell was Jason supposed to do with *that*? "You could have fooled me. It seemed you came here that day with an agenda to push me as far as you could."

The gray eyes so like their father's pinned him with a sincerity Jason couldn't quite believe. "I did. I hated you." He shrugged. "You hated me. We're even."

"Except for the part where you left me bleeding and scarred for life." Both inside and out.

"And I regret that." He sipped his whisky. "But tell me, brother, if the situation had been reversed, what would you have done?"

Jason wanted to say he would've helped him, that he would've ensured the staff knew it had simply been a fight between brothers and not the violent unhinging of a madman. But he couldn't. Even now, if he were presented with the opportunity to ruin Ethan, he'd take it. Isn't that what he was hoping to gain by helping Bow Street?

Polishing off his drink, Jason went to the sideboard and poured another. "So you want to be a gentleman and you think to gain my support to accomplish that?"

Ethan blinked at him, as if he wouldn't have put it that way. "I *am* a gentleman and I'd hoped to take my place as your half brother. It seemed that might work best if we weren't trying to kill each other."

"If you're a gentleman as you claim, where have you been these last seven years? Why emerge now?"

Ethan finished his whisky and then set the glass atop Jason's desk with a loud clack. "It doesn't matter. I was foolish to think we could overcome the past."

How Jason wanted to just ask him outright about his activities. Was he taking over the theft ring? Was he responsible for the theft on Curzon Street? However, he presumed Bow Street wouldn't want him to be so unsubtle. "If I thought I could trust you, things might be different."

Ethan's stare was probing, expectant. He looked more like their father than ever. "So try."

Jason set his glass down on the sideboard and leaned forward. "Give me a reason."

With a loud exhalation, Ethan looked at the floor for a long moment. When he raised his head once more, his features were tightly stretched. "I'm not what they say. Not now. I'm trying to change."

"How?" Jason wanted details. He moved a step forward. "What are you trying to change?"

"Hell," Ethan muttered. "Just give me some time. Will you do that? Soon, I'll tell you everything."

And until then, Jason was simply supposed to have faith in the person who'd destroyed his life? No one was that indulgent. "Why not now? If you tell me, it would go a long way to establish trust."

"It would also go a long way to getting you killed." His gaze was intense. "Just be patient, will you do that?"

"You clearly know what I've heard. Put that with the

Ethan Jagger I know, and I have no choice but to believe you're up to no good."

"You're so goddamned suspicious." Ethan shook his head and murmured, "Just like your mother."

"What did you say?" Jason's self-control suddenly and completely snapped. He lunged at Ethan and slammed him backward into the bookshelf. Ethan's head made a dull thud as it hit the wood of the shelf, but he didn't seem affected. He pushed back at Jason and swung out, catching his jaw with his knuckles.

Scalding rage poured through Jason, stripping him of rational thought. He only wanted to punish this man who'd done nothing but hurt him and his mother. He sent his fist toward Ethan's face, but the blighter dodged the strike. Ethan moved quickly with his own fists, driving them into Jason's sides, first one then the other.

Jason grunted and lashed out again. This time he caught Ethan's cheek with the first blow, though he missed with the next. Ethan was fast, his defenses good. He punched Jason in his scarred cheek.

"You move slow, old man," Ethan growled.

White fury blinded Jason for a moment as he grabbed Ethan's upper arms and threw him against the other bookcases. His frame slammed into the wood, and several books fell from the shelves. Jason drove his fist into Ethan's gut, and relished the whoosh of air he exhaled and the grunt that followed.

Ethan slid to the side and found his footing. He sent another fist into Jason's side, sending a searing burst of pain along his ribs. The bastard knew exactly where to hit. And then it dawned on Jason. Ethan was fighting like a pugilist.

"Have you been working out with your fighter?" Jason asked, his breath coming in harsh pants as he sent another pair of punches toward Ethan's face. He only connected with one, but it was a good hit to Ethan's nose.

Ethan brought his hand to his nose and rubbed a knuckle over the end. "Yes. Father would've been very proud."

The son of a bitch. Of course Benjamin Lockwood would've been proud. The only thing he liked better than his whores was fighting. And leave it to Ethan to take after him *and* rub it in Jason's ruined face. Jason roared with rage and reached for Ethan's neck. Just as his fingers were closing around the collar of Ethan's shirt, hands pulled him backward. Jason tried to throw them off. His vision tunneled until all he could see was Ethan's taunting face.

"Let him go, my lord." North's even tones broke into the fiery haze in Jason's brain.

"You'd best leave," Scot suggested from somewhere to Jason's right. He had to be talking to Ethan.

Jason threw one of his retainers off him, freeing his left arm. "No, he can't go. I'm not finished." He swiped out at Ethan, trying to grab his cravat and hopefully choke him with it.

But Ethan was too fast again. He moved quickly out of his reach and then delivered a sharp jab to Jason's ribcage again—in the same spot he'd already hit twice before.

This prick was *not* going to best him again.

Jason reared up and pulled his right arm free. Then he dove on top of Ethan and tackled him to the floor. Ethan's head grazed the desk as he fell. Jason pulled his hand back to deliver a blow to his face, but someone grabbed his fist and held him fast.

Hands hauled him up and away from Ethan. "Let me go, goddammit!" he roared.

"Get him out of here," North said. From where his voice originated, Jason guessed he'd been the traitor who'd stopped him from hitting Ethan.

Two footmen helped Ethan up. Ethan's hand went to the back of his head and when he brought it down, blood striped his fingers.

Ethan's mouth lifted in a semblance of a smile as he sent a mocking gaze at Jason. "Get what you wanted?"

Jason pulled at the men—what, three of them?—holding him. Fingers dug into his biceps; they weren't letting him go. He glared at Ethan with all the malevolence boiling his insides. "Not even close."

"Then I'll look forward to the next time." Ethan nodded at the men holding Jason. "Evening, lads." Then he turned and left the office.

The door closed after his departure, and the men released Jason. He strode for the door, intent on going after Ethan and pummeling him into dust, but Scot got there first, his back slamming into the wood. He shook his head. "Not now. You've got a house full of people."

Those words permeated Jason's brain like no others could. Scot may as well have said, "Do you want a repeat of seven years ago?" If he took his fight with Ethan outside of this office, everyone at the party would see the outburst and perhaps conclude that Jason really *was* mad. Then his parties would cease, and he wouldn't allow Ethan to take his sole enjoyment from him too.

He strode to the sideboard and poured another whisky. The door clicked, and when he turned back to the room he saw that only North remained. His butler regarded him with wary eyes. He said nothing, but stood between Jason and the door.

"I won't go after him," Jason said, gripping his whisky as if it were the only friend he had. But he knew it wasn't. North and Scot were more than retainers who valued their jobs. They'd saved Jason from making a colossal mistake—again—because they cared.

North nodded once, but didn't relax. His gaze lost a bit of their guardedness, but his tense posture said he was still vigilant.

If Scot were here, he'd ask questions, but North would simply wait for Jason to speak, if he wanted to. And Jason didn't want to. He tossed back the rest of his drink and set the glass behind him on the sideboard.

At length, the door opened. Scot stepped inside and held the door. Cora swept into the office, her scarlet skirts brushing over Scot's boots.

"Darling," she said, coming toward Jason.

What the hell had Scot done bringing her here? Was she supposed to somehow provide solace? He didn't want that. He didn't want *her*. Not now.

As she moved closer, he wanted to retreat, but couldn't because he was already up against the sideboard. He slid to the side a bit.

Cora's forehead creased with concern. Her dark eyes looked over him curiously, lingering on his cheek, which was surely reddened from Ethan's blow. "Are you all right?"

"I'm fine," he ground out. "You should go."

"No, let me help you, darling," she cooed.

He didn't want sympathy or coddling. He wanted release. And then he realized he could get that with her. Take her upstairs to the bedroom they usually used and fuck her until he was senseless. But he didn't want that either. He didn't want *her*. He wanted to nurse his anger and plan his next move.

He pierced her with his darkest stare, knowing he looked ferocious. "No. Get out."

Her eyes flashed with some emotion—pain, perhaps. But Jason didn't apologize. He couldn't. She turned, and Scot opened the door for her, shutting it firmly after she exited.

Jason tried to force the tension from his shoulders by shaking his arms out. That was when he realized his hands were shaking of their own accord. He curled his fingers into fists and glared at his retainers. "What the hell were you thinking?"

"I thought she might help," Scot said without a trace of regret, his hand still on the door. "You and she get on well. And have for quite some time."

"That doesn't mean you bring her to me after what just happened. You feel the need to guard me from my guests, but you bring her in here as an offering?"

Scot let go of the door. "She's not a guest, she's your mistress." Now there was a trace of apology to his tone, and he added, "Isn't she?"

Jason scowled at his valet. "No." He didn't want to think about Cora right now. He wanted to plan Ethan's downfall. He pinned North with a vicious stare. "How'd that bastard get in without my knowing?"

North took a step toward him. "Might I pour you another glass of whisky?"

"Don't patronize me. How did he get in?"

"I'm not certain, my lord." He clenched his jaw. "It could be that he presented his invitation to the footman and I was perhaps otherwise detained with a guest."

Possibly, but Jason rather thought the blighter had snuck in.

North refilled Jason's glass. "Here. I'm not patronizing, I'm fortifying. Put yourself back together and go back out there when you're ready. And smooth things over with Miss Stroud. You upset her."

He'd sought feminine companionship any way he could get it for so long, and now he didn't want it. At least not from her. For some reason, Lydia Prewitt's dark-as-hell eyes appeared in his mind. Sparkling. Flirtatious. Expectant, as she'd been on the street yesterday. And he'd been obnoxious.

He drank his whisky and threw a nod at North and Scot so they'd leave.

Jason's gaze raised to the portrait of the man who'd created two men who despised each other and who potentially had the power to ruin each other. "What a bloody mess you made. All because you couldn't be faithful." Jason wouldn't make that mistake. He wouldn't make promises he didn't intend to keep. Which is why long-standing relationships with women had no place in his life. He wasn't his father.

He threw back the rest of the drink, relishing the hot trail it burned down his throat. Then he quit the office in search of Cora Stroud so he could tell her she was no longer welcome in his bed.

Chapter Eight

LYDIA ADJUSTED THE cap covering her blond curls as she made her way down the back stairs of her town house. Quietly, she opened the door and stepped into the scullery. She'd waited to leave until she knew all the servants would be occupied in other areas. She hurried across the empty space and out the door, then rushed up the exterior stairs. Without a backward glance, she headed east toward her destination: Lockwood House.

Dressed as a maid in a plain dress, apron, and cap, she drew no one's attention. Anxiety coursed through her veins. She'd never ventured anywhere by herself. It was beneath her station, Aunt Margaret would say, unseemly.

It actually felt quite liberating.

Exhilaration overcame her anxiety until she thought about where she was going. What would Lord Lockwood say when she infiltrated his den of disgrace?

She mentally shook her head. He'd hosted another party two nights ago. Aunt Margaret was only too eager to spread that information, and already Society was abuzz with his continued indiscretion. Did he not realize he couldn't hope to gain invitations to events like the Whitmore Ball if he insisted on hosting vice parties? Clearly not. And it was also clear he needed someone to tell him so. Lydia had elected herself that person.

Which only brought her anxiety back to the fore. He hadn't exactly been welcoming during their last encounter, and now she was going to march right into the beast's lair and put her reputation at risk. She was counting on being unrecognizable in her borrowed maid's costume. Perhaps borrowed wasn't the right word. Aunt Margaret's maid, Coxley, had no idea Lydia had pilfered her extra uniform—she was closest to Lydia's size. Hopefully Lydia would be able to return it before its absence was noted.

Obtaining the maid's clothing and escaping her aunt's town house had been challenging enough, but the true test would be getting back in. She didn't want to think about that now; it would only heighten her nervousness and she'd likely turn back in fear. Better to focus on her upcoming interview with Lord Lockwood.

Why was he still having vice parties? No, that wasn't the question she wanted answered most. Why did he have vice parties at all?

She could still hear Aunt Margaret cackling with glee, saying how Lockwood couldn't possibly improve himself. How his bastard half brother was going to fare better than he.

The bastard half brother who wanted a meeting. That was the second item on her agenda to speak with him about today, right after the vice party discussion. And all the while she supposed she ought to flirt if she wanted to encourage Mrs. Lloyd-Jones's scheme. But did she? There was no easy answer. She wanted out of Aunt Margaret's house, but Burke had to be a better option than shackling herself to someone like Lockwood. However, so far her choices were nonexistent. Which made this party doubly important. If she could help Lockwood regain his footing in Society, she would change people's perceptions about her, and maybe then she'd finally attract a husband.

Fifteen minutes later, after traveling at a brisk pace, she arrived at Lockwood House. Though the afternoon was cool and overcast, she was quite warm due to the exercise. She slowed as she passed the massive house, trying to determine how to enter. There was no visible servants' entrance, so she turned into a narrow alley that ran along the side. Where the house terminated, a stone wall started and encircled the back garden. She didn't spy a gate and frowned. Now what?

She walked back to the street and decided she had no other choice than to approach by the front door. She couldn't very well loiter outside any longer and risk being recognized. Although, she rather hoped she was unrecognizable in her maid's attire.

A few moments later, she rapped on the ebony door—a fitting color for Lockwood House. The door cracked open to reveal a tall, dark-haired butler garbed in black and gold livery.

His gaze swept over her quickly and settled on her face. "I regret to say we do not have any open positions at present."

She affixed a sunny smile on her face. "Oh, no, I'm not here for employment. I'm here to see his lordship."

The butler's dark brow arched almost imperceptibly, the only reaction he displayed. "I'm afraid I couldn't bother his lordship with your . . . trifles." His tone wasn't arrogant or condescending, but matter-of-fact. She appreciated that.

"Tell him Lady Lydia Prewitt is here to see him. And please, for the love of my reputation, let me inside."

The door swung wide, and she stepped into a massive marble-tiled foyer. She felt a moment's panic as she realized she was inside the storied Lockwood House. But it was too late now. She was here. What's more, she had business to conduct.

He inclined his head for her to follow him. "Come with me."

He led her across the impeccably clean marble floor to a doorway and ushered her into a sitting room with a wide window facing the street. The door closed behind her and she moved farther into the room. It was tastefully decorated in ivory and gold, though the styles and fabrics were probably two decades old.

She wandered the room looking for clues about this house, this man, but there were no portraits or interesting décor that might reveal something. Maybe the ceramic figurines of a shepherd and his flock on the mantel were dear family artifacts. She somehow doubted that. What had she expected? Portraits of naked women? A shiver danced along her flesh as she again realized she was *inside* Lockwood House. What happened in this very room during one of his infamous parties?

The door clicked and she swung around. Lord Lockwood entered and closed the door behind him. He didn't advance, just stood and studied her thoroughly.

He was dressed in flawless attire—buff breeches and a blue coat. A rich brown waistcoat peeked from beneath his lapels, and a pristine cravat encircled his throat. His features were relaxed, his scar standing in stark relief, a potent reminder that he might look amenable, but that beneath the surface lurked a man of strong passion.

Lydia ignored the pounding of her heart and forced herself to recall her errand. "Good afternoon, my lord.

I hope I'm not disturbing you."

He cocked his head to the side, regarding her as if she had sprouted an extra arm. "Lady Lydia, you've arrived at Lockwood House dressed in a maid's costume. Nothing about your visit *isn't* disturbing. I've asked North—my butler—to call a hack, and a footman will see you home."

She refused to be deterred. "I realize how this may seem, but I assure you my reasons for coming here are sound. But you're right, I don't have a lot of time before I will be missed at home, so I appreciate the hack."

His eyes widened a fraction. "Before you will be missed? Did you sneak out?"

Now it was her turn to look at him as if he'd lost his mind. "Do you think I simply announced to my aunt that I was going for tea at Lockwood House?" His mouth quirked the barest amount, but it was enough to make her smile. "No, of course not. Hence my costume." She gestured to her maid's gown. "I've come to offer my assistance."

He blinked at her. "Your assistance? Why am I suddenly filled with trepidation?"

"Oh, you needn't be. Do you mind if I sit? I walked over here rather quickly and I'm a bit tired."

"Certainly, please excuse my boorishness." He indicated an ivory settee with slender stripes the color of burnished gold.

She took a seat. "Thank you." When he continued to linger near the door, she said, "Won't you join me?"

He eyed the space beside her with a wary gaze. Then he walked to a burgundy chair situated across a table from her and took that instead. He didn't want to sit by her, but then she supposed that would be scandalous given that they were unsupervised in his home. Good Lord, what had she been thinking? Why did she assume this man—this notorious purveyor of vice—would be harmless?

She had to stop letting her mind wander. "My lord, I've come to speak with you about your, er, parties."

He blinked once. Twice. "You've come to talk about my parties? I begin to see why this meeting is clandestine—aside from your sheer brazen lunacy in coming here."

"And that's precisely the problem. We must remove the stigma surrounding your home."

"'We'?" he repeated. He shook his head. "Let's assume for a moment that Lockwood House is simply a gentleman's residence—no vice parties. Your calling here unchaperoned is still the height of impropriety."

She narrowed her eyes at him playfully, vaguely aware that she was still flirting with him and probably oughtn't. "You're not really going to lecture me about impropriety, are you?"

He smiled fully then. "Point taken. What do you want to say about my parties? And don't ask if you can secretly attend. I've never allowed another young lady to do so, and I won't start now."

She leaned forward, her eyes wide. "Other young ladies have asked?"

His eyes shuttered and his features darkened. "If you've come to accumulate gossip, you may as well wait in the foyer for your hack. I have no patience for such nonsense."

She felt the heat rushing to her cheeks and wished she could stop it. She settled back against the settee, hating that was always what people expected from her. She would need to work harder to change that assumption, and wasn't that the reason she was trying to help him? "That's not why I came. Please be assured that anything I learn today will be kept strictly between us."

"Forgive me if I don't quite trust you completely." His eyes were still guarded. "I'm afraid my experience with your aunt makes me skeptical."

Understandably so, given Aunt Margaret's clear dislike of him. Lydia wanted to know the details of that experience from his perspective, but she didn't have time to ask for specifics. If her errand proved successful, there would be plenty of opportunity to ask him in the coming days.

She offered him a smile to try and set him at ease. "Fine, I shall have to demonstrate that you can trust me. As I said, I'm here to help you. You seem to want to reestablish your place in Society, but you can't if you continue to have vice parties. Indeed, I'm shocked you had one the other night after your success at the Whitmore Ball."

"It's what I do." He leaned back in his chair with a shrug. "And anyway, what success? I left early. I barely spoke to anyone. I only danced with one person."

Her. She tried not to think of his strong hand fanning over her back or of the arousing way in which he'd glided her across the floor. "But surely you understand that you won't be invited anywhere if you continue to host these parties?"

"Really, why?" he asked, seeming genuinely interested.

He wasn't that obtuse, was he? "Because they're

unseemly!"

"It's ridiculous," he scoffed. "Do you know how many people from your precious Society attend those parties? You'd be scandalized. And, no, I won't tell you any of their names."

Lydia hated that she wanted to know. Hated that her aunt had engendered within her a need to know, if not to wield information that shouldn't matter a whit to her. "I'm not asking you to," she said softly. "I'm trying to help you, but perhaps this was a mistake."

"Why would you want to help?" His gaze was direct, intense, scalding her with a heat she didn't want to feel in his presence. He didn't trust her and probably didn't even like her. Why indeed.

She had trouble thinking of an answer without dredging up everything she'd learned from Mrs. Lloyd-Jones. Perhaps they'd discuss those things, but not today. "Aside from simply wanting to help you, doing so will make me the toast of the *ton*."

He looked rather skeptical. "So helping me helps you?"

"Yes. People will see that I'm more than a gossip." She realized she was trying to persuade him as much as anyone. If he didn't believe she'd changed, she had little hope of convincing anyone else.

"What do you suggest?" he asked, still sounding suspicious.

She folded her hands in her lap and raised her chin. "A vice-*free* party."

He leaned forward again, his jaw dropping slightly. "A what?"

"Host a regular party. Not a full ball, but a soirée with food and music." She clapped her hands together to punctuate her offer. "I'll help you with the arrangements."

He stared at her for a long moment. "You want me to invite Society to Lockwood House for a *soirée*?"

"Precisely."

"No one would come," he said incredulously.

"That's where you're wrong." A smile crept over her face as she thought of people's expressions when they received the invitations. "People will be clamoring to be invited. Lockwood House is a place of mystery, of scandal. It's dangerous. Exciting. To have the opportunity to see it without risking one's reputation will have people here in droves. But we won't invite droves. The guest list will be quite exclusive."

His mouth twitched with amusement. "You've put a lot of thought into this."

"I have."

"And you mean to keep coming here so we can plan this?" He shook his head. "I'm not comfortable with that. You mustn't risk your reputation."

He may not trust her or like her, but that simple statement meant more to her than any of that. He *was* a gentleman—somewhere inside. "I'll come with a chaperone. And I'll ensure everyone knows our relationship is above reproach."

He stared at her, but she sensed his mind working. He didn't like her aunt and was weighing whether her help was worth putting up with Margaret in some capacity.

"I won't be chaperoned by my aunt, if that's what you're worried about. I believe Mrs. Lloyd-Jones will be pleased to play the part." Yet, Lydia still had to convince Aunt Margaret to allow it. She had to believe she would get something out of it, that Lydia would obtain some unknown secret of Lockwood's. She'd promise her aunt whatever she had to. Not only would this scheme get her away from her aunt for a goodly amount of time, the potential for a permanent departure through marriage to an eligible bachelor dangled before her like sweetmeats on a tray.

He still looked skeptical. "You really think people will come to a party here?"

"I'm certain of it. Two weeks hence." She briefly held up her forefinger. "And no more vice parties."

"All right," he said, "but I want to invite Lady Aldridge."

She snapped her gaze to his. "I believe she's still ill. At least she was when I last tried to call on her. That was the day I met you as you were getting into your coach." And he'd all but insulted her.

His gaze drifted off briefly before settling back on her. "Please accept my apology for my behavior that day. I should not have inferred you were like your aunt. That was rude of me." His voice was soft, his gaze tinged with heat.

"Thank you." She smoothed her hand over her lap. His gaze followed her movement and lingered on her hand or her lap. Or both.

Now was the time to address the second item on her agenda. "I think you should invite Mr. Locke."

Lockwood's mouth tightened, and his entire frame seemed to tense. "Why?"

She needed to tread carefully. "It's part of the mystique. Until your ill-advised vice party the other night, your encounter with him at the Whitmore Ball was the talk of the town. It still is, but your continued disregard for societal norms has captured people's interest."

He exhaled, and his shoulders lost some of their tension. "You may have to repeatedly remind me why I want to do this. I'm content out here on the fringe with my . . . unacceptable proclivities."

The way he said the last brought a shiver to her skin. Again, she wanted to ask for more details. What proclivities, and why did he like them so much? Though she didn't have the luxury of time, she couldn't seem to stop herself from asking, "Why did you start having vice parties in the first place?"

He was silent for a very long moment. Lydia inwardly cringed and wished she could take the words back. In fact, she was about to apologize and tell him to disregard her question when he spoke. Softly but deeply. "Because they're the only kind of parties I can have."

She shook her head. "That can't be true."

His gaze held hers. "But it is. I don't wish to delve into the specific details, but Society consciously excluded me. I had to cultivate new relationships and new methods of entertainment. Now, after years of hosting these parties, I quite enjoy them. Indeed, I'd be loath to give them up."

She clasped her hands together in her lap to focus the energy swirling through her. *Society consciously excluded me.* She'd planned to ask him what was wrong with Society, but given what he'd said, she already knew. Who would want to be a part of something by which they'd been rejected?

There was something in his expression—something in the way his eyelids dipped just slightly. Anger or sadness lurked just beneath the surface.

She probably ought to let the subject go, especially given her lack of time, but she wanted to get at the heart of why he felt like these parties were all he had. "So you'd choose vice parties over Society? They provide you with that much . . . pleasure?" She couldn't keep from blushing.

"Since I've only recently been reaccepted into Society—on a very limited scale—there isn't really a choice. But yes, I enjoy my vice parties very much. However, please understand my *pleasure* derives from playing host and providing a pleasurable evening for my guests, not from satisfying my own vices." He cocked his head to the side. "And why do *you* want a place in Society? I would think that someone like you would be intimately aware of its artifice and whimsy. I like knowing where I stand and what I can expect. I also like living by my own rules and not those of some silly arbiters of fashion or taste."

His words stirred her. If she hadn't already committed to wanting to distance herself from gossip, she would have done so now. She also knew she couldn't be content hosting sinful parties on the "fringe" as he put it. "You are entitled to your opinion, of course. I, however, like the entertainments Society has to offer, and I like the people. Well, some of them anyway." Even enduring the ones she didn't like was far better than spending her days conversing with sheep. Which is precisely what she'd be doing if she didn't wasn't very careful. "If you aren't interested in reclaiming your place in Society—and you absolutely deserve one—I suppose there's no reason to have this soirée." She didn't bother hiding the disappointment from her voice. She wanted to help him now more than ever.

"I suppose there isn't," he said softly. "But I'll do it anyway."

She snapped her gaze to his. "You will?"

He lifted a shoulder carelessly as if he'd just decided to buy an ivory cravat instead of a white one. "Why not?"

She'd been about to say *because you don't care what anyone thinks of you.* And she suddenly wished she could feel that way. That she could be happy with only her own approval, and maybe that of her father, though she already knew he didn't much care where she lived or what she did. How freeing it would be to walk your own path—and yet how lonely.

The butler's entry, however, prevented her from speaking. "The hack is waiting, my lord. Dockley will see her home."

"Thank you, North." Lord Lockwood stood.

Lydia knew she should leave, but didn't want to. And not just because she loathed returning to her aunt's. She felt comfortable here—at Lockwood House of all places. With him. Just as she had the first day she'd met him. Perhaps Mrs. Lloyd-Jones's matchmaking skills were more astute than Lydia realized. *That* provoked her to jump up and seek her departure.

He moved toward her and offered his hand. "Come, 'tis time you're on your way. Your costume is convincing, but if anyone sees your face they'll know in a trice who you are."

A bolt of fear shot down her spine. "Your staff won't say anything?"

"No, I have the most discreet retainers in London.

Just keep your face down when you get outside. I'd offer you a mask—we keep plenty on hand—but that would draw even more attention at this time of day."

She took his hand and again experienced the burst of heat she always felt when he touched her.

He didn't release her, but held her hand as he walked her to the door. "How do you plan to get back into your house undetected?"

"The same way I left, through the scullery." She hoped to get in without anyone seeing her. They'd have to report it to Aunt Margaret. In fact, Lydia would insist. Once, a maid had covered for Lydia and the consequences for her had been so severe that Lydia hadn't allowed any of them to do it again.

Lockwood arced his head down to look at her. His gray eyes were inquisitive. "You risked a great deal coming here."

She didn't flinch from his gaze. "Nothing I'm not willing to lose." This small taste of freedom would be worth any punishment Aunt Margaret threw at her. Unless she put her in a coach to Northumberland. But given how much her aunt relied on her to obtain gossip, Lydia doubted she'd actually do it.

North held the door open, and Lockwood escorted her into the foyer.

She could imagine him as a gracious, charming host. And maybe he was at his vice parties. Perhaps that was why they were so popular. Throwing a successful party was a skill, regardless of the themes involved.

He walked her to the front door and then brought her fingers to his lips. The touch of his mouth against her glove barely penetrated the fabric, but the charged look in his eyes shot all the way to her soul. "You intrigue me, Lady Lydia. I look forward to how we might proceed."

Oh, this flirting was growing dangerous. Never mind what she'd risked in coming here today—what was she risking by aligning herself with this self-proclaimed devil?

She withdrew her hand and exited Lockwood House. Though she hadn't attended one of its notorious parties, she felt scandalized just the same. But that wasn't the worst part. No, the worst part was that she'd liked it.

Chapter Nine

JASON WATCHED LYDIA walk to the hack and frowned as Scot hurried by her. North held the door open to admit his brother. Scot swiped his hat from his head. His breathing was labored, as if he'd run a long distance.

"Devil nipping at your heels?" Jason asked.

"Not yet, my lord. I was down the pub as usual." Scot habitually visited one of his favorite pubs on afternoons when Jason didn't require his services. "Seems Aldridge House takes an ale delivery twice a week. Only today they didn't accept delivery because the house was in an uproar. Lady Aldridge died this morning."

Jason couldn't keep his jaw from dropping. He snapped his mouth shut and inclined his head at North to shut the door. "What? How?"

"Laudanum overdose."

Jason shook his head sadly. A shame the widow had to follow her husband to the grave in such quick succession. She was far too young to lose her life. "She'd been ill. Perhaps she took too much laudanum by mistake."

Scot's countenance, however, implied that nothing was ever that simple. "Or perhaps she took too much on purpose. She was quite devastated by his lordship's death."

"I'm not sure I'd believe her capable of suicide," Jason said. Her reputation before Aldridge's death had been that of a vivacious young woman with a pleasing complement of wit and charm. Still, no one knew what people were truly capable of. After all, no one had ever guessed Aldridge had been running a theft ring.

Scot inhaled deeply as his breathing slowed.

Jason clapped him on the shoulder. "I appreciate you delivering the news with the utmost haste, although you didn't have to run."

Scot shrugged. "I knew you were interested in Lady Aldridge and whatever she's doing with Jagger. If you don't mind, I'm going to grab an ale."

North arched a brow. "Didn't you just come from the pub?"

"I *ran*." Scot gave his brother a harassed glare and took himself toward the kitchen.

Ethan. Jason clenched his jaw. Why was his half brother always at the root of something bad?

"My lord, you don't think he was somehow involved?" North asked sharply.

Did he? Ethan had claimed he was trying to change and had pleaded with Jason to trust him. Those were not the sentiments of a man who would be involved in the death of a young widow. Still, his sudden relationship with her and his apparent background as a criminal were too coincidental to ignore. "I don't know."

Jason turned to go to his office and assumed North would follow, which he did. Despite the terrible news, Jason felt a curious lightness he hadn't felt in a long time, maybe never.

"My lord," North said, falling into step on Jason's right. "Why did Lady Lydia come here dressed in a maid's costume?"

"She was on a secret mission." He wanted to smile at her daring, even if it was a bit foolish. She continued to surprise him, and he liked it. "I'm hosting a party in a fortnight."

The space between North's brows briefly gathered, revealing his confusion. He was likely trying to determine what Lydia's secret mission could possibly have to do with a party. Instead of asking, however, he only said, "I'll get started on the invitations."

Jason waited to reveal the truth until they reached the office so he could appreciate North's full reaction. He moved to stand beside his desk and faced his butler. "Not a vice party. A *real* party. A *soirée*. Lady Lydia is helping me reestablish my place in Society."

North stared at him, his mouth agape. "I beg your pardon?"

"You heard me correctly. We're to host a real party. No invitations delivered late at night by black-liveried footmen, and no masks. At least I don't think there will be masks. She said it would be a party with food and music, but not a full-blown ball."

North continued to appear nonplussed. "Why?"

Jason tried not to laugh at his butler's confounded state. "To present me as an acceptable member of Society. To show them all that I'm not to be feared or reviled." She hadn't said any of that, but they were the reasons Jason had agreed.

And maybe, *maybe* because she looked at him with those gorgeous chestnut brown eyes and made him feel like he wasn't feared or reviled.

"It's your fault," Jason said. "You're the one who encouraged me to venture back into Society."

North regained his composure. "How foolish of me

in retrospect," he said dryly. "I take it you will not be inviting Mr. Jagger again?"

"On the contrary." Jason still wasn't certain that was a good idea, particularly given how his last visit to Lockwood House had ended, but he was more curious about his half brother than ever. And though they had come to blows again, Jason couldn't stop thinking about how genuine he'd seemed in trying to start anew. It was unsettling.

"Do you think he'll come after what happened the other night?" North asked.

"I do. We have unfinished business." Jason believed Ethan would jump at another chance to reconcile—if that's what he truly wanted. But what if it wasn't? What if he were still in the midst of a criminal lifestyle and Jason was to be his next victim?

"You said Lady Lydia is helping to plan this party?" North asked.

"Yes, you'll take all instruction from her."

"Given Lady Lydia's involvement, Lady Margaret will have to be invited," North noted. "Can you tolerate that?"

Damn. Jason hadn't considered that she'd be here in his house. She hadn't been to Lockwood House since before his mother's collapse.

"I'm afraid I must." Just the notion of that harridan in his house made his head ache. Jason massaged his temple. "In the meantime, where am I going tonight?"

North clasped his hands behind his back. "A musicale at Lord and Lady Compton's. However, no new invitations arrived again today."

Yesterday had been the first day since the Whitmore Ball without invitations. He had to credit the vice party with the deficit. It seemed Lady Lydia's help would be welcome. Except, what the hell was he doing? He didn't *care* about any of that . . . did he? He wondered if he would see Ethan at the musicale and knew that was the reason he cared. So long as Ethan was out there enjoying Society, Jason would be too.

"Will that be all, my lord?" North asked.

"Yes." Jason fixed his gaze toward the bookshelves but focused on nothing in particular. He didn't see his office. He saw a pair of rich chestnut eyes looking at him with unabashed interest. They still lingered on his scar, but not as much as they used to. Her pink lips smiled more often than not, revealing endearing little dimples. She was proving to be as unlike her aunt as he could hope.

Hope?

What could he possibly want from her? She was a marriageable young woman and since he had no interest in marriage, he should be steering clear of her. Why, then, was he planning the precise opposite?

Because, as he'd told her, he made his own rules. He could indulge their mutual flirtation without overstepping. And once he'd determined what the hell Ethan was up to, he'd part ways with the alluring Lady Lydia and return to his existence on the perimeter.

THE HACK DROPPED Lydia off on the corner. She kept her face averted, as Lord Lockwood had recommended and made it to the servant's entrance of her aunt's home. Exhaling with relief, she mentally braced herself for the last little bit of luck she needed. But it was not to be.

The housekeeper, Mrs. Erickson, stood near the door to the scullery into the kitchen. Her concerned gaze fixed on Lydia and swept over her gown.

Lydia closed her eyes briefly. She'd have to tell Aunt Margaret everything. Not because Mrs. Erickson would tell her, but because Lydia didn't want to put any of the servants in the position of having to lie for her. She wouldn't allow any of them to lose their positions on account of her folly.

She put on her sunniest smile, which was completely at odds with the foreboding swirling in her belly. "Good afternoon, Mrs. Erickson. Has my aunt returned from her calls?"

Worry lines creased the housekeeper's kind face. "You know she hasn't." Her gaze dropped to Lydia's attire. "Is that Coxley's dress?"

"Yes, but she doesn't know."

Mrs. Erickson nodded. "Let's get it back quickly then." She held her arm out and gestured for Lydia to hurry up the back stairs.

Lydia didn't move. "You must tell Aunt Margaret. She won't hesitate to—"

Mrs. Erickson put up her hand to cut Lydia off. "I didn't see anything."

Lydia forced her heavy feet across the bricked floor. "For now. But if I think for a moment she's figured anything out, I'll tell her I threatened you."

On occasion, Aunt Margaret was more than verbally abusive. She'd raised a hand to Lydia more than a few times, though not in the past couple of years. Once, a servant had intervened on Lydia's behalf and had been summarily dismissed without reference. Lydia had vowed that no one would suffer because of her again.

Mrs. Erickson clearly remembered the same occurrence, for her eyes turned sad. "Go."

Lydia hurried up the stairs and changed out of the maid's costume as quickly as possible. She'd replaced the garments in Coxley's room and was just coming down from the topmost floor when she heard her aunt's voice coming from her sitting room.

"Where is Lydia?" Her voice climbed to a near-shriek, and Lydia knew it wasn't the first time she'd posed the question.

She hurriedly went to the sitting room and forced herself to remain composed despite her frantic emotions. "I'm here, Aunt Margaret. I was upstairs."

Aunt Margaret's cheeks were flushed and she was yanking her gloves off with violent tugs. "Looking through your mother's things again?"

There was a small trunk of items that had belonged to Lydia's mother in a room upstairs. Lydia had brought it with her from Northumberland as a means to keep the memory of her mother close. When Lydia sought solitude, she went up and spent time with her mother the only way she could—by touching things that had belonged to her. Aunt Margaret never ventured to the top floor, and the servants never intruded on Lydia when she was up there.

Today, it was a blessed excuse. "Yes." She smiled and tried to look as cheerful as possible. "Did you have a nice afternoon?"

"I did not." The dark glint in her narrowed eyes studied Lydia as if she could discern her secrets.

The butler backed out of the sitting room and closed the door without a word. Lydia hovered near the doorway, her legs wobbling. She didn't like the flush in her aunt's face or the shadows in her gaze. Had she somehow learned that Lydia had gone to Lockwood House?

Aunt Margaret slapped her gloves against her palm. "Mrs. Lloyd-Jones was at Lady Dunthorpe's this afternoon. I overheard her saying the most outrageous thing."

Lydia tensed, but she tried to act nonchalant. "Indeed?"

"She was talking to Mrs. Horwatt about available bachelors and had the audacity to include Lockwood in her accounting." Her voice dropped to a deceptively soft tone. "And do you know what she said next?"

Fear gathered in Lydia's chest. She shook her head.

"She said she hoped *you* would catch his eye." She skirted the furniture, stalking toward Lydia with heavy steps. "Have you any idea why she would say such a thing?"

Lydia forced herself to exhale. Talking to Aunt Margaret about helping Lockwood was certainly out of the question now.

Aunt Margaret came to stand in front of her. She smacked her gloves against her palm again. "You'll disabuse Mrs. Lloyd-Jones of this folly. Lockwood isn't fit to be anyone's husband. He belongs in an institution or under the care of a physician like his demented mother."

How Lydia longed to defend him. "I'll speak to Mrs. Lloyd-Jones."

"Good, but it's not enough. I want him gone. For good." She tipped her head to the side and stared at Lydia. "You agree, don't you? His presence isn't to be borne."

Lydia gritted her teeth before saying, "Of course. But what can we do? It's not as if we can force him to behave a certain way or—"

Aunt Margaret's gloves slapped against Lydia's face with a force that shouldn't have been possible from a woman of her age and stature. "You stupid girl. We can manipulate anything we like. How in the world do you think I got rid of his mother?"

Lydia's jaw dropped before she could help herself. The gloves hit her face again, and this time the buttons smacked her jaw, stinging her flesh. Aunt Margaret hadn't raised her hand to her in years, why now?

Because of Lockwood. She'd said Harmony Lockwood hated her, but clearly the feeling was more than mutual, and it extended to Lady Lockwood's son. So much so, that Aunt Margaret was completely irrational about him.

"Close your mouth and listen to me." Aunt Margaret's eyes were overbright, and Lydia wondered if *she* hadn't gone mad. "You will do precisely as I say and nothing else."

Lydia blinked through the pain in her cheek and jaw. "Yes, Aunt Margaret, but I wonder if I might make a suggestion?"

Aunt Margaret's breathing had become rapid with her anger. "What? And this had better be worthwhile."

It was a bold risk, but Lydia had to do something. "What if I assisted Lord Lockwood with a party?" Aunt Margaret's nostrils flared, she sucked in air and then lifted her hand.

Lydia couldn't help herself from moving back to avoid the coming blow. "Just listen, please! Only think of it—the best of Society inside Lockwood House. His secrets there exposed. It's precisely what you want."

Even as she offered this scheme, she tried to think of how she could preserve him from humiliation and degradation.

Aunt Margaret's eyes narrowed and she stared at Lydia, though she didn't seem to be seeing her as she weighed her proposal. "I would have to be invited."

"Of course." Lydia hadn't told him that, but he was rational and would understand.

Aunt Margaret's eyes narrowed skeptically. "What would 'assisting' him entail? You can't be going to Lockwood House and acting like you're his wife." She sneered as if that were the most distasteful thing she'd ever heard, and maybe it was.

"No, Aunt. I would give him a guest list. I would tell him how to decorate, what food to serve, what musicians to hire."

"And once we're inside?" Aunt Margaret sniped. "What exactly do you hope to expose—and you'd better have specifics."

She didn't, and so she frantically came up with something and strove to make it sound *specific*. "He keeps a guest list of attendees for his vice parties. I might even be able to find it before the party, actually, if you allow me to visit Lockwood House." She had no idea if such a list even existed, and even if it did, she wouldn't want to actually find or reveal it.

"No, you can't be seen at Lockwood House before this party. That would be a disaster." She shot Lydia a suspicious glare. "Besides, I don't want you spending time with that scoundrel."

"But—" She regretted the utterance as soon as the

gloves smacked her face again. She'd been about to argue that helping him plan a party—a regular, non-vice party—would put her, and by extension Aunt Margaret, in a favorable light. However, Lydia ought to have realized that Aunt Margaret wouldn't agree, because in her experience, one only achieved notoriety by tearing other people down.

"You may provide him with guidance by letter. I will read each one before they are delivered, as well as his responses. You will have no secrets from me, Lydia."

Of course not. Lydia's only privacy was in her mind. She forced a placid smile to mask her bitter disappointment. "As you wish, Aunt Margaret."

Aunt Margaret turned from her. "Go on. The Comptons' musicale is tonight. Make sure you cover that mark on your face."

Lydia brushed her fingers over the throbbing pain along her jaw and felt a tiny welt. "Yes, Aunt." She sounded defeated, but that would please her aunt. A broken spirit was the most malleable kind.

Chapter Ten

LYDIA TRAILED HER aunt into the Comptons' drawing room with her head held high. Inside, she was in turmoil, but she would never let it show. Society had no idea of the despair darkening her soul, and they never would.

Lady Compton welcomed them with a broad smile. After exchanging the necessary pleasantries, Lydia left her aunt as quickly as possible. She searched for Audrey, but was waylaid by a pair of young ladies, Miss Rowe and Miss Bryant.

"Lady Lydia!" Miss Rowe exclaimed. "You must tell us about Lord Lockwood. I can't believe you danced with him. Is he horribly clumsy?"

Lydia stifled the urge to scowl. Instead, she leaned close as if imparting a secret. "Actually, he's quite graceful for such a large man. I was most impressed."

Miss Bryant's eyes widened. "Never say so! He's just so . . . frightening!"

"Nonsense," Lydia said with just a touch of venom.

"Oh, but that ghastly scar." Miss Rowe shuddered. "Did you have to keep your gaze averted?"

Lydia's patience was thinning. "No."

Miss Bryant gave a tiny shriek. "There he is!"

Lydia resisted the urge to turn and look at him. She was actually hoping to avoid him. Things would be smoother with Aunt Margaret if she stayed away from him—at least publicly.

At last, she caught sight of Audrey in the corner.

"Please excuse me."

Audrey smiled as Lydia arrived at her side. "I love your new gown, Lydia. That amber looks wonderful with your coloring."

"Thank you, I'm quite pleased with how it turned out." Lydia said, glad for something to take her mind off Lockwood and her aunt.

Audrey lowered her voice. "Lord Lockwood is staring this way."

Apparently, he wasn't going to make avoidance easy. Lydia didn't turn to look. "He's not coming over here, is he?"

"He's talking to Lord Sevrin of all people."

Of course; they were friends. Sevrin had frequented Lockwood's parties before he'd married. "Good. Will you let me know if Lockwood moves in our direction?"

Audrey darted a glance toward Lockwood. "What's the matter? Don't you like Lord Lockwood?"

"Yes, but I don't need to be seen with him at every event, do I?" Lydia *had* to increase the distance between them. If Aunt Margaret had been furious about Mrs. Lloyd-Jones's comments, she would be positively enraged if she thought there was a consensus building that somehow linked her to Lockwood—which was asinine, as they'd only danced a single waltz.

Nights like this almost made her wish she could be happy in Northumberland married to a miller or a farmer whilst raising children and cats. But no, she had to appease Aunt Margaret, which meant going about her usual business. She pasted a smile on her face. "I can't adorn the corner tonight. Let's go find someone to talk to."

She caught Lockwood out of the corner of her eye.

He was looking in her direction, but she didn't return his regard. Though her neck prickled, she kept moving. Why did she have to like him? Her life would be so much easier if he was the scary beast everyone assumed him to be.

But no, he was considerate and witty and he made her heart sing. And if Aunt Margaret had her way, she would end up crushing him.

JASON WATCHED LYDIA talking to Miss Cheswick. He returned his attention to Sevrin, with whom he'd been hoping to speak. "Though you've only just returned to Town, I'm sure you've heard about my half brother."

"Mr. Ethan Locke? Yes, I've heard about him, though I haven't made his acquaintance, and you'll understand when I say gossip doesn't interest me much." His smile was droll. If anyone knew about the pitfalls of rumor and innuendo, it was Sevrin.

"This is not rumor and something only you will fully understand: Locke is better known as Ethan *Jagger*."

Sevrin's eyes widened and he moved closer to the wall, drawing Jason with him. "*He's* your brother?"

"*Half* brother." If nothing else, Sevrin was acquainted with him as Jagger the pugilistic sponsor, but what else did he know? "How much do you know about him? And do be honest. I suspect he's a criminal."

Sevrin kept his voice low. "You'd be right. He coerced me into fighting for him by threatening to expose Philippa as the woman I was seen with that night at your party." So, in addition to being a criminal, his half brother was a right prick. Sevrin continued,

"I'd agreed to find him a permanent fighter, but when I took too long, he brought Philippa to the fight in Dirty Lane."

Jason had watched that bout, and he'd seen the masked woman seated beside Ethan. He hadn't realized she was Lady Philippa. "Wait, didn't you fight for him again in Cornwall? I'm surprised you didn't use your considerable pugilistic skills on *him*."

Sevrin's eyes darkened. "I didn't entirely hold back. But I must admit there is something about him that soothed my anger. He understood my need to fight, appreciated it even as he exploited it. It's why I fought for him in Cornwall." He paused a moment, then lowered his voice even further. "There's something else. One of his men—a nasty brute—kidnapped Philippa in Cornwall. I was able to stop him before things got . . . ugly." The way he said the word and the intangible aura of menace Sevrin elicited gave Jason an idea of what precisely that meant.

Jason continued to wonder how Sevrin hadn't beat Ethan to within an inch of his life. "What role did Ethan play in all of that?"

"That's just it: none." Sevrin frowned. "He was actually rather upset to learn what his man had done. He went so far as to apologize. What's more, the kidnapper was killed in prison. I have no proof, but I wonder if Jagger was behind it."

Once again, his half brother was at the center of some evil. It didn't make sense that Ethan *wasn't* involved, regardless of what Sevrin believed. Perhaps Ethan had simply convinced him otherwise by using his infamous charm—something he'd always employed to gain his own ends. The servants at Lockwood House had adored him when their father had brought him for visits. It seemed even a man like Sevrin wasn't completely immune. "I pray you aren't being naïve."

"I didn't say we were bosom friends," Sevrin said wryly. "No one knows what happened in Cornwall, and for Philippa's sake, I'd like it to stay that way."

Jason's gaze flicked to Lady Sevrin, who was now engaged in conversation with Lydia and Miss Cheswick. "Of course. But you said Ethan was a criminal. Are you aware of any other criminal activity beyond kidnapping and coercion?"

"He works for Gin Jimmy." Sevrin shrugged. "I couldn't say what Jagger does, but when Philippa and I were brought to him, he certainly seemed a prince lording over his subjects. He had quite a gang of brutes."

Now Jason had firsthand testimony of his brother's crimes, even if it wasn't anything he could take to Bow Street. "Thank you for telling me."

Jason must have let his animosity show, for Sevrin cocked his head to the side and said, "There's no love lost between you, is there?" When Jason failed to respond, Sevrin's voice grew soft. "That's unfortunate. I'd give anything to have my brother back."

Unable to share that sentiment, and strangely discomfited by it, Jason completely changed the subject. He looked toward Lydia again. She was still talking with Lady Sevrin, but Miss Cheswick was no longer with them. "Speaking of your wife, it's past time we were properly introduced."

Sevrin shot him an inquisitive glance. "Did you know who she was that night at Lockwood House?"

"Not precisely, but I didn't believe for a moment that

she was just some paramour you'd brought along." As had many people, so Jason added, "A supposition I never repeated."

Sevrin sighed. "She's too damned elegant, too perfect. No demimondaine could carry herself as she does. Come." He led Jason to his wife and, more importantly, to her companion, Lydia.

Lydia registered their approach, but quickly averted her eyes to Lady Sevrin. Sevrin took care of the introductions.

"Lord Lockwood, I'm delighted to make your acquaintance," Lady Sevrin said with a mischievous sparkle in her eye. They had, of course, already met when she'd mistakenly intruded into one of his vice parties. Sevrin had rescued her, and though it had been a bumpy road, things had turned out splendidly for them. If a scoundrel like Sevrin could find redemption, perhaps there was hope for Jason after all.

Jason took her hand and bowed. "The pleasure is mine."

"You already know Lady Lydia," Lady Sevrin said, her gaze flicking to Lydia who continued to avoid meeting his eyes. What the devil was wrong with her? Had they not just entered into a partnership that very afternoon?

"Indeed. Good evening, Lady Lydia." When she didn't offer her hand, he boldly took it and pressed a kiss to the back of her glove. He felt her muscles tense, and her gaze finally snapped to his. But her brown eyes were flat, lacking their usual sparkle.

"Lord Lockwood." She pulled her hand from his grasp. "Please excuse me, I see someone I must speak with." She turned and left.

Jason frowned. Someone stopped her less than ten feet from them. He couldn't hear what was said, but he picked up her response. "Yes, he hosted one of those parties." She sounded resigned, indifferent.

This time he heard the other woman's comment. "Judging by the company he keeps, he's not rehabilitated at all. One must wonder if he should be allowed to mingle with our most impressionable members of Society. Like you, for instance. I should think you'd prefer to keep your distance."

"I am trying, yes," Lydia said.

Jason's insides turned to ice. What game was she playing? Was she setting him up for a humiliating failure? Was she hoping to push him over the edge into madness as her aunt had done to his mother at that dinner party seven years ago? Anger swirled in his gut, and it took every ounce of will he possessed to not stalk over to her, grab her by the arm, and drag her somewhere to get the truth.

He excused himself from the Sevrins and walked around the periphery of the room. As he watched Lydia move from person to person, likely spreading her poison, his mood blackened.

He saw Miss Cheswick in the corner. Perhaps she could provide some insight as to what the hell Lydia was doing. "Miss Cheswick, it's a pleasure to see you here."

She smiled. "Lord Lockwood, good evening."

"Propping up the corner, I see. Do you enjoy attending these events?"

"I know it seems I mustn't, but I do. I'm more of an observer, and that suits me fine. Do *you* enjoy attending these events? Tell me," her voice lowered dramatically, "are your parties more entertaining?"

He laughed softly, liking Miss Cheswick. "Naturally. But never say I told you so. Why isn't Lady Lydia keeping you company?"

Miss Cheswick pressed her lips together and wrinkled her nose. "She's just being Lydia. She really is harmless." The look she gave him was serious, and perhaps a bit pleading. She wanted him to believe what she said.

The words he'd overheard stirred his anger once more. "Harmless? I'm certain she's harmed plenty of people. Isn't she a gossiping viper just like her aunt?"

Miss Cheswick flinched, and he wished he'd worded things differently. "She isn't really. If you knew her as I do, you'd see that. But then no one knows her as I do," she finished sadly.

"Then help me know her." He lowered his voice to a whisper and leaned toward Miss Cheswick. "When the music starts, send her to the portrait gallery."

"That's hardly appropriate," Miss Cheswick said, sounding scandalized.

"Perhaps not, but I suspect you'll do it anyway." He sent her a challenging look, hoping that Miss Cheswick possessed the rebellious spirit he thought she did.

Miss Cheswick shook her head. "I don't know if she'll come."

He gently pressed his fingers to her forearm. "Please ensure that she does."

Miss Cheswick nodded. He strode away from her, meandering through the drawing room into a smaller room next door where people still mingled. He moved into another room and then at last came to a corridor that led to the portrait gallery where he squandered the next half hour staring at paintings. He paced near the doorway. When he heard the strains of the music start up, he paused. She wasn't coming.

He leaned against the wall and laid his head back against the plaster. A moment later he heard the whoosh of skirts before a flash of amber entered beside him. He reached out and snatched her hand, spinning her around so that she came to face him. But he pulled harder than he intended—or maybe she was just lighter than he anticipated—and she connected with his chest.

Her brown eyes were wide as she stared up at him. He wrapped his arm around her waist and continued holding her hand.

He meant to assault her with questions and demand she give him the truth, but he was speechless at the look of fear in her eyes. He'd never frightened her before. What had changed in the hours since he'd seen her last?

Her upturned face was pale and beautiful in the soft light of the gallery. "I shouldn't have come," she whispered, pulling back.

He held her close, tightening his grip around her waist. "Don't go. I won't let you. Not yet." Letting go of her hand, he stroked his thumb along her jaw. She flinched. "What's wrong? Did something happen this afternoon after you left Lockwood House?"

She hesitated the barest fraction before she shook her head. He didn't believe her. In fact, now he *knew* something had occurred. "Tell me what happened this afternoon."

"Nothing," she said, but the response came too quickly and with a higher pitch that verified she was lying.

He moved his thumb back, applying a bit more pressure and this time she blinked and pulled away. He gently held her chin and tipped her head to the side and saw a faint red blemish, though it was carefully masked with a cosmetic. Fury shot through him. "What is this?"

"Nothing."

"Stop saying that," he said more sharply than he intended, but anger was swirling inside him. "Tell me how this happened." He looked into her eyes. "And don't lie."

She swallowed and his eye was drawn to the gentle column of her throat. "Please, don't ask me." The words came out ragged.

He wouldn't force her. She'd been through enough today. "Was this because you came to see me?" Rage fought against the overwhelming tenderness he felt for the woman in his arms. He'd never been assaulted with such an urge to protect someone other than his mother, who'd always seemed powerless. But Lydia wasn't the same. She was strong, and he wanted her to remain that way.

"I should go," she whispered, sounding hollow and broken.

Yes, she should. But he had to know. "If your aunt did this to you, I demand you tell me. I can't—"

She wrenched her head back from his touch. "You can't what? You don't have any say. Please, let me go."

He cupped the back of her head and drew her mouth to his. He longed to free her mind from this moment, to give her a sense of joy, of bliss. And maybe he wanted that for himself, too.

He moved his lips over hers. She didn't resist, but

she didn't kiss him back. He tilted his head and massaged her waist, which served to bring her more firmly against him. She felt like heaven, her body curving into his with an innocence that was as heady as lust. No, headier.

She'd never been kissed before. He'd bet Lockwood House on it. Her mouth relaxed against his, and he ran his tongue along the edge of her lips. She gasped, and he took the opportunity to slip inside her wet heat.

Her hands came up against his chest. He froze for the barest moment, afraid she meant to push away. But then her fingers tangled into his lapel and cravat as if she were hanging on for her life. Perhaps she was.

His fingers dug into the back of her skull as he deepened the kiss. He opened his mouth wider and she followed suit, inviting him to show her what to do. Tentatively, her tongue brushed against his. He nearly groaned with the sweet agony of it. His cock hardened between them, and he hoped she wouldn't cringe. Christ, if anyone saw him now—seducing an innocent—he'd never recover.

He ought to stop. Not for his sake, but for hers.

Except her hand crept over his collar and cradled the side of his neck. It would be so much better without her bloody gloves on, but he would take what he could get. Her touch was hesitant, but bold. Her hand moved to the back of his neck and copied what he was doing to her, holding him to her as if she never wanted to let go.

He stroked his tongue more insistently in her mouth as his desire climbed. He had to stop soon, but she felt so damned good. Vaguely he remembered why he'd wanted her to come here. And it hadn't been to kiss her. At least not consciously. He pulled back to look at her, but her eyes were still closed.

"Lydia," he said, his voice blackened with lust. "Look at me."

She opened her eyes. They were glazed, pleasured. His cock grew.

"I'm going to protect you from her."

"You can't. It doesn't matter. Just . . . I don't want to talk about it. Can't you just kiss me again?" She tugged on his head.

He could do more than that.

He spun her around until her back was against the wall. Her eyes flared in surprise, and she inhaled sharply. He smiled wickedly. "I'd be happy to. Shall it be a chaste kiss here?" He brushed his lips against her cheek and felt her shiver.

"Or perhaps here?" He trailed his lips along her jaw and pressed his mouth to the underside of her chin.

She cast her head back against the wall, which elongated her porcelain neck in unparalleled elegance.

"No, I think here." He dropped kisses down her neck and along the edge of her collarbone. He opened his mouth against her skin and licked her flesh. She jerked. He closed his lips on her and gently suckled, careful not to leave a mark.

She moaned softly and tangled her fingers in his hair.

He kept his right hand on her waist and splayed his left over her shoulder. She arched her head back farther and pressed herself up into his mouth, silently begging for more. With Herculean effort, he slid his mouth back along her collarbone and up her neck.

"I think I might like your mouth best." Then his lips were on hers, but this time she met him with naked fervor. Her hands clutched at him, holding him hostage to her burgeoning desire. Her mouth opened and she angled her head to receive his intrusion, then thrust her tongue out to make her own conquest.

He pressed against her, finding that divine cleft between her thighs in which to nestle his cock. Visions of her skirts pushed up to her waist and her bare flesh spread to his hungry gaze nearly drove him mad. He rotated his hips in mindless need.

She gasped into his mouth again, but didn't push him away. He dragged his hand down the front of her gown and cupped her breast. She was firm and soft, delightfully round. His fingers pulled on her through the fabric of her gown, working their way to the tip.

Voices broke into his sexual haze.

He stopped kissing her, but didn't pull away. She heard the voices too, because her panicked gaze found his. He shook his head and whispered, "Shhh," against her mouth.

Her eyes were full of fear.

"The gallery. No one will be in there," came a tittering feminine voice.

"Lead the way," said her male companion.

Lydia's eyes widened further. Jason reluctantly withdrew his hand from her spectacular breast and flattened his palm against the wall above her head. He spoke as quietly and urgently as possible. "They're coming from your left. They'll likely enter through the door you just came in. We're going to exit through the other door to your right. We must time it right. Move as silently as you can. Nod if you understand."

She nodded. He felt her heart thundering against his chest. He clasped her hand, gave her an encouraging stare, and then—because he couldn't resist—he kissed her quickly.

Keeping his tread light, he pulled her to the other door and peered around the jamb. The couple was tangled in an embrace in the adjoining chamber. He watched and waited.

Lydia's hand gripped his tightly. He felt a slight tremor in her frame.

The couple moved. Just as they passed through the doorway, he pulled Lydia out of the gallery. He didn't pause, but kept going through to a sitting room. They were on the opposite side of the house from the ballroom, where the musicale was going on. He didn't want to take her there yet. She needed to regain her composure.

"Do you know where the retiring room is?" he asked.

She stared at him blankly, as if she didn't understand the question. Then she blinked. "There's a small sitting room near the—"

"I don't care where. Go there now. Don't come to the musicale for ten minutes. Plead a headache and go home."

She nodded.

He squeezed her hand. "You'll be fine. Go."

After a last lingering look, she pivoted without a word and left. He watched her amber skirts swing against the doorway as she exited and quashed the urge to go after her, sweep her into his arms, and spirit her away to Lockwood House like the blackguard he was.

But no, he'd let her go home to that bitch who'd marked her face. And if that didn't make him a blackguard, what did?

Chapter Eleven

WHEN LYDIA ARRIVED in the retiring room, she was greeted by a small group of women who were just a bit older than herself. All married, they were avoiding the musicale so they could sit in here and gossip. Their eyes lit when Lydia entered, but she gave them a weak smile and went directly behind a screen for privacy.

She prepared to tune them out but then distinctly heard the words "Lady Aldridge" and "death." Her ears pricked up.

"So sad," one woman said.

"But to take your own life?" this woman sounded offended. "The death of her husband is tragic, horrific even, given the circumstances, but suicide is such an ungodly act."

Suicide? How? Lydia wanted to ask, but the new and improved version of herself bade her to keep her mouth shut.

"I can't imagine they'll have a funeral. What a shame. I quite liked her."

Another woman nodded. "She had a tremendous eye for fashion."

"Well, at least she had the grace to simply overdose on laudanum," said the third woman, an acerbic-tongued young baroness. "I daresay that's the tidiest way to do it."

Lydia had heard quite enough and was actually a little nauseated by what she'd overheard. She left the retiring room and quietly returned to the ballroom where the musicale was still going on. Feeling nearly as maudlin as when she'd arrived that evening, she took up a position near the wall behind the rows of chairs that were set up.

But then she caught sight of Jason staring at her from the other end of the row. He leaned against the wall, arms crossed, eyes boring into her with seductive intensity. Her thoughts immediately veered from melancholy to libidinous.

Jason?

Apparently she couldn't think of him as "Lockwood" anymore. He'd become a friend. No, not quite that. He'd become something far more dangerous.

She looked away from him, lest her face heat to a noticeable degree. It was bad enough that the rest of her was on fire thinking of his mouth on her flesh, his hand covering her breast, his thighs nestled against hers.

Think of something else.

His party. She could easily help him plan the event via letter as her aunt had decreed, but it wouldn't be as much fun. Especially since she wouldn't be seeing him, which meant no opportunity for more kissing. Maybe they could meet secretly. They could take care of the arrangements in person then and she could kiss him again. Perhaps he'd touch her breast, even remove her gown. There was no telling what they might end up doing. Goodness, with one embrace he'd turned her into a wanton.

Think of something else!

Back to the party. She'd completely forgotten to talk to him about the fact that they'd have to plan it via letter. But then how could she? Their mouths had been rather occupied.

Oh, devil take it, she couldn't escape the recollection of his devastating embrace. It crowded every corner of her mind. She burned to finish what he'd started. If they hadn't been interrupted, perhaps they'd be doing just that.

Her gaze drifted to Jason's. He was still staring at her. Overwhelmed, she turned and left the ballroom again and stopped short when she nearly ran into his half brother.

"Mr. Locke," she gasped.

He reached out and lightly touched her elbows to steady her. "Lady Lydia, you look flushed. Are you all right? May I take you for a turn on the terrace?" He let her go and offered his arm.

The music droned on behind her. She didn't want to go back in, not when the only entertainment was battling her attraction to Jason. "Yes, thank you." She linked her arm through his, and he led her back through the drawing room.

She looked askance at him and thought that while he possessed the unscarred face, he was somehow the lesser for it. She suddenly recalled that he was a friend of Lady Aldridge's. "Please accept my condolences regarding Lady Aldridge. Such a sad end, and after tragedy already struck the poor woman."

He peered at her sideways. "You already heard?"

She smiled wryly. "This is London, Mr. Locke. You're new to town, so perhaps you don't understand how quickly information moves."

"There are, it seems, few secrets."

"There are plenty. The challenge is in uncovering them." Which Aunt Margaret expected Lydia to do with him. But she couldn't do it. Did his relationship with Lady Aldridge really matter, particularly now that she was dead?

"And is that your goal with me?" He gave her a sidelong glance as he guided her out onto the terrace.

"No, my goal with you is to help you and your brother reconcile." At his startled expression she said, "That is what you want, isn't it?"

His answer was a long time coming. "It is."

"You don't sound certain." She surveyed the terrace, illuminated with several lamps. There was no one out here—the footman stationed just inside the drawing room door didn't qualify.

"I'd hoped Jason and I could leave the past, well, in the past. But it seems we cannot."

She stopped and turned toward him, removing her arm from his. "You've spoken to him?" She'd failed to arrange a meeting as Locke has requested, but it seemed he'd found his own way.

"I went to one of his parties at Lockwood House, and we . . . talked."

They had? Jason hadn't mentioned it. But why would he? He made no secret about not liking Locke—at least he hadn't to her. She recalled the tension in him when they'd come face-to-face at the Whitmore Ball and realized she'd avoided discussing Locke, beyond suggesting Jason invite him to his soirée. For the first time, she was overly sensitive to another person's feelings.

She scrutinized Locke's profile. "Did you achieve what you wanted?"

He faced the dark garden, his gaze sweeping over a landscape they couldn't see. "Not really. It didn't go well."

She was dying to ask for specifics, but doubted he would share them. Furthermore, she was doing her level best to keep her tongue in check. It wasn't easy. "I didn't notice any more scars, so it can't have gone too badly."

He pivoted toward her and flashed a smile. "Perhaps they're hidden."

Lydia drew back, suddenly wanting to seek Jason out and check him for injuries.

Locke's gaze reflected mild surprise. "I think your opinion of my brother may have elevated since our last meeting. How curious." He turned back toward the garden. "Don't worry, he's fine."

She was relieved, but wasn't completely uncaring when it came to the man before her. "Are you all right as well?"

"You needn't worry. It was a tussle between brothers."

If they were still fighting, things couldn't be going very well. However, she'd managed to persuade Jason to invite Locke to his party. Perhaps she could help them resolve their differences. "Will you tell me why he hates you? And before you accuse me of trying to obtain gossip, that is not my purpose. I agreed to help you—secretly—and I will. But I need to know more."

"Very well, but I tell you this in the strictest confidence and perhaps against my best judgment. Don't make me regret it," he said darkly. Lydia nodded and he continued, "I have more than enough regrets already. Not the least of which is pushing my brother out a window."

Lydia couldn't keep from recoiling. Though he'd said

before that he might've pushed Jason, her mind had maintained it was some manner of accident. "You pushed him on purpose?"

"I didn't intend to. Things . . . spiraled out of control. Violence is—or was—the one language we both understand. We were in constant competition. When I was young, my father brought me to Lockwood House. I think he hoped Jason and I would be friends, but Jason hated me even then. His mother made sure Jason treated me as if I were beneath him. She was rather awful to me, as well."

Clearly, Lady Lockwood's jealousy and madness had greatly affected their relationship. "How sad for both of you. So you grew up resenting each other?"

"Yes, though Jason more than I. I was relatively happy in my youth. I lived with a mother who loved me, had a father who spent a great deal of time with me, and yes, he loved me too. When he died, things changed." Locke's speech had started pleasantly, but by the time he'd finished, his tone had darkened to ash.

"What happened?"

Locke stared at nothing for a moment, then shook his head. "The specifics don't matter, but I found myself alone and without funds. I went to Lady Lockwood for assistance, but she turned me away. And Jason did nothing to stop her. From that point on, our resentment was quite mutual."

Lydia was rapt, but not because she ever wanted to repeat this. She was wrapped up in their story, in their heartache. "What brought about your fight seven years ago?"

"We hadn't seen each other in years. I'd heard about his mother's collapse." He shifted uncomfortably. "I'm not proud of it, but it made me happy to see that Jason was alone like I was. I went to see him—yes, to gloat—but also to find some letters that my mother had sent our father."

"And did you find them?" she asked softly, her heart breaking for these two boys who were never given a chance to embrace brotherhood.

"No. We fought instead."

"I'm sorry." And she truly was.

"I'm the one who's sorry." He exhaled, and she heard the regret in that soft, weary sound. "He tore up his house amidst our battle. He was beyond furious—mad, even. Most of his retainers left his employ that day in fear. Then they related the event and his behavior to everyone who cared to listen. When Jason attempted to return to Society after his wounds had healed, he was shunned."

What a horrible, tragic tale. For both of them, but the altercation had irrevocably changed Jason's life—and was perhaps the catalyst for the life he led now as the isolated scoundrel who hosted parties of sin. "Do you understand that fight caused him to lose his standing? Whatever plans he had or dreams he nurtured were destroyed."

Locke's stare was steady, intense. "Don't think for a moment I don't know what that fight cost him. It's why I need to make peace with him."

She understood and appreciated his sentiment. "But why now, after all this time?"

His eyes crinkled briefly with amusement. "So curious," he murmured. He grew serious once more. "But I'll tell you. I'm dissatisfied with my current lot and wish to change it. For most people, having family means having someone who cares. Like it or not, Jason is all I have left. I'm hoping it's not too late." His voice trailed off and he looked away.

Lydia understood completely, and for that reason she vowed in that moment to do whatever necessary to unite these two brothers. "Jason will come around eventually."

Locke's expression was doubtful, but he nodded. "Thank you. Now, there's one other thing I need to ask you." His eyes were uncertain, which was odd. He always carried an air of purpose, of power. He actually seemed a bit vulnerable, which had to be her imagination. "I want to learn to dance."

She hadn't been expecting that, and her lack of a thoughtful response proved it. "Oh." She rushed to add, "I can recommend a dance master to teach you."

"No, I'd prefer not to advertise my inability."

Perhaps he was vulnerable after all. Lydia felt a chuckle bubbling in her chest, but she kept it buried. "I see. And you want me to teach you?"

"If you could. I'm a fast learner. Just the waltz would be sufficient. Those other dances look dreadfully complicated." He shook his head in distaste.

She felt as if they were friends now, and decided she could provoke him a bit—as friends ought. "Mr. Locke," she asked in her most sweetly inquisitive voice, "are you angling for a wife?"

He laughed. Loudly. Richly. Gentlemen didn't laugh like that. "No. You amuse me, Lady Lydia. I see why my brother likes you."

"I'll have to consider how to teach you, but once I've puzzled it out, I'll send a note. I understand you're at the Bevelstoke?"

"Yes. I see nothing remains secret, not that my address was meant to be." He then took up her hand, surprising her. "My brother is lucky. I hope he realizes it."

Lydia withdrew her fingers from his grip. "I don't know to what you refer, but I'm certain Lord Lockwood appreciates his fortune."

Locke's smile was weary. "He never has before, but perhaps like me, he'll try to change."

WHEN LYDIA REENTERED the ballroom awhile later, Jason decided that was his cue to leave. Staying at the musicale in her orbit was only going to cause a furor as he walked around in a constant state of abject lust.

He pushed away from the wall and departed. An hour later, he was in the back room of the Lamb and Flag Tavern, a place called the Bucket of Blood where one could take in a good fight on any given night. Two men were in opposite corners readying themselves for a bout. The room was dark and smelled of all manner of men: gentlemen, working men, criminals. It was a place where station didn't matter, where the thrill of the fight lured each and every one of them. And perhaps the promise of a purse from a well-placed wager.

But Jason wasn't betting tonight. He wasn't even sure he'd enjoy the fight. He was tense, pensive, and he kept watching the door.

The fighters moved to the center of the room. Jason lingered near the wall. It wasn't the best vantage point, but seeing the fight was only part of the reason one came here. The other part was simply the atmosphere:

electric, alive, heady.

The bout started with the clang of a bell. Instantly, the temperature in the room spiked along with the noise. The smell grew sharper as everyone's excitement surged.

"I wondered if I would see you here."

Jason turned at the sound of Ethan's voice. How the hell had he moved so close without Jason realizing? He'd been watching the door just to see if Ethan would enter.

Tossing him a wary glance, Jason said, "I wondered the same."

"Did you?" Ethan sounded surprised. He was angled toward the fight, but he was watching Jason.

"This seemed a neutral enough place to perchance meet." Jason hadn't realized until that moment that he'd come here *hoping* Ethan would show up.

Ethan laughed. The sound was rich and deep. It reminded Jason of their father. Or maybe it was just that they were watching a fight together, as Father had made them do on countless occasions in their youth.

Jason shifted uncomfortably. "What do you want?"

With a shrug, Ethan turned his attention to the match. "Nothing specific. I thought we might enjoy the fight together."

Though Jason was watching the bout, he wasn't seeing anything but the many ways in which this encounter with Ethan could resolve, starting with a rematch of the other night at Lockwood House. Indeed, Jason expected to feel a rush of anger and an urge to pummel Ethan into the filthy floor. But, strangely, he felt only a skeptical weariness and found himself trying to discern his half brother's emotions.

"You aren't looking to reenact what's going on over there, here in our little corner?" Plenty of fights broke out in the Bucket of Blood, and a tussle between two gentlemen—or at least two men who *looked* like gentlemen—would be more than welcome.

"I didn't come here to fight with you, no." Ethan was quiet a moment and the sounds of the fight and the noise of the spectators threatened to smother Jason's tumultuous thoughts. At length, Ethan looked toward him again. "Do you remember coming here with Father?"

"Of course." Jason heard the snap in his tone, but couldn't moderate his emotions when it came to his perfidious father.

Ethan nodded. "I loved those nights. Except, you never paid me much attention." His smile was tinged with regret. Had he wanted Jason's attention? Worse, had he wanted Jason's affection?

Jason inwardly squirmed. He didn't like the direction this conversation was taking. They weren't brothers in the true sense of the word. Still, how would it have been to experience these fights with a younger brother? Someone with whom he could laugh and carouse. Someone with whom he could share the trials and troubles of becoming a man. "I couldn't. You were an affront to my mother. To me."

"Your mother despised me. As if it were my fault I'm the bastard of her husband's mistress." His tone was resentful.

Jason turned toward him, his mind blocking out the sights and sounds around him. "It was your fault that you were a jackass. You were always disrespectful to her, and you marched around Lockwood House as if you could be the heir."

Ethan stared at him and shook his head. "I was jealous of you. You were—*are*—the heir. Your mother made it clear I would always be beneath you."

It sounded awful coming from Ethan now, but Jason understood his mother's bitterness and anger. "She was devastated by your very existence, and for Father to parade you in front of her and treat you like a member of our family was a gross insult. I won't debate you as to whether that's right or wrong. It's how she felt and I can't disrespect that."

Ethan's gaze was steady, his mouth set in firm lines. "And I can't respect it."

Jason looked toward the fight. "We're the products of our stations. I can no more enjoy your presence than you can tolerate mine."

"You're wrong." The determination in Ethan's voice drew Jason to turn his head back. "My parents don't define me. I'm my own person, and I thought you were too. I was hoping we could reach an . . . accord."

Bewildered at why this man would seek him out now and try to repair an insurmountable breach, Jason shook his head.

A sharp elbow caught Jason in his back and he pitched forward. Ethan caught him and as quickly let him go. Angry that he'd fallen into his half brother, Jason spun around in search of the miscreant who'd collided with him. "Watch yourself," he snarled.

"Wot's 'at?" A scruffy-faced young man wearing a too-large coat with a cut that was far too fine for his ratty person swiped a dirty finger across his nose. He shoved Jason again. "Mind yerself."

Jason launched forward and pushed him back, the

emotion he'd restrained during his conversation with Ethan erupting forth. The lad bared his teeth and took a swipe at Jason's face, but Jason easily ducked. When he brought his head back up the young man's face had turned ashen. His dark brown eyes were affixed to something. Jason pivoted.

Ethan was staring the lad down. He looked none too pleased. In fact, he looked downright enraged. But where Jason felt like his anger was a living, breathing thing that sometimes broke out of its cage, Ethan's seemed cold and resolute, something he kept leashed— but just barely.

"Jagger," the young man croaked.

Ethan moved to stand beside Jason. "Don't touch this man again. He deserves your respect, if not your admiration." His words could've frozen the Thames.

"Yes, sir." The lad straightened, cast a nervous glance at Jason, and then turned to go.

But Ethan grabbed him by the shoulder of his coat, the wool bunching up in his fist. He spun the young man around. "Apologize."

His dark brown eyes were wide with fright. "Beggin' yer pardon, sir."

"*My lord,*" Ethan prompted darkly.

"Beggin' yer pardon, m'lord," the young man choked out.

Ethan let go of the lad's coat and brushed his palm over the wool. His lips spread in a malevolent smile. "And my name is Mr. Locke, not Jagger. Make sure your friends know that too."

He nodded vigorously and scampered away into the mass of bodies. A few people had turned to watch the altercation, but now they returned their attention to the fight. Jason stared at his half brother.

Ethan's expression was placid. He was seemingly unaware of what he'd just done, but then maybe he was. It wasn't any man who could scare the breeches off someone with only a frigid stare. But perhaps Ethan did it with such ease and frequency that he simply didn't realize how it appeared.

"I'm quite capable of defending myself," Jason said.

Frustration etched into the lines around Ethan's mouth. His eyes narrowed again, but this time with ire. "Is it wrong to want to help my brother?"

"No." It seemed Jason wasn't able to say anything without being provoking. He forced the next words between his lips. "Thank you." And then he had a hundred questions about why the lad had seemed so afraid and why Ethan had instructed him to address him differently. Then everything Sevrin had told him earlier came back to him in a flood, and Jason's questions were answered. Sevrin had said Ethan lorded over people. In his criminal role, he commanded fear and respect. He was, perhaps, the head of his own little kingdom the way that Jason was the ruler of vice among Society.

There was one question, however, he did want to ask. He pressed closer against the wall, knowing Ethan would move with him. "Why did you tell him not to call you Jagger?"

"That's not my name any longer."

Jason couldn't keep himself from shaking his head in disbelief. "Calling yourself something different doesn't change who you are."

Ethan slid him a hooded look. "And who am I?" His voice was soft, but sharp as a finely honed blade.

Jason studied him a long moment. "I'm trying to figure that out. I understand you're a criminal. What other kind of man can inspire fear in people with a well-focused stare?"

"A lord?" Ethan offered sardonically. "That Duke of Holborn could scare the piss out of a gent who's just used the privy."

A smile broke over Jason before he could censor it. Holborn was a formidable old son of a bitch. He sobered. "Do I need to be afraid of you? Not that I would be, of course."

Ethan inclined his head. "No, you do not." He lowered his voice so that Jason had to lean in to hear him. "It's best if you don't ask me anything else."

"Best for whom?"

Ethan's stare was dark and deliberate. "You."

This was the same tack he'd taken at Lockwood House. His evasion only made him look guilty, and his secrets only made him look like a blackguard. "That sounds like a threat."

"Not from me. Didn't I just prove that I'm on your side?"

"Stepping in to stop a young man from foolishly picking a fight with me isn't precisely being on my side. Just because you don't want someone else pummeling me doesn't mean you weren't eager to do it yourself just a few days ago."

Ethan's nostrils flared. "You started that."

Jason was reminded of the quarrels they'd had as boys when Father had brought Ethan to Lockwood House. They'd been relegated to the nursery together and had fought over toys, books, the nurse's attention, and most of all, their father's affection.

He turned his head and stared at the sea of men, heard their laughter and cheering, felt their camaraderie. Suddenly he wanted that. It had been too long since he'd enjoyed something like this with someone who wasn't in his employ—which wasn't to impugn Scot, who was an excellent companion at an event like this. Jason looked at his half brother again, who was still staring at him with that probing gaze. "If you want me to trust you, you'll have to earn it. Right now I have no reason to believe anything you say. Furthermore, I'm inclined to thrash you for what you did to Sevrin and his wife."

Surprise flashed briefly in Ethan's gaze before his eyes shuttered. He was quite good as masking his thoughts and emotions when he chose, but Jason was beginning to be able to read him. "Did Sevrin tell you about that?"

"He told me all about your interactions. You ought to be in gaol for what you did."

Ethan scowled, but there was a hint of regret in the twist of his lips. "I didn't hurt them. Well, that's not exactly true. Some of my men might've been a little rough with Sevrin, but only because he was fighting them." The corner of his mouth ticked up. "He's a brilliant fucking pugilist."

"So I've seen," Jason said. "You might apologize to him."

"I have. Or didn't he mention that?"

How could Ethan be so cavalier? He really *ought* to be in gaol. "You can't continue like that. I won't be privy to any criminal behavior on your part. You're very lucky Sevrin doesn't bring charges against you."

"I fully acknowledge that." Ethan's jaw clenched,

making it seem the words were very hard to say. "You're going to have to trust that I'm trying to change."

Jason didn't have to trust anything. They might've made a small bit of headway tonight, but they were a long way from brotherly love—if they'd ever achieve that. He wanted to make sure Ethan understood his position. "If you do anything to further ruin me, I'll destroy you."

Ethan gave a small bow. "I give you permission."

Was this the same man who'd cowed a young man just a little while ago? The same man Bow Street suspected of running a theft ring? The same man who'd perhaps been romancing Lady Aldridge? Jason kept his voice low. "What were you doing with Lady Aldridge?"

Ethan had pivoted toward the fight and now cast Jason a sidelong glance. "I told you: no questions."

"And I told you: You have to earn my trust."

Ethan shook his head. "Not that way."

His patience rapidly dissipating, Jason straightened and adopted a normal tone. "Then we're done here." He took a step, but Ethan stayed him with a firm, but not rough, hand on his arm.

"For now. But I'll see you again soon."

Jason shook him off, uncomfortable with the almost brotherly gesture. "You're clearly used to being in command, but not with me."

Ethan glanced down. "Just so long as you don't expect me to lick your boots."

Jason recalled he had demanded something like that years ago. Was it any wonder they weren't close? "Fine, we've both been pricks. I'll endeavor not to be one now. Happy?"

Though he didn't smile, Ethan's eyes lit with something that might have been mirth. "Immensely."

Chapter Twelve

THE NEXT DAY, Lydia drafted a letter to Jason. It included her proposed guest list as well as the musicians he should hire. After Aunt Margaret reviewed it—and made her own adjustments—it was posted and delivered.

There was a slight chance a response would arrive today, but Lydia wouldn't hold her breath. She resolved herself to a day without hearing from him. Or seeing him, since tonight she and Aunt Margaret planned to stay in.

Thankfully, Audrey called to break up the monotony of Lydia's day. She greeted her friend in the sitting room facing the street. "Audrey, I'm so glad you've come to save me from expiring of boredom."

Audrey smiled as she removed her bonnet. She set her hat on the settee and leaned toward Lydia. "Is your aunt about?" she whispered.

"She's napping." Lydia went and closed the door, then joined her friend who'd sat down on the settee.

Audrey huddled close. "What happened with Lord Lockwood last night? I was hoping to talk to you after the musicale, but I had to leave with my grandfather." She frowned in regret.

Lydia's heart fluttered as she recalled her interlude with Jason in the portrait gallery. She'd relived his kisses a thousand times since then, which had led to a rather sleep-deprived night. But Lydia didn't care. "It was the most spectacular evening of my life."

Audrey's eyes widened. "Did he kiss you?"

Warmth rushed up the back of Lydia's neck. "Yes."

Audrey's entire face lit up, and she clasped Lydia's hand. "I'm so happy for you! You're happy, aren't you? You seem happy."

Lydia squeezed Audrey's fingers. "I'm practically giddy. But you know how Aunt Margaret feels about him. So for now, I have to tread cautiously." Lydia had told Audrey all about her aunt's hatred of his mother and her glee in anything negative that befell him.

Audrey shook her head. "There's nothing she can do if he offers for you. Then you'll be free of her, and you'll be happy."

Would she be happy with Lockwood? Sharing stolen kisses was one thing, but leg-shackled to a man with a reputation for sin? Actually, she didn't mind the sin part—after all, she had enjoyed his kisses rather a lot— so long as he was still included in Society. Which he hadn't been for quite some time. A situation he seemed rather content with.

She let go of Audrey's hand. "I didn't say I was going to marry Lockwood. Nor has he asked." He hadn't even indicated courtship, but then she suspected the kiss and subsequent kisses had caught him as unaware as they'd caught her.

"Oh." Audrey's face fell and her voice drooped with disappointment.

"Come now, don't be melancholy," Lydia cajoled. "I'm helping him to plan a party. One without his usual entertainments."

Audrey blinked at Lydia in wonder. "Your aunt is letting you do that?"

Lydia cocked her head to the side. "In a way. I tried

to convince her that it would be a social boon for me to help him, but she didn't agree. So I had to promise that I would expose the secrets of Lockwood House."

Audrey touched her arm. "You wouldn't."

"Of course not. But I had to say it to gain Aunt Margaret's approval. Furthermore, she's reading every letter that goes between me and Lockwood House so she can 'supervise' the planning."

Audrey set her hands in her lap and gave Lydia a look that was a bit . . . Machiavellian. "You should have just helped him secretly. If you posted your missives to him through me, your aunt would never know. I'll make sure he gets them."

"You would do that?" Lydia straightened, her mind cavorting ahead of her tongue as she considered Audrey's brilliant idea. But she didn't want to get her friend into any trouble. "I hate for you to risk your own reputation by helping me."

Audrey lifted a shoulder. "What are best friends for? Besides, I'm already a wallflower. No one would care if they learned I was corresponding with Lockwood House."

Lydia hated that Audrey thought she was beneath everyone's notice, but there was nothing she could do to change that since she was, unfortunately, correct. How foolish they all were too, because when it came to friendship and loyalty, Audrey had no match. "What a relief it will be to tell Aunt Margaret I'm no longer helping him. Thank you so much. I'm touched you'd risk so much to help me."

Audrey blushed, and Lydia knew it was because she was unused to such praise. Her family rarely consulted her about anything. "As I said, I've very little to risk.

You, on the other hand . . . " Her gaze flicked to Lydia's chin—and presumably the mark there. "You don't have to stay with her."

"And what would I do? Return to Prewitt Hundred to live amongst the sheep? I have no friends there and certainly no prospects." She shuddered.

"No, but I could ask Grandfather if you could stay with us here in London."

Lydia's heart swelled at her friend's kindness and concern, but it wouldn't solve her problems. "My father wouldn't allow it. He sends my allowance provided I remain under Aunt Margaret's chaperonage. Besides, I wouldn't put it past Aunt Margaret to publicly ruin me if I crossed her."

Audrey audibly inhaled. "She hasn't threatened that, has she?"

"Not directly, but she's fond of reminding me that my position is enviable, that any young woman would delight to be under her care and protection, that I should feel extremely fortunate and demonstrate proper respect, given the tenuousness of my position." The threat was clear enough to Lydia.

Audrey's lips rippled in a soft frown. "I see." She was quiet a moment, then a look of distress marred her features. "But then why would you help Lord Lockwood at all? If the risk of your aunt's wrath is too great, why chance it?"

Lydia considered this. It was most definitely a risk, but she felt as if her time were running out. She didn't know how much longer she could endure Aunt Margaret's demands, not when she really and truly wanted to put gossiping behind her. "Because for once I have the opportunity to help someone instead of tear them down."

Audrey smiled softly as she nodded. "I understand. And I'm so proud of you."

Her words meant more to Lydia than anything. She was more determined than ever to help Lockwood be a success. He deserved nothing less, and she wouldn't let her aunt ruin him. "I should write a letter to Lockwood now, if you truly don't mind delivering it?"

"I offered, didn't I?" Audrey's gaze was direct and very comforting. "This will work, trust me."

Lydia stood and went to the small desk in the corner.

"Don't forget to tell him to respond via me," Audrey said.

Lydia nodded as she pulled out a piece of parchment and dashed off a note informing Jason of her plan. She folded the paper and gave it to her friend as she sat back down beside her. "Here. I shall be on tenterhooks until you deliver a response."

Audrey tucked the letter into her reticule. "I'll post it straightaway. Or perhaps I'll have a footman personally deliver it."

Lydia touched her friend's arm. "I don't want to get you into any trouble, and sending your footman to Lockwood House may draw unwanted notice."

"Pshaw. Like I said, no one will notice." Her eyes sparkled with mischief, and Lydia wished all of London could see how smart and beautiful her dearest friend was. Lydia put her arm around Audrey's shoulders and gave her a squeeze. "Someone will notice you some day, and I daresay it's going to be even more glorious than my portrait gallery rendezvous with Lockwood."

"That would be very nice," she said softly. "Very nice indeed."

"Oh, that reminds me!" Lydia straightened. "I must tell you something, but you can't tell a soul."

Audrey's eyes widened in mock outrage. "Lydia Prewitt, how many secrets have you entrusted to me over the years? You know I would never reveal anything on pain of death. Didn't I just offer to be your secret courier?"

Lydia laughed. "Yes, but this isn't *my* secret, it's someone else's, and I don't want it repeated for a change." The irony in her tone was thoroughly intentional. "I'm going to teach Mr. Locke how to dance. Actually, I think you should help me. It would be easier for me to direct him with a partner."

"You want me to partner him?" Audrey looked a bit spooked. "I rarely dance."

"Don't be silly. That doesn't mean you don't know *how*. Besides, I don't trust anyone else besides you to keep this a secret."

"Why *is* it a secret?"

"People already question where he came from, and he's a bastard to boot." Lydia realized she'd extended her campaign of assistance to Lockwood's half brother. Perhaps if she helped enough people, she'd be able to cancel out the hurt of the gossip she'd spread. But no, life wasn't an accounting ledger and she couldn't really expunge the things her aunt had forced her to do. She'd do good because it was right. "He's simply trying to fit in."

Audrey's eyes took on a far-off look. "I can understand that." She refocused on Lydia. "Of course I'll help. But if you conduct the lessons here, there's no way it will be a secret. Your aunt will broadcast the news everywhere. We'll have to do it at my house."

Lydia wasn't sure that was the right solution either. "If Mr. Locke is seen visiting, that could raise eyebrows."

Audrey laughed. "Maybe it will help my reputation. Really, Lydia, I don't have anything to lose."

"Everyone is capable of being ruined." Lydia didn't want that to happen to someone as kind and thoughtful as Audrey.

"Not if you don't care what other people think," Audrey said quietly.

Was that true for Audrey? Did she not care what others thought of her? She certainly didn't care about her wallflower status, and didn't see the point in being popular. It was, Lydia acknowledged, interesting that the two of them had become such close friends.

Lydia stood. "I'll write another note for you to deliver to Mr. Locke at the Bevelstoke. I don't want to risk Aunt Margaret seeing me correspond with him either." She sat at the writing desk once more and turned to Audrey. "When shall we do it?"

Audrey shrugged. "Thursday?"

"Thursday it is." Lydia penned the letter, folded it, and gave it to Audrey.

Audrey tucked the missive into her reticule along with the note to Jason. "Locke won't mind that you're involving me?"

Lydia was a touch nervous about that, but had explained her reasoning in the letter. She'd also explained that Audrey was the most trustworthy sort— more than Lydia—and since he'd seen fit to entrust her with his secret, he'd have to accept Audrey into the bargain.

And if he didn't? Lydia chose not to think about that.

LATER THAT AFTERNOON, Jason sat in his office with Scot, regaling him with the story of his encounter with Ethan at the Bucket of Blood.

"You didn't discuss the Curzon Street robbery with him?" Scot asked.

Jason shook his head. "He wasn't forthcoming. I tried to ask him about Lady Aldridge, but he wouldn't say anything beyond asking me to trust him. Can you imagine?" Jason still wasn't prepared to ignore a lifetime of animosity and blindly trust Ethan—particularly when he was a criminal and clearly hiding something. Or somethings.

"Pity I haven't been able to learn anything at the Bevelstoke." Scot crossed his arms. "Jagger genuinely seems like an ordinary gentleman who just happens to employ a somewhat odd-looking manservant."

Yes, Ethan was quite accomplished, but then a criminal like him would have to be.

"When do you plan to see him next?" Scot asked. "And can I come? I think I need to see this for myself." He'd been shocked that Jason and Ethan had shared a conversation without coming to blows.

Jason leaned back and stretched his legs out beneath the desk. "He'll be coming here for my party."

Scot rested his elbows on the arms of the chair and leaned forward. "Do you really think you can pull off a 'vice-free' party?"

Before Jason could answer, North entered bearing a letter. "This was just delivered, my lord."

As it was written in a feminine hand, Jason wondered

if it was from Lydia. He tore open the missive and read its contents.

Jason,

I will need to help you plan your party in secret. Do not be concerned about this! All correspondence will be filtered through Miss Audrey Cheswick. We are confirmed on the date of two Fridays hence?

Additionally, I should like to set up a meeting at Lockwood House so that I can ascertain the entertainment space and perhaps sample some of your cook's offerings. Please advise.

Yours,
Lydia

Yours.

Was she his? He didn't necessarily want her to be—the whole marriage avoidance thing—but the signature gave him a thrill nonetheless. He suddenly couldn't wait to see her. "North, do I have an invitation to something tonight?"

"You do not, my lord."

Jason suddenly realized he was at least partially smiling and only hoped he didn't look like a mooncalf. He schooled his features into indifference. "Tomorrow?"

North inclined his head. "A dinner party."

"That from your lady?" Scot asked with more than a hint of teasing in his tone.

Jason gave him a mock glare. "It's from Lady Lydia. She is not *my* lady." He turned his attention to North, whose eyebrow was raised just the faintest bit. He would never offer cheek like Scot—not that Jason would've cared since he liked the camaraderie he shared with both men—but the subtle reaction was telling. "Out with it, North."

"Has Lady Lydia given any further instruction?"

"No. She only confirmed the date of the party. She already sent the guest list and the names of musicians, correct?" Jason trusted North to handle everything, just as he did for the *other* parties.

"Indeed, my lord."

Jason recalled the other part of her missive. "And we need to plan for her to tour Lockwood House."

Scot leaned forward in his chair. "She's coming here?"

"Are you sure that's wise?" North asked. "I can easily describe the room situations to her via post."

Jason wasn't sure it was wise at all, particularly given how badly he wanted her. "Perhaps."

Scot grinned at his brother. "He *wants* to bring her here."

North arched a brow in response.

Scot winked obnoxiously at Jason. "You going to show her the dress-up room?"

He hadn't thought of that, but now images of her in the fantasy room crowded his mind. Oh no, inviting her here wasn't a good idea at all. "No, I simply require her help. What the devil do I know about planning a legitimate party?"

Scot shrugged. "You host the most illicit parties in London and now you want to invite a young miss into your lair. I'd say you know next to nothing about planning a legitimate anything."

North coughed, but it sounded suspiciously like he was covering up a laugh.

"What an insolent pair you are," Jason said without heat. He speared both men with a suffering stare. "I'll think about whether it's appropriate to arrange a meeting here."

"Sounds like you care about her," Scot said without even a hint of sarcasm.

Yes, he supposed he did, but he was still a bit reticent. So far she'd proven herself to be different from her aunt—just how much remained to be seen. "I do."

"When's the wedding?" There was the sarcasm.

Jason raised his eyes to the ceiling. "Oh, for Christ's sake, caring about her doesn't mean I'm going to marry her."

Scot, ever the nosy-Jones, cocked his head to the side and asked, "Why'd you show Cora the door then? You've never kept on with anyone so long, and her departure seemed abrupt."

Jason wasn't entirely sure except that after she'd come to his office and seen him in that state, he just couldn't take her to bed again. "I was ready for a change." But for marriage? He'd completely written that off.

Scot unfolded his arms and held them up in surrender. "All right." His eyes were mischievous as he turned them back toward Jason. "But if you're ready for a change and Lady Lydia isn't your preference, I know a couple of Cyprians you should invite to the next party. One of them is new to Town. Tall, blond, legs to here." He held his hand up to a thoroughly hyperbolic height above his head.

"Thank you, Scot," North said crisply. "If you spent half as much time focusing on your duties as you do tossing up skirts, you'd be the most sought-after valet in town."

Scot rolled his eyes. "I was so hoping Sarah would work that stick out of your arse."

"Yes, well, we can't all be as loose as you."

Jason didn't bother hiding the smile their bickering brought to his lips. They were brothers through and through—teasing each other, supporting each other, loving each other. Was there any chance he and Ethan could have the same? Jason had never, ever imagined it. And now?

North gave a small bow to Jason. "I have duties that require my attention, my lord." He threw his brother an accusatory glance that clearly asked whether Scot should be doing something.

"What?" Scot said, looking up at his brother in mock innocence. "His lordship isn't unhappy with my performance."

Pursing his lips, North turned and left.

Jason shook his head at Scot. "Would it kill you to give your brother a rest?"

Scot leaned back in his chair and waved his hand. "I already owe him for saving my life. If I didn't give him a ration of shit now and again, he'd be absolutely insufferable."

North *had* saved his brother. He'd pulled him off the street just after he'd succumbed to joining a theft gang. Then he'd talked Jason into giving him a position in the stable. Scot had hated it, but he'd done a good job and when Jason's staff had abandoned him after his fight with Ethan and after he broke Lockwood House up in a rage, North and Scot were the only ones who'd stayed. In a way, they'd both saved him.

A galling question pervaded Jason's brain: Who'd saved Ethan?

The painful and somewhat shocking answer was quite clear: no one.

Chapter Thirteen

LYDIA'S HEART BEAT in triple time as Jason stepped into the drawing room of Mr. and Mrs. Horwatt's fashionable town house in Hanover Square the following evening. He looked outrageously handsome in black evening clothes, his snow white cravat in stark contrast, just as the scar on his face was in direct opposition to the utter beauty of everything else about him.

His gaze found hers and his lips spread into a small smile, which only increased her excitement. Her belly tumbled over itself and she wondered how she'd ever be able to eat a thing at dinner.

She slid a look at her aunt, who was deep in conversation with Lady Dunthorpe. They both glanced toward the doorway, which gave Lydia to believe they were discussing Jason's arrival. Lydia's protective instincts kicked up and she had to restrain herself from walking over to speak with him.

Aunt Margaret had been pleased to know that Lydia would not be participating in the planning of Jason's party any longer, though she'd been disappointed at not learning Lockwood House's secrets. Her disappointment, however, was short-lived when the invitation to the party had arrived that morning. She planned to use the event as an opportunity to unmask all of the seedy things that happened at Lockwood House. Lydia had pretended to support her cause while trying to determine her aunt's plot, which wouldn't be easy.

She needed to speak with Jason, but couldn't do so in front of her aunt. She needed to get him alone for just a few moments. It was too bad Audrey wasn't here to aid her.

Trying to appear as nonchalant as possible, she crossed the drawing room and quietly asked Mrs. Horwatt where she could find the retiring room. Armed with directions to the back corner of the town house, Lydia made her way to the doorway. This brought her into Jason's proximity and she murmured, "Follow me to the retiring room in a moment, but be discreet."

She didn't look back to see if he had heard what she said, but trusted that he had.

A few moments later, she was pacing a small sitting room. It was well lit, with multiple lamps and a pile of coal burning in the grate. It was also where anyone might show up for a respite. Perhaps it was not the best place for a private meeting.

The sound of the door opening drew her attention— and her anxiety. She exhaled as Jason walked inside and closed the door behind him.

He frowned, which was not the reaction she might've liked. "Lydia, this is not a good idea."

"I need to speak with you." She moved toward another doorway and gingerly opened the door.

Jason came up beside her, eliciting a shiver along her neck. "What are you doing here alone?" he whispered.

"Trying to find a more appropriate place than the retiring room where anyone can enter."

The door led to a small dining chamber, perhaps the breakfast room. A round table sat in the center and was encircled with a half dozen chairs. Lydia moved inside, and Jason quickly followed.

He closed the door and frowned again. "It doesn't appear to have a lock."

There was another door on the opposite wall, but Lydia didn't want to open it. What if it led to the grand dining room where they were to have dinner soon? She hadn't been to the Horwatts' home before and didn't want to take the chance.

Meanwhile, Jason had propped a chair from the table against the door and was now doing the same to the second door.

"Is that really necessary?" she asked, though she was pleased he was going to such lengths to preserve her reputation.

He completed his work and directed his full attention upon her. "More necessary than you suggesting I follow you." He kept his voice low as he moved to stand in front of her. "What is so important that you've decided to completely flaunt Society's rules?"

His eyes were full of concern. She touched his lapel gently with her fingertips. "Perhaps you're having an effect on me."

He inhaled sharply. "Lydia. Unless you'd like to have an effect on *me*, you'd best get to your point."

Why was flirting with him so much *fun*? But no, she hadn't beckoned him here for an assignation, though that sounded rather delightful . . . She shook her head. "I wanted you to know that my aunt plans to come to your party and ferret out your secrets."

He blinked at her. "What secrets?"

"You *know*," she said. And when he continued to look perplexed, she added, "What happens during your vice parties . . . "

He stifled a laugh. "Those aren't secrets. It's simply polite not to repeat them, though I'm sure some do."

"Oh." Her mind traveled a path in which she thought about some of those things and wondered how alike they were to what she and Jason had been doing at the musicale the other night. "So you're not worried about my aunt ruining your party? That is, I'm afraid, her intent."

"I would expect nothing less from her."

Lydia flattened her palm against his chest, feeling his heart beating strong and sure despite the layers of his clothing. It seemed hers danced with the same rhythm, but that was certainly fancy. "You never should have invited us. Although now that you have, I couldn't possibly convince her not to come."

His hand came over hers and she wished their gloves to perdition. She wanted to feel the heat of his skin against hers. "It will be fine," he assured her. His gray eyes bored into hers with promise. "I'll be ready for her."

She should leave now, before their joint absences were noticed, but she didn't want to. Once upon a time he'd called her bold, and he'd said he liked it. She hoped what she was about to do wouldn't disturb him. She moved so that their bodies nearly touched. Without breaking eye contact, she pulled the glove from her right hand. Then she lifted her hand to his face. "May I?"

He stared into her eyes, seemingly entranced. "Yes."

Lightly, she touched her fingertip to the top of his scar, just beneath his eye. "Did it hurt terribly?"

His breath caught. "Yes."

She traced slowly down his cheek, her finger gliding over the ridge of flesh. "How many stitches did you take?"

"Twenty-one."

There was a slight bump just past the middle. "Were you conscious?"

"For every single one."

She reached the end and set her fingers against his jaw. "I'm sorry." Then she stood on her toes and pressed her lips to the base of the scar.

He groaned and turned his face to capture her lips. The kiss wasn't gentle or soft. It was hard, demanding, and sent a stark flash of need straight to her soul.

His arms came around her and pulled her against his chest, crushing her breasts. But it felt wonderful. Though she knew it was pointless—they had no future together—she'd ached to be held by him again. She angled her head and opened her mouth. His tongue was ready, sweeping into her mouth hotly. Desire lightened her head and sped her pulse.

She curled her fingers along his jaw and wrapped her other hand behind his neck, though she still clutched her glove. He swept her around and lifted her to sit on the edge of the table, all the while deepening their kiss so that she felt open and exposed to his hunger. A word she'd only heard murmured crept into her brain and seemed the perfect description: *erotic*.

His hands urged her legs apart. She complied and he moved so that her inner thighs rubbed against his outer. If she'd felt exposed to his kiss, this was something far more invasive. But deliciously so.

His mouth left hers to trail down her neck. She encouraged his descent by throwing her head back and giving him free access to her throat. He could have whatever he wanted. She wanted him to *take* whatever he wanted.

His hand slid up her side, caressing her hip and then her ribcage before settling beneath her breast. His thumb brushed up over her nipple. She sucked in a sharp breath.

His tongue licked at the flesh above her fichu and she wished every single garment she was wearing would simply fall away. But his reason was far more present than hers and he pulled away. "Not here. Not now."

He pressed a kiss to her naked palm. A long, hot, wet, kiss that made her squirm against the table. Then he took her glove from her other hand and held the opening so she could slide her hand inside. When the white silk was at last encasing her arm, he stepped back. "You're the most dangerous young lady I've ever met. If you'd still like a tour of Lockwood House, I'll arrange it."

She wondered if "it" meant more than just a tour, or if that was just her aroused imaginings. She should say no. She should do whatever was necessary to refrain from being alone with him, but she simply couldn't deny how good he made her feel. How no one else had ever come close to making her feel the things he did: alluring, desired, *liked*. "Yes, I want it."

He nodded imperceptibly. "Look for my note. Now, go back into the retiring room." He moved the chair away from the door and opened it a sliver. After peering into the room, he pushed the door wider and gestured for her to move inside.

She was alone in the retiring room before she had a chance to say anything. *Like what?* "Thank you?" or "I can't wait to kiss you again?"

She shuddered, as much to clear her thoughts as to push the feel of his mouth and hands away from her. She had to get a hold of herself before she went back to the party.

Miraculously, she not only made it back to the drawing room, she also made it through the dinner without making a complete cake of herself. Of course, it helped that Jason was seated on the other side of the table and at the opposite end.

After dinner, Lydia was playing cards with her aunt, Mrs. Horwatt, and Lady Rowe when Jason and the other gentlemen reentered the drawing room. She'd relived their assignation—for it had definitely turned out to be one—in her mind several times. Aunt Margaret kept glaring at her for not paying attention, but Lydia simply apologized and then covered a fake yawn to infer that she was tired.

After glancing in Jason's direction, Lydia was careful to keep her gaze averted. But her head snapped up when Aunt Margaret said, "Really, Johanna, I'm a bit scandalized you invited Lockwood."

Mrs. Horwatt looked stricken. "But why? I thought it would be devilish fun to have him here. Moreover, I thought you would appreciate his presence."

"I do not. He's an absolute bounder. And mad as any inmate in Bedlam. 'Tis only a matter of time until he loses his mind like his mother." Aunt Margaret's dark eyes lit. Lydia tensed. She'd seen that look a hundred times. Her aunt was up to something.

"Lord Lockwood," Aunt Margaret called sweetly.

Jason's eyes narrowed slightly—not enough to draw notice from those around him, but Lydia was attuned to the nuances of his expressions. When had that happened?

He moved closer to their table. Mrs. Horwatt looked up at him nervously. Lady Rowe's features were expectant. Aunt Margaret's expression was calculating. Lydia tried to think of a way to avert the coming disaster, and surely it was going to be a disaster if her aunt was successful.

"Lord Lockwood," Lydia said with her sunniest voice. "It's so lovely to see you here tonight. How are you enjoying your evening?"

His gaze was appreciative, but decorously so. If anyone knew they had earlier shared a passionate embrace, it wouldn't be because he'd let it show. "Quite well, thank you." He turned his attention to their hostess. "Mrs. Horwatt, I must thank you for extending me the invitation to your fine home. Dinner was excellent and your husband's port superb."

Mrs. Horwatt preened a bit beneath his compliments, though Lydia noticed the woman couldn't help staring at Jason's scar with an expression of distaste. Unaccountably, Lydia wanted to kick her under the table.

"I'm sure any dinner you were invited to would be excellent," Aunt Margaret said with just a touch of acid. "We must be grateful you're able to comport yourself as you ought. The last time I attended a dinner party with a Lockwood, things didn't turn out very well."

Lydia froze. Aunt Margaret couldn't be referencing the dinner party at which Lady Lockwood had suffered her mental break? But of course she was. Lydia looked up at Jason expectantly, her breath tangled in her throat.

Jason's gray eyes hardened, but he forced a thin smile. "I'm sure these fine ladies don't care for ancient history, *Lady* Margaret."

"Of course they do, my boy." Her contrived familiarity caused him to flinch.

"Well, I don't." He turned then, which was a bit rude since he didn't excuse himself, but Lydia didn't fault him in the slightest. She glanced at the other ladies to gauge their reactions. Mrs. Horwatt looked confounded, and Lady Rowe looked a bit disappointed. Lydia now wanted to kick *her* under the table.

"See what I mean?" Aunt Margaret said to her tablemates. "He possesses a modicum of manners, I suppose, but blood will win out. He's young yet. His mother didn't completely lose her mind until she'd reached middle age. It's only a matter of time before Lockwood does the same, and I ask you, do we really want to witness that in public?"

Lydia actually bit her tongue to keep from accusing her aunt of wanting such a spectacle. That it was, in fact, what she was hoping to provoke right now.

But Jason spun around with such vehemence that all conversation around them stopped. Lydia stared up at him, silently pleading with him to just go. His eyes found hers, and after a long moment he seemed to understand. The muscle in his jaw, clenched so tightly when he'd turned, released, and Lydia exhaled the breath she'd been holding.

Jason bowed to the ladies at the table. "Good evening. Thank you again, Mrs. Horwatt, for a— mostly—delightful evening." Then he turned without sparing Lydia even the briefest glance, and she hoped it was because he didn't want to be seen doing it. Though she feared it was because he couldn't bear to look at Margaret's niece.

THE FOLLOWING MORNING, Jason was preparing for an afternoon meeting with his solicitor when North interrupted him in his office. "My lord," he said, "Lord Carlyle is here to see you."

Jason frowned. What could he want? Their last meeting had ended with them possessing opposite opinions regarding Ethan. But now Jason had to admit his opinion was at least slightly different. Jason nodded once at North. "Show him in."

A few moments later, Carlyle entered his office and offered a small bow. "Good morning, I hope I'm not disturbing you."

"Not at all. Please, sit." Jason gestured to one of the chairs on the other side of his desk.

Carlyle perched on the edge of the seat, his back ramrod straight. His demeanor was a bit excited or agitated even. "I came to talk with you about Jagger."

Jason sat back in his chair as if he couldn't care less about Ethan, but he was utterly alert and eager to hear what Carlyle had to say. "What about?"

Carlyle frowned. He set his hand on his bent knee. He seemed to be searching for the right words. "I'm afraid he might be involved in the theft ring after all."

"Oh?" Jason kept his tone even. "Why is that?"

"There have been two robberies in Mayfair of late."

"Two?" Jason gave up the pretense of pretending this topic didn't interest him. He sat forward in his chair and clasped his hands atop the desk. "I read about the one on Curzon Street. There's been another?"

Carlyle nodded. "Last night. On South Audley Street, near the park."

"And you think Ethan was involved?"

"I don't think he actually committed the crime, but yes, I fear he may be involved." Carlyle didn't look pleased to say it.

Jason didn't hide his confusion. "What changed your mind? At our last meeting you cautioned me to give Ethan the benefit of the doubt. You believed he was trying to change."

"I *hoped* he was trying to change, and now I realize my error. Hoping someone has reformed isn't the same as their having done it."

That was it? "You simply decided you were mistaken about him? What evidence do you have linking him to the thefts?"

Carlyle's eyes widened a fraction before he masked his reaction. "It seems I'm not the only one who has changed his mind. You suddenly need proof to believe he's taken Aldridge's place?"

Jason shrugged, unwilling to share any alterations in his opinion, largely because he wasn't sure he was ready to accept them. "You were quite persuasive."

"As it happens, I have knowledge that gives me pause. While it's not firm proof that he's taken Aldridge's place, it certainly casts him in an unfavorable light. He may have been involved with Lady Aldridge's death."

Jason's blood chilled. "Tell me what you know."

Carlyle inclined his head. "It's why I came." He leaned forward and set his hand on Jason's desk.

"Jagger's manservant—a fellow called Oak—is a cohort from his past life. He visited Aldridge House on several occasions leading up to Lady Aldridge's death."

This didn't sound good. Jason's gut clenched. "What was he doing?"

"Delivering laudanum."

Which would not have been odd if Oak had been an apothecary's assistant or some manner of delivery boy. But he wasn't. He was Ethan's manservant and a likely criminal. Still, there could be a plausible and *legal* explanation for his actions.

Jason's jaw clenched as he looked at Carlyle expectantly. "Is there more?"

"Bow Street is beginning to believe she was murdered. She began taking laudanum after her husband died, but in recent weeks her intake increased to the point where she was barely conscious."

Bloody hell. Jason had wondered if she'd suffered the same fate as her late husband, though in a thankfully less grisly fashion, but hadn't really believed Ethan could be responsible. Carlyle, it seemed, didn't agree. "You think Ethan is behind her death, that he somehow orchestrated her overdose by laudanum? How would that even be possible?"

Carlyle's expression was grim. "Lady Aldridge's maid reported that her ladyship's laudanum use increased after she began to be seen with Jagger. Then even those brief public appearances halted. Bow Street has carefully questioned all of the retainers and anyone else who had contact with Aldridge House. Given Lady Aldridge's rapid decline, Bow Street believes the laudanum delivered by Oak was a stronger concoction than what she'd previously taken. Lethally so."

"And Bow Street simply offers you their information?" That was bloody convenient. "Is there some sort of former constable club that allows you such access?"

Carlyle smiled wryly. "Something like that." His features darkened. "I hope that I'm wrong and there's some explanation for Jagger's manservant's involvement."

"Perhaps Ethan had no knowledge of what Oak was about. Or, maybe Ethan is acting out of fear. You said yourself that Ethan works for a dangerous man and that his choices may not be his own." Jason wasn't sure he believed Ethan would follow anyone's orders. Ethan didn't seem the sort of man to fear much of anything, nor would he play the role of a puppet.

With his lips pressed together in a tight line, Carlyle didn't seem to believe it either. "Let's hope it's the former—that he isn't aware of Oak's actions. Because if it's the latter, Bow Street won't care who was in charge. Ethan will hang."

Jason tried to ignore the feeling of dread creeping over him. He shouldn't care what happened to Ethan. But the violent fury roiling in his gut, that for the first time was in defense of Ethan instead of directed at him, said he did. "What do you propose?"

"Let's pay him a visit."

While Jason wanted to know what Ethan had to say about his manservant's deliveries to Aldridge House, he feared it would be a wasted errand. "He's not going to tell you anything."

Carlyle's eyes narrowed. "Why do you say that?"

"Because I've spoken to him on more than one occasion and he refuses to discuss anything regarding

Lady Aldridge."

Standing, Carlyle took a deep breath. "Maybe I can persuade him to talk. It was, after all, my occupation."

Jason doubted Carlyle would succeed where he'd failed, but he was too curious about these developments to decline the invitation. He stood and moved around the desk. "Let's go."

Thirty minutes later Carlyle's coachman dropped them off in front of the Bevelstoke. A footman admitted them to the building.

Carlyle led Jason up two flights of stairs. They made their way down the corridor until they reached at door at the end. Carlyle knocked. They waited, but there was no response. Carlyle tried a second time, and again they were greeted with silence.

Carlyle glanced in his direction. He slipped his hand into his coat and withdrew something.

"What are you doing?" Jason leaned over his shoulder to see.

"Exactly what you think. You're blocking my light." Carlyle indicated the sconce behind Jason.

"Is this legal?" Jason asked, wondering not only about the lawfulness of their activity, but also whether Ethan was inside and simply ignoring the summons.

"It is for me." Carlyle peered at him sideways. "If you're uncomfortable with this, you're welcome to leave. We're only going to look around."

Jason supposed there was no harm in that. "What if he's inside?"

Carlyle shook his head with a small smile. "Men like him come to the door—or have their lackeys come to the door. Precisely because they don't want to be barged in on. You don't have to join me, but if I find something inside, don't you want to know about it?"

Unable to argue with Carlyle's logic—he'd been wanting to get to the bottom of Ethan's plans for some time—Jason moved to the side to allow Carlyle space and illumination to complete his work. A moment later, the lock was successfully released and the door sprung open.

Carlyle stepped inside tentatively, silently. A wide window on the opposite wall let in a stream of midday sunlight. Jason followed him into the apartment, closing the door behind him. Carlyle disappeared into a doorway to the right.

The main room wasn't terribly large, but it was well appointed with a round mirror decorated with gold scrollwork over the mantel, a pair of dark green chairs, and a gold settee bearing green pillows stitched with gold thread. The corner to the left of the door contained a cupboard and some shelving along with a small table and a pair of chairs.

Carlyle emerged from the doorway shaking his head. "No one here." Then he went to a desk near the windows and looked through the papers stacked neatly atop it.

Jason moved closer. "What are you doing?"

Carlyle didn't look up. "Searching for anything that might tell us what your brother is about."

It felt a bit wrong to enter Ethan's lodgings without his permission and rifle through his things, but how else was he to learn the truth when Ethan wouldn't trust him? Furthermore, what was Jason going to do with that truth? Watch him be thrown in gaol or, as Carlyle had said, hang? Or was there a slim chance Jason wanted to help Ethan? He didn't have an answer for that right now.

"I'll look in here." Jason went to the doorway Carlyle had already investigated and moved through it into Ethan's bedchamber.

Again, a window shed light on rich appointments—a large four-poster bed hung with dark red curtains and covered in matching silk stitched with a silver pattern of flourishes, a massive armoire in the corner. Everything was ordered and neat, like the sitting room. Another doorway led to a small alcove with a pallet where his manservant presumably slept. This seemed a likely place to begin, but there was only the pallet and a quick search revealed nothing.

Jason turned back to the bedchamber. His eye caught a small box atop a bedside table. He went to it and opened the lid. Nestled in scarlet velvet were a few baubles, some stickpins, a handful of gold rings, and a pocket watch. He picked up one of the rings. It contained a garish ruby. He dropped it and plucked up another. He froze. It was emblazoned with an L and perfectly matched the one he'd inherited when Father had died. The one Jason never wore.

He looked at it closely. The inside and edges of the ring were quite smooth, indicating frequent wear. Had their father given this to him or had Ethan had it made? Either one was a discomfiting thought. Frowning, Jason dropped it in the box and slammed the lid down.

The box moved, revealing a corner of paper beneath it. Jason slid the case aside and picked up a folded piece of parchment.

On it was a list of addresses. Some had marks next to them. Jason's gut clenched as he read that one of the addresses was Curzon Street. This list could possibly incriminate Ethan in the thefts. His instincts told him to pocket the parchment until he could investigate it further, when he was back at Lockwood House, but Carlyle entered at that inopportune moment.

"What did you find?" he asked, his inquisitive gaze fixed on the paper in Jason's hand.

Jason didn't think he could disregard the paper as nothing, not with the way Carlyle was intently advancing. So, Jason committed the contents to memory as best he could before handing the parchment to Carlyle. "It's a list of addresses."

Carlyle scanned the paper. "There are addresses on Curzon Street and South Audley Street." He was frowning when he looked up at Jason. "This doesn't look good for him."

For whatever reason, Jason took a defensive stance. "Are those the addresses of the robberies?"

"I don't know, but Bow Street will."

Jason's neck prickled. "You'll give that to Bow Street?"

Carlyle nodded, but he didn't look happy about it. "I told Teague I would let him know if I learned anything."

Irritation sparked in Jason's chest. "Is that why you came to see me today? As some sort of agent of Bow Street?"

"No, I sought you out because I thought you were interested in determining your brother's motives for showing up in Society. You were all but certain he was here to take over Aldridge's theft ring, but now you seem far less so." He tipped his head to the side, his eyes taking on an inquisitive sheen. "You said you'd spoken to him more than once. If he's convinced you to trust him, I'd like to know how."

"He hasn't." Jason could unequivocally say that. "However, I saw a little of what you spoke of—he seems a man bent on improving himself." Jason gestured to the elegant bedchamber they were standing in.

"Indeed," Carlyle said with a touch of sadness. "Though I'd hoped he was trying to do so within the law."

Jason realized he'd hoped so too, but refused to feel disappointed. He shouldn't have expected things to turn out any differently where his half brother was concerned. "Ethan's business isn't mine. You're going to take that to Bow Street now?" He indicated the list in Carlyle's hand.

Refolding the paper and tucking it into his coat, Carlyle nodded. "After I drop you at Lockwood House." He looked remorseful. "I said I would be the first to drag him to Bow Street if I thought he was doing anything illegal."

So he had. But whereas that had once filled Jason with satisfaction, he now felt only anxiety. No one had saved his brother, but maybe now it was time someone did. Not just any someone—Jason.

Chapter Fourteen

LYDIA WAITED IN Audrey's private sitting room the following afternoon for the arrival of Mr. Ethan Locke. They'd moved the furniture a bit to allow for waltzing space. Audrey sat in her favorite floral chair while Lydia walked circuits around the room.

"Why are you pacing?" Audrey asked.

"I'm worried this wasn't a very good idea. What if someone sees Mr. Locke come to your house? What if one of the servants spreads the information?"

Audrey laughed. "They won't. I concocted a scheme that would allow Mr. Locke to gain entrance without drawing notice."

Lydia wanted to ask how, but decided her brain was already too full of tumbling thoughts. She reluctantly sat beside Audrey. Energy still coursed through her, but then she'd been fraught with tension since the dinner party the other night. Her secret tour of Lockwood House was supposed to take place tomorrow, but she had yet to receive the details of her visit from Jason and suspected he'd changed his mind after the way Aunt Margaret had prodded him at the Horwatts'. She ought to be relieved, but she was scandalously disappointed instead.

Audrey patted Lydia's knee and regarded her with a depth of concern that no one else—save Mrs. Lloyd-Jones, perhaps—afforded her. "What's really bothering you?"

Lydia found she couldn't quite verbalize it. There was

Jason and whether he'd decided he didn't want anything more to do with her. There was Aunt Margaret, of course, and whatever she planned to do at Jason's party, plus her ever-present harping about gossip and maintaining their place in Society. And then there was Mr. Locke and keeping his secret. Lydia was happy to do it, but was still anxious should Aunt Margaret discover what she was up to.

In the end, Lydia forced a smile and waved her hand. "Oh, it's a multitude of things, none of which matter all that much."

"I like this new you," Audrey said softly. "I mean, I liked you before, but now everyone shall like you because they can finally see what I see—a caring young woman who only wants to be accepted. And I know that is what's most important to you."

It was. "How is it that we came to be such good friends? Fitting into Society's mold doesn't seem to matter all that much to you."

Audrey laughed. "Perhaps that's why. Because I don't necessarily care how people see me, I was able to be your friend—and I mean no offense by that. I know you acknowledge the fact that your aunt and her demands on you have made your social success less than what you wanted."

"It's true." Lydia didn't bother hiding the defeat in her tone. "I had such wonderful expectations when I first came to London." She'd begged and begged her father to let her have a Season, but he wasn't interested in leasing a town house and squiring her around to parties and balls. He came to town to sit in the Lords and to visit his mother, and he always stayed at his club. And Lydia's grandmother was unable to sponsor

Lydia because she lived in a small town house with her two spinster cousins. Lydia had been thrilled when Aunt Margaret had agreed to take her in and guide her through a Season. But here she was six Seasons later with a disappointing social standing—she was feared of course, but not especially liked—and no husband. All she ever wanted was to find a place in Society where she could have a circle of friends, a home, a family. She had none of those things, save Audrey, who had to be worth at least a half-circle of friends. Lydia clasped Audrey's hand and smiled. "I'm so glad you understand."

The door joining the sitting room to Audrey's bedchamber opened and in walked Mr. Ethan Locke.

Lydia gaped at him. "Did you come in through Audrey's bedchamber?" She swung an incredulous look at Audrey, whose cheeks had turned a faint pink.

Audrey inclined her head at Locke. "There's a leaf on your sleeve."

Locke plucked the yellowing foliage from his moss-green coat. "Thank you, Miss Cheswick." He looked at Lydia. "Yes, I came in through Miss Cheswick's bedchamber. She was kind enough to direct me up a tree outside her window. She is quite enterprising." He slid her an appreciative glance.

What the devil was going on here? Was Locke flirting with Audrey? Lydia rather hoped he was. A little excitement would be good for Audrey.

Locke offered them a belated bow. "Good afternoon, ladies. Thank you for helping this poor gentleman."

He was anything but "poor," at least in his appearance. He was elegantly dressed with tan breeches, boots polished to a high sheen, and a smart white cravat sporting a small, jeweled pin that caught the sunlight streaming through the windows.

Locke moved toward Audrey, and Lydia was reminded of her childhood cat who stalked birds in the garden. "I'm pleased to finally make your formal— acquaintance, Miss Cheswick."

Audrey held out her hand. "Mr. Locke, it's a pleasure. Actually, this isn't a formal acquaintance either, since we're meeting in *secret*." Her tone was daring, but the faint flags of pink in her cheeks told Lydia that her friend was nervous, as she often was around gentlemen.

Locke took Audrey's hand and pressed a kiss to the back. He smiled lazily at her while she—slowly— withdrew her hand. "The pleasure is mine, but I'm delighted to share it with you."

Audrey placed her hand in her lap but said nothing. Lydia couldn't tell what she was thinking. Goodness, no one had probably ever flirted with Audrey. Did she even recognize it?

Locke turned to Lydia, breaking her reverie. "How shall we begin?"

Lydia nodded. "You said you wanted to waltz, so we'll start with the most sedate version."

Mr. Locke regarded Audrey. "Dare I hope you're to be my partner, Miss Cheswick?"

Audrey nodded.

"It would be my honor," he said, offering his hand.

Audrey—again, very slowly—took his hand. He was wearing gloves, but she was not. Lydia wondered if she would've preferred to wear them too and made a mental note to ask her for the next lesson.

"Waltzing isn't terribly difficult," Lydia began. "Audrey, show Mr. Locke where to put his hands."

Audrey guided Locke to the middle of the space they'd cleared. He was staring intently at Audrey, and Lydia didn't want him frightening her.

"Mr. Locke," Lydia began, "you look nervous. This really is rather simple. There's nothing to be alarmed about."

"I think he looks bored," Audrey said, her gaze locked on his. "In fact, I think he may even look beleaguered." She lowered her voice a bit. "You don't have to do this, you know. No one will care that you don't dance. I rarely dance and no one even notices."

"But no one's watching you," Locke said.

Lydia opened her mouth to take him to task for pointing that out, but shut it again after he whispered, "It's criminal."

Audrey glanced away then, and Lydia realized two things: Locke *was* flirting with Audrey, and Audrey knew it.

"Position your right hand at her back," Lydia said when it appeared neither Audrey nor Locke was going to move. "You don't need to touch her firmly, just a light brushing of your fingertips is sufficient."

That hadn't been how Jason had touched her when they'd waltzed, but she didn't see the need to encourage it here. It was all fine and good for Locke to flirt with Audrey, but his mysterious background did not recommend him for anything more permanent.

Locke complied with her directive and lightly splayed his hand across Audrey's back. Because Audrey was quite tall, the top of her head came to his eyes. The top of Lydia's head only came to Jason's mouth. When had she noticed that detail?

"Lady Lydia," Locke drawled, "We await your direction."

She really needed to pay attention! "You'll clasp hands, but it's your right hand that will guide your partner around the dance floor."

He flexed his hand against Audrey's back and frowned. "That feels odd."

"Are you left-handed?" Audrey asked.

"Indeed I am," he said, "how very astute of you."

Audrey cocked her head to the side and regarded him with a mischievous sparkle in her eye. "Left-handed people are said to be related to the devil."

Lydia blinked. Where was her shy friend?

Locke's lips curved up. "Yes, they are. And I'm sure you'll find I'm no exception."

Lydia coughed delicately. "Might we return to the lesson? The waltz is done in three-quarter time to the music. The foot movements are a bit difficult to master, but the most important thing is to keep moving. If you don't, other couples will run into you."

"That might be entertaining," he drawled.

Audrey giggled. "Oh it is, when it happens."

"But let's avoid it, shall we?" Lydia said. "Mr. Locke, you're going to start with your left foot."

He did so, and Audrey automatically stepped back.

"Excellent, now you're going to step forward and to the right with your right foot, making a right angle with your foot."

Locke followed her instructions, and Audrey went along.

"Move your weight to your right foot, Mr. Locke, and then slide your left next to it."

"Good. Now you'll do the reverse. Step back with your right foot." He did, and Audrey followed. "Move your left back and to the left—the opposite of what you did with your right going forward."

He gave a single nod and complied.

"Put your weight back on your left foot and slide your right over next to it."

After he completed the step, Lydia clapped her hands together. "Now you simply repeat it. I'm going to count as you do it. We're not going to worry about moving or turning or toe work yet, let's just master the steps."

"How bloo—" He coughed. "How complicated is this dance?"

"Do you need to walk through it again?" Audrey asked. "You felt a trifle uncertain on that last step back."

Locke's mouth twisted into a faint scowl. "No. I think I have it. Though I'm skeptical about adding in turns or 'toe work'. I am ready on your count, Lady Lydia."

"And on one, two-three, ONE," she called out. "Two, three, one, two, three." She went slowly at first. Locke followed her cadence and moved as he ought. After three practice steps, Lydia went a little faster, and Locke kept up. For the first step. Then on the second he kicked Audrey in the shin.

"Ow." Her eyes narrowed slightly, and she withdrew her hand from his shoulder to massage her leg beneath the hem of her skirt.

Locke watched her. He opened his mouth to say something, but then snapped it closed. He tried to step back, but Audrey kept a hold of his right hand with her left.

"I'm fine," she said. "Lydia, count again."

Lydia counted, more slowly again, and he did fine for a series of five steps. "A little faster," Audrey said.

Lydia complied and counted more quickly and this time, he managed three steps before nearly kicking Audrey again. However, he corrected before he did any damage, and Audrey smiled at him encouragingly.

"Excellent work, Mr. Locke!" Lydia said. "Shall we take a break?"

Audrey released Locke's hand and shoulder and stepped back. "I'll go and fetch a tea tray."

Once they were alone, Locke turned to face Lydia. "My brother is having a legitimate soirée at Lockwood House. What do you know about this?"

Though her involvement was supposed to be secret, she found she wanted to tell someone other than just Audrey. And since she and Locke shared confidences, she decided to trust him. "It was my idea, though that's *my* secret that I'm sharing with you," she said pointedly. "He ought to show Society he's not just the scoundrel who provides those other entertainments."

He chuckled. "I should have known you were managing this. And did you tell him to invite me?"

"In fact, I did. I'm glad he took my advice."

"Thank you." He studied her with interest. "You're wrongly cast as an air-headed gossip with little awareness of loyalty."

"You mustn't believe everything you hear." She nearly choked on those words since she'd always relied on people doing precisely that.

Audrey returned without a tea tray. She paused just over the threshold and clasped her hands. "Mr. Locke needs to go. My grandfather has returned home early."

Locke frowned with disappointment. "What a shame." But then he flashed a terrifyingly handsome smile, and Lydia saw a glimpse of what Jason might've looked like without his scar. And decided that she definitely preferred him with it. It wasn't only that it gave his countenance character and a touch of vulnerability. It gave him depth and showed his strength—both inside and out.

"Until next time, ladies." Locke bowed again and took himself off through Audrey's bedchamber once more.

Lydia turned to Audrey and cocked her head to the side in mild bafflement. "You directed him through your *bedchamber*?"

Audrey's eyes widened innocently. "It's not as if I *met* him there." Then her eyes narrowed playfully. "You don't get to judge, not when you're sneaking about with Lord Lockwood."

Immediately, Lydia's muscles tensed. She'd forgotten about her worries regarding Jason during the dance lesson, but now they came roaring back.

Audrey pressed her lips together, something she often did when she was worried. "Oh dear, what did I say?"

"It's nothing," Lydia said, refusing to be concerned about Jason Lockwood's plans. His kisses might be divine, but she had no future with someone like him. His social standing might cost her a respectable circle of friends, he would saddle her with a notorious home, and his family was rife with madness. It was fine to maintain a friendship with him, but anything more would be foolish—she could never love a scoundrel.

Chapter Fifteen

IT HAD TAKEN time to organize everything for Lydia's visit today, not the least of which had been how to get her here. Jason had ended up enlisting the surprisingly enthusiastic help of Mrs. Lloyd-Jones. Lydia was to have gone to her house for an afternoon call, but would then travel to Lockwood House in a hack.

Things had come together perfectly, with the exception of Mrs. Lloyd-Jones insisting on coming along. Jason hadn't been able to argue the propriety, and it was for the best, since he couldn't keep kissing Lydia, no matter how badly he wanted to.

Jason strode into the foyer near the appointed time of Lydia's arrival with North at his side. "Everything is ready for Lady Lydia's visit?"

"Yes, my lord. Everyone has the afternoon off save Cook, who is busy in the kitchen, and of course me." They'd cleared the house to protect Lady Lydia's reputation—he trusted his staff implicitly, but took the measure anyway.

"Cook is working on the samples for the party," North said. "We'll bring them up upon Lady Lydia's arrival."

"Very good." Jason pivoted on his heel. "I'll await her in the drawing room."

North nodded, and as Jason made his way through the foyer, he thought he heard the sounds of a coach out front.

A few minutes later, North showed Lydia into the

drawing room. She wore a long-sleeved ivory dress with a small floral pattern topped with a green bodice that drew his eye directly to her breasts. He immediately snapped his gaze upward lest he be caught staring. This meeting was not starting on the right note—not if he meant to keep his hands to himself. It was especially good then that she hadn't come alone.

Alone. He looked behind Lydia for her chaperone. "Where's Mrs. Lloyd-Jones?"

Lydia wasn't looking at him, she was studying the room. "She wasn't feeling well, and when her sister—Miss Vining—also pleaded a headache, she sent a maid with me instead."

"A maid?" he dumbly repeated as his body shot to awareness.

"She's gone to the kitchen," Lydia said, perhaps a touch shyly. She had yet to meet his eyes. Where was the brazen girl who'd traced her finger along his scar?

A maid in the kitchen wasn't going to do a thing to protect Lydia's reputation. "Is that all right, or would you prefer her to chaperone?"

Her gaze finally found his, and the edge of her mouth ticked up. "It's all right. I suggested she have tea."

He had the sense Lydia was nervous, so he sought to set her at ease. He extended a bow. "Welcome to Lockwood House," he said, winking at her playfully, "again."

"Thank you. Do you mind if I remove my bonnet?" Her fingers were already tugging the ribbons from beneath her chin. She pulled the hat from her lush blond curls and set it on a table near the doorway.

The look she gave him when she turned around was

filled with trepidation. "I wanted to apologize for my aunt's behavior at the dinner party. I admit I was worried you meant to cancel today's tour, especially when I didn't hear from you until so late yesterday."

He hated that she'd gone the better part of the week thinking he was perhaps angry with her. He'd been so focused on whatever Ethan was doing that it had never occurred to him to send a note of confirmation. He definitely hadn't intended for Lydia to think he judged her for the things her aunt said and did. "There's no need to apologize for your aunt. In fact," he injected his tone with a light sarcasm hoping to convince her that he didn't blame her, "you could apologize until you drew your last breath, and there would still be no way to forgive her. You, on the other hand, did nothing that requires forgiveness. Indeed, I should thank you for saving me from making the situation worse."

Lydia smiled warmly, and he relaxed. "I'm glad you feel that way. I was disappointed the evening was ruined by her comments."

"Nothing could have ruined that evening." Damn, why had he said that? As if the memory of his unfinished seduction weren't already something he had to work hard to forget. He should probably send her on her way right this minute, but he didn't. Apparently he wasn't a scoundrel for nothing.

Before Jason could adequately gauge her reaction, North appeared in the doorway with a tray of food. He set it on a table near the center of the room. A table that was usually adorned with a barely-clad Cyprian during vice parties. *Do not think of Lydia in that position.*

"A selection of food that Cook is suggesting for the party." North executed a bow and then departed. Jason noted the bounder left the door open. What the hell use was propriety at this juncture? She was a young, unmarried woman who was secretly visiting Lockwood House without a proper chaperone. An open door was utterly pointless.

Lydia went to the tray and perused the items, her gaze landing on the pair of oysters. "These look splendid for the buffet. I love oysters."

Jason couldn't help but think of Casanova's diet of fifty oysters a day. He resisted the urge to eat even one, because really, his lust didn't require any assistance at the present moment. He directed his attention to the pheasant and the blood pudding and the sliced ham. "The food will do?"

"It looks excellent, and I'm sure it tastes divine." She glanced around the drawing room. "Will this be our main room for entertaining?"

"Yes."

She did a half-circuit before pausing to ask, "And what is this chamber's function during your vice parties?"

"Lydia." He stared at her as he fought to expel images of Lydia attending one of his vice parties from his mind. "Why on earth would you need to know that?"

Her face lit with a guilty smile. "Sorry. I'm naturally curious. Anyone would be."

"Everyone is." He prowled toward her. "Have you come here today to discover all the answers and then share them with London's finest?" As soon as he said it, he wanted to bite the question back. "And now I'm sorry. I was teasing you and it wasn't well done of me."

She fixed him with an ardent look. "I shall keep

everything you tell me today inviolate."

He shouldn't spoil her naiveté and reveal any of the details of his parties, but he was enjoying their time together more than he thought possible and couldn't seem to stop himself. He moved to walk beside her as she completed her circuit. "This is where guests come when they first arrive. We keep the illumination somewhat dim."

"Everyone wears a mask, do they not?" she asked, sounding a trifle breathless, which only served to heighten his infernal desire.

"Yes, unless they go directly to the gaming room. Several gentlemen come here just for the cards or billiards and don't care who knows it."

She flicked him an inquisitive glance. "The Marquess of Wolverton sometimes attends for those purposes, or so I've heard."

Jason nodded, his mind wavering on what to share and what to keep from her, to preserve her delightful air of innocence. "I invite only certain gentlemen, and they must present their invitation to gain entrance."

She paused and turned her upper body toward him, rapt. "What about women?"

"I would never risk a lady's reputation by inviting her directly, but if one chooses to attend—or if she isn't a lady at all—we don't typically turn her away. My retainers are instructed to use their judgment regarding whom to admit."

"So if I appeared in a mask without an invitation, I'd be welcome?" she asked.

He pressed his lips together. "I don't recommend you try it. You recall what happened to Lady Philippa."

She inclined her head. "Lord Sevrin did try to rescue

her."

While that was true, they'd been discovered nonetheless. "And you see how well that turned out."

She gave him a small smile. "Actually, it turned out perfectly for them. They're quite happy."

"You're correct. I only meant their road to happiness wasn't easy—it was paved with secrets and scandal."

She glanced away from him, her voice growing soft. "I shouldn't care if my road to happiness was rife with disaster and heartache, just so long as it led to happiness."

Not for the first time, he wondered at the cause of her sadness. He sensed it there, just beneath the surface. To all appearances she was lively and confident, but maybe it was because he was on the outside looking in that he saw a young woman fighting for her place.

She turned to face him with a bright smile. "I hope it's all right that we use this room as a congregation point as well. Then we'll have the music and dancing here later in the evening. What other rooms should we plan to use?"

He held out his arm. "Next door is a smaller drawing room. I thought we would use it for the dinner." He led her into the room where his guests typically engaged in illicit embraces. "We'll move this furniture out and set up a buffet."

"We'll need some tables and chairs for people to sit and enjoy the food if they choose," she said, surveying the room.

"Of course, North will take care of that." He knew she would ask about the function of this room during a vice party and sought to head her off. "Don't ask me for specifics about this room. Guests come here when they wish for a modicum of privacy."

She turned her questioning gaze on him. "Don't you offer rooms upstairs for that sort of thing?"

A rush of heat flooded his lower half. "*Bloody hell.* Pardon me, Lydia. How on earth do you know all of this?"

"I'm a dreadfully good listener." Her gaze caught his, and she imparted this information as if they were bosom friends. In that moment he knew he absolutely did want to know her. "If you position yourself next to the right people at certain events, you can overhear some very interesting things."

He was rapt. "Such as?"

"Such as Lord Compton took Mrs. Horwatt upstairs at one of your parties last year."

He blinked. "But people are masked. How do they know?" He could only imagine Compton's friends had spread the tale. Who else would've known? He recalled that Mrs. Horwatt's face had been entirely covered.

Lydia's eyes sparkled mischievously. "If Lord Compton is the one imparting the information, it's safe to say it's accurate, is it not?"

"The blighter!" But then he was hardly shocked by Compton boasting of his sexual prowess. It's what men—most men—did. "So you have more than a vague idea of what happens here?"

"Yes, though I don't suppose you'd take me upstairs to see what all the fuss is about—since you've warned me against sneaking into one of your parties."

The scoundrel in him wanted to. The scoundrel in him wanted to carry her upstairs right this instant to the very first room he found and finish what he'd started the other night. But even he acknowledged that he wasn't a *complete* blackguard, and so he led her into the next room.

He tried very hard not to focus on the heat of her gloved fingers burning through his sleeve or the sound of her skirts rustling against her legs. He took a deep breath to calm his lust and immediately regretted the action for now his senses were full of her spicy floral scent. What was that flower? *Hyacinths.*

"The billiards room?" she asked, her gaze landing on the baize-covered table at the opposite end of the room.

"Yes, this is where gentlemen gamble away their fortunes."

She peered up at him. "Do you gamble?"

"Infrequently. And when I do, I prefer to wager on fights."

"Pugilism? Did you watch Lord Sevrin fight?"

"I did." Though, he'd spent more time watching Ethan in his elevated seating area and wondering why in the hell Sevrin had agreed to fight for him.

She shuddered delicately. "Such a brutal sport. I admit I don't see the appeal."

"Women rarely do. Which is not to denigrate your sex. I only mean that men seem to derive pleasure from watching others physically triumph over others."

"While women—some women—enjoy emotional victory over others," she murmured. She shook her head then shot him a deeply curious look. "Why do you watch?"

He shrugged, his memory traveling back to his youth when his father had started taking him to fights when he was maybe nine years old. They had been wonderful evenings, the only times he'd felt truly close with his father. He'd take Jason to eat at a pub and then they'd watch the fight. Jason had felt like such a man next to his father. But then he'd drop Jason at Lockwood House and continue on to his mistress's, ruining what had been a perfect night. Still, Jason had longed for the next time. In fact, he'd lived for it.

Until Father had started bringing Ethan along. Then those special nights had turned into torture. Eventually, Jason had stopped going with them. But he'd still gone to fights. It was a torment of which he couldn't seem to deprive himself. He'd wanted to recall and relive the only blissful memories he had of his father.

"Jason?"

Her softly spoken use of his name jarred him—pleasantly—back to the present. He liked watching her lips say his name. Almost as much as he liked tasting them.

"I heard you got into fights when you were young, that you broke someone's arm at Eton and were sent down for it." There was a gentle inquisition in her voice. She didn't sound like the scandalmonger she was purported to be. She sounded like someone who genuinely cared.

He'd almost forgotten there was a host of stories and rumors she'd likely heard about him. Yet, she was here anyway. Was it because she didn't believe he was the mad, violent, promiscuous lord he was painted as?

"Not to sound defensive, but the other boy started it and was also sent down. I think he hit me because he thought I'd tripped him. But it was really just his own clumsiness. We were young and foolish and got quite carried away." He grimaced. "I'm sure the characterization you heard was far worse than the reality."

She looked at him unflinchingly. "I knew there was an explanation for it. Regardless of what I've heard, you've yet to display a violent nature to me. But you were going to tell me why you liked watching fights."

"I was?" He wasn't, but now he wanted to tell her. "I used to attend fights with my father. They're good memories."

She nodded, then looked away. "I understand."

He thought she just might. He wasn't certain, but he knew her father was still alive and somehow inexplicably absent from her life. And since she lived with Margaret, he'd deduced her mother was no longer with her. "Your mother died long ago, didn't she?"

"She passed when I was nine."

So young to lose her mother, but presumably she'd had a strong feminine presence in her life—even if it wasn't a very good one. "And did your aunt raise you?"

She seemed weary, sad. "I'm sure it seems that way, but no. I went to live with her for my first Season and since I'm still unmarried, my father allows me to remain with her."

Her father was Lord Prewitt. Jason suddenly recalled that he spent most of his time at his country seat. "Your father is in Northumberland?"

"Yes." Clear lines of distaste fanned from her pursed mouth. "He loves it there."

"You don't?"

"It's the middle of nowhere," she said matter-of-factly. "There's nothing for an unmarried lady to do save milk cows or embroider. Visiting the nearest neighbor requires an overnight stay."

He thought of her dressed as a milkmaid sitting on a stool in the barn and couldn't reconcile the elegant Society miss at his side with such a provincial image. "Surely you didn't milk cows?"

"I did." She surprised him with a smile. "I liked doing it when I was a girl. My mother taught me, actually."

He glimpsed the pure young girl she'd been and sensed her aunt had changed her, perhaps in ways she didn't like. But maybe he was projecting his own opinions on her. "Have you been happy with your aunt?"

She removed her hand from his arm and walked to the billiards table, keeping her gaze averted from his. "Happy enough. What other games will you offer at the party besides billiards?"

He wanted to press her for a truer answer, but her abrupt change in topic told him she was done discussing it. And since he didn't enjoy talking about his father, he understood.

He followed her toward the billiards table, but stopped short, giving her space. "The usual card games. And hazard. However, I won't allow the wagering to go as deeply as at my other parties."

She turned from the table. "We don't want anyone losing a fortune."

And then, because he wanted to see the vivacious young woman he'd come to like—and he liked her even more after today—he held out his arm again. "Come, I'll take you upstairs."

Her eyes widened. "You will?"

"If you wish."

She hesitated the briefest moment and Jason held his

breath. Then she nodded once and took his arm. He led her from the billiards room and back the way they'd come. In the foyer, he guided her up the wide staircase.

She peered up at him in blatant curiosity. "Where are we going first?"

He chuckled at her blatant interest. "You swear you're not here to collect information for nefarious purposes?" He didn't really believe she was, but wanted to hear her say it one more time.

"I swear." She paused on the stairs, and he turned to look down at her. "Once upon a time, I would have, but not any longer. I truly only want to help you succeed."

He saw the honesty in her eyes and knew she was different from her aunt, that spending years in that harpy's company hadn't forever marred her sensibilities. He turned and continued up the stairs. "I'm afraid it's not all that exciting. The rooms are really just a series of bedchambers."

She frowned. "But I thought there was a special room upstairs."

He knew precisely to what she referred, but was again a bit shocked at how much she already knew. "Some call it the 'dress-up room,' others call it the 'watching room,' and still others call it the 'prop room.'"

Her eyes were wide as she tried to puzzle what each of those descriptions could mean—apparently there were still things he could reveal. She turned to him as they reached the top of the stairs. "And which do you call it?"

He smiled. "The fantasy room."

Her intake of breath stirred his imagination. "How

many fantasies have you realized there?"

"None." But he had plenty sparking in his mind at the present.

Her brown eyes were curious, beautiful. "Why?"

"Because I've never used that room." He turned to the left and gently pulled her along. "It's this way."

He led her down the corridor and turned left along the western wing. The corridor terminated in a curved alcove. Two chaises were set against the walls. "This is where people wait their turn for the room. It's quite popular. In most cases, people put their names in as soon as they arrive."

She looked from one chaise to the other and turned her head to look up at him. "You said it was also called the watching room. How does that work?"

He wasn't at all sure he should be explaining this to her, but why not? She was a grown woman well past the blush of her first Season. "If the people using the room agree to it, others may watch what they're doing. There's another room next door with little holes to look through."

Just telling her about this was incredibly arousing. His skin felt hot. Maybe it would be better if they weren't touching. He moved away from her, withdrawing his arm from her fingers, and opened the door.

He stepped to the side and allowed Lydia to move in past him. She sucked in her breath again. "It's beautiful."

Her gaze was fixed on the bed. There went his cock again. It was a spectacular bed, if he did say so himself, but that was the point of it being in this room. It was a massive four-poster, plenty large enough for several people, and covered in opulent purple silk.

"It's so big," she breathed. "Did you have it custom made?"

"Ironically, no. It was my father's bed, just as this was his bedchamber." He'd never told anyone that. He was apparently unable to censor himself with her today.

She turned toward him. "If this is the viscount's room, where do you sleep?"

He'd never wanted to sleep in his father's bed and since it was too large to be moved, he'd had a new viscount's chamber designed in the east wing. But it was sacrosanct—to him—and he'd never taken anyone there or allowed anyone to use it. "I made some renovations when I inherited."

"I see." She walked toward an armoire against the wall. Jason had a moment's panic. There was one with clothing and another with objects designed to enhance pleasure. Since he never used this room—and rarely even went inside—he wasn't sure which was which. He dearly hoped it was the former but suddenly recalled it was the latter. He rushed to step in front of her, placing his back against the armoire.

He smiled down at her. "You don't want to open this one."

She looked at him expectantly, her mouth forming a moue. "I thought you were going to show me the room?"

"I think I'm corrupting you quite enough, and this armoire is for people of a certain experience."

She didn't look convinced. In fact, she looked determined. "What's in there?"

He exhaled. He could tell her. It didn't mean he had to show her. "Objects used in amplifying desire and satisfaction. If you were familiar with sexual acts, I could explain them more fully, but I'm guessing you're not."

She blushed again, this time a far darker shade of pink. "I know enough."

He pivoted and opened the armoire a sliver. He reached inside and grabbed the first thing his hand found. "Enough to know what this is?" He wasn't even sure what he'd grabbed, but now saw that it was a slender leather thong. It could actually be used for a variety of things, but he vowed not to share them all with her. Even his perversion had its limits.

Her gaze fell on the thong for a moment before rising back up to meet his. "No, I don't know what that is for." Her lips pursed, and he could see that lack of knowledge frustrated her.

"So inquisitive," he said, fingering the soft leather. "This is used to secure someone to the bed. Or I suppose a chair, or any other piece of furniture. Or perhaps it's just used to lash someone's hands together."

Her eyes widened and her nostrils flared. "Why?" she whispered hotly, stirring his desire. It was impossible to have this conversation without envisioning her tied to his bed, her lush body splayed for his appreciation and enjoyment—and hers.

"Some people find pleasure in being restrained during sexual acts. They have to trust their partner—or partners," he really ought to stop trying to shock her, "and completely give themselves over to their care."

She glanced at the thong again. "Do you enjoy . . . that?"

The heat in the room spiked. He was finding it very

hard not to touch her, kiss her, tear her clothes from her. "I have—once or twice—but it depends on the partner. And before you ask, I typically stick to just one, regardless of what you may have heard."

"Typically?" she asked, her voice climbing.

"Lydia, do you really want to know every detail?" He leaned forward, hoping for another waft of her spicy hyacinth scent. *There.* He nearly closed his eyes in lust. "I find a little mystery goes a long way."

She reached out and touched the leather, her fingers brushing against his. "It's very soft."

"You wouldn't want it chafing your skin, would you?" His cock was now fully erect. How much time did they have until she had to leave? *No.* He couldn't even consider it.

"No." Her dark eyes were luminous and still so full of curiosity. And he wanted to appease every last inch of it. "May I have it?" she asked.

Nothing could have shocked him more. That wasn't precisely true, but it was close enough. "Lydia, what in God's name are you doing to me?"

Her look turned apologetic. "Sorry, that was overbold of me." She let go of the thong. "Show me what else there is to do in here."

He'd already told her about the watching, and he'd showed her a prop. That left the dress-up. He took her hand and led her to the other armoire in the corner, dropping the thong on the edge of the bed as they passed it. He opened the armoire doors wide, exposing an array of clothing, mostly gowns in vivid colors with daring cuts that no respectable lady would be seen wearing.

"Oh," she breathed, her fingers reaching out to

stroke a rich, crimson velvet. "These are beautiful."

"Guests may wear them, though I daresay they scarcely last long on one's frame."

She let go of his hand and looked through them, pausing at a maid's uniform. "Why is this here?"

"Some like to play different roles. There are military-style uniforms." He gestured to a bright lobster red coat. "For women who always fancied shagging an officer."

Her nostrils flared at his use of crude language. "I see. And I also begin to see why you call this the fantasy room." She turned toward him. "There's something for everyone here. But I want to know what's in here for you."

"Nothing. Until now." He gazed down at her upturned face, recalled the imprint of her soft lips under his, the feel of her warm hands cradling the back of his head.

Her hand came up and splayed against his chest. "I want you to do it. I want you to have your fantasy. Right now."

Though they'd been flirting for quite some time, he was still surprised by her words. But, God, how he wanted it, too. "I don't think that's wise."

Her eyes narrowed. She tugged her glove from her hand and tossed it on the bed behind him. As she worked the second glove off, she pinned him with a hot stare. "If you don't, I'll have mine. And that involves me using that leather thing to tie you to the bedpost." She speared him with a bold stare and laid her palm against his scarred cheek.

He flinched.

"What is it?" she asked, her eyes wide with concern.

The touch of her hand burned his flesh, but in the best possible way. "How can you touch my scar so easily? And you don't stare at it anymore. Why?"

"Because I don't see it any longer. It's simply part of you. It's no different than any other part of you—that of which I've seen." She let her gaze travel over his body in slow deliberation. "I find you beyond attractive, Jason. This scar," she traced her thumb along its base, "is simply one of your many splendid parts, and without a single one of them you wouldn't be Jason Lock—"

He devoured the rest of his name from her lips. Lust raged through him with the power of any madness that had ever darkened his soul. But this wasn't dark, it was light. Blinding, beautiful, soul-wrenching light.

Her hands clutched at his cravat and worked their way to the back of his neck, pulling him down into her embrace. Her mouth opened to his with a ferocity that matched his own, her tongue sliding against his with hungry strokes.

He encircled her waist and hauled her up so that her breasts were pressed against his chest. A hundred fantasies, all with her as the focal point, swirled in his mind. She was clothed, she was naked, she was bound, she was free, she was masked, she stared at him with beckoning eyes.

He lifted her completely from the ground and carried her to a chaise positioned in front of the fireplace. Gently, he set her down on the chaise, but she pulled back from his kiss. "What's wrong with the bed?" Her mouth was red and wet.

He leaned forward and licked her lower lip, then nibbled at the supple flesh with his teeth. "This is my fantasy, isn't it?"

"I beg your pardon," she said softly, with a smile in her voice. "I don't know if your fantasy involves this, but I hope you don't mind if I encourage you to touch my breast. You've come frightfully close on two occasions now, and I'm afraid I can't let a third opportunity pass me by."

She lifted her fingers to the green bodice of her gown and released some hidden fasteners. The bodice gapped open, revealing the pale ivory of her chemise. The tops of her breasts swelled over the edge of the undergarment.

He stared at the tempting curve of her bosom and was nearly engulfed in a dizzying whirlwind of desire. He squeezed his eyes shut. This wasn't supposed to happen. He needed to put an end to this right now.

But when he opened his eyes, met hers, and saw the wondrous curiosity in their depths, he was lost. "I wouldn't want to disappoint you." It was more than that—he couldn't *bear* to. Without breaking eye contact with her, he brought his palm to one of her breasts and cupped her through the chemise. The nipple instantly hardened, and her flesh heated against him. Her eyes widened almost imperceptibly, but he registered the shared lust rushing between them.

"Lydia, we need to stop this."

Her gaze was steady and didn't carry a hint of trepidation or remorse. "I know." She palmed the back of his head and drew him down to kiss her.

Just one more, he told himself, as he took her mouth. He took his time exploring her lips and tasting her mouth. She tipped her head back with the softest of moans, her hands clutching him as if she might fall without him to secure her.

She pushed her breast into his hand and he teased the nipple with first his thumb and then added his forefinger, pulling on the nub. He pivoted her and laid her back against the arched curve of the chaise. He settled one knee between her legs and left her mouth to drop kisses along her jawline. She arched up, but he wanted her to lie still and pliant against the chaise. He kept his hand at her breast, but splayed the other softly against her neck and held her down. Her eyes opened, but there was no alarm, just hot desire burning in their chestnut depths.

"Lie still," he commanded softly.

She did as he bade, letting her head fall back against the gold velvet. He moved his hand down her neck, stroking her flesh with his fingertips. Then he found the straps of her chemise and slid them down her shoulders. He kept going, peeling the chemise and the top of her gown down her torso until her breasts were completely exposed to him. Her pale flesh gleamed in the mottled afternoon light finding its way past the edges of the curtains in the windows.

He left the gown and chemise around her forearms, knowing she was, in effect, restrained. He sensed she'd wanted to try that, and it was only one of a thousand fantasies he'd had about her since entering this room.

He lowered his mouth to her breast and covered her nipple with his mouth, swearing to himself that after this taste, he'd wrap her back up and send her along her way. She gasped and surged up against him. He felt her struggle with her hands, as though she wanted to clasp him.

She wriggled, trying to get her arms free. He

wouldn't stop her, in fact, enjoyed her movements. Could she focus on getting free while he made love to her breasts?

He suckled her flesh, drawing the nipple deep into his mouth. He licked and kissed her, giving this part of her the same attention he'd given her mouth. But he didn't ignore her other breast. He stroked and massaged the delicious mound, reveling at how perfect she felt in his grasp.

Finally, she got her hands free and her hands locked around his head, holding him close against her. "Jason," she breathed, again and again.

Her hips moved, and he felt the heat of her core against his knee. He pressed upward, giving her something to move against. And she took his lead with abandon, her thighs closing around him with sharp need.

He cupped her breasts firmly and moved his mouth to devour the second one as he'd done the first. She moaned softly, her fingers digging into the back of his head and her hips grinding down against his knee. He longed to replace that appendage with his cock and drive into her. She felt so good, so perfect.

She arched her chest up, offering herself to his mouth, glorying in his attention. It was more than he'd allowed in his fantasy. And it was more than he should allow in reality.

Reluctantly, terribly, hesitatingly, he pulled away from her breast. "Lydia, we have to stop. If nothing else, you're nearly out of time."

She reached down and pulled the skirt of her gown up, revealing her stocking-clad leg. "Then you'd better hurry."

Chapter Sixteen

LYDIA KNEW IT was brazen, knew she should refasten her dress and let him escort her downstairs. But she couldn't. She'd never felt such sensations before. She'd never had anyone look at her like that before, let alone touch her in this manner. And maybe she never would again. She knew the beauty and singularity of this moment, probably better than she knew anything else in her life, and she'd be damned if she would let it go, even if it meant she was ruined.

"Please, Jason, don't stop. I don't want you to."

He drew in a ragged breath and focused on her face, and she sensed instinctively that it took everything in his power not to continue with what he'd been doing. She felt a tremor in his hands as they cradled her breasts.

"I am many, many things, most of them horrid, but I am not a defiler of innocents."

No, she wasn't ready to let this moment go. A joy she'd never known was so close she could taste it. "I don't feel the least *defiled*." And because his eyes widened the barest bit and she could see that he was weighing her plea, she added, "As you said, we have very little time. There isn't a moment to waste." For some indefinable reason, she needed this. Needed *him*. "Please."

He stared at her another long moment and then finally stood. Her heart clenched, and began to wither as he moved away from her. Tears stung her eyes—but why? She'd already decided they had no future together, that a marriage with him wouldn't give her what she wanted. She tried to convince herself that he was doing the right thing, while she was the one behaving scandalously. She would've laughed at the paradox if she hadn't felt so wretched.

The sound of the door closing was heavy in her ears. She sat up to refasten her dress, but his words froze her movements. "What are you doing?"

She blinked up at him and realized he'd only left her to close the door. "Did you change your mind?" Hope blossomed in her breast as the return of desire heated her veins.

"I didn't change it—I made it up. But maybe I should—"

Grabbing his hand, she pulled him back down to the chaise, reclining back against the velvet. Then she tugged his head down and kissed him. She wouldn't give him the chance to change his mind, not when she sensed happiness just beyond her grasp.

Copying some of the things he'd done to her, she used her tongue to lick his mouth and her teeth to tug at his lips. She angled her head and slid her tongue deeper into the hot recesses of his mouth. He tasted divine—like her favorite fresh-baked bread, like the warmest summer day, like how she imagined happiness should taste.

His hand slid down her ribcage and cradled her waist, his palm massaging her through the layers of her clothes. She wished they had more time. She'd demand to be naked against him.

Then his hand dipped lower, skimming over her hip and thigh to the hem of her gown where it lay just above her knee. He pushed the fabric up, exposing her bare thigh, and letting it bunch at her waist, while the skirt fell to the side of the chaise.

"Lydia," he gasped, lifting his head. "There's not enough time to do what I want. To make this right and good for you."

"I assure you this is plenty right and outrageously good for me." She pushed her breasts up against his chest, loving the feel of his strength, even though he was clothed, against her bare flesh.

He smiled down at her, a heart-stoppingly *erotic*—there was that word again—smile that flooded her core with heat and want. His hand came against her most intimate flesh. She flinched, surprised at the contact, but willed herself to relax even as he whispered, "Easy," against her ear.

His tongue traced the outer edge of her ear while his fingers stroked between her legs. "You're so soft and hot and wet." His words enflamed her as powerfully as his touch. "There are so many things I want to do to you—*for* you. But I can't today. You feel ready. Are you ready, love?"

She nodded, unable to find speech amidst all of the sensations rioting through her. His thumb teased the nub of flesh at the top of her core, swirling over her with expert precision. It was more than she could stand and not nearly enough all at once. Then his finger slid along her folds and pushed inside, giving succor to her need.

"Yes," he said, his exhalation sending a shiver down her neck. "Open for me." He withdrew his finger and then pumped it forward again, filling her with white-hot bliss. His thumb worked the nub while his finger moved in and out. "If I had time, I would put my mouth on you down there. I'd lick you here." He glided his finger over the sensitive flesh. "And suck you here." His thumb pressed against the nub and her hips bucked as pleasure flooded every part of her.

He pulled and pressed on her flesh, massaging it with frantic, enraptured caresses. The pleasure exploded into something hotter, brighter. It was magnificent. And then his fingers were inside her again, stroking her with a rhythm that sang straight to her soul. She lost control, let her head cascade back, her thighs fall apart, her heart swell.

His hands left her briefly, and she was vaguely aware of him working the buttons of his breeches. Fabric brushed against her thighs and then she felt hot flesh against hers.

His eyes fixed on hers, and she was entranced by how bright they seemed—like the sun shining behind a thin layer of gray clouds. "I will die if you tell me to stop, but I will. I'll do anything for you."

Briefly—very, very briefly—she wondered if she *should* stop him, if there was any point in preserving her virtue for a marriage that might never happen. And just as quickly, she rejected the idea. Nothing would ever feel as right and wonderful as this. *Nothing.* "You can't really expect me to deny you when you say things like that. Jason, whatever you do, *don't stop.*"

She moved her hand down to her thigh. "Show me what to do."

He guided her hand between them and closed her fingers around his shaft. He was hot and hard, but his flesh was soft, too. She ran her palm along his length and wrapped her fingers around the head. He groaned.

"More time." The words were a curse and a plea.

"*Another* time," she said, guiding him instinctively forward.

His hand covered hers as he pushed against her folds. He nudged once, twice, rubbing against her in exquisite torture. "Look at me, Lydia. This will sting, I think."

Then he plunged into her, swiftly, but with great care. She gasped—yes, it stung—as her flesh stretched around him. She moved her hand to his hip and gripped him tensely, waiting to feel the pleasure he'd given her moments before. That couldn't be all.

He rested within her a moment, his breathing coming in ragged pants against her ear. Then his thumb was on her again, teasing her, tormenting her, stirring her passion. Moist heat welled in her core and he moved, creating a delicious friction.

His movements were slow at first, but then they picked up momentum. He withdrew further and then surged forward, filling her each time with blinding pleasure. "Wrap your legs around me, love," he said, his voice low and rough with desire.

She followed his instruction and he sheathed himself even deeper. She groaned low and loud as need built within her again. She wanted him to move. Needed him to move. "Move."

He rotated his hips against hers, grinding against her, but only barely withdrawing. She craved the friction of his cock sliding in and out of her and tried to pull her hips back, but she was flush against the chaise.

Desperate to reach her climax again, she pushed at his hip, urging him to give her what she wanted. He withdrew sharply, leaving her empty and starved. Then he plowed forward, filling her again until ecstasy threatened. Again, he drew back, and again he filled her. She moved her hand to his backside and guided him as he thrust forward and back.

"Lydia, hold on to me, love, because I have to let go."

It took her a moment to understand what he meant, but then she knew. He thrust into her with fast and frenzied movements, his breathing frantic as he gave her pleasure upon pleasure. She met every one of his thrusts with one of her own. The hunger inside of her built until he pushed her to the very top of her ascent. Then his mouth covered hers in a blistering kiss, and she toppled from heaven, savoring every blissful moment of her fall.

With a groan that sounded as if it also carried a curse, he left her. Her climax slowly dissipated and when she opened her eyes, he was kneeling beside the chaise, his head bowed.

She reached out and touched his arm. "Are you all right?"

His gaze found hers and he nodded mutely before standing up and going to a small dresser. He turned from her, and from his movements seemed to be tidying himself.

When he came back to her, his breeches were fastened. His eyes were dark and held a tumult of emotion. He didn't look pleased or satisfied, and Lydia inwardly cringed. She sat up quickly and readjusted her skirts to cover herself.

"It doesn't usually end so abruptly." His tone was flat and she couldn't tell what he might be feeling, though he looked . . . penitent. "I withdrew to prevent a child."

Oh. "Very thoughtful of you, thank you." She wondered if he'd even enjoyed it.

"I don't mean to be a brute, particularly after sharing such a heavenly occasion," her heart warmed at his words, "but you really are running out of time."

She nodded and quickly refastened her dress, then stood. With broad strokes of her palms, she tried to smooth the creases in her skirt. Then she went to a wide mirror positioned on the wall opposite the chaise to tidy her hair. As she tucked a few errant strands back into place, she caught Jason's reflection near the chaise. She spun about, her eyes wide. "Do people use this to watch too?"

His gaze was dark, wolfish and utterly personified the scoundrel he was supposed to be. She knew in that instant that he'd not only watched their coupling—he'd enjoyed every single moment.

A sharp rap on the door terminated all thought and kindled sharp beads of apprehension. She froze in place, petrified that her ruin was at hand.

Jason went to the door and opened it just a crack. He spoke in low tones and then turned back to Lydia. "It's time for you to go."

Relief, though subtle and incomplete, coaxed her into motion. "Just a moment." She hurried back to the bed and plucked her gloves from the purple coverlet, quickly donning them as she made her way to the door.

He ushered her from the room and as they neared the stairs, she saw his butler descending the last few steps. Presumably he'd been the one at the door.

By the time they reached the foyer, North met them with her bonnet in his hand. His attitude and expression were deferential as he delivered her hat into her care. If he was aware of what had transpired upstairs—and surely he must be—he didn't show it.

"Thank you." She set the bonnet on her head and tied the ribbons beneath her chin with quaking fingers.

"You look lovely," Jason murmured close to her ear.

She nodded imperceptibly and then gave the butler a broad smile. "And thank you also for taking care of the arrangements for the party. I'll send a list of decorations to procure."

"Certainly, my lady. I await your direction. You'll be pleased to hear the positive responses are coming back by the dozens."

"Of course they are. This is to be the party of the Little Season. No one will want to miss it. In fact, we should make sure people don't try to sneak in."

"I think we can be prepared for such an occurrence, my lady." If his tone was a bit ironic, Lydia didn't blame him. Of course—they managed people trying to sneak in all the time.

Mrs. Lloyd-Jones's maid entered the foyer. North opened the front door, and with a final, uncertain glance at Jason, Lydia left Lockwood House with the maid trailing behind her.

When she and the maid were settled in the coach, Lydia forced herself to draw even breaths to calm the frantic beating of her heart. What had just happened?

She'd behaved like a complete wanton. With Jason Lockwood!

She was beyond ruined, or would be if anyone knew. But no one did. And she had to hope they never would. She glanced at the maid seated across from her. If she was aware that anything untoward had occurred, she didn't reflect it either. However, as with North, Lydia had to assume the worst.

"How was your tea?" Lydia asked, grateful that she didn't sound as if she'd just surrendered her virtue to London's blackest scoundrel. But then, really, what did that sound like?

Heavenly.

That she couldn't even summon the tiniest twinge of remorse should have been alarming, but it was instead comforting. She couldn't feel regretful. She *wouldn't.* Not when a life of uncertainty stretched before her. Not when she could treasure and relive this memory for the rest of her days.

"It was lovely, my lady," the maid answered. "The cook gave me some of the cakes for the party. They were delicious." She smiled beatifically, and Lydia wondered if it was possible that she didn't know what had transpired. Lydia would likely never know for certain and would simply have to pray for the best.

And try very, very hard to make sure nothing like this happened again.

THE DOOR CLOSED behind Lydia. North turned to face Jason. "Was it a productive visit, my lord?"

As usual, North was unreadable. He had to be aware of their activities in the fantasy room. Though, he behaved as if he didn't.

"Yes. I do believe Lady Lydia got what she came for." Oh, that sounded quite sinful. God, he really was a scoundrel if he couldn't even summon a sliver of regret. And he couldn't. She'd met him more than halfway, and he'd long ago made a conscious decision to ignore Society's rules.

North clasped his hands behind his back. "It seems, however, that she should have had enough time to make her list of decorations while she was here. I could've started on those arrangements right away."

Jason frowned at his butler. It seemed he wasn't going to simply ignore what had transpired. "Why don't you just say what you want to say?"

"Very well. Do you think it wise that you took Lady Lydia to the prop room?"

He gave North a thoroughly sardonic stare. "Clearly you don't. Though, I daresay it's none of your business."

North's lips pursed very briefly, but it was enough for Jason to register that he was offended—or at least pretending to be. On exceptionally rare occasions, North could be a bit dramatic like his twin. "Just so, my lord." He continued to look at Jason as if he wanted to say more.

"Well, what else?" Jason said, surrendering.

"You'll forgive me for being bold."

Jason grimaced, fearing what would come next. "I'll consider it."

North's nod was stiff and exceedingly deferential. "Is there any reason you couldn't court Lady Lydia? She might make you a lovely wife."

One very perturbing reason. "Margaret Rutherford."

A pained expression flashed very briefly over North's features. "There's no way you could overlook their relation?"

Margaret's vengeful streak was endless, and to go with it, she had patience. It was a ruthless combination, and Jason would spend his life looking over his shoulder, waiting for the viper to strike. Despite that, he recognized that he ought to offer for Lydia. He wasn't so far gone that he didn't recognize that. But he couldn't. Just as he couldn't bring himself to regret their time together, he couldn't consign himself to marriage, especially to Margaret's niece.

"Not another word, or I may have to rethink whether I want to tolerate your insubordination." It was an empty threat, and North knew it.

North's eyebrow climbed very high before he nodded deferentially.

"What the hell?" Scot called as he entered the foyer from the back corridor. "I go to the pub for a pint and I come back to his lordship reminding you of your place?" He chuckled gleefully, utterly unaware of any tension, but maybe that was because the only tension was in Jason's mind. *Christ, what had he just done?*

"I wasn't taking your brother to task," Jason told Scot. "He's trying to be . . . helpful."

Scot looked between them, his gaze settling on Jason. He opened his mouth, snapped it shut as if he'd decided silence was the better part of valor in this instance, and then dipped his head. When he looked up once more, there was a mischievous sparkle in his eye. "I'll wager I'm more helpful than he is. Would you care to hear what I learned down the pub this afternoon?"

Jason crossed his arms, grateful for a subject to occupy his mind other than the colossal mess he'd just made with Lydia. "Please."

"Ran into a former footman of Lady Aldridge's. He left his post a fortnight or so ago. Said he couldn't stand to work for the underbutler—he'd been Lord Aldridge's valet and they gave him the position after his lordship passed."

"He just offered this information?" Jason asked.

Scot shrugged. "Eh, you know how I am. We got to talking over an ale, and pretty soon he was spilling his life story."

Yes, Jason knew how that happened. Scot made everyone as comfortable as if they'd known him all their lives. And this footman was no exception, evidently. "What else did he tell you?"

"He said the underbutler was haughty and inserted himself into every part of the household. He was very involved with caring for Lady Aldridge, which the footman found odd. He personally sent the orders for her laudanum and made sure her maid gave it to her regularly."

Was the underbutler perhaps working with Ethan's man, Oak? Jason wondered whether Bow Street was aware of this information regarding Aldridge's former valet. He ought to share it, particularly since he'd told Teague he would. However, Jason was reluctant to add fuel to the fire building around Ethan.

Compassion for his half brother? Seducing innocents? What in the bloody hell was *wrong* with him?

"My lord?" North asked, breaking into Jason's thoughts. "Will you be informing Bow Street?"

"I don't know." With a frustrated scowl, he turned and marched toward his office, expecting North and Scot to follow, which they did.

Once inside, he poured a glass of whisky and dropped into his chair behind the desk. When he'd finished taking a sip, Scot was seated in another chair while North continued to stand, as was his wont.

"If I tell Bow Street, this only adds to what they

already have against Ethan."

"The list?" North asked.

Jason had told them both about the paper he'd found after he'd returned home from the Bevelstoke yesterday.

Scot settled back in his chair and crossed his legs at the ankles. "Sounds like you don't want Jagger to be guilty."

Jason didn't know what he wanted, but he kept hearing his half brother asking him to trust him. He had a sudden thought. North was quite familiar with the city, Mayfair in particular, as he'd come south from the lowlands of Scotland to find work in a grand London house. "North, your memory for details is remarkable. Do you by chance recall whether the Chaunceys live at number nineteen Curzon Street?"

North considered a moment and then firmly answered, "They do not, my lord."

"That was the address on the list I found at Ethan's."

"Perhaps there was another address on Curzon Street?" North asked.

Jason searched his brain—he'd been quite particular about memorizing the list. "No, the only address on Curzon Street was number nineteen." He looked up at North. "What number was the South Audley Street robbery?"

Once again, North provided the necessary detail. "The newspaper said it was number sixty-three."

Jason's felt a triumphant surge. "That wasn't the address on the paper. I don't know what his list was for, but it doesn't seem to be related to the robberies."

That still didn't explain Ethan's manservant's potential role in Lady Aldridge's death. Jason hoped the laudanum deliveries were simply what they seemed: a retainer delivering medicine. Though, the fact that it wasn't *her* retainer didn't instill confidence. And what did the underbutler's behavior have to do with the matter—if anything? He ought to let Bow Street sort things out—they'd presumably come to the same conclusion regarding the list that Jason had and had perhaps already stopped their investigation of Ethan. However, Jason somehow doubted his half brother would get off so easily.

Scot leaned forward and leaned his elbow on Jason's desk. Then he set his chin in his palm. "Both Curzon and South Audley Streets being on the list seems rather coincidental."

Jason didn't like Scot's train of thought, because he didn't believe in coincidence.

"Well," Scot said thoughtfully, "what if the list *is* to do with the robberies and the addresses on it are some sort of code?"

North frowned at his brother. "That's a bit fanciful, even for you."

"No, I don't think it is. My criminal history is thankfully brief," he shot North an appreciative glance, "but I remember getting directions in code once."

So, the list might be incriminating after all. Damn. It was time to talk to Ethan—and time for him to be forthcoming.

"Why don't we let Bow Street do their job?" North suggested.

Scot gave a little shrug and leaned back in his chair. He regarded Jason with a knowing smile. "How did you and Lady Lydia fare with party planning this afternoon?"

Damn, and he was just putting her from his mind. "Fine."

Scot arched a brow, looking more like his twin than he would've liked to know. As he'd done earlier, he opened his mouth and snapped it closed. He dropped his chin to his chest and remained quiet.

Jason seized his silence to redirect the conversation. "Are we set on how to protect Lockwood House's more . . . interesting aspects?" He'd told them both about Margaret's unknown plan to try to ruin the party.

North inclined his head. "The doors to the prop room will be locked, and two footmen will be stationed outside. Additional footmen will stand guard at the top of the stairs and at the top of the servants' staircase."

Jason's "vice-free" party, as Lydia had called it, was going to require nearly as much security as his vice parties. "Excellent."

Scot sat up and rubbed his hands together. "Any chance we can cook something up that would satisfy Lady Margaret's curiosity? Mayhap we can launch an offensive instead of waiting for her to make her move."

Jason was shocked to discover he didn't want to stoop to her despicable level. "The additional security will be enough."

Scot exhaled his disappointment.

North coughed. "Might I make a suggestion, my lord?"

Both Jason and Scot turned their heads to look at him.

"I could have Sarah follow Lady Margaret at the party—at a discreet distance, of course. She could ensure nothing unfortunate occurs by Lady Margaret's design."

Another brilliant idea from his ever-reliable butler. Jason gave him a look that said he forgave him for his earlier cheek, but really there was nothing to forgive. North was merely playing the part of Jason's conscience—to an annoyingly excellent degree. "A sound notion, North."

Scot rolled his eyes as he threw his head back against the chair and looked up at the ceiling. "Pray, don't inflate his ego any more than you already do."

"Your jealousy is unattractive, brother." North elevated his chin and left the office.

Scot leapt to his feet and sent Jason a faux glare. "Thank you. He'll be insufferable at dinner."

Jason shook his head as Scot followed his brother's departure. He'd long envied their brotherly relationship, and it was, he acknowledged, why he liked them so much, why he considered them as close as his own family, and why he tolerated—no, *encouraged*—their familiarity.

But they weren't family, and Jason's was woefully small. Only his mother, an odd cousin or two . . . and Ethan. And just like that, he opened himself, if only a little bit, to the idea of having a brother.

Chapter Seventeen

LYDIA TRUDGED UP the stairs toward her bedroom. Maybe she needed a nap. The brisk walk she'd just taken hadn't helped to improve her mood, but she suspected nothing could until she heard from Jason.

Three days had passed since their tryst, and she hadn't received a bit of communication from him. She was frightfully worried that he utterly regretted their encounter and she had settled into a state of despondence because of it. She didn't expect him to profess his undying love—she wasn't even sure she wanted that—but his cold disregard was more painful than she could've imagined.

"Lydia!" Aunt Margaret's voice halted Lydia as she was passing the open door of the upstairs sitting room. "Come in here!"

Feeling as if her feet were encased in bricks, Lydia turned. She wasn't in the mood to suffer Aunt Margaret, but she was unfortunately at the woman's mercy. "Yes, Aunt?"

Margaret didn't look up from the stack of missives in her lap. "Come here. There are letters for you."

Letters! Maybe one was from Jason. The bricks evaporated from her feet and her lungs swelled up as excitement jolted her into the sitting room. She eagerly went to Aunt Margaret, who thrust a piece of paper at her, again without looking up.

The parchment was flat and had clearly been opened. Lydia suppressed her outrage. "Did you read this?"

Finally, Aunt Margaret raised her gaze, though she looked anything but remorseful. Indeed, she looked harassed. "It's from your father."

Smothering a scowl, Lydia went to sit in a chair and perused the brief letter. Two sentences in, her stomach dropped to her feet, and she felt as if she'd run up three flights of stairs.

He wasn't going to fund another Season.

After six years, he'd decided it was time for her to come back to Northumberland. Mr. Jarvis's wife had died last winter and he was looking for a replacement. A *replacement?* Could he not have used a . . . *kinder* word?

"It appears you're out of time."

Lydia looked up and couldn't decide if Aunt Margaret's expression was smug or unsympathetic. Both, she supposed. And Lydia couldn't stifle her ire any longer. "You read my letter?"

Aunt Margaret's eyes narrowed, pitching her brows low. "You should know by now that you don't have *any* secrets from me."

The frigid way in which she delivered the statement sent shivers of dread down Lydia's spine. What did she know? Had she somehow learned of Lydia's activities the other day? Sweat beaded the back of her neck, and her extremities went cold.

Aunt Margaret leaned over the oval table separating her from Lydia and tossed two more pieces of parchment in her lap. "Your other letter. Or should I say 'letters.'"

Lydia glanced down and recognized Audrey's hand. *Oh, no.* Aunt Margaret had opened Audrey's letter, too. And since there was a second piece of paper, Lydia determined that Jason's latest missive had been enclosed. What had he written? Nausea tossed Lydia's belly until she truly thought she might be sick.

Slowly, Lydia shuffled the papers to bring Jason's to the top. Only, it hadn't been written by Jason; it had been penned by North and contained a brief update about invitation responses and flowers. Lydia relaxed slightly, but the letter was still damning. Now Aunt Margaret knew she'd continued to help with Jason's party.

Working past the anxiety balled in her throat, Lydia asked, "What are you going to do?"

"The question is, what are *you* going to do?" Aunt Margaret said softly. "You have two very distinct choices: Help me ruin Lockwood's party or take the first mail coach to Northumberland."

Lydia clutched the stack of papers in her trembling hands. "My father didn't ask me to return immediately." He'd said he'd come to collect Lydia in a month's time.

"Lydia, you reside here by my good graces. Yes, your father gives me a stipend on your behalf, but it has always been my discretion to send you home at any time. I am quite content to decide that time is now, though I admit I will be disappointed. We had a very good alliance, and I simply don't understand your rebellion." She actually sounded let down, as if Lydia had once been a source of great pride and had now failed her. But then, that's probably how she saw things in her twisted way.

Lydia straightened her shoulders. She was proud of the way she'd changed, even if Aunt Margaret wasn't. "I don't enjoy ruining people's evenings or worse, their lives. When I was popular last spring after the wagering incident, people began to genuinely like me." Until Aunt Margaret had drawn her into her web of gossip once more.

"You're still popular," Aunt Margaret said dismissively.

"More like feared."

Aunt Margaret stared at Lydia as if she were a lunatic. "It's better than being nothing, like your pathetic follower, Miss Cheswick."

Lydia inhaled sharply. "Audrey isn't pathetic. She's a true friend. I'd rather have one of her than a legion of people cowering at my feet."

Aunt Margaret smirked. "Lucky for you, then, that you have both."

Lydia's endurance snapped. "Is it too much to want love? A husband? A family of my own?"

"In a word, yes. You can have the latter two—if you really want them—but love is for fools. When will you realize the world is ruthless? If you don't guard yourself, including your heart, you'll be the one who's ruined. You're so terribly close . . . " She let the innuendo hang in the air.

Fear froze Lydia's veins to ice. What else did Aunt Margaret know?

Lydia scrutinized her aunt's currently placid features for any indication that she knew of Lydia's indiscretion, but there was nothing. Perhaps she was only referring to Lydia assisting Jason. "You're angry with me for helping Lord Lockwood."

"Certainly," she answered in a matter-of-fact tone. "You know I can't tolerate him. Your betrayal is a slap in my face. I won't have it. You'll help me ruin his party on Friday, or I'll send you packing immediately. Do you understand?"

Quite clearly, but how could Lydia possibly promise to ruin Jason? Even if he wished they'd never met, she was long past the point of being able to consider hurting him.

Aunt Margaret watched her shrewdly. "I can see that you're weighing your decision carefully. Let me make it easy for you. Help me ruin his party, and I'll let you stay until you marry. *I'll* fund your expenses and convince your father to let you stay. If you refuse, you'll be on your way to Northumberland by this time tomorrow."

A devil's bargain—and one she couldn't accept. However, if she didn't, Jason would be ruined. Unless she was at the party to hopefully stop whatever her aunt planned, which meant she couldn't leave for Northumberland until after.

She'd have to agree to help Aunt Margaret—at least ostensibly.

Still, once Aunt Margaret witnessed Lydia working against her at the party, Lydia would find herself traveling north come Saturday. But it would be worth it to help Jason. He deserved to find happiness—even if it wasn't with her.

"Fine. I'll help you." They were difficult words to utter, and they sounded that way: dark and scratchy as if saying them were the equivalent of carrying a load of stone across London.

"Good girl." Aunt Margaret flashed a terrible smile. "I'm not asking you to do anything you haven't done before."

How Lydia wished she could refute that, say she'd

never sunk to such depths, but it wasn't true. She *had*. Mortification sliced through her.

Aunt Margaret lowered her tone as if she were imparting a secret—a dramatic tool she enjoyed. "Do remember that no matter where you are—London or the wilds of Northumberland—I have the power to ensure you're never accepted."

Lydia's throat constricted. How could she be so cruel? What had happened to make her such an awful person?

"Now," Aunt Margaret said sitting straighter and adopting a business-filled tone, "I saw from the letter that Lockwood is expecting nearly one hundred and fifty guests on Friday." Her eyes glowed with excitement. "So many will witness his humiliation."

Lydia resisted the urge to scream. She could help Jason best if she knew what Aunt Margaret was scheming. "What do you plan to do?"

Aunt Margaret shook her head, her lips curving into an imperious smile. "Oh, no. I don't trust you enough to actually share the details with you beforehand. But you'll know it when it happens, and I'll expect you to spread the information like a wildfire in midsummer."

"Yes, Aunt Margaret." Lydia didn't bother trying to sound enthused. What was the point when Aunt Margaret was well aware she was consenting against her will?

Aunt Margaret scooted forward on the settee and pursed her lips in a thoroughly patronizing manner. "I know you think I'm harsh, but I only want what's best for you. I want to protect you from the vultures of the ton."

Lydia wanted to argue that *they* were the vultures.

Aunt Margaret's eyes narrowed, but her smile remained. "And yes, the surest way to guard yourself is to be one."

JASON MOVED THROUGH the Lamb and Flag Tavern toward the Bucket of Blood. He didn't know whether Ethan would be here, but hoped so, particularly since he'd sent a note after failing to run him to ground at the Bevelstoke, despite multiple visits.

Not that Ethan had responded. No, Jason's sole correspondence that day had been a letter from Miss Cheswick stating she could no longer act as intermediary between him and Lydia. She hadn't indicated why, which concerned Jason, but he'd have to deal with that problem tomorrow. Tonight, he needed answers from his half brother.

"Lockwood."

The deep sound of his name drew Jason's attention to a corner of the Lamb and Flag's common room, where Ethan was seated.

Jason weaved past a few tables and took a chair to his left. "I wasn't sure you would come."

Ethan's hand was casually wrapped around a glass of whisky atop the table. "I wasn't sure I would either, but it seems safe enough for now."

He couldn't expect that cryptic comment to go without notice? Jason reached for the bottle of whisky and filled the sole empty tumbler, the rim of which was chipped. "You're concerned about your safety?"

Ethan held up his whisky. "A toast?"

Jason stared at him a moment, wondering if he could

actually share something so . . . civilized with this man. Maybe it would help loosen Ethan's tongue. Jason raised his glass. "To sharing a drink."

"I'll drink to that." Ethan finished his whisky and poured another. "I've been avoiding a certain Bow Street Runner."

That explained why Jason hadn't found Ethan at the Bevelstoke. "Why?"

Ethan shrugged. He didn't appear particularly concerned, though his gaze made a steady and continuous perusal of the premises. "I'm just not in the mood to speak with him."

How could Ethan be so careless when he was being investigated? Especially when evidence was starting to mount against him—if Carlyle was to be believed. But maybe Ethan didn't know. "I know why he wants to find you."

"Oh?" Ethan asked with an air of nonchalance. "I don't suppose it has something to do with the list that went missing from my bedchamber at the Bevelstoke?"

Jason swallowed a mouthful of whisky before responding. Of course Ethan had discovered its disappearance, but did he suspect Jason or Carlyle of taking it? Jason didn't plan to lie about being there. "It does."

"Who gave it to Bow Street?" Ethan's eyes and voice hardened. "Please tell me it wasn't you."

"No. It was Carlyle."

Ethan's lip twisted with disappointment. "I figured. I assumed you hadn't gained expert lock-picking skills. But you went with him?"

Jason shifted uncomfortably. He hadn't felt right about going into his rooms, but Ethan hadn't left him much choice. "How else was I supposed to learn your plans? It's not as if you were being forthcoming." Ethan's eyes narrowed slightly and Jason added, "For what it's worth, I hadn't planned on showing him the list. He caught me with it just after I'd found it."

Ethan appeared nonplussed. "Thank you."

Jason shifted in his chair and took another swig of whisky. He wasn't sure he was ready for gratitude. "Don't thank me yet. I'd planned to demand you reveal what the hell you're doing—something I'm still going to demand."

"Ah." Ethan inclined his head. "You want to know why I had a list of addresses—some of them on streets where robberies have occurred as of late."

Thank God Ethan wasn't stupid. Jason could suffer a lot of things from his half brother, but didn't think he could tolerate foolishness. "Yes."

"I'm afraid that falls under the category of Things I Can't Tell You."

Jason slammed his fist on the table and leaned toward Ethan. "Horseshit! I'm sick of this game. Either you want to change or you don't. You can't expect me to trust you if you don't demonstrate a little trust yourself."

Ethan's eyes glittered coldly in the dim light of the common room. "It's nothing personal, brother. I don't trust anybody." The words were uttered with an edge of steel, but underneath there was an inflection of bitterness and regret.

That sounded . . . lonely. "No one at all?"

"And just who would I trust?" Ethan set his glass down. "My mother is dead. Our father is dead. You've made no secret about the fact that you wish I were dead. Or at least you did until very recently."

Jason didn't like the uneasiness creeping up his spine. "What about your mother's protector? I thought he'd taken you under his wing."

Ethan's laugh was dark and hollow. "He was a corrupt magistrate, so yes, I guess you could say he tutored me well. But he was all I had until he was hanged. There is no one I would trust."

"Not even me?"

"Not even you." Ethan swept up his glass and took a drink.

Jason gritted his teeth. How could they possibly move forward if Ethan held him in such disregard? Maybe they couldn't. But Jason would try—just this once. He flattened his palm against the pocked tabletop and took a deep breath. "If you told me, perhaps I could help you."

Ethan narrowed one eye in a rather skeptical manner. "You want to help me avoid Bow Street?"

That wasn't the underlying issue, and Ethan knew it. "I want to help you be safe. Not just for now, for good."

Christ, when the bloody hell had that become something Jason would ever want to do? A fortnight ago, he would've dragged Ethan to Bow Street, or brought Teague along to this meeting. But for whatever reason, he wasn't ready to consign his half brother to gaol—or worse.

His mouth slightly agape, Ethan leaned back in his chair. For a moment, he settled his gaze on Jason then he went back to scanning the common room. "I'm not sure that's possible." For the briefest moment, Jason detected a flash of something in his eyes—resignation, maybe?

"I won't know unless you tell me. Christ, Ethan, I'm offering you more than I ever thought I would." Jason's patience thinned. "And it's a singular offer. If you shut me out again now, we're finished and Bow Street can bloody well hang you." Though he said so, Jason wasn't sure he could let it happen.

Ethan leaned forward abruptly and slapped his palms on the table. "You're a persistent jackass."

Persistent—like Lydia. Perhaps she was rubbing off on him. He didn't mind. "And you're as slippery as Blackfriars Bridge in December."

Ethan grinned as he turned his hands up and swept his knuckles across the table, holding his arms wide. "I don't know any other way." He sobered as he wrapped his fingers back around his whisky glass. "I have a plan. I can't share the details because I don't want to endanger you. It's bad enough that we're sitting here having a conversation."

"Who the hell should I be afraid of?"

Ethan lowered his voice. "More quietly, please. You don't need to be afraid. I'm just dodging Bow Street." But would there be others? "I don't want them thinking you're in league with me."

Jason didn't like the sound of that. "It certainly seems as if you're doing something illegal."

"It doesn't matter what I'm *doing,* it only matters what Bow Street *thinks.* Anyway, I won't tell you the specifics."

"That's the best you can do? 'I have a plan.'" Jason shook his head. "Not good enough."

Ethan glowered at him. "You've a surly streak, don't you? I have a plan that will show I am not responsible for these thefts."

Jason ignored his taunts, but was vaguely aware their conversation bore many similarities to those between Scot and North. "Does that mean there's someone else?"

"Yes." Ethan dragged out the word as if he were hesitant to say more. Ultimately he did, however. "Someone Bow Street isn't investigating."

Finally, something remotely informative. But still only remotely. "Who? And don't try to tell me you don't know. You're too intelligent not to have already figured it out."

Ethan grinned. "Was that a compliment?"

"You're not answering me."

"See? Surly." Ethan sipped his whisky. "Of course I know, but I'm not telling you. Not yet anyway."

Jason didn't see any point in trying to persuade Ethan to tell him. So he tried something else. "Tell me how I can help with your plan."

Ethan slid him a dubious glance, but then nodded. "Try to keep Bow Street off my back."

Jason couldn't think of how to do that. "What do I tell them?"

"I don't know." He was quiet just a moment before continuing, "Maybe say you spoke to me and I didn't know anything about the list? Perhaps infer it was staged in my apartment." Ethan seemed rather good at coming up with things.

Jason hoped he wasn't being lied to, particularly when he was being asked to lie. "If I find out you're using me for some vile purpose—"

Ethan cut him off. He looked a bit exasperated. His expression reminded Jason of North when Scot annoyed him. "I know, you'll personally cart me to the hangman's noose."

Strangely, Jason felt a burst of amusement. It was like they actually were . . . brothers. "Something like that."

"I should go." Ethan swigged back the rest of his drink and set the empty glass on the table. "Thank you for your concern. For your help. For . . . everything." There was a question in his tone, as if he couldn't quite believe what Jason had offered. But then Jason couldn't quite believe it either.

Jason finished his drink as Ethan scooted back his chair and stood. "Keep me informed," Jason said. "I'll do my best to steer Teague—and Carlyle—but remember that I make a better ally than an enemy."

"I've already determined that." He gave his head an infinitesimal shake. "And I'll be damned if that doesn't shock the hell out of me."

As Jason watched Ethan leave, he muttered, "Me too, brother. Me too."

Chapter Eighteen

THE DAY OF Jason's vice-free party arrived, and as Jason made his way downstairs in his evening attire, he was surprised to feel a burgeoning edge of excitement. It wasn't the same as with his other parties, but he wasn't loathing the upcoming evening. Perhaps that's because he would finally see Lydia again. Did she regret making love with him? Damn, what if she was too embarrassed to come?

He swore under his breath, castigating himself for not communicating with her before now. But how was he supposed to do that when Miss Cheswick had ceased her role as go-between?

North moved to meet him at the bottom of the stairs. "You look splendid, my lord."

Jason had donned full evening wear, including dancing slippers—something he never did for his usual parties, at which he typically wore whatever he damn well pleased. However, tonight was a momentous occasion for several reasons, and he thought he should look the part. "Thank you. I would ask if all is ready, but I know better than to insult your skills. Tell me, though, which do you prefer to execute—a party like this or our usual fare?"

North clasped his hands behind his back and inclined his head. "I must admit your typical parties are easier to coordinate, but perhaps it's because they have become routine."

"Ouch." Jason pretended to flinch. "Don't let

anyone hear you say my vice parties are 'routine.'"

The barest flicker of humor passed over North's features. "Never, my lord. I didn't mean to imply they weren't exciting. Time to position yourself in the drawing room. Guests will be arriving at any moment," North said just as the footman opened the door.

Jason hurried to the drawing room and languished only ten minutes before Lydia swept in on the heels of her aunt. His gaze was immediately riveted to Lydia. She was stunning. Her pale blond hair was swept into an elegant style with curls edging her temples. A pearl necklace with an antique cameo graced the slender column of her throat and led his gaze to the delicious swell of her breasts above the lace trim of her dark coral-colored silk gown.

"Lockwood," the old biddy called out in her nasally grating tone, effectively destroying the desire Lydia had stirred within him. "How sporting of you to invite us into your home after all this time. I haven't been here since . . . well, I'm sure you'll recall."

Jason clenched his hands into fists. *The time you provoked my mother into a fit during which she banished you from Lockwood House.* He forced an indulgent, albeit nasty, smile. "I'm glad you recognize the magnanimity of my invitation."

He abruptly turned his focus to Lydia. She looked beautiful, vibrant, and he knew he had to get her alone. If only to apologize for behaving like an utter cad.

He took her hand and bestowed a kiss on her knuckles. He stroked his thumb along her wrist before reluctantly letting go. "You look lovely this evening, Lady Lydia. I look forward to a dance with you later."

"As shall I," she said softly, her chestnut-colored

eyes searching his face. There was an air of uncertainty about her, as if she was trying to determine his motives. Yes, he definitely needed to speak with her alone.

"Don't count on Lydia to dance with *you*," her aunt nastily interjected. She fixed Jason with a haughty stare. "Come, dear." She ushered Lydia away from him, and Jason caught sight of North's wife, Sarah, trailing after them. She'd watch Margaret's behavior this evening— and keep Jason informed if aught was amiss.

Jason spent the next half hour greeting guests, many of whom hadn't been to Lockwood House in several years—people he would never invite to his other parties. His gaze kept straying to Lydia, who remained with her aunt. Though he couldn't hear their conversations, he could see the disparaging way she looked at Lydia, and the meek way in which Lydia responded to her behavior.

Fury boiled inside of him. He longed to throw Margaret out of Lockwood House and keep Lydia under his protection. His fury dissipated as he realized the implications of that. What was he thinking? Was he ready to make a commitment to someone? Could he possibly trust someone enough to open himself in that way? Could he trust *her*?

He scanned the drawing room looking for Scot and found him stationed near the door to the sitting room. He made his way in Scot's direction and was pleased when the valet met him partway. "My lord?" he asked, adopting a far more formal demeanor this evening. Jason would've been amused if he weren't trying to figure out how to get Lydia alone.

"Bring Lady Lydia to my office," he said so quietly he hoped Scot had heard him.

"Now?" Scot asked, verifying Jason's words had been audible enough.

Jason answered with a quick jerk of his head and then took himself immediately to his office to hopefully improve his disposition with a glass of whisky.

Ten minutes later, the door opened and Lydia stepped inside. He was beside her in an instant, closing the door with alacrity. He took her hand and drew her into the office. Her gaze was guarded.

"You wanted to see me?" she asked, her tone as apprehensive as her eyes.

And he hated that. He wanted to erase the doubt from the lines etched into her forehead. "Of course I wanted to see you," he said.

Her frame relaxed slightly, but her wariness didn't vanish. "I wondered. You've been dreadfully quiet."

"Because Miss Cheswick sent me a note asking me not to correspond with you." But he knew that sounded pathetic. They'd made love a week ago and he hadn't said a word to her since. He was the worst sort of scoundrel.

She gave a single nod. "My aunt learned I was still helping you with the party. She wouldn't allow further correspondence." Her gaze turned questioning. "Would you have written to me?"

He opened his mouth, but realized there was nothing he could say that wouldn't sound awful. She deserved better. "I'm sorry about what happened."

Her shoulders drooped for the barest second before she threw them back and lifted her chin. "I'm not."

Oh, she was a brave and beautiful thing. Why didn't she do that to her aunt and put the old harpy in her place? Because after years of living in her shadow,

Lydia was tired and defeated. He was suddenly and thoroughly sick that he'd allowed her to go back to that monster's house, and contemplated whether he should whisk her away to Gretna Green. Except he didn't want to leave London with Ethan in his current predicament.

He cupped her face in his hands. "You are a rare and wonderful woman, do you know that?"

He felt the warmth in her cheek as she turned her face into his palm. "When you say it, I almost believe it."

"Believe it," he said, determined to show her. "I want to take you away from Margaret."

Her eyes widened. "She's determined to ruin tonight. I feel terrible for encouraging this party. I should probably stay as far away from you as possible."

He hated the agony in her voice. He wanted to see her smile. "That's going to be very difficult when you're my wife. If you want to marry me, that is."

Her lips parted, and she stared at him a long moment. "You really want to marry me?

He rubbed his thumbs along her jawline and tried to coax a smile from her lips. "Yes. Is that so difficult to comprehend?"

"Yes." She shook her head. "I mean no. That is, you can accept me despite my aunt?"

"It's not as if you adore her and I'll be forced to endure the Christmas Season in her company."

Lydia giggled, which released the tension bunching Jason's shoulders. "No, never that."

"So you'll marry me then?" His breath tangled in his throat as he waited for her response.

"Yes." She reached up and wound her arms around

his neck, pulling him down for a kiss.

Her mouth was warm and sweet, her lips parting to invite him inside. His tongue met hers and they danced while her body pressed up into his. Desire flooded his loins, and he worked to keep himself in check. He hadn't planned on making love to her here. But he'd be damned if images of doing just that weren't crowding his mind and feeding his lust.

She suddenly broke the kiss and disappointment threatened to cool his ardor—which was probably a very good thing. However, what she said next had the complete opposite effect. "Is the door locked?"

He forced his brain to overpower his body, at least for a moment. "Lydia, we have to go back to the party."

"We have a little time, don't we? Besides, I'm your fiancée now, even if we haven't announced it yet." Little lines pleated the space between her brows in an adorable fashion. "You'll have to write to my father, and that will take at least a week. Plus the time to receive a response. Which means the banns won't be read for probably a fortnight. Jason, it could be weeks until we're alone together again."

Jason could barely form words. His body had quite taken over his faculties, and he could only seem to think of ways in which to make love to her that wouldn't crease her dress or ruin her hair.

"The door?" she prompted.

Right. Jason went and locked the door.

She was smiling seductively when he turned back. His cock lengthened, and he suddenly knew just how to make this work so she wouldn't look as if she'd been tupped.

"Lydia," he rasped, his voice sounding as if he were speaking his first words after a weeklong sleep, "do you trust me?"

She nodded, her lips still curved like a siren's. "Of course."

"Then turn around."

Her smile slipped into an adorably confused frown. "But I thought we were going to—"

He couldn't help kissing her. Quickly. Deeply. "We are, but I want to preserve your hair and gown. Will you trust me to show you?"

She nodded, and he reminded himself how innocent and inexperienced she was. Perhaps this was too much.

"Lydia, we can wait—"

It was her turn to interrupt him with a smoldering kiss. "I cannot." She slid her hands beneath his coat and ran her palms up his chest and over his shoulders. "You can at least remove this, can't you?"

He shrugged out of the garment and longed for the day when he'd be naked against her.

"You're so beautiful," she breathed as she ran her hands back down his chest. "I wish you could take all of this off."

Nothing she said or did could have stirred him more. He lowered his mouth and took hers in a bruising kiss. He wrapped his arms around her and pulled her up tight to his chest. Her hands cupped the back of his head. She suckled his tongue in brazen fashion—where in the hell had she learned to do that?—and he was lost.

Or he would be if he didn't focus on what he needed to do. They couldn't be caught. Not here. Not tonight.

With supreme effort, he dragged his mouth from

hers and spun her around before he changed his mind and simply tore her clothes away and shagged her senseless in every way possible.

God, he really was a reprobate.

He guided her forward two steps to his desk. With a sweep of his hand, he pushed the items on top to one side. "Put your elbows on the desktop."

She turned to look at him over her shoulder but didn't say anything. Her eyes were dark, the pupils enlarged. Then she put her elbows down and pitched forward. The curve of her arse was perfectly delineated beneath the fall of her gown. With hands trembling from desire, he lifted her skirts, exposing first stocking-clad calves, then bare thighs, and finally her perfectly rounded behind. He ran his hand over the soft flesh and kneaded her. Then he gripped her hip and leaned over her, whispering against her ear, "Spread your legs."

She complied, moving her thighs apart. He trailed his fingers down to the cleft between her legs and found her moist heat. He slid his fingers along her folds, pleasuring her with slow, steady strokes. Her hips moved in time with his touch. She was exquisite. He eased a finger inside of her. Welcomed by her moisture and the movement of her body, he stroked once, twice. She widened her stance to give him greater access, and he took it, working her flesh with increasingly rapid thrusts.

She moaned, and he needed no further encouragement.

He unbuttoned his clothing and took his cock in his palm. He imagined her back bare and pale, her muscles flexing. *Next time.* He leaned forward and kissed the back of her neck. "Try to be quiet. I know I'm going to have the devil of a time."

Then he guided himself into her heat. She moved her thighs apart even more and pressed back, pulling him into her more quickly than he would've gone. But it was such bliss. She was so much more than he ever expected. Far more than he deserved.

He situated her skirts on her lower back and gripped her hips. Slowly, he moved inside of her. She was so hot and wet, but with just the right amount of friction to tease his cock. It was a very good thing they didn't have much time, because he didn't want to make this last. He wanted her to feel like he did—overwhelmed with need, desperate for release. He wanted to own her.

He increased his speed, thrusting in and out of her with sure and steady strokes. Her hips moved with him and her breaths came in hard little pants that only spurred his lust.

"Faster," she urged.

He had to stop himself from winding his hand in her hair. Instead, he cupped the back of her neck and drove into her with sharp, rapid strokes. He leaned over her, and put his mouth against her ear. "Is this fast enough?"

Her hands were fisted on the desktop, her ivory gloves pulled taut over her knuckles. "Yes." She gasped, and he felt her muscles contract around his cock.

He suckled her ear and nibbled the lobe. He felt her shudder beneath him.

"Yes, come with me, Lydia." He thrust into her and kissed her ear, her neck, his tongue licking her flesh.

She made a strangled sound and cast her head back,

elongating her neck. He wanted to suck her, mark her with his lips and tongue, but he didn't. There'd be time for that. A lifetime.

His orgasm crashed over him, and he just managed to pull out before he spilled himself inside of her. He realized it didn't matter, but until they were wed, he would take nothing for granted.

Then, because no moment had a right to be as perfect as this one, a rap sounded on the door.

She jerked upright, her skirts thankfully surrendering to gravity and shielding her lower half once more. She turned wide eyes to his.

He held his finger to his lips and gestured for her to move toward the fireplace so she was out of sight from the doorway—provided he was able to keep the door from opening more than a sliver.

Quickly tidying himself with a kerchief from his desk, he buttoned himself back up and made his way to the door. He was relieved to open it a crack and see only North on the other side.

Except North looked far more distressed than Lydia just had. And since North never looked anything beyond mildly amused or irritated or any other emotion, Jason beckoned him to come in. "What is it?"

North caught sight of Lydia, and his nostrils flared before his gaze settled on Jason. "We have uninvited guests."

Jason had wondered if people would try to come without an invitation, but judging from his valet's demeanor, he deduced it was more serious than that. "Who?"

"Perhaps you should just come and see for yourself." North looked at Lydia. "Things are, ah, focused on the drawing room at present, so if you wait a moment and then make your way to the gaming room, you shouldn't draw any notice."

Lydia's cheeks flushed, but she nodded.

Jason hated that their delightful tryst had to end this way. He sent her an encouraging glance and then followed North from his office. Upon entering the drawing room, he froze. They'd thought they'd prepared for whatever Margaret had planned, but he never saw this coming.

Standing in the center of the room was Cora Stroud. And she was decadently, shockingly, unremorsefully, nude.

Chapter Nineteen

JASON STARED AT Cora. Her eyes widened as she realized, likely from Jason's dark expression, that she wasn't supposed to be there. She'd worn a green banyan to cover her body, but it was pooled at her feet. Jason swept the silk from the floor and wrapped it around her. "I'm sorry," he murmured, hating that she'd been degraded in this fashion. Though a Cyprian typically delighted in showing her body, Jason wouldn't allow it for the sake of humiliation.

Margaret Rutherford sauntered toward the table, her eyes glowing with triumph. "We should've realized you couldn't host a staid party. Just look at you. Where did you leave your coat? Upstairs in your notorious room of debauchery?"

Bloody hell. He hadn't put his coat back on after his tryst with Lydia.

He really *couldn't* host a legitimate party.

"This was a mistake," he said quietly, meaning both the presence of Cora and the others—a quick scan of the room revealed at least a half dozen of her demimonde sisters—and the fact that he'd tried to execute this disaster of a party in the first place. "I didn't invite her or any of the others."

Another Society matron standing just behind Margaret echoed the harpy's sentiment, "The mistake was ours in thinking this wouldn't be your typical party." Murmured agreement erupted around the room.

"Lockwood, this is disgraceful!" An elder

gentleman—someone who didn't come to his other parties—shook his head disdainfully. "I never imagined you would provide such lewd entertainment, but apparently you're as off-kilter as your mother." He shook his head again, took his gaping wife by the elbow and escorted her from the room.

Jason expected others to follow, but instead of the departure triggering a mass exodus, everyone continued to stare and whisper. In fact, more people filed in from the adjoining sitting room. Anger simmered through his frame. Despite his best efforts, it looked like Margaret was going to get exactly what she wanted.

"Yes, I'd say he's at least as off-kilter as his mother. And far more scandalous." Margaret glanced around the room at her rapt audience. "At least Lady Lockwood didn't defile her family's name by allowing such lasciviousness in her home."

The sound of his mother's name from that harpy's mouth ignited his fury. He moved in front of Cora and glared fire at the woman who'd made it her life's mission to destroy what was left of his family. "What did you have to do with this? Did you invite them here?"

"Me?" Margaret widened her eyes in a profane display of mock innocence. "Why would I need to? Aren't they your usual guests?"

"We'll go," Cora murmured, turning toward the door.

"No." Jason didn't want her or the others skulking away in shame. The night was ruined anyway. The room fell quiet. "Lady Margaret is correct. You are my typical guests, as are several people in attendance this evening." Jason heard a few people gasp. "But I am not in the business of spreading gossip or doling out humiliation. *Lady* Margaret, I demand you apologize to these women."

Several intakes of breath punctuated the silence, but none more than the loud gasp he heard from the doorway. *Lydia.* She was supposed to be in the gaming room. He hated for her to become involved in this.

"I have nothing to apologize for," Margaret said haughtily. "And I would never stoop to addressing these women, let alone apologize to them for anything."

Mr. Rawlings, a middle-aged gentleman Jason recognized as a sometimes-guest at his vice parties, stepped forward. "Really, Lockwood, you can't expect her to do that."

"I can," Jason spat, "and I do." He didn't give a damn what these people thought of him or his party. He longed to ask Rawlings if he'd spent time with any of the courtesans present. But he wouldn't do what Margaret did, not even to those who would condemn him.

Rawlings stared at him in bewilderment. "But they're . . . beneath us."

"In your mind," Jason said. "However, they are people just like you and me, and they've been lured here to provide some sort of entertainment that requires their humiliation. I won't tolerate that." When Rawlings continued to look harassed, Jason curled his lip. The man enjoyed Lockwood House on any other night and yet he was going to stand here and act as if he were above it all? Fuck him, and everyone else who felt the same. "Besides," Jason drawled in the worst tone he could manage, "I like them better than most of you."

Raising her chin, Cora stood straighter. "Thank you, Jas—my lord."

Margaret's lips spread into a malicious grin. "I think it's now fairly clear why you removed your coat. Perhaps you were waiting for your paramour." The look of victory in her eyes stole the last vestige of Jason's patience.

"There's a very good reason I removed my coat." He glanced at Lydia, who, like most everyone else, was staring at Cora. What he was about to say would accomplish two things: shut Margaret the hell up and show Lydia that Cora wasn't the one he wanted. "I took my coat off to kneel upon it when I proposed to your great-niece just a few moments ago. I'm delighted to say she's agreed to become my wife."

The resulting gasps were louder than the last series— and more drawn out. Apparently wedding Lady Lydia Prewitt was more shocking than inviting courtesans to a Society soirée.

At last, Margaret's mouth gaped and her eyes widened in horror, which gave Jason a spiteful sense of pleasure. Then she directed her attention to Lydia. "What have you done?"

All eyes swiveled to Lydia in the doorway. She'd looked lush and vibrant after they'd made love, but now she was pale, and her shoulders were low, giving her the appearance of someone who wished she could fade into the background.

Uneasiness spread through him. He shouldn't have announced their engagement in such a fashion. Damn, he was so woefully out of practice.

Margaret laughed then, a brassy, grating sound. "I'm

sure my niece was eager to accept your proposal. It's the only way she can avoid returning to Northumberland since her father has decided it's time for her to come home."

Pink swathed Lydia's cheeks, and she glanced at the floor before straightening her spine and pressing her mouth into a firm, daring line. Though she was trying to look courageous, the initial look in her eyes told Jason everything he needed to know: that Margaret spoke the truth.

Defeat crushed the happiness Jason had felt just a short time ago. Had that really been tonight? In that moment he saw only Lydia before him, and felt as if he were hanging in limbo. "Is what she says true? Did you accept my proposal because you didn't want to go home?"

Lydia glanced around. "Can we talk about this later? People are listening."

Anger and hurt propelled him toward her. "I don't give a damn if the Archbishop of Canterbury is here. This is between you and me." He turned back toward the drawing room. "Everyone, *out*. The party is over."

North appeared at his side. "My lord," he said softly, but urgently, "why don't you allow me to escort Miss Stroud and the others out? The party isn't ruined."

The hell it wasn't. Everyone was staring at him with a mixture of disgust, fear, and pity. Tonight's events would appear in every gossip column from here to Edinburgh. He was disgraced. *Again*. But he didn't have to stand there and suffer it. He wanted them all gone. *Now*. "Why isn't anyone moving?" he demanded.

People began to gravitate toward the foyer, North, Scot, and another footman ushering them along. Jason turned back toward Lydia, who'd moved away from the doorway so people could file through it. Her lips were pressed together and the pink had faded from her cheeks leaving her quite pale.

Margaret's nauseating voice sounded beside him. "Marrying my great-niece won't save you." Her mouth lifted in a delighted smirk but then her eyes lit as Ethan moved past the departing guests and stepped into the drawing room. "Look everyone, Mr. Locke has arrived. And just as we've all been cast out." She pretended to pout, then curved her lips into a slick smile. "I daresay Locke would make a better husband than his brother. No tainted blood from the mother, you know."

Ethan hastened to Jason's side. "Let her go," he murmured.

Looking incredibly pleased with herself, Margaret sauntered by them toward Lydia. She took Lydia's arm almost gently. "Come, dear, it's time to go. I know it seems things are a mess right now, but no one will expect you to actually marry Lockwood. This proposal nonsense will be dismissed as the ravings of a madman."

Lydia's eyes were dark with regret.

Ethan tightened his grip. "Let her go too. You can fix this later."

Jason threw his brother's hand off his arm and glared at him. "You can leave with them." With a final searing glance at Lydia, Jason stalked to his office and slammed the door. He went straight to the sideboard, but instead of pouring a drink, he swept the glasses and bottles to the floor.

His gaze landed on his half-cleared desk and he envisioned Lydia bent over it, as she was just a short time ago. Then he shoved everything atop it onto the floor.

The door opened, but Jason assumed it was one of his meddling retainers and didn't turn to see who it was. "Not now."

"Yes, now." The door clicked shut.

Ethan.

How had Jason come to recognize his voice already? He threw him a furious glower. "I told you to leave."

"I'm not very good at following directives." His gaze took in the mess on the floor. "How in the hell are we supposed to have a drink now?"

"We aren't."

"Ah, well, I'm sure one of your men will bring some more. It's not as if everyone couldn't hear that you'd broken what sounded like an entire cabinet of wine." Ethan picked his way over the broken glass and spilled liquor and assumed a position leaning against a bookcase. "Tell me why you threw everyone out."

Jason stared at Ethan. Maybe he'd overestimated the man's intelligence after all. "I should think it would be obvious."

"No. Some courtesans showed up at your first normal party." He shrugged. "Like you said, it was a mistake. You bundle the nude one up and send them all on their way. Everyone has a chuckle and then they eat dinner. Yes, there would be gossip, and yes, it wouldn't be the party you'd hoped for, but really, Jason, what the bloody hell was your intent anyway?"

What *had* been his intent? He'd embarked on this silly foray into Society for the purposes of keeping up with his brother. Only, he didn't need to do that anymore.

Then Lydia had asked him to host this party. She'd

told him it would be good for him—and for her. And since he didn't give a damn about where he fit into Society . . . He'd done it for her.

But he wasn't going to tell Ethan that. If his brother could guard secrets, so could Jason. "It doesn't matter. I meant what I said. I don't care about any of them. The party was a ridiculous idea."

Ethan shook his head. "It wasn't. It's just too bad you had to invite that bitch. But then I suppose you have to put up with her if you're marrying her great-niece."

Jason wasn't sure that was going to happen after what he'd just done. In fact, if he were to place a wager, he'd say the odds were against him. "I doubt it will come to that."

"Marrying her or tolerating the bitch? I hope you don't mind, but I do believe that's how I'm going to refer to your great-aunt-in-law."

Jason wasn't in the mood for Ethan's humor. He wanted to be alone. With a drink. He looked at the shards of glass littering the floor and the whisky pooling around them. That was a problem.

"Jason?" Ethan snapped his fingers. "You're really in a state." He frowned. "Is this how you were after our fight?" he asked softly, his voice filled with remorse.

Jason looked at him then, the mere mention of that day rousing his anger once more. "No, it was much worse, but then you didn't stay to find out. I've learned to manage my rage since then. You ought to be thankful because if I hadn't, you'd resemble that lot." He gestured to the debris.

Ethan slowly nodded. "I suppose shattered glass and ruined whisky are better than broken ribs." He patted his chest.

Jason considered having another go at his brother's nose. "You deserved those broken ribs."

"I did." His voice dipped. "But you didn't deserve what happened to your face. Or your reputation. If I could go back to that day and change it all, I would."

Jason wasn't feeling brotherly or sympathetic. "Why, because then you wouldn't be in your current mess?"

Ethan's eyes narrowed. "There's no need to be a jackass. I can't change what happened seven years ago, but I can help you now."

What a bloody hypocrite. "And I'm just supposed to let you do that when you'll scarcely allow me to do the same?"

Ethan crossed his arms over his chest. "Maybe it's because I owe you more than you owe me. Now, what are you going to do to fix this cocked-up party?"

"Not a damn thing. It's over."

"I mean," he said, raising his infernal eyebrow, "what are you going to do to set things right with Lydia? There was a moment in which everyone present was deciding whether you were a reformed reprobate or a genuine scoundrel—and you announced your engagement to a young woman who clearly gives a shit what Society thinks."

The uneasiness he'd felt earlier in the drawing room after revealing their engagement grew into full-blown apprehension—and regret—as he realized what he'd done. Jason sat on the edge of his desk. "She's not ruined—at least not by that. No one would fault her for not marrying me. In fact, she'll weather the entire debacle just fine if she does what her aunt suggested and says there was no engagement at all, that I'm simply a blathering lunatic." He slammed his fist on the desk, furious with Margaret's meddling. "Dammit, I was trying to show Lydia that I wanted her, not Cora."

Ethan dropped his arms, his expression grim. "I understand, but your timing was atrocious."

Jason stared at the detritus on the floor. He'd lost control again. Maybe not as badly as seven years ago, but his performance in the drawing room wasn't going to change any opinions about him.

Except for one.

He'd devastated the one person who'd wanted to see him succeed, who'd put her faith in him. And that made him feel like a failure more than anything else he'd ever done. What's more, he wasn't sure he'd be able to make it right.

Then, just as he'd feared, just as he'd guarded against all these years, his heart cracked into pieces as jagged and varied as the glass cluttering his floor.

LYDIA WOULD have hid in her bedchamber all of the following day, but Aunt Margaret had demanded her presence at the midday meal. Lydia was already seated when her aunt bustled into the room wearing a pinched expression.

"There you are at last! You're such a coward—you can't bury your face beneath your pillows. You're more popular than ever, which is exactly what you wanted, isn't it?" The question could have been phrased many ways, but Aunt Margaret delivered it with a healthy dose of venom.

Lydia scowled at her, seeing no reason to pretend she felt anything but loathing for the woman who'd been her guardian. "You know I didn't." She'd wanted to be liked and accepted, not pitied as the fiancée of a madman or derided as the fiancée of a blackguard.

Aunt Margaret took her chair at the table, and the footman began to serve their luncheon. "Well, as I said last night, you've certainly decided to shackle yourself to the wrong fellow."

Upon leaving Lockwood House, Aunt Margaret had spent the entire coach ride home raving about her success and Lydia's foolishness. Lydia had done her best to ignore her, which hadn't been too difficult with Jason's outrageous behavior haunting her memory.

Lydia wondered if she could ignore her again today and intended to find out.

However, that didn't stop Aunt Margaret from continuing to rant. "Fortunately you have me to save you from the mess you made. No one expects you to marry Lockwood, especially not now."

Because his actions last night had "proved" he was at least a scoundrel and perhaps a little bit mad. Lydia had spent half the night trying to decide if she ought to marry him or not. She had fallen in love with him, but if he meant to continue his ribald lifestyle after they were wed, she couldn't endure it.

She couldn't make a final decision until after she explained that her father recalling her home was irrelevant to her accepting his marriage proposal. And he had to explain . . . well, quite a lot. She understood why he'd become so angry—Aunt Margaret had done everything in her power to provoke him—but he'd bungled things horribly. What did he expect her to do now? Meekly follow him to the altar with all of London ridiculing her? Maybe he didn't care about his reputation, but she did. A life on the fringe would be no life at all. Even Audrey would have to discontinue their friendship.

"Though you failed to help ruin his party, I'll offer you another chance to remain in London." Aunt Margaret eyed her skeptically. "If you throw Lockwood over, I'll convince your father to let you stay here."

Another devil's bargain. "So if I cry off, you won't care that I don't want to help you gossip any longer?"

Aunt Margaret twisted her lips in a manner that demonstrated more disgust than disappointment. "If it means the complete ruination of that crazy scoundrel, yes."

Then, because Lydia could think of no reason to censor herself, she simply let go of the emotions she'd held inside for so long. "How could you do that to him? His life was ruined seven years ago—and you played no small part in that by continually badgering his mother. You've done the same to him at every opportunity over the past weeks. What did he ever do to you? Not his father, not his mother, *him*. You're carrying on a feud that doesn't need to exist. I can only imagine you're doing it for the simple pleasure of watching others be humiliated." She recalled the conversation she'd had with Jason in the billiards room at Lockwood House about people needing to watch others in pain and decided her aunt was simply. . . sick.

Margaret set her fork beside her plate. "When you've been brought as low as I was, you want to see those responsible share in your suffering. And that includes those they hold most dear. Revenge isn't pretty, Lydia, but it is very, very satisfying." She stood up from the table. "So what will you do, break Lockwood's heart or run away to obscurity?"

Hopefully there was a third choice where she and Jason resolved things and married. How Lydia would love to see Aunt Margaret's face if that happened. In the meantime, she'd put her off. "I don't know."

Aunt Margaret pursed her lips, and as if she could read Lydia's mind, said, "Don't be stupid and think to marry him anyway. Mark my words, he's as mad as his mother. Outbursts like the one he had last night preceded her mental collapse. It's only a matter of time before he follows suit." The relish in her tone was palpable.

Jason had been provoked—by Aunt Margaret. Lydia had to wonder if her aunt had also provoked Lady Lockwood's outbursts. She claimed not to know what had pushed Lady Lockwood over the edge at that dinner party, but Lydia was suddenly certain it had been Aunt Margaret's taunts and innuendos.

Aunt Margaret exhaled and then clucked her tongue. "You likely find me heartless, but really Lydia, having a heart will only cause you sorrow." She turned and departed.

The footman swept up the dishes, and Lydia, her mind overrun with thoughts, meandered from the table to the adjoining drawing room. She went to the windows and looked at the small terrace and garden behind the house.

Lydia stared at the garden until she heard her aunt leave the house. She relaxed slightly knowing that Aunt Margaret had gone, but the ultimatum she'd delivered weighed heavy on Lydia's mind. She turned from the windows as the butler entered.

Tate clasped his hands behind his back. "Lady Lydia,

Lord Wolverton is here to see you."

What on earth was he doing here? And to see her? Lydia turned fully toward the door. "Show him in."

She instinctively smoothed her skirt and curved her lips into a welcoming smile.

The broad-shouldered gentleman strode into the drawing room. He looked around and assessed the space before settling his gaze on Lydia. "Good afternoon, Lady Lydia, I do hope I'm not disturbing you."

"Not at all. However, my aunt is not at home." Lydia couldn't imagine why he was here to see her, particularly when he was of an age with Aunt Margaret. Although, Lydia had never known the two of them to speak, which made his call even more curious.

"That is just as well because I came to see you." He looked around again then said, "Is it too much trouble to ring for tea? Perhaps you've a maid who can bring it in?"

It was an odd request—Tate, the butler, could easily serve them—but perhaps Lord Wolverton did things differently in his household. She smiled at him and went to ring the bell pull. "Our housekeeper can bring up a tray."

Tate reentered, and Lydia instructed him to have Mrs. Erickson deliver tea.

As soon as the butler left, Lord Wolverton gestured for her to sit and then followed suit, depositing his tall frame on a blue patterned settee. "You have a butler and a housekeeper? But perhaps not much else given the size of the house?"

Was he making small talk? Lydia wasn't sure what to make of his questions, but didn't wish to be rude. She situated her skirts around the gilt legs of her chair. "We've three maids, and a trio of footmen. Our housekeeper does the cooking with the assistance of one of the maids."

He nodded. "I see. A good complement then." He smiled benignly. "I do hope you won't find the reason for my visit to be too forward, but after last night's . . . *activities* at Lockwood House, I simply had to pay you a call."

Lydia assumed he'd come to ascertain whether she was actually going to marry Jason or declare him a madman. She didn't know about the former and would never do the latter. Adopting her haughtiest tone, she said, "I'm afraid I'm not interested in discussing what happened last night. Perhaps you should return when my aunt is at home."

He chuckled. "No, no, my dear. That isn't why I came. In fact, I called hoping to find you at home without your aunt. I believe she's probably out recounting last night's debacle to anyone who will listen, no?"

Yes, and unlike Lydia she had *no* problem advertising Jason's "lunacy" to the entire population of England. Lydia suddenly felt very weary and only wished to get to the point of this visit. "Then why have you come?"

"To lend support, which I suspect you're in need of after last night. You surprise me, Lady Lydia. I'd always assumed you were a model of your aunt. I'm quite delighted to see you are not. You are not to blame for anything that occurred at Lockwood's party. The battle between your aunt and Jason Lockwood's family is old and complicated." Wolverton's very gray and very bushy brows dipped low over his eyes. "Perhaps you'll allow me to share with you some things you likely don't know about your aunt. Some things that might put her in a different light."

Lydia stared at him, her curiosity more than piqued. But no one ever dared gossip about Aunt Margaret. "You're not afraid of upsetting my aunt?"

"Not at all. I'm not the least bit afraid of your aunt. I do believe, however, that she is quite afraid of me." His eyes twinkled as if he appreciated that fact. She ought not care that he gloated. Aunt Margaret certainly deserved such treatment. However, Lydia found she didn't have the stomach for it—even at her aunt's expense.

Mrs. Erickson entered with a tea tray and poured out. When she departed, Wolverton picked up his tea and took a long sip. "Has your aunt ever told you about her youth? Her first Season?"

"Yes. She said she was close to becoming engaged to Lord Lockwood, but that he threw her over for the current Lady Lockwood."

"*He* threw *her* over?" Wolverton laughed deeply. "I suppose that's not terribly far from the truth, but it sounds as if she neglected to share a detail or two. He did drop her like a stone—but only after she gave him her virtue." His eyes hardened. "You see, some gentlemen think it acceptable to enjoy a lady's charms and then cast her aside to become another man's problem."

Lydia was glad she hadn't yet picked up her teacup for she surely would have dropped it like Miss Vining had done weeks ago when Jason had appeared at Mrs. Lloyd-Jones's tea. "Lord Lockwood sounds a perfect reprobate." Did people know of this? Had it contributed to Jason's reputation? She was worried then that her face drained of color because she realized that Jason had done the precise same thing to her—though he hadn't cast her aside. Yet.

He wouldn't. But his hurt expression and his outrageous behavior pervaded her mind.

He might. He hadn't rushed over here today to apologize or assure her that the engagement was actually real.

She tried to keep her attention focused on the conversation at hand instead of her wild imaginings.

"Yes, Lockwood was quite the scoundrel." Wolverton shook his head with disdain. "However, you can't blame him entirely. Your aunt was desperate to marry. When Lockwood turned his attentions elsewhere, she came after me."

Lydia tried to follow along. How was it Wolverton knew these intimate details? Unless Lockwood had shared them. "Did Lockwood warn you away from her?"

"No, in that respect he was a gentleman." He sighed with regret. "I'm afraid I learned of your aunt's indiscretions firsthand . . . though I'm not proud of my own actions. I was carried away. I wanted to marry her. Until I realized she hadn't been honest with me."

And now Lydia could see that her aunt hadn't been honest with her either. She'd said that Jason's mother had employed dishonest measures to steal Lockwood, that Harmony Lockwood had spread lies about what her aunt had done to entice him—lies that now seemed to be the truth.

Furthermore, Aunt Margaret had also given herself to Wolverton. Despite all of her aunt's cruelty and machinations, Lydia felt a pang of sorrow for the young woman who'd made foolish choices and likely seen her dreams crushed. She began to see how her aunt had perhaps become corrupted. She'd acted rashly and had paid for her behavior, though she'd amazingly avoided ruin. Perhaps she'd then set out to ensure she was never on the wrong end of scandal.

Lydia internally shook herself and focused on Lord Wolverton who'd gone back to sipping his tea. "I take it your engagement to my aunt wasn't publicized?"

"No, no, it was never that formal. She enticed me, I professed my love, things . . . progressed, and when I discovered she was no longer pure, I told her I couldn't marry her. Please understand, I would never have gone down that path with her if I hadn't fully intended to wed her. And I still would have, if it hadn't been clear that she was using me to provide a name for her unborn child." Lydia couldn't stifle her gasp. Wolverton grimaced. "Perhaps I'm the lesser man for it, but I couldn't commit my life to someone who would do that."

Lydia was shocked by every one of his revelations. "What happened to her child?"

"I assume she lost it. She never left town to whelp." He shrugged. "I'm telling you this so that you can perhaps understand the reasons for your aunt's hatred of Lockwood and his family. I'm sure she sees your fiancé as a copy of his father—just as I mistakenly took you for being like your aunt." He shook his head and his mouth spread in a self-deprecating smile. "I should have known better than to judge you like that."

Lydia was surprised by Wolverton's kindness. She'd also wrongly cast him as a frightening peer who fancied himself above everyone around him. "Why didn't you tell anyone about what my aunt had done?"

Wolverton's face wrinkled into an expression of distaste. "I don't care for gossip, and I saw no reason to ruin her. As it was, certain gentlemen talk amongst themselves, and she was all but ruined anyway. It's a pity, but I'm afraid the situation was of her own making."

Lydia picked up her teacup and took several sips because she didn't want to say that it took at least one other person to create that situation. Indeed, the whole conversation made her uncomfortable, largely because she was guilty of the exact same indiscretion.

Lord Wolverton set his teacup down. "Tell me, Lady Lydia. How do you plan to wield this information?"

Lydia blinked at him. "I don't."

Wolverton drew back in mild surprise, but quickly covered by shaking his head. "Not publicly of course, but from what I could see last night, you might want to strike back at your aunt. It's clear she doesn't hold your fiancé in very high esteem."

No, she didn't, but revealing that Lydia knew of her scandalous past wouldn't change her opinion of Jason. And anyway, it might not matter. Not if there wasn't a marriage. "I think it's best to leave the past where it belongs—in the past."

"You're a far kinder person than she is. To your credit." He tipped his head in her direction. "I noticed the cameo you were wearing last night at Lockwood House. It's an exquisite piece, is it a family heirloom? It looks to be early last century, at least."

Lydia recalled the necklace she'd been wearing, it was one of her favorites. "You've a good eye, it's from around 1700. It belonged to my great-great-grandmother."

"It's very special. Well, I suppose I must go," Lord Wolverton said, getting to his feet. "Will I see you and your aunt Monday evening at Lady Holborn's soirée?"

Lydia saw no reason not to voice her fear. "I'm not sure I want to face anyone after last night."

"You mustn't be embarrassed. Lockwood's the one who came out looking bad, not you. Unless you still plan to wed him. But I'm sure you were well aware of how people would treat you if you married him when you accepted his proposal in the first place." He paused, his gaze calculating. "Did you accept his proposal?"

Here was the moment where she could deny everything and leave Jason to look the crazed fool. But she couldn't do that. "I did."

Wolverton's nose twitched. "I see. Well, it's not too late for you to recover. Think about what you'll do next." His gaze turned earnest. "And don't make a choice you'll regret. Life is far too short, Lady Lydia."

Lydia smiled at him, appreciating his kindness and support. "Thank you, Lord Wolverton. I look forward to seeing you Monday."

He grinned down at her as he walked her to the door. "The pleasure will be all mine."

Chapter Twenty

JASON AMBLED INTO the breakfast room in the middle of the afternoon, his head aching and his stomach rumbling. He stopped short at the sight of Ethan seated at the table devouring a plate of eggs, kippers, and freshly baked bread.

Ethan glanced up and waved his fork. "About time you came down," he said around a mouthful of food.

Jason took in Ethan's clothing and though much of last night was a blur—they'd become blindingly drunk after North had tidied the mess and replenished the liquor in the office—he was fairly certain his half brother was wearing the same costume as the night before. "Did you sleep here last night?"

"You don't remember offering me the use of your 'gold room'?" Ethan smiled as he forked another piece of ham. "You were rather soused."

With a scowl and a grunt, Jason sat at the table and waited for the footman to bring his plate. But as soon as it was placed before him, he wondered if he wanted to eat after all.

"Bring him an ale," Ethan said to the footman.

Jason glanced at Ethan. "Your prescription for the effects of a drunken evening?"

Ethan lifted a tankard and held it up in toast. "It's served me well."

Jason could only imagine, and he had to agree. He'd spent a good amount of time inebriated after Society had ostracized him and when women had turned away in disgust and fear.

"Will you call on Lydia this afternoon?" Ethan asked, setting his ale back on the table.

Jason picked up his fork and moved some food around his plate. "No."

Ethan glared at him. "Why the hell not? Last night you decided to beg her forgiveness. Don't tell me you changed your mind, or I might have to beat the shit out of you."

Due to the amount of whisky he'd imbibed, Jason remembered no such thing. He did need to beg her forgiveness, but he didn't want to go to Margaret's house to do it. "Leave it for now. I'd rather talk about your plan."

Ethan cut a bite of ham and speared it with his fork. "It's really too bad you don't remember last night. I told you all about my plan." His mouth spread into a wicked grin.

"Horseshit." Jason stifled the urge to throw his plate at Ethan's head. The footman delivered Jason's ale, and Jason eagerly took a swig. *Delicious.* And just what he needed, thanks to Ethan. Was this what brotherhood felt like?

Ethan sat back in his chair. "Why won't you go talk to her?"

"I didn't say I wouldn't talk to her, I only said I wasn't going today." He scowled at Ethan. "I also asked you to leave it alone."

Ethan's stare was relentless. "I won't. And from what your loyal servants told me, you shouldn't hesitate."

"What the bloody hell did they tell you?" But Jason could guess. Since when had their lips loosened to such an extent? And to a man Jason had spent most of his life hating?

"Don't be angry with them," Ethan said. "I plied them with whisky too. Damn, your valet can drink."

Yes, Scot had an awe-inspiring tolerance for alcohol. But North? "I'm surprised that worked with my butler. He doesn't typically indulge."

"I had that impression, but I also think he had a rough night. Do you remember him telling us he caught one of your guests upstairs in your—prop room, is it?—with one of the courtesans?"

Hell. So his "legitimate" party really *had* turned into a vice party. "No, and perhaps I would've been better off not knowing at all. "

Ethan half smirked. "When did you become such a coward? You're a blackguard. Embrace it. You endorse debauchery, and even provide it. From what I can tell, you don't give a damn what anyone thinks about that, so screw them all. Live your life and marry Lady Lydia."

As if it were that simple. Did she even want to marry him after last night? "I don't even know if she'll have me. And I won't discuss anything this important with Margaret hovering over our shoulders."

"Then what will you do? You can't just wait around for an opportunity. Your already-scarce invitations will surely wither completely after last night's performance."

Jason massaged his aching temple. Ethan was right. And inviting Lydia here again wouldn't do. She'd already risked her reputation more than once to visit Lockwood House, and last night he'd thrashed it to within an inch of its life. No, he had to go to her, but not at Margaret's. "There has to be somewhere I can see her."

Ethan stood. "As it happens, there is. I'll get you into the Holborn soirée on Monday."

Jason gave up the pretense of eating and shoved his plate away. "How the hell are you aware of the ton's social calendar? Furthermore, how are you so well placed that *you* can get *me* into Holborn House?"

Ethan flashed a grin. "I'm a nosy bastard. And I have ways of getting into places. In this instance, I can probably acquire an invitation via Sevrin—he's rather close with Saxton." Who was Holborn's son.

"Your master plan is for me to attend this party, find myself alone with Lydia, and persuade her to marry me?" Jason doubted the likelihood of each of those separately, but all together they seemed damned near impossible.

Ethan gave a beleaguered sigh. "I know you won't like me saying this, but trust me. Please?"

Jason slouched back in his chair and looked up at Ethan. "Do you know what? I will. For *this*. Which means you better not cock it up."

Ethan clicked his heels together in a ludicrously formal fashion and bowed. "I won't let you down."

It wasn't Ethan who worried him. Jason would be lucky if he wasn't cut by everyone at the party the moment he walked in. Not that he ultimately gave a damn what anyone thought. That sparked an idea, and his chest began to lighten. He might be able to win her over yet. "On second thought, I don't want an invitation. I'd prefer to maintain the element of surprise. Get me into the soirée some other way." He fixed his brother with a mocking stare. "I assume that won't prove difficult for you."

Ethan grinned. "Not at all. See you Monday."

He departed, and a moment later North entered. If he'd overimbibed the night before, it didn't show. His dark hair was tamed and neat as usual, his livery impeccable. Jason scrutinized North's features looking for any sign of weakness—the man was practically an automaton. But there! A faint swath of purple beneath his left eye. Jason smiled, glad to see his butler wasn't completely immune to indulgence.

"I'm glad to see you at last, my lord. I trust you're feeling well."

"Not quite, but I'll get there. I fear I don't remember much of what transpired after the party ended. Ethan says you found someone upstairs with one of the Cyprians. Who was it?"

"Blaylock."

Idiot. "Strike him from the list, and everyone else who stood around the drawing room gawking."

"That will decrease your numbers by about twenty, I'd say." North paused, but clearly wasn't finished. "You don't mean to continue hosting your old style of parties now that you're getting married?"

Of course he couldn't, if he were married. But damn he would miss them. They gave him comfort. Enjoyment. Identity. He knew precisely who he was in that world. Without those parties, who was he?

"My lord?"

Jason realized he hadn't answered North's question. "I'm not ready to write off vice parties yet. I'm not certain I still have a bride." If Lydia turned him down, he was going to immerse himself in a steady stream of the goddamn things.

North inclined his head and then squared his

shoulders. "If I might say so, my lord, it's good to see you and Mr. Jagger together. He seems to genuinely care for you." North seemed surprised to be saying that.

Jason had to begrudgingly admit he'd begun to care about him in return. "I hope whatever plan he's executing will come to fruition soon. Otherwise, our reconciliation will be very short-lived."

North tipped his head to the side. "So you have reconciled then?"

Yes, he supposed they had. Jason nodded, still bemused over *that* turn of events. It seemed miracles really could happen. Perhaps he could hold out hope for a future with Lydia after all.

Come Monday, he'd find out.

AFTER REFUSING TO join Aunt Margaret at church the next day, Lydia kept her afternoon appointment at Audrey's grandfather's townhouse. Would she still be welcome here if she married Society's most infamous bachelor?

She stepped out of the coach and blinked up at the fashionable house in Berkley Square, which Audrey had called home since spending the summer here a year ago. Her grandfather was alone, and they got on very well together. Theirs was an enviable relationship.

Today's visit had been set several days ago—before Jason's party—and was to be Mr. Locke's next dance lesson. Lydia wondered what Mr. Locke thought of what had happened. Had he spoken to Jason? Their interaction the other night seemed different, as if they'd reached some sort of accord, which surprised her.

Aunt Margaret's footman held open the gate, and Lydia walked up the path to the door. The butler, Spool, showed Lydia to their usual sitting room where Audrey was waiting. She immediately stood and met Lydia as she entered.

Audrey's eyes crinkled anxiously as she clasped Lydia's hands. "Lydia, I am so sorry about Lockwood's party. I wish I could have been there to support you." Audrey, her parents, and her grandfather had been invited, but her parents had refused to allow her to attend.

"Thank you. It was an utter disaster, but then that's precisely what Aunt Margaret wanted."

Audrey gaped. "She's responsible?"

"Mostly." Lydia hesitated, though she didn't know why. Audrey had likely already read what had happened, what Jason had done. Furthermore, she was Lydia's dearest friend so of course she could confide in her. Oh, but the entire affair was so . . . humiliating. And the longer she went without hearing from Jason, the angrier that made her. "I'm sure you read the accounts in the paper. About Jason."

Audrey squeezed Lydia's hands and drew her further into the sitting room. "I did. But I'm withholding my judgment until you tell me what actually happened. Did he really remove his coat to propose?"

Despite all that had happened, Lydia couldn't keep from smiling as she recalled the *real* reason he'd removed his coat. But just as quickly the smile faded from her mouth. Recalling their time together was only a painful reminder of what she'd risked and probably lost. Though she might not be with child—and she could only pray that was the case—she was now no better than Aunt Margaret. No, that wasn't precisely true since she had no plans to entrap some unwitting gentleman into marriage. But if she didn't marry Jason, what on earth was she going to do?

Despondently, she withdrew from Audrey's comforting grip to remove her gloves and bonnet and set them on a table.

"Oh dear," Audrey said, touching her mouth briefly in concern, "you don't look at all happy."

Lydia shrugged, feeling helpless. "Should I be? I went from happy fiancée to social pariah in the span of thirty minutes. Which I could endure if I thought Jason supported me. But I don't know where he stands."

"He's likely just trying to sort out how to make amends," Audrey said firmly. "In his defense—forgive me—I understand why he might not call on you at your aunt's house."

Lydia could understand that too, but that didn't mean it was right. "He's left me quite adrift."

Audrey nodded, glancing at the floor. "What will you do?"

"That depends on him, but I don't have an infinite amount of time. My father wants me to come home, and anyway, I'm not exactly marriageable anymore. . . "

"Nonsense!" Audrey's eyes narrowed. "Things are going to work out with Lockwood."

Lydia appreciated Audrey's optimism, but she had to be realistic. "And if they don't?"

"You'll find someone else." Though the tone of Audrey's voice didn't sound as if she believed that— only it couldn't be for the same reasons Lydia *knew* she wouldn't. Because Lydia hadn't told Audrey why she wasn't marriageable.

"I won't find someone else," Lydia said quietly, her gaze locking on the patterned carpet beneath her feet for a moment. "I've ensured no one else will have me. Unless I dupe them."

Audrey's expression wrinkled with confusion and then of a sudden her eyes flared wide. "Oh!" She rushed to put her arm around Lydia's shoulders. "You poor dear. I've made my judgment. At least about Lockwood. He's an utter cad. A scoundrel. The worst sort of reprobate."

Lydia couldn't help but smile at her friend's staunch support.

"I do hope you're not talking about me." Mr. Locke entered the sitting room.

Audrey jumped and spun around. "Goodness, you surprised me!"

He bowed. "My apologies. But I do hope that doesn't make me—what did you say?—'the worst sort of reprobate.'"

"No, I'm afraid I was referring to your half brother." Audrey's eyes darkened with outrage.

He offered a benign smile. "Could I ask you to refrain from completely consigning him to hell? At least until after tomorrow night?"

"Why?" Audrey queried with a suspicious tone before Lydia could ask the same thing. "What's going to happen tomorrow night?"

"I'm afraid I can't say." He turned his attention to Lydia. "You'll be at the Holborn soirée, I hope?"

"I will," she said cautiously, not at all sure she trusted this man or his brother not to make an absolute disaster of that event too.

"Excellent. Are we ready for my dance lesson?" Locke asked, appearing quite satisfied. Did he not realize Lydia's future was hanging by the damaged thread that was Jason's whim? Whatever he planned to do tomorrow night could affect her reputation more deeply than he already had.

Lydia crossed her arms, feeling rather justifiably mutinous. "I think I may change my mind and stay at home."

Locke's face darkened. "No. You can't do that." He took a step forward and then stopped short as if he forgot where he was and who he was with. He took a deep breath. "*Please*. You must go to the party."

She wasn't ready to agree, though her curiosity would surely get the best of her in the end. "I'm quite angry with him."

Locke held up his hands. "And you have every right to be. I took him to task myself."

"You did?" Audrey asked, sounding impressed.

Locke turned toward Audrey and gave her a grin tinged with a hint of wicked. "Of course. What sort of gentleman would I be if I hadn't?" He shot Lydia a pleading look. "Please trust me that he won't do anything to upset you or impugn your reputation."

In lieu of answering, Lydia pursed her lips together. She wasn't sure she trusted either of them, but what more did she have to lose?

Her heart.

She narrowed her eyes at Locke. "I think it's time for your lesson."

"By all means." Locke offered Audrey a courtly bow. "Shall we dance?"

Chapter Twenty-one

JASON SNUCK UP the servant stairs of Holborn House on Ethan's heels. It seemed a criminal background was useful for certain things. Such as stealing into a duke's house.

Anxiety-induced perspiration dampened Jason's palms beneath his gloves. He'd gone over and over what he needed to do, but that didn't mean it was going to be easy. No, he feared it was going to be the hardest thing he'd ever done. But he'd do it. For Lydia.

Ethan led him through a door into a deserted sitting room and then turned to face him. "You wait here and I'll go find her."

Jason hadn't informed Ethan of his plans. "No, this plan requires I find her at the party."

Ethan stared at him as if he were daft. "If you go out there, it'll be a catastrophe. You can't just march into the middle of the party."

Though his plan seemed preposterous, Jason had thought it through and was convinced it was necessary. And if he was very lucky, it would be successful to boot. "Why not? People might ridicule me? Or think I'm crazy? Or say I'm a degenerate? I hate to disappoint you, but they do that already."

Ethan rolled his eyes but released him. "Fine. But don't say I didn't try to stop you."

Jason straightened his coat and strode from the room aware of Ethan on his heels. They followed the sound of people and eventually came upon a massive chamber. It wasn't a ballroom, but it was far larger than a typical drawing room. There was furniture, but it had been arranged around the perimeter so that people could mill about—and perhaps later dance—in the center. It was the perfect location for what Jason had planned.

The moment he stepped into the room, heads turned. He registered no one's identity as he methodically searched for Lydia's cream complexion and dark eyes. She was the only person he cared about, the only one he wanted to see.

Conversation began to die out. The hair on the back of his neck prickled and his anxiety vaulted to new heights, but he ignored everything save his quest to find Lydia.

Ethan touched his arm and inclined his head toward the far wall. Lydia stood with Miss Cheswick and another young woman, a redhead Jason thought might be Lady Saxton, the Duke of Holborn's daughter-in-law. Jason immediately cut toward them.

He didn't think the room could grow quieter, but with each step the silence seemed to increase, as if it were a living, breathing entity that could consume them all. People fell away from his path, creating an ever-widening space in the middle of the room.

Ethan leaned close and muttered, "I hope you know what you're doing," and then moved away from him.

Jason stood utterly alone in the center of a sea of expectant and censorious faces. But the only one he focused on was Lydia's.

"Lady Lydia," he said loudly and clearly. Then he dropped to one knee. The entire room let out a gasp loud enough to make Lydia flinch. At least, he hoped that was why she flinched.

Once it was silent again, he gathered his courage. "I want to apologize for announcing our betrothal the other night. It wasn't well done of me. I earnestly beg your forgiveness."

Murmurs broke out, but Jason couldn't hear what anyone said. Not that he cared. All of his apprehension, all of his concern was directed at Lydia. Her reaction, her opinion, her forgiveness was all that mattered.

He waited for her to speak. To move. To do anything but stand there and stare at him as if he was far crazier than anyone purported him to be. As one moment became two, his palms grew damper and his neck began to outright itch.

"Lydia?" he ventured softly.

She blinked, but otherwise continued to stand as still as a statue. "I appreciate your apology. And I accept it."

"Thank you." He exhaled with relief. But that was only one part of his scheme. The easy part.

Time to put everything out there. He sucked in a breath and forged onward. "I regret what happened the other night. Though I had no part in orchestrating what occurred, I could have handled things better. I'm . . . a hothead." He offered a meek smile, but was discouraged when her features remained guarded. No, that wasn't quite right. She looked as if she were about to be run down by a coach and four.

Still, he had to carry on. "If I'm guilty of anything, it's of being too passionate." More murmurs. "I suppose it's why I hosted vice parties in the first place." Because it was the only way he could get human interaction. But he wouldn't bare his soul about that here. Later, he would more fully explain to her why he'd started them, why he needed them.

"However, with you as my wife," he continued, somewhat surprised at how sure and strong he sounded given what he was about to say, "Lockwood House will no longer be the center of Society's debauchery." He'd chosen his words carefully. If he was going to humiliate himself in this fashion, he'd remind every single hypocrite that they were no better than him.

"Are you saying you'll give up the vice parties?" a deep voice asked from somewhere behind Jason.

He didn't turn, keeping his gaze focused on Lydia, whose returning stare was intent. But he couldn't tell whether she was pleased or not. Damn it, why wasn't she giving him even a bit of encouragement? Clearly he was doing something wrong.

The man's question came back to him. Though it pained him to voice the answer, he did so, praying it would warm just a fraction of Lydia's cool demeanor. "Yes, I'm giving up the vice parties."

The murmurs grew louder as people discussed this shocking development. Jason didn't even try to make out what they said. He only wished Lydia would say something. Anything.

"Looks like your plea is falling on deaf ears, Lockwood." *That* voice he recognized.

Margaret. Somewhere to his left.

"A pretty speech, to be sure, but she's too shrewd to accept him," someone said just loudly enough that Jason could hear. "Marriage to him would scarcely be better than returning to . . . Where does her father live?"

"Anything would be better than shackling herself to a lunatic like him. Just look at him there. Down on his knee. He's making an utter cake of himself."

Margaret moved into his line of sight then, taking a position near to Lydia, but not directly beside her since Miss Cheswick and Lady Saxton hadn't moved.

Miss Cheswick leaned down and said something close to Lydia's ear. How Jason wished he could hear what she said, but he couldn't. Lydia nodded though, and hope burgeoned in his chest.

And was quickly squashed.

"I don't know. I'm not sure . . . " Lydia said, her voice soft and wobbly.

Margaret reached around Miss Cheswick and patted Lydia's arm. "Well done, gel." Then she shot Jason a superior smile.

"Hear, hear!" someone shouted, followed by a clap. Then a second. Then a third. Soon dozens were applauding.

Lydia looked at Miss Cheswick and then at Lady Saxton, then her stunned gaze settled on Jason. He saw her mouth form the word no, even if he couldn't hear her over the suddenly thunderous sound of applause in his ears.

Not knowing whether she could marry him was the same as a refusal. She either loved him or she didn't. There was no middle ground. He'd put everything out there for her, had even offered to relinquish his vice parties, and for what? For her to take his heart and smash it to the ground.

He stood on surprisingly firm legs, but then he felt as if his entire body was made of wood. His blood, his heart, his very soul had solidified into a cold, hard mass.

People moved toward Lydia and surrounded her so

that he could no longer see her face. Others turned toward him, some with pitying looks, others with smirks of disdain. He felt a hand on his shoulder and knew it was Ethan.

But Jason didn't want his help or his comfort. He only wanted to get back to the life he thought he'd left behind. The only life he apparently deserved.

LYDIA STRUGGLED TO free herself from the pressing mass around her. She barely registered who anyone was or what they said, though she was aware of Audrey's hand on her arm, trying to guide her to freedom. She ignored everything but Audrey's touch as they made their way through the cluster of people.

At last Lydia was able to see the center of the room, but Jason wasn't there any longer. She frantically searched for him among the throng, to no avail. He'd gone, and she couldn't blame him.

How could she have just stood there?

She been utterly, fantastically, and quite literally speechless. His heartfelt plea had shocked her. Not because he'd made it, but because of the manner in which he'd delivered it. He'd come here in front of the highest echelon of the ton and laid himself bare.

And her response had been no better than what he'd done to her the other night. Shame burned her face as she envisioned the hurt in his eyes. His scar had paled with pain while she'd fought to find the words to tell him that she loved him. Why had she muttered nonsense?

Because she'd panicked. She'd been afraid to throw

her status and reputation away. But as her peers gathered round to cheer her wise decision, she realized this moment would define the rest of her life. And what she wanted most wasn't a lofty status or a pristine reputation. She wanted *him*. A scoundrel, yes, but a scoundrel who'd just publicly offered to change his life for her. And that frightened her more than anything.

"You're smart to have turned him down," someone said beside her. "Well done."

"Of course she refused him," Aunt Margaret's voice cut through the dissonant noise surrounding Lydia. "She's a good girl."

Now she was "good?"

"I'm not," she said. She reached for Audrey's wrist and squeezed it. Audrey turned. Her face was flushed. Lydia needed someone to hear what she said. "I'm not good."

Audrey pulled her forward and linked their arms. "Come with me quickly."

It wasn't quick, but eventually they were free of the drawing room and Audrey was ushering her down a slender corridor. Vermillion skirts swished ahead of them, and Lydia realized Lady Saxton—Olivia, as she and Audrey called her—was leading them.

Olivia opened a door and swept them into a small room with a dainty set of furniture, including a pale yellow chaise. "You poor thing." Her eyes were full of compassionate warmth. "Do you want to lie down?"

Lydia eyed the chaise and for some ridiculous reason could only think of Jason's fantasy room. Agony tore through her. "I want to go home."

She didn't really, at least not to Aunt Margaret's. But she had no other options.

"You're welcome to come to Saxton House with me." Olivia smiled. "Provided you don't mind a newborn."

Lydia stared at her, and again words were slow in coming. Finally she ground out. "Why? I was horrid to you when you came to Town. I deserve all of this."

Olivia shook her head firmly. "No, you don't. No one does."

The door opened, and Lydia's stomach dropped to her feet. If that was Aunt Margaret, she feared she might scream.

But it wasn't Aunt Margaret. It was Philippa. She too gazed at Lydia with empathetic concern. Which made sense, given that she could understand Lydia's plight better than anyone.

"How are you?" she asked tentatively.

"I don't know." She felt cold and hot and nauseous. "That's not true. I feel awful. I just let him stand there—kneel there—and I did nothing. I'm the most horrible person."

Audrey hadn't left her side and now squeezed her shoulders. "You're not. You're human. You'll talk to him. He'll understand."

"How can he, when I'm not sure I do?"

"Do you love him?" Olivia asked.

Lydia nodded. More than ever. More than she ever dreamed possible. Which only turned the blade deeper in her gut. "But you saw him out there. He doesn't care what anyone says or thinks. He says he'll give up his vice parties, but I know how much they mean to him. I tried to change him, I thought it was to help myself, but I think I really just wanted to conform him to the man I wanted him to be, instead of the man he is. And it turns out I love the man he is."

Olivia gave her head a tiny shake. "Then what's wrong?"

"He said he'd give up his vice parties for me." Lydia still couldn't believe he'd said that—and so publicly. "What if he grows to resent that? What if he grows to resent *me?*"

"He won't," Philippa said. "Lockwood risked a great deal to come here tonight. I'd wager he's as ready to give up what's important to him as you're ready to thumb your nose at that lot out there."

"You are, aren't you?" Audrey asked.

Lydia never imagined she'd be able to turn her back on wanting approval and acceptance, but she'd found something far more precious. "I'm more than ready. I just hope it's not too late."

"Never." Philippa smiled encouragingly. "I followed Ambrose all the way to Cornwall."

"Luckily for me, Lockwood House is much, much closer." Then Lydia hugged each of her friends in turn.

After spending a good hour in seclusion, she ventured back to the party and suffered people's commentary and congratulations. With practice, she thought she could learn to not care what people thought of her or said about her. At last, it was time to leave and she was ensconced in the coach with Aunt Margaret for a blessedly short ride home.

Aunt Margaret nodded approvingly. "I'm quite proud of how you handled yourself this evening, though you shouldn't have disappeared for so long. You've more than won your freedom to stay with me. I'll write your father first thing in the morning."

Oh no, she thought Lydia had humiliated Jason on

purpose. "No, you won't. I'll write to him to inform him of my upcoming nuptials. Provided Jason will still have me."

Aunt Margaret gaped at her. "You've lost your mind. You'll be a pariah."

"Perhaps." Lydia shrugged. "Perhaps not. Philippa came through her marriage to Sevrin all right."

The coach stopped in front of Aunt Margaret's townhouse. Aunt Margaret scooted forward in her seat. "Not according to everyone. I'm shocked Lady Holborn would deign to include one such as him, but I suppose she did so to satisfy her son. Though look at what *Saxton* married." She rolled her eyes. "He could've had any young woman, and he chose that nobody." She returned her dark, malicious gaze to Lydia. "You'll be utterly ruined if you marry Lockwood."

"*When* I marry Lockwood." Lydia refused to consider the alternative. "And I don't care. Though I'm sure you'll do everything in your power to make us miserable."

The door of the coach opened, and the footman offered his hand to Aunt Margaret. "I won't have to. Lockwood solidified his exclusion from Polite Society tonight and if you're foolish enough to wed him, you'll join him in perdition," she said, taking the proffered hand and stepping down to the sidewalk.

Lydia followed her from the coach and trailed her to the front door. Now that she'd decided to embrace what she really wanted—Jason—she saw no reason to mince words with Aunt Margaret anymore. "Stop directing your hate at Jason and his mother. They aren't the ones who hurt you."

Aunt Margaret stopped short of the door and spun

around. Her dark eyes were furious in the light cast from the street lamp. "Who told you?" Her voice had dropped in tone and volume.

Lydia moved closer to her aunt. She didn't want to battle anymore, not when she was hopefully about to start a very happy life. Gently, Lydia touched her arm. "Wolverton explained everything, but he only wanted me to understand. I wish you'd told me. Maybe I could have helped you let it go."

"Let what go?" Aunt Margaret snapped as she drew her arm away from Lydia. "I can't believe Wolverton exposed my past to you, but I suppose I should be thankful he's remained quiet all these years."

Only she didn't sound appreciative. She sounded bitter. "Is that why you spread gossip?" Lydia asked. "So that people will fear you, and you'll never have to suffer it yourself?"

Aunt Margaret's eyes widened briefly, but then her face shuttered. "It doesn't matter why I do it. And I don't want your pity." With a grunt, she turned around. "Where's Tate? Why hasn't he opened the door?"

The footman who'd ridden on the coach rushed forward and opened the door. The foyer was empty. Eerily so.

Lydia stepped inside behind Aunt Margaret. "Something must be amiss."

Aunt Margaret turned to the footman. "Go and find Tate."

He nodded and took himself off.

"I'm going up to bed," Aunt Margaret said crossing to the stairs. "I hope to heaven Coxley is there waiting for me." She was halfway up the stairs when they heard running footsteps.

"Lady Margaret!" the footman called before his feet carried him into the small foyer. "You've been robbed! A group of men came into the house and tied everyone together downstairs."

Aunt Margaret paled, and Lydia rushed up to steady her lest she fall down the staircase. As she patted her aunt's shoulder, she turned to the footman. "Please send the coachman to Bow Street to fetch a Runner." It was all she could think to do. Lydia realized she was trembling. She stopped the footman just before he reached the front door. "Is everyone all right?"

He nodded briskly. "I think so, your ladyship. Just scared." He departed, and Lydia turned her attention back to Aunt Margaret.

"Let me help you up to bed, then I'll send Coxley up." Lydia guided Aunt Margaret slowly up the stairs.

"No, I prefer you sit with me. For a bit." She sounded small, frightened.

Lydia had never heard her like that. She put her arm more firmly around her aunt's shoulders. "I'll sit with you as long as you like."

"Thank you. I do hope they didn't steal my jewelry— or yours." She flicked Lydia a glance.

Lydia thought of the pieces that had belonged to her mother and felt a pang of sorrow. "I hope so, too." But more importantly she was glad no one had been hurt. Now more than ever she realized the importance of living her life to be happy, and she hoped Aunt Margaret finally saw it too.

Chapter Twenty-two

"MY LORD, MY lord!" Scot burst into Jason's bedchamber with North on his heels, fully rousing Jason from the slumber he'd been half-enjoying. Only half because it had taken him all bloody night to get there.

"Is the house on fire?" Jason asked, rubbing a hand over his eyes as he sat up.

Scot looked at his brother. "Do you want to tell him?"

"No, you do it," North said, his expression foreboding.

Jason looked between his retainers with mounting frustration. "I don't care who does it, but one of you better—and fast."

"There was a robbery last night," Scot said darkly.

His tone set off an alarm in Jason's mind. That, and the fact that they'd charged into his room, which they'd never done.

"Who?" Jason asked with more than a bit of trepidation.

"Lady Lydia."

Jason had almost been expecting her name. Who else would have caused these meddlesome servants to behave in such a fashion? What he hadn't expected was the fear that settled deep into his chest. Particularly after the manner in which she'd thoroughly denied him last night. He ought to despise her, oughtn't he? No, because regardless of their non-future together, he still cared about her. "How do you know this?"

"Mr. Teague is downstairs," North said.

"You couldn't have started with that information?" Jason threw the coverlet off and went straight to his dressing chamber. He knew Scot and North followed him and so continued the conversation. "What else do you know?

North paused in the doorway while Scot immediately went to gather Jason's clothing. "Nothing."

Jason turned to Scot. "Then get me the hell dressed."

Scarcely ten minutes later, Jason appeared downstairs in the front sitting room where Teague was standing before the windows. He turned when Jason greeted him.

"I'm sorry to bother you so early, my lord, but I wanted to inform you of last night's robbery. Your butler told you?"

Jason nodded. "He did. How is Lady Lydia?"

"She and her aunt are anxious, but they weren't home when it happened. They returned from a party to find their retainers bound together in the scullery." Teague frowned. "That makes it different from the past few robberies, which were perpetrated without the residents being disturbed. Those thieves went in, took what they wanted, and no one realized until after the fact."

Jason was relieved Lydia hadn't been there when the theft occurred. "Why was this one done differently?"

Teague's expression was grim. "I don't know, but it's notable because we haven't seen a robbery like this in Mayfair since Aldridge died. Whoever planned it knew things about the house and staff and knew Lady Margaret and Lady Lydia would not be at home."

Jason's blood ran cold. He knew what Teague was going to say. "You think Ethan—Jagger—is involved."

"We have his man, Oak. He told us Jagger did in fact take over Aldridge's gang and that they're responsible for the recent thefts. He also said the list you found was coded."

Jason didn't want to believe Ethan had lied to him or that he'd been foolish enough to succumb to Ethan's treachery. And he really couldn't believe Ethan would target Lydia's house. Not the Ethan he'd come to know. If he'd had anything to do with robbing Lydia, scaring her . . . Jason would make sure he hanged.

Jason tried to think rationally over the blood roaring in his ears. "But you said this theft was different. Couldn't someone else be responsible? Ethan told me there was another person."

"*He* told you that?" Teague sounded skeptical. "I think it probable that he lied to you."

Jason felt like he'd been punched in the gut. Repeatedly. Especially when he thought of things Ethan had said—that he'd spoken to Lydia several times. It was logical to think he'd had opportunity to learn about her household. And he'd been more than aware that Lydia wouldn't be home last night. He'd ensured she would be at the Holborn soirée. Jason's veins felt as if they'd turned to ice.

"There's more," Teague said. As if Jason needed to hear more. He was ready to string Ethan up himself. "Oak was taking orders from Jagger when he brought a particularly strong tincture of laudanum to Aldridge House the week that Lady Aldridge died so that when she took her regular dosage, she was actually overdosing."

The lying son of a bitch. He clenched his fists. "Are you going to arrest Ethan?"

"Yes." Teague grimaced. "But first we have to find him."

Jason wanted answers. And then he wanted that bastard to suffer. "Allow me to help."

"I was hoping you'd say that. Carlyle seemed to think the two of you had reconciled."

He'd spoken to Carlyle? But of course he had when Carlyle had delivered the list. Jason couldn't summon even a bit of irritation toward the men, not when every fiber of his being was focused on the hatred he currently felt for his half brother. "Not anymore. I'll find him for you. And then you can ensure he gets exactly what he deserves."

After seeing Teague out, North returned to the sitting room. "My lord, would you care for breakfast?"

"No, I'm going out." Jason turned and strode to the foyer. He doubted Ethan would be at the Bevelstoke, but Jason couldn't just sit at home and do nothing. He was too fraught with furious energy.

As expected, Ethan wasn't at the Bevelstoke. In fact, he'd scarcely been there at all in the past week, according to the footman at the door.

Frustrated and simmering with unsatisfied anger, Jason directed his coachman to Carlyle's house. Perhaps he could help run Ethan to ground.

It was still very early—far earlier than Jason or any other gentleman was typically about. London at this hour of the morning was a strange and somewhat beautiful thing. It was quiet, peaceful, and seemed more purposeful, perhaps because of the people bustling about their business instead of carelessly seeking their pleasure. And maybe Jason noticed because he was about business instead of his usual pleasure-seeking.

A short time later, his coach stopped in front of Carlyle House. He had to convince Carlyle's butler to awaken his lordship, but after a few minutes, he was shown to Carlyle's office to await the man.

A maid brought a tea tray and after Jason had downed half a cup, Carlyle arrived. He was simply dressed, and Jason imagined he did so by himself. A man with his background likely had no use for a valet. Jason barely did, but only because he relied on him as a person. As a friend.

"To what do I owe this early morning visit?" Carlyle asked, sitting behind his desk. "Moss said you had an urgent matter."

"Margaret Rutherford's town house was robbed last night."

Carlyle grimaced. "Your fiancée lives there. I'm very sorry that happened." He said the words with an empathy that only one who'd experienced the same sensation could demonstrate, because his wife had been the victim of a similar crime.

Jason didn't bother correcting him about his betrothal state. "Bow Street has testimony from Ethan's manservant that ties Ethan to the thefts and to Lady Aldridge's murder."

Carlyle's frown deepened. "I'm sorry to hear that."

"Why? You'd already begun to suspect him."

"That doesn't mean I wasn't hoping to be wrong. Your brother saved my wife's life—and mine. I hate to see things turn out like this for him."

Two hours ago, Jason might've believed Ethan was capable of a selfless act, but now he couldn't see past the fact that he'd gone after Lydia. She might not want him, but he couldn't simply turn off his feelings for her. "Help me find him."

Carlyle leaned back in his chair. "Jagger's very good at avoiding detection. He's skillfully eluded Bow Street for over a week, yet he's been to Lockwood House and a handful of other places."

Jason knew how to draw him out. "He'll come to see me. I just need to get him a message."

Carlyle tapped his forefinger on the arm of his chair. "He'll know soon that Bow Street wants to arrest him."

"Then I'll offer to help him." It was nothing he hadn't already done. Ethan wouldn't suspect a thing. "Can you find a way to ensure he gets my note?"

"I won't be able to find him myself, but I know people who are able to communicate with him." Carlyle pulled a piece of parchment from his drawer and slid it across the desk to Jason along with a pen and ink.

Jason considered what to write and then scratched out a note asking Ethan to come to his party on Thursday evening. He said he'd help him escape Bow Street and even signed it *Your Brother*, which curdled his stomach more than a little.

Carlyle took the paper and folded it. "It may soothe you to know that I do think your brother was trying to change. I've seen the potential in him for quite some time, then last spring, when my wife and I were taken hostage by Aldridge and his gang, Jagger let us go free."

Jason refused to be duped by Ethan. If he'd acted kindly, it wasn't because he was benevolent. It was because he had a reason that would somehow benefit him. "That doesn't soothe me at all, actually."

Carlyle nodded. "I'll see this is delivered today."

Jason stood. "How will you ensure he gets it?"

"I'll make sure he knows it's from you. You said he'd listen to you. Is there any chance at all he won't?"

Ethan had gone out of his way to forge a relationship with Jason, and they'd shockingly reached an accord. "None. He trusts me." He said he didn't, but Jason didn't believe that. Ethan was a lonely boy who was starved for someone to care about him. And Jason would use that to bring him down.

A quarter hour later, at his direction, his coach slowed in front of Lydia's house. It looked fine, untouched even. However, inside, Lydia—and even her godforsaken aunt—were likely upset and frightened. Jason felt a nearly painful urge to rush into the house and offer comfort and protection. But neither of those were his responsibility. She'd made that perfectly clear.

He rapped on the roof, and the coach drew forward. As he moved away, he cast one last glance at the house and saw the flutter of a drape in an upstairs window. He felt a twinge in his chest and then turned away, for he was certain that if he looked hard enough, he'd see Lydia. And if he did, his heart would surely break all over again.

LYDIA'S HEART CLENCHED as she watched Jason's coach pull away down the street. She turned from the window as Aunt Margaret walked into the sitting room.

She still looked pale this morning, and her eyes lacked their typical hard edge. Lydia wondered if last night's robbery had somehow softened her.

"Why the devil do you look so forlorn?" Aunt

Margaret demanded.

Apparently not.

"Last night was a bit of a trial, don't you think?" Lydia saw no reason to mince words with her aunt any longer.

Aunt Margaret moved into the sitting room and took her usual chair. She peered up at Lydia with disappointment shadowing her gaze. "I gather a night of sleep—or even a half-night—didn't prompt you to change your mind. You're making an utterly foolish decision if you marry him."

"I'm not. I love him, not that I expect you to understand that." Lydia was certain her aunt had no concept of the emotion.

Clenching her jaw, Aunt Margaret glanced away. "I loved Lockwood, the cad. Wolverton, too, if you can believe it. And you can see what love did for me." When she looked back to Lydia, her eyes gleamed with pain. "I was a fool to give myself to Lockwood, but he was immensely popular and I desperately wanted him to choose me. His son was the same way in his youth. Women fawned all over him. He could've had any of them and likely would've broken hearts like his father if I hadn't intervened."

Lydia's jaw dropped. "What did you do?" Though she already knew. "You pushed his mother into her breakdown, didn't you? Is everything you ever told me a lie?"

Aunt Margaret pursed her lips, but didn't flinch beneath Lydia's anger.

Lydia's heart ached for Jason, and her animosity for the woman seated before her intensified. "You're a horrible person."

Her dark eyes were defiant. "Yes, I'm a horrible person, but with damned good reason." Her lack of remorse was disgusting, but completely expected.

"Why?" Lydia asked. "Why did you make it your life's work to ruin people? It's not as if anyone knew of your transgressions."

Margaret—sometime during the past few moments Lydia had stopped thinking of her as "Aunt"—gripped the arms of her chair. "What was left to me? My mistakes weren't common knowledge, but men talk. I became a spinster. And I wasn't going to fade into the wallpaper like your silly friend Miss Cheswick. I made the best of my lot, and now I'm one of the most revered people in Society."

Lydia felt sorry for the woman. She was absolutely delusional. "You aren't revered—you're feared. That's not the same thing. And saddest of all, you're still alone. Well, that isn't going to happen to me."

She haughtily lifted her chin. "You won't be happy. Marrying Lockwood will seal your fate in exile."

Anger curled Lydia's hands into fists and stiffened her spine. "I *will* be happy and not in spite of marrying Jason, but because of it." Yes, some people would shun her, but she'd learned those people didn't matter. Her true friends and people of good substance wouldn't turn their backs on her. "And you're wrong—there are plenty of people who will be happy for me, and for Jason."

She gave Lydia the most awful, vindictive look. "I've made it my life's work to ensure the Lockwood family is miserable. You won't be spared once you become part of it." She meant to continue her campaign of gossip, and she'd try to push Jason over the edge just as she'd done his mother.

Lydia stalked forward and stood before her chair. She glared down at the woman who'd made her life hell for far too long. "You won't bother me or Jason. If you do, I'll ensure all of Society knows everything I learned from Wolverton."

Margaret blanched. "You wouldn't."

No, she wouldn't, but Margaret didn't need to know that. Since she always thought the worst of people, she'd have no trouble believing Lydia's empty threat. "There's only one way for you to know for certain."

She stared up at Lydia a long moment before blinking and then turning her head away. "I taught you too well."

"No, you didn't, because unlike you, I take no joy in having to use information against you. I only wish there was a way for you to let go of the past."

Margaret's shoulder twitched, but she kept her gaze averted.

Lydia shook her head to clear the anger and disappointment away. It was time to let joy—and hope—in. She'd thought she couldn't find happiness loving a scoundrel, but she'd been so very wrong.

But how to persuade him to receive her? He'd probably instructed his staff to ensure she wasn't allowed within fifty feet of Lockwood House. Or, perhaps she didn't need to persuade him. Perhaps she only needed to persuade his butler.

Chapter Twenty-three

JASON FELT BETTER than he had in days. The vice party—which he'd scheduled as soon as he'd arrived home from that disastrous Holborn soirée—was in full swing, his half brother would soon be in the custody of Bow Street, and Scot had arranged for a new Cyprian to meet him upstairs. He prowled from room to room like a caged animal while he waited for Ethan to arrive.

Scot found him in the drawing room. "Your entertainment for this evening awaits."

Jason scowled at him. "I'm not ready yet. I told you: after Ethan arrives and Teague carts him away." The Bow Street Runner was waiting in Jason's office, and several other Runners were stationed about the house.

"I'm aware of what you said, but I thought I'd let you know anyway." He glanced away. "And there's, ah, one more thing. I had to put her in your bedchamber."

Scot had Jason's full attention now. "You did *what?*"

"I didn't have any other choice. All of the other rooms are full. You've quite a crowd tonight. Seems that everyone wanted to come after what happened last week."

Of course they had. "You're an idiot," Jason growled, his good mood evaporating. "You knew I didn't want to see anyone this early, and you put her in *my* bedchamber. Get her out."

"I would, but I promised Lord Faversham that I'd procure a certain young lady from the next room." Scot was already hurrying off.

Jason swore. "I'll tell her myself."

He strode from the drawing room and quickly made his way upstairs. A couple was draped against the wall at the top of the stairs. Apparently he *was* short on space this evening. He made his way quietly past them.

When he got to his private wing, the corridor was brightly lit. They kept it that way to discourage people from venturing that way. An excess of light meant a dearth of privacy, and that was never a good thing.

He paused when he reached the door. What would he find inside? An image of Lydia—naked for once—spread across his bed invaded his mind, and he suffered a wave of lust so strong and so striking that he was suddenly certain he'd not only throw the Cyprian out of his room, he'd throw her out of the house. No, it was more than lust. It was love. He realized in that moment that he didn't want to be with anyone else, and he feared he never would.

He opened the door and hadn't planned to close it, but what he saw made him slam it shut.

Lydia—and yes she was fully, gloriously nude—was reclined upon his bed, her left arm raised against the bedpost.

Speech completely abandoned him as he stared at her gorgeous body, pale and perfect in the candlelight. It took every ounce of self-control, and he had precious little at this moment, not to throw himself on her.

"What are you doing here?" he croaked.

"Scot said you were in need of company. I hope you don't mind, but I thought I'd try out that thong." She pulled her hand, and Jason could see her wrist was tethered to his bed.

His cock roared with lust. But his mind interceded

with a dose of much-needed sanity. He couldn't continue with her. "Lydia, as much as I might like to take advantage of your . . . offerings—" His mouth went absolutely dry as his gaze settled on the delectable globes of her breasts. He swallowed. "Does anyone besides Scot—and I'll assume North—know you're here?"

"No." There was a note of cheer to her voice that made him want to scowl again. Why was she happy when he was still miserable?

Why was she even *here*, particularly during a vice party? "You refused me in front of half of London."

She grimaced, her lovely features wrinkling briefly. "I didn't mean to. You caught me quite by surprise. I'm afraid I panicked."

He stared at her, dumbfounded. "And you waited this long to tell me?"

She laughed then, a beautiful sound that filled him with hope. "That's rich coming from the man who made me stew in misery for three days after publicly humiliating me."

He flinched. "Perhaps my also public apology wasn't enough, then."

"No, I don't think it was. You'll have to make it up to me for quite some time." She raked him with a thoroughly seductive stare. "Starting right now."

Desire pulsed through him. He moved toward the bed, coming around the side to where her wrist was bound. "What are you saying?"

"That I want you. I want to marry you. I want a future with you." She notched up her chin. "And I'm not leaving until you agree."

He smiled then, admiring her ingenuity and

persistence. But was their love enough?

"Lydia." He forced himself to turn from her tempting curves and stare at the wall. "None of this changes who I am or what I've done. Society thinks me a crazed degenerate. I'll never be accepted the way you want to be, and what's more, I don't want that."

"I know." Her voice was soft, small. "I never should have expected you to. I think I spent too long under Aunt Margaret's tutelage. I lost sight of what was really important, if I ever really knew. And maybe I didn't before I met you. Being with you was the only happiness I have ever known. I'll take you any way I can get you—reprobate, lunatic, scoundrel."

He snapped his gaze back to hers. She was staring at him with those dark, seductive eyes and he felt like he could see all the way to her heart. A heart she was offering him if he only had the courage to accept it.

Fear froze him in place and blurred his vision. If he opened himself to her, let her inside . . . it was all he had left. He didn't know if he could risk it.

She pushed up from the bed, and with her free hand, stroked his ruined cheek. "I love you, Jason. Every damaged, mad, and lonely piece of you."

The fear curdled in his gut, sparking a bead of nausea. "What if I *am* mad like my mother—"

Her touch grew firmer, cradling his face with warmth and security. "You aren't. Together, we will keep the demons at bay. Your mother didn't have a partner, a soul mate, someone who would fight for her. You do."

His vision came back into focus and fixed on her heart-wrenchingly beautiful face. Happiness was so close . . .

"Let go with me, Jason," she coaxed, her fingers

stroking his scar, "be with me."

He closed his eyes and slowly fell forward, his mouth finding hers as he crushed her into the bed. Her lips were soft, inviting. They opened against his and kissed him with aching tenderness.

He did as she asked and let go, not because he couldn't withstand the tumult inside of himself, but because he wanted to give and take and share this moment with her. He slanted his head and intensified the kiss, opening his mouth and plunging his tongue into her heat. She answered him with fiery need, her hand curving around the back of his neck and holding him down to her.

Beneath him, her body was warm and soft. The mounds of her breasts pressed into his chest, making him realize he was wearing far too many clothes. He cupped the side of her neck and broke his mouth from hers. Her lips were red and moist, her cheeks flushed. *Beautiful.* He nipped at her lips and kissed her neck, unable to keep from trying to devour her whole.

"I don't suppose you could untie my hand?" she asked breathlessly. "I can't really feel anything beyond my wrist."

He smiled as he sat back and worked the thong free. "For prolonged restraint, it's best to leave your hand flat when bound." He took her hand down and gently massaged the extremity as he laid it down on the bed beside her head. "Like this. And, I'd move you to the center of my bed." He scooted her to the middle of the wide mattress, keeping his hand on hers so that her arm was extended. He kneeled beside her as he reached over and took her other hand. "Then I'd bind this hand in the same fashion." He stretched the arm flat so that she was spread eagled, at least on the top half.

She gazed up at him with eyes that had darkened to the color of soot. "And my legs?" she asked with a gravelly voice that was equally shaded.

"The same." His cock throbbed almost painfully as he envisioned her thus. Some day he would do that to her, and he would give her a pleasure she had never known. But not tonight. Tonight he had other plans. First, he needed to dispose of his clothing.

He stood up, and she frowned. "Easy, love," he said. "I'm just joining you in my natural state."

Her eyes slitted as he removed his coat. "I was going to offer to help, but I think I'd rather watch."

God, she knew exactly what to say to entice his desire to burn even hotter. For that, he'd give her a show. Divested of his coat, he sat on the bed to remove his boots—he never bothered with evening attire for his vice parties—and stockings. Then he got up and turned toward her, his fingers working at his cravat. Slowly, he loosened it and pulled it free. Playfully—God, when had he ever been that?—he tossed it onto the flat plane of her alabaster stomach.

She picked it up and held it to her lips. He nearly groaned with want.

Returning to disrobing, he stripped off his waistcoat with more impatience than he'd removed the cravat. He tossed it to the floor and then pulled his shirt from his breeches.

Her gaze was glued to his torso, her lips parted in anticipation. He went slowly, methodically drawing the linen over his head so that his flesh was bared inch by inch.

In the brief moment that the shirt blocked his vision

as he pulled it over his head, she'd gotten to her knees in front of him on the edge of the bed. Her eyes found his. "I got tired of watching."

"Tired? You looked rather engaged, to me."

Her gaze dropped to his chest and her hands splayed over his pectoral muscles. "Jason," she breathed. "You are . . . spectacular." Her fingers dug into his flesh and her mouth descended on him, her lips pressing eager kisses along his sternum.

Giving up on his demonstration, he pulled his breeches open with frantic tugs, loosening one of the buttons in the process. Hastily, he shoved the garment down his legs, bending at the waist and then capturing her mouth in a kiss as he kicked the breeches aside.

Her hands wound around his neck and pulled him down as she backed across the bed. He moved on top of her, pressing her into the mattress, his body fitting against hers with absolute perfection.

Their previous times together had been mind-numbingly good, but this was different. There was nothing between them, and it wasn't just the absence of clothing. They were in a new place, ready to trust each other and look to a future. This needn't be a hurried coupling or the potential last time.

The thought was altogether humbling.

And he wanted to remember this night for as long as he lived. He settled his hips against hers, and she widened her legs so that he was nestled between her thighs. The heat of her core beckoned his aching cock, but not quite yet.

Wanting to taste her, he licked and kissed a path to her breasts, cradling and massaging each one as he laved and sucked their exquisite softness. Her soft moans filled his bedchamber, and he was infinitely glad no other woman had ever shared this space with him.

She coaxed him with words, murmuring "yes" over and over, and with action as she tangled her fingers in the hair at his nape and arched her breasts up. He drew a nipple deep into his mouth and tongued the sweet tip. Her head fell back, and her legs opened further.

He moved his mouth down the slope of her belly, licking her soft flesh while he continued to tweak her breasts. Then he moved one hand down between her thighs and delved into her moist heat. She gasped as he gently pushed his finger inside of her. Her hips rotated against the mattress, and he rubbed his thumb against her clitoris. She jerked then, and he sensed her climax building.

He marveled at her lack of inhibition and rejoiced in her delight. He'd never had a lover who wasn't practiced and . . . professional. Lydia was innocent and generous, and he longed to make every moment good—no, spectacular—for her.

He moved further down, laving kisses along her hipbone and then across to her mound. He pressed down on her nub as he licked along her soft folds. She cried out his name and her thighs clenched. He braced his palms against her flesh and held her open while he tongued her.

She tasted spicy and sweet, and the musky scent of her womanhood mixed with the hyacinth fragrance she used. Her hips arced up and then back in a circular motion as her orgasm gathered.

Keeping a hand braced on one of her thighs, he used the other to pump into her softness, his fingers working in tandem with his mouth to bring her world crashing down. He slid in and out of her as he sucked on her nub. She grew wetter, hotter, her hips moved faster. He stroked faster, suckled harder. Then she cried out, and her muscles tensed as she came.

He rose up on his knees and gazed down at the beauty of Lydia in the throes of her orgasm and then buried himself deep inside of her.

Chapter Twenty-four

WAVE AFTER WAVE of pleasure threatened to sweep Lydia away. She had no idea where she ended, had no sense of space at all, but then he thrust inside of her and she knew precisely where she was—and it was the only place she wanted to be.

She opened her eyes and watched him as he moved in and out of her. Her body quivered with the aftershocks of her climax, or maybe it was still going on. She had no idea. She only knew how good she felt, how incredible this man was.

He slowed his pace, gliding forward and pulling back with slow, penetrating strokes. Every sensation was focused where their bodies were joined. She clasped his hips, urging him to move a bit faster, to increase the friction to that achingly blissful degree.

But he only gave her a half smile, his gaze locking on hers as he continued his maddeningly measured assault.

"Jason," she pleaded, coming up off the bed.

He only pressed her back down, going with her and sealing his mouth over hers. "Shhh. We've always had to hurry. I don't want to. Not this time."

She tasted a salty musk on his tongue and realized, shockingly, it was the taste of herself.

She must have reacted because he pulled his head up and smiled down at her. "Does that bother you?"

Even more shockingly, it didn't. She shook her head and pulled him down for a longer, deeper kiss.

His hands cradled her head as he leisurely drew on

her lips and mouth. Gradually, he moved more swiftly, coming in and out of her with more rapid pulses. She wound her legs around his hips and urged him to move even faster.

He sat back again and slowed the pace once more. She groaned, but then his finger stroked that sensitive spot between their bodies and ecstasy washed over her. He splayed his hand over her hip and pumped into her with joyous precision, each thrust bringing her to a new plateau of pleasure.

He fell forward once more, his mouth covering her breast. His tongue was hot as he licked her nipple and then sucked at her tortured flesh. She didn't know how much more she could take. Every part of her felt hyper-sensitive. She was utterly captive to his touch.

She'd closed her eyes at some point, but then his thumb stroked her bottom lip and she opened her lids to see him above her. His mouth still wore the faint smile he'd sustained this entire time. She'd never seen him so . . . happy.

"Are you ready now?" he asked softly.

"I've been ready for quite some time in case you hadn't noticed."

His hips rotated against hers, his cock moving deeper into her and withdrawing so quickly as to leave her feeling completely bereft. His lips spread into a grin. "I noticed. But don't tell me you haven't been enjoying every moment. I won't believe you." With each word he drove in and out of her and now he picked up speed, thrusting into her with a delicious force that made her cast her head back against the bed and squeeze her eyes shut as she came apart around him.

He shouted as he buried himself deep into her core.

She clasped his back, drawing him down on top of her and relishing his heat and strength. He was spectacular, and he was hers.

Minutes later, she trailed her fingers through his hair, tracing shapes in the dark locks, enjoying the press of his big body atop hers. He lifted his head and looked at her. The smile was gone, but now there was a sense of wonder in his gaze that made her feel shy.

"What?" she said, her hand stilling against his head.

He shifted to her side, his body leaving hers. But he drew her to turn so they faced each other. "You are far more than I ever dreamed."

She knew precisely how he felt. She snuggled against his chest, splaying her hand against his warm flesh. "I'm so glad I don't have to go anywhere. Would it be terribly scandalous if I stayed the night and snuck home at dawn?"

Instead of laughter, which she fully expected to hear, he drew away from her with a muttered curse. He bounded from the bed and began to dress.

She frowned as she sat up. "Where are you going?"

He flashed her a smile that put her at ease, but didn't satisfy her curiosity. "I have a party going on downstairs."

She moved to the edge of the bed. "Surely they don't need you to play host. Don't forget, I know what goes on down there—and up here—and I doubt you'll be missed."

"I'm expecting Ethan."

"Really? May I come with you?" she asked, swinging her feet over the side of the bed. "Scot can fetch me a mask—"

"No." He didn't look at her as he continued his

hurried toilet.

"Why not?" She stood up anyway and plucked her chemise from the floor where she'd left it.

He pulled his boots on. "Because Bow Street is here, and they'll be arresting him. I don't want you around that."

She held the garment to her chest and gaped at him. "Arresting him? Whatever for?"

"Theft. Murder. Maybe some other crimes." He sounded utterly careless.

Lydia quickly donned her chemise and grabbed his wrist. "You can't let Bow Street arrest him."

Jason paused in buttoning his waistcoat. "He was responsible for the theft of your things. I will most certainly allow them to arrest him. It's the reason I invited him to come tonight."

Her knees wobbled. "I can't believe it of him."

Jason's eyes narrowed. "Why?"

"He approached me weeks ago—at the Whitmore Ball—and asked me to arrange a meeting between the two of you. And I taught him to waltz."

Jason simply stared at her. "Why the hell didn't you tell me any of this?"

"Because you were seeking revenge against him." She cocked her head to the side, realizing that had somehow changed over the past few weeks. She suddenly wondered why he hadn't told her about that. "Besides, it's not as if you've kept me abreast of your relationship."

"You should have told me he approached you." He pressed his lips together, appearing quite different from the man who'd been in bed with her moments before. "And where did you teach him to dance?"

"At Audrey's house."

"He involved Miss Cheswick in his schemes?" Jason sounded very annoyed.

Lydia found her stockings and sat on the bed to don them. She adopted a defensive tone, feeling as though she needed to vindicate herself. "I would hardly call learning to waltz a 'scheme,' but asking her to help was my idea. She was more than happy to do so."

Jason shook his head as he finished buttoning his waistcoat. "He's a criminal, Lydia. He has been for years. Bow Street has evidence he's behind the robberies and that he was involved in Lady Aldridge's death."

Lydia's hands trembled. He couldn't have been. Not when he'd been so charming. "There has to be an explanation. Have you tried to speak with him?"

"Many times. He would never tell me what he was doing. He said he couldn't trust me, that he couldn't trust anyone." He pressed his lips together until the flesh around his mouth and the length of his scar turned white. "I was a fool to believe his lies."

She recollected what Ethan had told her at the musicale when he'd asked her to teach him to waltz. "He didn't choose to be a criminal—at least, it wasn't his first choice. He was alone in the world. You and your mother turned your backs on him."

Jason speared her with a furious stare. "Don't defend him to me. I'm sorry for his lot, but we all have choices and he chose to target your house. Furthermore, he's been lying to me for weeks." His lip curled making him look particularly fearsome. "On second thought, I'm not sorry for him at all."

A knock on the door caught both of their attention.

Jason helped Lydia into her gown, which took an agonizing few minutes. "Come," he called when they were finished.

Scot, followed quickly by North, stepped into the bedchamber. Their faces were pale and drawn. Or rather, Scot's was. North's was just pale.

"What is it?" Jason sounded alarmed, but looking at his retainers, he ought to be. Lydia was.

"One of the footmen—Kerr—has been found dead," North informed him, his attention fixed on Jason as if Lydia wasn't there.

The blood leached from Jason's face. "Hell. Where?"

"Outside in the alley near the back wall. Dockley went to relieve his post and found him. His throat had been slit, my lord. And his livery was stripped from him."

Lydia clasped Jason's hand and squeezed it.

"Is Teague still in my office?" Jason asked.

"I'm afraid Mr. Teague received a message and left awhile ago," North said.

Jason let go of Lydia's hand as Scot came forward with his coat and helped him to don the garment. "Damn, did he say where he was going?"

North shook his head once. "He did not, my lord."

"Did the other Runners leave with him?" Jason tugged his coat in place.

North frowned. "I'm not certain."

"That's all right, North. Send someone to Bow Street—even if Teague isn't there, someone should be able to find him." Jason turned to Scot. "Gather some footmen and try to find Ethan—he should have arrived by now. I'll be down as soon as I can."

Both men nodded and took themselves off with

alacrity.

Jason turned to her and clasped her shoulders. "I don't want you here when they take Ethan. I'll send one of my footmen up to see you home."

"I still can't believe Ethan would do this. He has to have changed." Her mind struggled to make sense of this. "Why would a criminal want to learn to waltz?"

"Lydia, Bow Street has proof—testimony from a man who works for Ethan. He directed Lady Aldridge's death." His eyes were sad. "I'm sorry to have to share such details with you, but you need to know what sort of man he is.

"I need to go." His gaze raked her from crown to toe, turning a bit wistful when he finished. "Do you need someone to help you?"

"No, thank you." Her hair undoubtedly looked a fright, but she'd manage.

He leaned forward and pressed a kiss to her temple. "I'll call on you tomorrow."

Lydia nodded and watched him leave.

With a heavy sigh, she found her slippers and slid them onto her feet. She still couldn't fathom Ethan stealing from her, let alone being responsible for Lady Aldridge's death. Good heavens, what would Audrey say when Lydia told her? She'd be just as shocked as Lydia. Perhaps even more so; Audrey had actually flirted with him.

After what seemed a least a quarter hour, there was a rap on the door. Lydia cracked it open to reveal a stocky footman she'd never seen before.

"I'm here to see you home, my lady," he said with a helpful smile. His face was kind and genuine, and he immediately set her at ease. "I'm Jimmy."

"Jimmy?" she asked, as he gestured for her to precede him. "You don't go by a surname?"

"No, my lady. I'm just Jimmy." He hastened beside her. "We must hurry. His lordship wants you on your way as soon as possible."

"Of course." She quickened her pace, and they were halfway down the stairs to the foyer when she realized she wasn't wearing a mask. If anyone saw her she'd be ruined—but did that really matter? Cheerfully, she acknowledged it didn't.

Jimmy hurried even faster when they stepped into the foyer, and ushered her out the door before anyone caught sight of her, but then they hadn't seen a soul. Which was odd. Shouldn't someone have been stationed in the foyer? Or were they all involved with the dead footman? Lydia grew a bit queasy as she realized death was very nearby.

She slowed as they walked toward the street, which was lined with a handful of coaches, none of which belonged to Jason. What vehicle was she to take? Confused, she turned to Jimmy, but he wasn't paying attention to her. He was turning his head this way and that.

"What is it?" she asked, alarm beginning to wind its way through her.

Jimmy took her arm and pulled her to the street. "We need to be hailin' a hack."

His voice subtly changed, triggering her alarm to erupt into full-blown fear. She tried to pull away from the footman's grasp. "I think I'd rather go back inside."

His grip tightened and after glancing up and down the street, he tugged her across, though she pointlessly tried to dig her feet into the stones.

"Let me go!" Her voice climbed, but the flash of steel silenced her immediately.

He'd pulled a knife from his boot and brought it to within an inch of her face. "Unless ye fancy a scar to match the one on yer lordship's cheek, keep yer mouth shut. Do as I say, and ye won't bleed." His crisp servant's diction had been completely replaced with the language of someone from a far lower class.

Lydia bit her cheek to keep from screaming and prayed Jason would find her. But he thought she'd gone home. He wouldn't realize she hadn't actually arrived there until tomorrow morning. By then, who knew what would have happened to her?

Fear iced her body as her captor pulled her along to God-only-knew-what fate.

Chapter Twenty-five

JASON RUSHED DOWN to the foyer and met North. "Has anyone found Ethan yet?"

"No, my lord. It's possible he hasn't arrived, or that he saw the Bow Street Runners stationed about and left." North clasped his hands behind his back in his usual stance, but there was a current of energy coursing through him, as though he were ready to spring into action at any moment.

Jason had been angry when Teague had shown up with four other Runners earlier in the evening. Ethan was far too smart, and if he sensed this was a trap, he'd leave and they might never find him.

Scot came through the foyer at that moment. He paused upon seeing Jason. "There's one Runner still here. He's out in the alley with Kerr." Scot's expression was grim, but carried a hint of fury. "I'd like to get my hands around the neck of whoever did that to him."

Jason felt the same, perhaps even more so since he suspected his half brother, who'd utterly and successfully duped him. "Still no sign of Ethan?"

"Not yet. Your guests sense something is wrong, but we've kept Kerr's death quiet. Though I don't know how much longer that will last."

Jason nodded. "I need someone to see Lydia home. I want her out of here as soon as possible."

North inclined his head. "I'll send someone to take care of it." He turned and departed with long strides.

Jason pivoted toward Scot, whose expression still

hovered somewhere between anger and sadness. "Where have you searched for Ethan?"

"I was about to go upstairs."

Jason's memory went back to his last vice party. Ethan had snuck into the billiards room undetected. He could very well have done the same thing tonight. "I'm going to the gaming room."

Scot shook his head. "I looked there."

"It's possible you didn't know what you were looking for." Jason hastened to the billiards room and quickly scanned everyone present as he moved through it. There were only a few men wearing masks, and none of them were Ethan. And whereas Jason hadn't been able to easily recognize him at the last vice party, he felt certain he'd know him anywhere now.

He reached the back of the room and stood near the terrace doors, one of which was open partway, presumably to allow the cool air inside. But what if it wasn't? Cautiously, Jason pushed the door wider and stepped outside.

A sconce on the exterior wall illuminated this area of the terrace. Jason stopped short at the sight of Ethan bent over a body. Ethan's eyes met Jason's. Slowly, he stood. A circle of blood was spreading from the body—it was Wolverton. Jason's gaze landed on a blood-covered knife dangling from Ethan's hand.

Jason moved forward haltingly, looking between the surely dead Wolverton and Ethan. "What have you done?"

Ethan turned toward him and stepped away from Wolverton. "I didn't do this."

Revulsion turned Jason's stomach. "It looks to me like you did." Jason turned his head and registered the arrival of Teague.

The Runner stepped out onto the terrace and moved next to Jason. "Put the knife down, Jagger."

"Teague, I thought you left," Jason said, returning his attention to Ethan.

"I did, but I've just returned, and not a moment too late, I see."

Ethan held up his hands. Blood dripped from the knife and landed on the stone like a scarlet raindrop. "I know this looks bad, but I didn't kill Wolverton."

Jason stared at him. "I defended you. I foolishly believed you'd changed. And you stole from my fiancée." He clenched his fists, hoping he'd finally have the opportunity to break the bastard's nose.

Ethan fixed him with an earnest stare. "I didn't steal from Lydia. It was Wolverton. I told you there was someone else involved."

And that someone was a marquess? It shouldn't have been impossible to believe since the Earl of Aldridge had been running a gang, but how many bloody noblemen were working for Gin Jimmy? Or was Ethan lying again? "Forgive me for not trusting you, but you've made that goddamned difficult. Do you have proof?"

"We do," Teague interjected. "I left earlier because I'd received a message directing me to Wolverton House. We found several stolen objects, including a necklace that belongs to Lady Lydia."

Jason exhaled. He was relieved to learn Ethan hadn't lied—at least about stealing from Lydia.

Teague took a step toward Ethan. "Did you kill Wolverton to eliminate your competition?"

"Why would I do that when I expected you to arrest

him?" Ethan glared at the Runner with equal parts contempt and arrogance, neither of which was going to help his cause. "Who do you think sent the note directing you to Wolverton House?"

Jason tried to make sense of everything and wished to hell his brother had trusted him with whatever plan he'd been executing. "Why are you standing here with a bloody knife?"

Ethan glanced at the weapon, and Jason caught the flicker of disgust in his eyes. "I'm telling you I didn't do this. I don't expect them to believe me, but I hope you do."

Jason didn't know what to believe. He'd spent far longer hating this man than he had liking him. And how did you have faith in someone who didn't have faith in you?

"Ethan, I'm going to have to arrest you for the murder of Wolverton and possibly the murder of Lord Lockwood's footman." Teague took another step. "And for organizing the death of Lady Aldridge."

Ethan backed up. "I didn't do that. It was Oak—he was following Gin Jimmy's orders. And Gin Jimmy killed Wolverton." He glanced at Jason. "One of your footmen is dead?"

Before Jason could answer, Teague asked, "You expect me to believe Gin Jimmy came out of his rookery to personally kill someone?" Teague's tone clearly indicated he believed no such thing.

Ethan's nostrils flared, and his gray eyes flashed with anger. "Yes, goddammit, he's in the house. He's wearing Lockwood livery. But you need to hurry, he may have slipped out by now."

Jason began to understand what may have happened.

"Why did Gin Jimmy come here tonight?"

"To kill Wolverton." Ethan gave a subtle nod, as if he were trying to communicate something additional to Jason. "Gin Jimmy thought he'd turned against him."

Jason thought he began to understand Ethan's plan. He *had* been trying to change after all. *He'd* turned against Gin Jimmy, not Wolverton. "And he killed my footman to obtain my livery because he wanted to blend in and escape more easily?"

"We need to find him," Ethan said. "It's good that he's wearing livery, so you'll know what to look for. I'm sure Teague doesn't know what he looks like."

"No." Teague looked conflicted. He glanced toward the house, but his stance was angled toward Ethan, his feet wide apart and his arms tensed. He was ready to fight. But he couldn't hold Ethan and go after Gin Jimmy. "Lord Lockwood, where is the Runner who stayed behind?"

"In the alley."

"I hate to ask you, but would you mind fetching him? I'm afraid I'm in need of another pair of hands with so many criminals about." He threw Ethan a dark glare. "Describe Gin Jimmy."

"He looks like your grandfather." Ethan held up his hand and indicated a height near his mouth. "Shorter, maybe five foot eight, a bit thick around the middle. White hair, clean-shaven, and he has a gold tooth. And of course, he now looks like another one of Jason's footmen."

Footman. A cold sensation raced up Jason's neck. North had sent someone to see Lydia home. He would've immediately recognized that Gin Jimmy wasn't one of their retainers, but Jason felt uneasy nonetheless. "I'll go get your Runner," he said a bit absently as he turned toward the house, intending to check on Lydia first.

The sound of a scuffle spun him back around. Ethan was standing over an unconscious Teague, still clutching the bloody knife.

Jason glanced at the weapon. "Christ, Ethan! You didn't kill him too?"

Ethan glared at him then dropped the knife beside Teague. "I haven't killed anyone. Tonight, anyway."

Jason didn't have time to be shocked by this revelation. He turned, needing to ensure Lydia had left safely. He rushed inside with Ethan on his heels. He nearly tripped over North, who was standing just inside the billiards room.

"The guests were becoming curious," North said. "I explained you were conducting business on the terrace and didn't wish to be disturbed."

Several men looked up from their games, but Jason didn't bother to send any of them reassuring looks. He doubted he'd be able to keep two murders quiet. It seemed Lockwood House really was an awful place.

"North, who took Lydia home?"

"I directed Pemley to send someone up to fetch her ladyship and see her home."

The cold that had settled into Jason's spine turned frigid. "Pemley's new."

"Which is why I didn't ask him to see her home," North said, his forehead creasing. "What's wrong?"

Ethan grabbed Jason's arm. "You think because this Pemley is new that he could've asked Gin Jimmy to take her home?"

Jason was certain the blood had drained from his

face. Ethan was already moving.

They rushed into the foyer where—miraculously—Pemley was at the door.

"Pemley!" Jason called. "Who took Lady Lydia home?"

The footman's cheeks reddened. "I don't remember his name, my lord. I beg your pardon."

"Was he older? About this tall?" Ethan gestured to his jawline. "His livery probably seemed a bit long for him."

Pemley nodded. "That's him. But he did as he was told. I saw him leave with Lady Lydia a few minutes ago."

Goddammit. Furious energy surged through Jason just as his muscles felt as though they were made of jelly.

"Come on." Ethan ran out the door and surveyed the street.

"Where would he go?" Jason's heart threatened to beat a hole in his chest. "Why would he take her?"

"To ensure he got away." Ethan turned and ran north. "He'll head back toward St. Giles. If he can get there, he'll be untouchable—it's why he never leaves. Do you know how fucking hard it was for me to get him out of there? And goddamned Bow Street couldn't even apprehend him."

Jason kept in stride with Ethan and tried to process what he was saying. "So you're the one who turned on Gin Jimmy."

"It was that or be his scapegoat for Lady Aldridge's death, which I may end up being anyway," he said darkly.

Ethan put his head down and increased his speed. Jason did the same. A few minutes and two streets later, their speed began to flag, but then Ethan spurred forward. "There he is!"

Up ahead, a man and a woman were turning onto Beak Street—the man clearly pulling her along.

Jason let out an inhuman cry and overtook Ethan in his effort to get to Lydia.

Gin Jimmy spun about, one arm locked around her neck and the other pointed at her side . . . with a knife.

Ethan lunged in front of Jason, partially shielding him, but Jason stepped around him. Ethan put his arm in front of his chest. "Stop. If you move, he'll kill her."

"What're ye doin', Jagger?" Gin Jimmy asked, his blade pressed against Lydia's ribcage.

Jason could barely contain himself, despite Ethan's arm restraining him.

"Let her go, Jimmy," Ethan said. "You don't need her. You escaped. Let's be on our way."

Gin Jimmy cocked his head to the side. "Somethin's odd about ye, Jagger. I'm beginnin' to think Wolverton might've been tellin' the truth. That ye set me up instead o' him. Why should ye give a shit about this bit o' fluff? She's yer brother's lady, ain't she? And I ken how much ye hate him. Why haven't ye gutted him by now?" His lips spread in a humorless smile. "Mayhap ye've been lyin' about how ye feel about him—like ye've been lyin' to me."

"You set me up, Jimmy." Ethan's tone was crisp and frigid.

Gin Jimmy's gaze was fierce and his mouth twisted with menace. "Ye weren't doin' yer job. Ye were supposed to take care o' Lady Aldridge, not squire her about town. Seemed yer fancy new place in Society had blinded yer vision. So I had Oak help things along."

While Jason was happy to learn that Ethan hadn't participated in Lady Aldridge's demise, he was far more concerned with Lydia at this moment. He pushed Ethan's arm away and stepped forward. "Lydia, are you all right?"

Her dark eyes were wide, frightened. Of course she wasn't all right. She was caught in the grip of a murderer. But at least she wasn't hurt. Yet.

"If you harm my fiancée, I'll kill you myself," Jason vowed. Indeed, he considered doing it anyway for kidnapping her and scaring the hell out of her.

"Jagger! Gin Jimmy!" A chorus of shouts and boots hitting stone sounded behind them. Jason looked back to see Teague and another man running their way.

Gin Jimmy snarled. He rotated his wrist. The knife flashed in the lamplight. Lydia's gasp twisted Jason's gut, and he lunged toward her.

Ethan moved like quicksilver, his hand catching Gin Jimmy at the base of his throat. Jason assumed he'd gone for the windpipe, but he'd missed. Still, it was enough for Gin Jimmy to loosen his grip on Lydia. Ethan grasped Lydia's forearm and yanked her forward. She stumbled into Jason's waiting arms.

Gin Jimmy raised his arm, and the knife blade glittered as he brought it down toward Ethan's chest. Ethan just barely moved in time, but the blade caught him in the upper right arm as he turned.

With a growl, Gin Jimmy turned tail and ran down the street.

Teague and the other Runner were almost upon them.

Ethan pivoted, his features drawn, his gray eyes furious. "I won't let them take me."

"Go," Jason said. Ethan had saved Lydia's life, and though he might be a fool, Jason was certain he hadn't killed Wolverton, nor had he orchestrated Lady Aldridge's death. "I'll explain what you were trying to do. How you were working against Gin Jimmy."

"It won't matter," Ethan said, sounding both defeated and remorseful. "They'll still come after me."

Jason kept one arm around Lydia, but he reached out and clasped his brother's wrist. "Let me help you. It's time to trust me. Go. I'll make sure you get a decent start."

Ethan smiled, and in it, Jason saw himself. Saw a future they could build together. He hoped they got that chance. Ethan took a step back, and Jason let him go.

"Thank you." Then Ethan turned and ran.

Jason turned his attention to the woman he loved. "Lydia, I need you to faint."

She gazed up at him, her eyes confused, her lips parted. She already looked halfway there.

"I need to distract Teague," he said urgently.

Her eyes widened with understanding, then fluttered closed. She exhaled dramatically, giving a little squeal as she did so, and dropped like a stone. Jason caught her before she hit the street.

He knelt, cradling her head on his knees, and leaned down. "That was brilliant. I love you." He felt her flinch. "No, don't open your eyes. Not yet. Let me deal with Teague first. Then, my love, we will get on with the rest of our lives."

She cracked open one eye briefly enough to glare at him. "I told you Ethan wasn't a criminal."

LYDIA CLOSED HER eye again and feigned unconsciousness. She hoped Ethan was able to get away.

"Where did he go?" someone demanded; Lydia thought it was Teague. She'd only met him the one time after her house had been robbed, but she recognized his voice.

"He got away," Jason explained. "I had to see to Lydia." He brushed his hand over her forehead.

He loved her. The knowledge filled her with warmth and joy.

She figured it was all right to awaken, and so she allowed her eyes to gently open. "What happened?" she asked weakly.

"You fainted," Jason said, his hand still stroking her hairline.

She sat up quickly. "Gin Jimmy!" she cried, hoping to put the focus on him instead of Ethan.

"I'm afraid he ran, but you're all right." Jason helped her to stand. He slid one arm around her back and held her close.

"Yes. Thank goodness for Ethan. If he hadn't gone after Gin Jimmy, I might be dead!" Lydia used all of her years and experience as an accomplished storyteller to sound as convincing as possible.

Teague frowned. "He's still wanted for murder." He flicked his gaze to Jason's. "Even you can't deny that he killed Wolverton—the knife he dropped on your terrace is his, it's engraved with the letters EJ."

Lydia felt Jason tense and cast him a sidelong glance. He clenched his jaw. "I'm sure there's a reasonable explanation."

"Doubtful." Teague turned to his companion. "Let's go." They took off in the direction both Ethan and Gin Jimmy had taken. Lydia prayed that Ethan would somehow evade them, but he was hurt.

She turned in Jason's embrace. "Will Ethan be all right? Jimmy stabbed him."

"I know." Jason stroked her shoulder with his fingertips in a circular motion. "But if anyone can emerge from this and come out on top, I have to believe it's Ethan."

She looked up at him. "Your opinion of him has changed."

"Yes." He frowned with regret. "That doesn't alter the past, however, and he was a criminal—regardless of what you want to believe. He may not have killed Wolverton, or stolen from you, or even had anything to do with Lady Aldridge's death, but I'm afraid there are plenty of other crimes he may yet be accused of."

She shivered. She couldn't reconcile the criminal with the man she'd taught to waltz or the man who'd flirted with Audrey. "We'll stand by him."

"'We'?" Jason asked.

"Of course, we're to be married, are we not?"

He pulled her tight against his chest and held her. "Yes, though I was afraid I was about to lose you. Are you sure you're all right?"

"Yes. He didn't hurt me. He was actually quite friendly at first." She pulled back, and they started to walk back toward Lockwood House. "Why was he wearing your livery?"

"He killed Kerr and took his clothes." Jason's arm was still draped around her back, and as he spoke, his hold had tightened. She could feel his muscles coiling with anger.

She laid her hand against his chest in an effort to soothe the tension in his frame. "But why?"

"To get inside Lockwood House so he could kill Wolverton."

Lydia realized that was the second time he'd mentioned Wolverton dying. She shook her head, trying to take it all in. "Why?"

"He was the one in charge of the gang who robbed your house."

Lydia stopped and gaped at him. "Never say so!"

"I'm afraid it's true. Ethan directed Bow Street to his house, where they found your necklace, among other things." He guided her forward once more.

She thought of the pleasant visit she'd shared with Wolverton not even a week ago, and she stopped short again. "He called on me last Saturday. He commented on my necklace, and he asked the most peculiar questions about our staff—how many maids we had and so forth."

Jason's mouth formed a grim line. "It sounds as if he was planning the theft."

She shook her head and started walking with Jason again. "How perfectly horrid. But I'm sorry he died. Why did Gin Jimmy kill him?"

"I'm not completely certain, but he apparently thought Wolverton had turned against him. However, Ethan is the one who was trying to get him captured by Bow Street." Jason fell silent a moment. "I still don't understand Ethan's plan. I wish we'd had more time together. I wish he'd trusted me sooner."

Lydia squeezed his arm. "You'll get your chance.

We'll find a way to prove he's innocent of these crimes."

"*These* crimes, but what of others?" Jason asked hopelessly. "I just found my half brother. I don't want to lose him again. Especially when I think of how different his life might have been if only we—my mother and I—had shown him some compassion."

They were nearly halfway back to Lockwood House. Lydia paused and wrapped her arms around Jason. "We won't lose him. I firmly believe that love conquers all, and you love Ethan. And he loves you."

"That might be taking things a bit far." He kissed the top of her head.

She wanted to argue with him, but she was suddenly bone-tired. "Can we hurry back to Lockwood House?" Plus, she wanted to hear more declarations of love.

"Of course." He took her hand, and they walked more purposefully toward their destination.

"Goodness, your last vice party is going to be remembered as quite a singular event. It will have been your most shocking party yet."

"My 'last' vice party?"

She peered at him askance. "I know you don't really want to give them up, but I don't want to preside over vice parties as Lady Lockwood." This was one point on which she refused to concede. He didn't have to go to balls or pretend to be nice to people, but she wouldn't become the viscountess of debauchery.

He was quiet for several strides, and Lydia worried that he was going to argue.

"All right. No more vice parties." He sounded sad.

"You'll really miss them?"

"Just the idea of them. After I was ostracized, they

were the only place I felt I belonged."

She thought for a moment, hating that he was going to lose something that had been a beacon for him during his loneliest years. "Perhaps we could have parties and invite those same people. We'd still have the gaming room—just no lasciviousness."

Jason laughed. "Something between your vice-free party and my vice parties?"

Her lips quirked up as Lockwood House came into view. "Something like that."

"All right. Now that I've made a concession, it's time for you to do the same."

She slowed her pace. "What's that?"

"You'll let me handle your aunt." He took her hands and looked into her eyes with love and sincerity. "I won't allow her to badger you any longer."

Warmth flooded her and she smiled up at him. "Thank you, but you needn't worry about her. I've ensured she won't bother us at all."

He shook his head. "I shudder to think of how you managed that."

"I'll explain it later—I'm afraid it's a rather awful tale." She wondered what he would think of his father's role in Margaret's past, but imagined he wouldn't be surprised.

They arrived at Lockwood House, where Scot and North were standing outside.

"Is everything all right, my lord?" North asked.

"Yes, Lady Lydia is safe, as you can see, and Ethan escaped."

North's mouth dipped into a serious frown. "I'm afraid the deaths of Kerr and Wolverton were discovered, my lord. Several of the guests left, and the others have congregated in the billiards room to discuss their theories on what happened."

Jason closed his eyes briefly and shook his head. He gazed at Lydia with regret. "I'm sorry. This is going to be a mess. Are you sure you want to marry me? You'll be plenty notorious, but not in the way you'd probably like."

She slid her arm around his waist and hugged him. "It's the only way I want—with you."

Scot elbowed his brother. "We'll make sure the entry is clear so you can go upstairs undisturbed."

"Thoughtful man, your Scot," Lydia murmured as Jason held her close to his side.

"Nosy as hell, but yes, very thoughtful."

She pulled back and looked up at him. "Actually, I have one more demand. I'd like to keep the fantasy room as it is."

He looked adorably confused. "But you just said you wanted vice-free parties."

She gave him a sly grin. "Oh, it's not for parties. It's for us."

His answering smile was so wicked and so full of promise that Lydia wished she could take him up there right this instant. But this was Lockwood House's final vice party, and she'd let it reach its natural conclusion.

"I can see I'm going to need to secure a special license for our wedding. I'm afraid I simply can't wait for the stupid banns to be read. Please tell me that's all right."

Love for this man poured through her. She cupped his beloved face. "It's more than all right."

Relief mingled with his joy. "Thank God you agreed. I don't know what I would've done if you'd insisted on waiting." He sobered briefly. "What about your father? Don't you want him here for the wedding?"

Her father's cold letter, including his reference to her as a "replacement" wife for Mr. Jarvis doused any charitable feelings. Furthermore, while Father would be pleased she was finally marrying, she doubted he would care if he attended the ceremony. A letter as cool as his would suffice. "We'll write to him in the morning."

He turned her toward the house and walked her up the steps to the front door. "You say that as if we'll be together."

She stopped and pivoted to look up at him, her arm linked securely through his. "And why not? You never answered me earlier—do you mind if I sleep here tonight?"

The door swung open as he reached down and swept her into his arms. "I insist."

And then he kissed her in full view of anyone— inside or out—who cared to watch. It was, Society would later say, a fitting end to the notorious vice parties at Lockwood House.

THE END

Thank You!

Thank you so much for reading *Never Love a Scoundrel*. I hope you enjoyed it! Would you like to know when my next book is available? You can sign up for my new release email list at http://www.darcyburke.com/newsletter/, follow me on Twitter at @darcyburke, or like my Facebook page at http://www.facebook.com/DarcyBurkeFans.

Reviews help others find a book that's right for them. I appreciate all reviews, whether positive or negative, and hope you'll leave one at your vendor or reading community website of choice.

Never Love a Scoundrel is the fifth book in the Secrets and Scandals Series. Don't miss the exciting conclusion of the series, *Scoundrel Ever After*, featuring Jagger and Audrey!

I appreciate my readers so much. Thank you, thank you, *thank you*.

Books by Darcy Burke

Historical Romance

The Spitfire Society

Never Have I Ever With a Duke
A Duke is Never Enough
A Duke Will Never Do

The Untouchables

The Forbidden Duke
The Duke of Daring
The Duke of Deception
The Duke of Desire
The Duke of Defiance
The Duke of Danger
The Duke of Ice
The Duke of Ruin
The Duke of Lies
The Duke of Seduction
The Duke of Kisses
The Duke of Distraction

Wicked Dukes Club

One Night for Seduction by Erica Ridley
One Night of Surrender by Darcy Burke
One Night of Passion by Erica Ridley
One Night of Scandal by Darcy Burke
One Night to Remember by Erica Ridley
One Night of Temptation by Darcy Burke

Legendary Rogues

Lady of Desire
Romancing the Earl
Lord of Fortune
Captivating the Scoundrel

Secrets and Scandals

Her Wicked Ways
His Wicked Heart
To Seduce a Scoundrel
To Love a Thief (a novella)
Never Love a Scoundrel
Scoundrel Ever After

Contemporary Romance

Ribbon Ridge

Where the Heart Is (a prequel novella)
Only in My Dreams
Yours to Hold
When Love Happens
The Idea of You
When We Kiss
You're Still the One

Ribbon Ridge: So Hot

So Good
So Right
So Wrong

Praise for Darcy Burke's

The Untouchables Series

THE FORBIDDEN DUKE

"I LOVED this story!!" 5 Stars

-Historical Romance Lover

"This is a wonderful read and I can't wait to see what comes next in this amazing series..." 5 Stars

-Teatime and Books

THE DUKE of DARING

"An unconventional beauty set on life as a spinster meets the one man who might change her mind, only to find his painful past makes it impossible to love. A wonderfully emotional journey from attraction, to friendship, to a love that conquers all."

-Bronwen Evans, USA Today Bestselling Author

THE DUKE of DECEPTION

"...an enjoyable, well-paced story ... Ned and Aquilla are an engaging, well-matched couple – strong, caring and compassionate; and ...it's easy to believe that they will continue to be happy together long after the book is ended."

-All About Romance

THE DUKE of DESIRE

"Masterfully written with great characterization...with a flourish toward characters, secrets, and romance... Must read addition to "The Untouchables" series!"

-My Book Addiction and More

THE DUKE of DEFIANCE

"This story was so beautifully written, and it hooked me from page one. I couldn't put the book down and just had to read it in one sitting even though it meant reading into the wee hours of the morning."

-Buried Under Romance

THE DUKE of DANGER

"Another book hangover by Darcy! Every time I pick a favorite in this series, she tops it. The ending was perfect and made me want more."

-Sassy Book Lover

THE DUKE of ICE

"Each book gets better and better, and this novel was no exception. I think this one may be my fave yet! 5 out 5 for this reader!"

-Front Porch Romance

THE DUKE of RUIN

"This is a fast paced novel that held me until the last page."
-Guilty Pleasures Book Reviews

" ...everything I could ask for in a historical romance... impossible to stop reading."

-The Bookish Sisters

THE DUKE of LIES

"THE DUKE OF LIES is a work of genius! The characters are wonderfully complex, engaging; there is much mystery, and so many, many lies from so many people; I couldn't wait to see it all uncovered."

-Buried Under Romance

THE DUKE of SEDUCTION

"There were tears in my eyes for much of the last 10% of this book. So good!"

-*Becky on Books...and Quilts*

"An absolute joy to read... I always recommend Darcy!"
-*Brittany and Elizabeth's Book Boutique*

THE DUKE of KISSES

"Don't miss this magnificent read. It has some comedic fun, heartfelt relationships, heartbreaking moments, and horrifying danger."

-*The Reading Café*

"...my favorite story in the series. Fans of Regency romances will definitely enjoy this book."

-*Two Ends of the Pen*

THE DUKE of DISTRACTION

"Count on Burke to break a heart as only she can. This couple will get under the skin before they steal your heart."

-*Hopeless Romantic*

"Darcy Burke never disappoints. Her storytelling is just so magical and filled with passion. You will fall in love with the characters and the world she creates!"

-*Teatime and Books*

League of Rogues Series

LADY of DESIRE

"The de Valery Code gave me such a book hangover! . . . addictive. . . one of the most entertaining stories I've read this year!"

-Adria's Romance Reviews

"A fast-paced mixture of adventure and romance, very much in the mould of *Romancing the Stone* or *Indiana Jones*."

-All About Romance

ROMANCING the EARL

"Once again Darcy Burke takes an interesting story and . . . turns it into magic. An exceptionally well-written book."

-Bodice Rippers, Femme Fatale, and Fantasy

"...A fast paced story that was exciting and interesting. This is a definite must add to your book lists!"

-Kilts and Swords

LORD of FORTUNE

"I don't think I know enough superlatives to describe this book! It is wonderfully, magically delicious. It sucked me in from the very first sentence and didn't turn me loose—not even at the end ..."

-Flippin Pages

"If you love a deep, passionate romance with a bit of mystery, then this is the book for you!"

-Teatime and Books

Secrets & Scandals Series

HER WICKED WAYS

"A bad girl heroine steals both the show and a highwayman's heart in Darcy Burke's deliciously wicked debut."

–Courtney Milan, *New York Times* Bestselling Author

"…fast paced, very sexy, with engaging characters."

–Smexybooks

HIS WICKED HEART

"Intense and intriguing. Cinderella meets *Fight Club* in a historical romance packed with passion, action and secrets."

–Anna Campbell, *Seven Nights in a Rogue's Bed*

" . . . fresh with a cast of well developed characters. Darcy Burke is an author on the move!!"

–Forever Book Lover

TO SEDUCE A SCOUNDREL

"Darcy Burke pulls no punches with this sexy, romantic page-turner. Sevrin and Philippa's story grabs you from the first scene and doesn't let go. To Seduce a Scoundrel is simply delicious!"

–Tessa Dare, *New York Times* Bestselling Author

"A great read with a gorgeous tortured hero and a surprisingly plucky heroine, I can't wait to read Ms. Burke's next book."

–Under the Covers Book Blog

TO LOVE A THIEF

"With refreshing circumstances surrounding both the hero and the heroine, a nice little mystery, and a touch of heat, this novella was a perfect way to pass the day."

–The Romanceaholic

"This novella has it all--action, romance, love and passion…a lovely story!"

–Rogues Under the Covers

NEVER LOVE A SCOUNDREL

"I loved the story of these two misfits thumbing their noses at society and finding love." Five stars.

–A Lust for Reading

"An excellent commentary on the power of gossip, but also a wonderful story about two people willing to overcome their differences and to trust in their love."

–Bodice Rippers, Femme Fatale, and Fantasy

SCOUNDREL EVER AFTER

"There is something so delicious about a bad boy, no matter what era he is from, and Ethan was definitely delicious."

-A Lust for Reading

"I loved the chemistry between the two main characters . . . Jagger/Ethan is not what he seems at all and neither is sweet society Miss Audrey. They are believably compatible."

-Confessions of a College Angel

Ribbon Ridge Series

A contemporary family saga featuring the Archer family of sextuplets who return to their small Oregon wine country town to confront tragedy and find love . . .

The "multilayered plot keeps readers invested in the story line, and the explicit sensuality adds to the excitement that will have readers craving the next Ribbon Ridge offering."
  -Library Journal Starred Review on YOURS TO HOLD

"Darcy Burke writes a uniquely touching and heart-warming series about the love, pain, and joys of family as well as the love that feeds your soul when you meet "the one."

-The Many Faces of Romance

I can't tell you how much I love this series. Each book gets better and better.

-Romancing the Readers

"Darcy Burke's Ribbon Ridge series is one of my all-time favorites. Fall in love with the Archer family, I know I did."

-Forever Book Lover

Ribbon Ridge: So Hot

SO GOOD

" ...worth the read with its well-written words, beautiful descriptions, and likeable characters...they are flirty, sexy and a match made in wine heaven."

-Harlequin Junkie Top Pick

"I absolutely love the characters in this book and the families. I honestly could not put it down and finished it in a day."

-Chin Up Mom

SO RIGHT

"This is another great story by Darcy Burke. Painting pictures with her words that make you want to sit and stare at them for hours. I love the banter between the characters and the general sense of fun and friendliness."

-The Ardent Reader

" ...the romance is emotional; the characters are spirited and passionate... "

-The Reading Café

SO WRONG

"As usual, Ms. Burke brings you fun characters and witty banter in this sweet hometown series. I loved the dance between Crystal and Jamie as they fought their attraction."

-The Many Faces of Romance

"I really love both this series and the Ribbon Ridge series from Darcy Burke. She has this way of taking your heart and ripping it right out of your chest one second and then the next you are laughing at something the characters are doing."

-Romancing the Readers

Acknowledgments

Like Jason and his scar, this book was a beast. Thank you to my E-Team: Emma for nitcritting this story to within an inch of its life, Erica for writing the best fanfic evah, Elisabeth for being available on IM pretty much whenever I needed you, and Erica JM for the truly excellent beta read. This book would suck without you.

Thank you also to the Northwest Pixie Chicks for our fifth (FIFTH!) annual retreat, at which I wrote scads and scads of this book despite gas leaks, one very frigid night, and a mysteriously staged knife.

Two lovely people made this book look fantastic: Patricia Schmitt and Martha Trachtenberg. Thank you to Trish for designing a cover I can't stop staring at and for being so much fun to work with. Thank you to Martha, whose editing skills are unparalleled and who is quite simply one of the most delightful people I've ever met.

I also want to thank some other dear friends who provide unflinching support: Janice Goodfellow and Lynda Aicher. And special thanks to Rachel Grant for so many things, but most of all for paving the e-formatting way and teaching me how to do it.

Finally, thank you to my family for your constant love and patience. I can't promise I'll make dinner more often, but I will always make sure your clothes are clean.

About the Author

Darcy Burke is the USA Today Bestselling Author of hot, action-packed historical and sexy, emotional contemporary romance. Darcy wrote her first book at age 11, a happily ever after about a swan addicted to magic and the female swan who loved him, with exceedingly poor illustrations.

A native Oregonian, Darcy lives on the edge of wine country with her guitar-strumming husband, their two hilarious kids who seem to have inherited the writing gene. They're a crazy cat family with two Bengal cats, a small, fame-seeking cat named after a fruit, and an older rescue Maine Coon who is the master of chill and five a.m. serenading. In her "spare" time Darcy is a serial volunteer enrolled in a 12-step program where one learns to say "no," but she keeps having to start over. Her happy places are Disneyland and Labor Day weekend at the Gorge. Visit Darcy online at http://www.darcyburke.com and sign up for her newsletter, follow her on Twitter at http://twitter.com/darcyburke, or like her Facebook page, http://www.facebook.com/darcyburkefans.